AN ALPENGLOW RIDGE NOVEL

Roped on the Ridge

ZEA KAYLEIGH GALAN

To you,
Even when broken, you're worthy of it.

Playlist

Dave Matthews Band – Crash into Me
Camille Parker – Peace
Don Louis, Sophia Scott – She's Trouble
No Doubt, Lady Saw – Underneath It All
Eddie Flint – Broken People
Carter Faith – I Just Wanna Dance
J.R. Carroll – Bandit (OurVinyl Sessions)
Anthony Ramos – Vicariously
Sasha Keable – WHY
Red Hot Chili Peppers – Scar Tissue
Tucker Wetmore – Wind Up Missin' You
Frank Walker, Nate Smith – Missing You
Tyler Hubbard – Dancin' In The Country
Morgan Wallen – Lies Lies Lies
Reyna Roberts – Louisiana
Doja Cat – Options (feat.JID)
Kane Brown – What Ifs (feat. Lauren Alaina)
Ariana Grande – Moonlight
Feist – The Bad In Each Other
Teddy Swims – Are You Even Real (feat. Givēon)
Gabby Barrett – Pick Me Up
Reyna Roberts, Tayler Holder – Another Round
Rascal Flatts – What Hurts The Most
Matchbox Twenty – If You're Gone
Lady A – Need You Now
Riley Green – Don't Mind If I Do (ft. Ella Langley)
Sophia Scott – Tumbleweed
Nessa Barrett – LOVE LOOKS PRETTY ON YOU

This is a romantic suspense novel that is suitable for mature audiences only. There are heavier themes in this book including, but not limited to heavy alcohol use, explicit sexual content, miscarriage (off page), profanity and violence that may be sensitive to some readers. For a full list of potentially sensitive content, visit my website:

www.zeakayleighgalan.com/cw

Also by Zea Kayleigh Galan

Alpenglow Ridge

Saddled with Finesse
Verse to Acclimate
Whisk til Peaked
Hope by the Horizon
Roped on the Ridge

Shades of Vengeance

Into the Blue

AN ALPENGLOW RIDGE NOVEL

Roped on the Ridge

CHAPTER 1

Maxwell Stewart

"WHAT DO YOU MEAN *no one?*"

I lean onto the counter instead of on the crutches I've been given. It's easier when you need the support. I've just now been allowed to move around since my surgery, but I can't go home. Not until I find out what's going to happen to that woman in there.

"Sir, I understand that you are concerned, but I really cannot give you more information than that since you are neither her family or emergency contact. She has not had anyone that claims to know her."

"Mack," Reese places a hand on my shoulder but I don't let go of the counter. "We can just wait for visiting hours. It's not long until then." I look over my shoulder at her. "Please," she adds. "I'm worried about you. You need rest, too."

"She has no one. I'm not leaving until I know she's going to be okay."

"Do you know her?" Her brows pinch. "Is there something you're not telling me?"

"No. I just..." I sigh and grab my crutches from where they lean against the counter. "I don't know." *She lost someone and I know what that's like.* No one should have to go through that alone. "I'll wait. You don't have to. You should be at home with your family for the New Year."

"Our family," she corrects me. *She's right.* They are my family. The only ones I truly have. "And you should be there, too."

"That's what I meant. I'm fine. I have my phone and my charger. You can get ahold of me if anything happens. I'm in a hospital. Nothing bad can happen to me here."

Indecision plays in her eyes as she considers what to say next. I know she's worried for me, but I want to make sure *she* is okay before I leave this place. "You need to rest and heal. Cory can probably bring you back later this week."

I didn't want Cory to bring me back. I wanted to stay here until I needed to leave.

"I don't want to argue about this anymore. If I need you, I will call. I promise. Go home and enjoy the rest of the time off you have until we have to get back into the fray."

"Mack." Her tone is firmer than before. A good sign that she will actually go home. "There is no way that I'm letting you come back to work when the holiday is over. I'm not budging. You will rest until the doctors say you can get back in the saddle."

The silence stretches between us. Normally, I would rush to fill it with placating words, but I don't. I won't. "I love you Reese, but I'm not going to argue with you about it now."

"Fine. We *will* talk later. Call me if anything—"

"I will." I allow her to help me to the two-chair bench in the waiting area. She drops the bag she brought for me onto the seat next to me with some essentials.

She squeezes me tightly. I feel every bit of her concern in that hug, see it in her watery eyes as she gives my arm a squeeze.

When she leaves, I slump back into the chair and let my hat fall onto my face, careful not to disturb the bandages on my nose, and shield me from the bright lights of the waiting room.

The terrified eyes I could make out through the frosty windshield on a slow collision course for me... The sound of crunching metal in the defining quiet of winter in Colorado. I'm watching the SUV slide across the road and off into the tree it found itself wrapped around. Nothing but red filters into my vision with the blood pouring from my nose and I try to wipe it away. Then, the pain blaring through my entire body with the snap of my left leg as my truck meets its demise as well.

"Mr. Stewart." I wake with a start when a nurse, or someone in scrubs anyway, taps my arm. I push the hat back on my head and sit up. "We just opened visitor hours."

I blink a few times and rub a hand over my face. It's rough under my hands. The five o'clock shadow is well past needing to be shaved, but I'll worry about that later. "Thank you," I say, my voice gruff with sleep. "Is she awake?"

"Not yet. I'm Rita, one of her nurses. We've been monitoring her, but she's still sleeping right now."

I nod and reach to grab my crutches, hoping to get my bag after that. The nurse grabs it for me and I mutter a *thanks* as she leads me back through the doors to her room.

The hospital smell is much stronger back here. It even assaults my broken nose that I can barely smell anything out of anyway. The nurse isn't going too quickly, so I'm able to keep up with her. I know when we're getting close to the room because I feel the same pull I did before. Couldn't explain it any other way than that.

I was drawn.

The nurse peers into the window on the door for a moment and then smiles at me when she opens the door for me to go in.

The room is not that large, but I still look around it anyway. Pale walls and curtains surround me. There's a chair beside her bed and I sit down in it.

She lies in the bed, frozen in time. Tubes are attached to screens with information showing that I don't know how to interpret. One of them has to be responsible for the beeping in the otherwise silent room. Though there is a mess of activity outside her door, in here, there is nothing but peace.

She looks like Sleeping Beauty.

Tawny brown skin like potter's clay or fall leaves still glows warm in the harsh lighting. Thick dark lashes fan out over her defined cheeks that are only minorly nicked up from the accident. A large bandage is taped to her forehead above strong eyebrows. Rose pink lips that make my fingers itch to feel if they are as soft as they look. I study every detail I can get my eyes on.

Rita startles me when she approaches to set my bag down beside me. "Kathryn is going to be up soon. Likely sometime today. They are reducing her sedative slowly."

Kathryn.

It suits her. I think any name she would have said would have been great because it's a relief to give a name to the beauty in front of me instead of referring to her as "her" in my head.

I take my hat off, dropping it somewhere behind me. "Can I stay here until then?"

"Visiting hours are over at eight PM. If she's not up before then or a change occurs, you'll have to go back to the waiting area."

The nurse taps the door on her way out to catch my attention again since I've returned to looking at Kathryn lying in her hospital bed. "Elevate that leg if you're gonna stare at her this whole time." I slide the bag I brought in front of me. She tilts her head to the side like *really* before she brings the other chair in the room for me to put my leg up on.

"Thanks," I say before she leaving again.

It's not long before I fall asleep again and the haunting memories assault me, but I can't stop them from coming. I wake a few hours after that and see the missed calls and text from Reese on my phone.

She should be spending time with her kids and husband, not blowing up my phone. She saw that I was fine this morning. Sitting up, I massage my exposed thigh through the pins and needles dancing up and down the lame thing.

I need to eat.

It's been a couple hours and admittedly, I slept for a lot of them. This chair is by no means a comfortable resting place, but I settled in anyway.

I feel settled being close to her.

It's a weird revelation and one that I will push to the back of my head because I'm here for a reason.

Even if I don't quite know what that reason is right now.

I know the cafeteria is on the bottom floor of the hospital, so I carefully grab my crutches and make my way over to get some food. It's not anything special they have to offer, but I tried taking the pain medication they gave me on an empty stomach and I think I should heed the warning to *take with food* more seriously.

It's all rote as I eat and check my phone. I answer texts and most importantly, let my sister know that I'm still okay so she doesn't come marching back up here. When I need more clothes and a shower I'll call Cory, her husband and my good friend, instead.

Sitting by the large window in the cafeteria, I look out at the snow as it falls and piles up again. It falls slow and otherwise peacefully. At one point, I loved the snow. I loved how the world seemed to slow down for it. I've lived in Colorado all my life and have never been in an accident because of it before. It took thirty-two years for my luck to change.

For the best or for the worst, I have no idea which as of yet.

Chapter 2

Kathryn Jeann Barker

Beep. Beep. Beep.

What's that sound?

Beep. Beep. Beep.

Where am I?

Beep. Beep. Beep.

Why am I aching all over? My head is killing me.

I blink my eyes open. Vision blurry and unfocused. It's like sand has crusted them closed and each blink hurts with the lights so bright around me. I squeeze them closed again. This feels like the worst hangover.

My throat is terribly dry and I cough to get relief.

Where am I?

I wince at the feel of something on my arm. Not on... in. Tentatively raising it, I panic. Why are there so many cords attached to me?

The beeping increases with my racing heart and two women come to my side with navy-colored scrubs on. "Kathryn? Calm down, sweetie. It's okay," one of them says. "My name is Amana and I'm one of your nurses here. They just lessened your sedative, so you might feel a little disoriented waking up."

"Where... Am... I?" I struggle to croak out.

"Rita, grab her that water." Turning to me, she says, "Kathryn, you're in the hospital in Harmony Hill."

Rita is back with a water cup, holding the straw out for me. I drink slowly and it feels better immediately. My head is still killing me though. "What's Harmony Hill?" I ask.

Amana's eyebrows pull together. She looks to Rita and they both look back at me. "Harmony Hill, Colorado. You were in a car accident on a county road not far from here three days ago. You came here with a concussion and minimal damage to your person. A few stitches but no broken bones. Does that sound familiar?" Amana asks.

"No," I feel myself frowning. "I've never left Louisiana…"

Rita speaks up next as Amana scribbles something on a clipboard. "Don't worry about that too much. The doctor will be in to see you shortly. Just hang tight, okay?"

I nod, but it's *not okay*. They leave the room and I look at my surroundings. How did I end up in Colorado?

Trying my hardest, I attempt to recall what I was doing yesterday. No, she said three days ago. How am I here right now?

Looking down at my arm again, I see the IV taped there, but it's everything else that confuses me. What are these tattoos? Little patchwork pieces of art span the length of my arm… no, both my arms.

There's whispering coming from outside the door that's rising in volume.

"I'll just be a second," a voice says before a man comes into the room on crutches.

He comes over quicker than I would expect for someone on crutches, but I don't recognize him. In a long-sleeved flannel shirt and, oddly enough, exercise shorts with a work boot on the foot that's not in a cast. He's kinda goofy looking with the big smile he has on his face for me. I don't know why he's so happy. There's a large bandage on his nose and deep purple bruising under both his eyes. He got into a fight with someone or something and it doesn't look like he won.

But those eyes. They stop my heart for a second. I've never seen eyes this color before. Even from the distance he stands, they're striking. They look like... like a chlorine pool that's sparkling in the summer sun. Clear and inviting, even with the bruising and bandage.

He smirks a little and waves toward his face, "Oh, this? You should see the other guy." Then, he winces. It's boyish and kind of adorable. "I-I didn't mean that..." He takes a step back from me and I watch him make space between us. "I'm sorry for your loss."

"My... Loss?" I say, my voice feeling like razor blades.

"I don't... I'm messing this up. Let me start from the beginning." He clears his throat and runs a hand through his hair. It's light brown and a little greasy but longer in the back where the front is only long enough to flop onto his forehead. "I'm Mack," he says. His smile is big, imperfect, and happy. It's infectious. I smile, despite my circumstances.

"Kathryn," I respond.

"I like it..." he gives me a sheepish look... "Of course, I already knew that since I've been awake longer than you have. I've been in this room more times than this, but they said you woke up, so I had to see you."

"See me?"

"Yea. See you."

"Why?"

His face turns more solemn, great clouds over his perfect blues. "To apologize."

"For my... loss."

He nods slowly. "I was in the truck your SUV came in contact with when you hydroplaned across the ice on the county road. The EMT managed to get you and me out of the vehicles but your friend... He didn't appear to be wearing a seatbelt... He didn't make it."

Nothing he's saying makes any sense. Ice? Is it winter? Clayton has never had ice on the roads. But I'm not in Clayton Terrace. I'm in Colorado. How random and... "What friend?"

He shifts his weight on the crutches and maneuvers over to the chair to the left of my bed. There's already a bag there. I don't recognize it, but there are an abundance of things I don't recognize. I'll add that to the list. "Sorry, my pits were starting to hurt." He stretches out his leg that has the cast and hands me the water bottle the nurse brought in for me. "Do you need help with this?"

I tentatively take the water bottle, but it is heavier than I expected. He never truly let go, so it's easy for him to help me move it closer to my mouth and drink. "What friend?"

He sighs. I get the feeling that he doesn't like to be the bearer of bad news. That sigh told me everything I needed to know so I brace for whatever it is he'll say next. "His name was Ethan Davey. Does that name mean anything to you?"

All at once, memories of a brown-haired boy flick through my mind. Us at five learning to ride bikes together. Then, us at sixteen trying our first beer. He always had a rebellious streak, but he had a heart of gold. What I remember most was his hugs. So many hugs. "Ethan," my voice breaks and tears roll hot and heavy down my cheeks.

Mack puts the water bottle down and picks up a crutch to hop on his good leg, closer to the bed. He uses a tissue to clean my face and when I open my eyes again, it's his blue ones peering down at me with all the understanding a friend could have.

I don't have any memories of this man who's at my bedside. Is he my friend? I don't know why he's the only one here or why I'm in Colorado, to begin with. There are too many feelings that sit heavy on my chest.

Ethan is gone.

How did I get here?

"I'm so sorry, Kathryn. Driving on the ice can be dangerous even for us who were born and raised here, too. I wish I had better words to say, but I know nothing can replace the loss of a loved one... I know that better than most." He looks down at the bed for a time. Bracing his arm on one side of the bed, he hugs me with the other free one. He smells like fresh cut grass, earthy and familiar, and leather as his warmth envelops me.

He moves back to the chair and picks up the bag, throwing it over his shoulder. Surprisingly there's a brown cowboy hat behind it that he plops on his head next. It's a little dirty and crooked, but it suits him. "Well, I'll let you get your rest. I think the doctor will be coming in soon." His sparkling eyes, a little dimmer than before.

Then, he's walking over to the door. He's... leaving, taking all the sunshine with him. "Mack," I say with a scratchy voice. He turns back around to face me. "Will you stay?" He blinks. "Please?" I ask.

The corner of his mouth lifts. "Of course."

It only takes a second before he's back by my side. That warmth that comes off of him in waves makes me shiver. I've never *felt* anyone who feels as cheery as he does.

At least, I don't think I have.

Searching through my memory for anything or anyone that resembles this guy is fruitless because I know he's a stranger. I can't for the life of me figure out why he's being so nice to me. It seems like Ethan was at fault in the car accident that injured us both.

He picks up the chart the nurse was writing on before and I look over the details they've filled in about me.

"The doctor is going to come in pretty soon. I think it's best if you say I'm your boyfriend..." His face flushes pink, despite the purple bruising and he stutters for a bit. "I mean, so they don't dismiss me right away. I—I want to stay here with you just to make sure everything is okay. If I can."

"Everythin' is not okay," I murmur. "I don't know how I'm in another state to begin with. No offense to Colorado, but I never even dreamed of comin' here. None of this makes sense to me." I point to the papers in the clipboard. "My last memories are of bein' twenty-three, but I'm apparently twenty-six!"

Beeping intensifies as my heart rate picks up. I'm panicking again and it's coming on fast. I'm hurting and helpless with only a stranger here to comfort me. My hand is enclosed in his and I haven't removed it. Odd.

A tall White woman with dark brown hair and a white lab coat comes into the room before I have more time to talk to Mack. "Hi, Kathryn. My name is Dr. Ruby Cresswell. And I've been overseeing your care while you've been here." She stands close to the end of my bed with her ramrod back and arms crossed over her clipboard. "Amana let me know that you were up and I thought I could come in and clarify some information about your condition and what is in store for you moving forward."

I nod my head and try to sit up a little bit more. Mack is already at my side to help me get comfortable. Dr. Ruby's eyes track Mack's presence and she sighs. It's not entirely irritated. She continues, "Mr. Stewart here has been anxious to come and see you since he was out of his own hospital bed. Whereas I'm happy to see that someone cares for you so strongly, I still need to ask if you would like him to be here to talk about your care."

"I would like for him to stay if that's possible. This is all very..." My sentence trails off because the words don't come. I can't describe how I feel in this moment. I'm floating in between a lot of unknown emotions because that's just it... Everything *is* so unknown.

"I understand," Dr. Ruby says. She flips through the papers on the clipboard and then meets my wary gaze. "Well, I suppose I should start with what we know from observing you for the past three days. There was a contusion, or blunt force trauma to your head from something in the vehicle that caused the large gash just at your hairline. We suspected that there might be some swelling in the brain since there is still swelling on the temple. Since you were unconscious, we chose to monitor you while allowing your body to calm down from the accident. Plenty of fluids and keeping you sedated was the best course of action. Thankfully you had an ID that allowed us to get you processed in the system and contact your emergency contact. The driver of your vehicle passed before we were able to get him into the hospital so he was not a viable contact. There was no other information that we could easily find but we would be more than happy to get someone on the phone for you now that you're awake."

"No," I hear myself say. Empty spaces fill the places where support should be. "I just want to know how, when, I can get out of this hospital and back to Louisiana."

"Unfortunately, now that you're awake, we would like to move forward with an MRI and some other tests to see how you are faring both, mentally and physically. The nurses mentioned that you were having trouble remembering recent events, which isn't uncommon, and should come back with time."

"How recent?" I ask.

"The last day or two might be foggy. You may get just flashes of the events as our brains are really clever. Sometimes, they do a good job of shielding us from painful things that happen to us. Other than that, you should remember everything without issue." My brows scrunch and I do my best to wipe that emotion from my face, but Dr. Ruby catches it anyway. "Is that not the case?"

"I—I don't actually remember how I got into the state or the accident."

"Confusion is also common. Rest assured that we will take the very best care of you while you're here in Harmony Hill. Let's start with the testing and move forward from there. Does that sound okay to you?"

"Sure," I manage to respond.

It didn't sound okay.

But I had no choice at this point.

CHAPTER 3

Jeann

AFTER MUCH TESTING OVER this past week, Dr. Ruby found that I needed to stay in the hospital for at least the next week to see if I would improve. They found only minor swelling that has since receded and is no longer worrisome with the MRI.

"Don't be afraid to find a new routine, Kathryn."

Kathryn was my Nana. We both are, since I'm her namesake. It was confusing while she was alive since she was as likely to be called out for being mischievous as I was. I started going by Jeann and she was Kathryn. She passed, a fact I don't love that I could recall only bits of, but still I prefer Jeann.

I don't correct her. Dr. Ruby doesn't need to know that because they're much bigger fish to fry. It's far more important that I can't remember how the hell I got to Colorado.

What the hell am I doing in the state in the first place?

"Memory is fickle with injuries like this. It may come back tomorrow, or next week or years from now. It may never come back at all. The important thing is to get back to your life in a fashion that feels right for you. Seek normalcy and trust your instincts. That usually helps since our brains are complex organs that can accomplish many things on their own."

I nod in understanding though it is still extremely unsettling to know that so much of my adult life is just gone.

Poof.

Why couldn't I have lost my teen years? Every criticism for being the weird one. Having one guy who liked me, only to use me and later tell his friends that I was easy because I was desperate.

What about losing my parents way too young? My mom and dad—gone.

Or my sister? I remember her face and laugh so clearly.

Why did I have to remember Ethan and feel the loss of my best friend?

Why couldn't those memories be gone?

I ball up the front of my gown and grit my teeth. I know what she said is meant to be placating, but it isn't.

It fucking sucks.

A hand gently cups my fist and I release my death grip on the gown.

Mack is here.

He's always here.

His consistent presence makes me doubt the truth of him not meaning more to me than he's let on. Why would someone who has only met me now have this much patience and consideration?

For a stranger.

And by all that I've been told—the stranger responsible for his injuries.

No, I wasn't driving, but I was in the car that gave him a broken leg and nose.

And still, he rubs gentle circles on the back of my fist until I release it.

This man is good.

He is a good person and he has a kind heart.

I don't deserve his kindness. He owes me none of this patience or consideration.

Yet, he gives it to me anyway.

"Will she be able to travel?" Mack looks over at me sitting in the chair of my recovery room while he sits in a wheelchair. It's only for the doctor's benefit. He refuses to use it otherwise. The relaxed expression he has is still far happier than my own.

If his face says, *I'm ready to help.* Mine says, *fuck right off and fall on a stick.*

My hand finally relaxes and he lets it rest on top of his on the armrest of the wheelchair. "You know? Go back to Louisiana?" He asks.

There's a scripted name on the back of his hand between the knuckle of his thumb and his wrist that says "Callan". I've noticed it before, but didn't ask who that is. I'm not going to now either, but I focus on it all the same as the doctor continues.

"Yes. It might be uncomfortable for her to be in a car or she may feel anxious, but that will lessen with time. I would advise traveling by plane to lessen the prolonged exposure she has to car travel."

Advise traveling by plane?

My lip curls on its own. I couldn't even afford a rideshare to get to the closest airport, let alone a plane ticket out of Colorado that far.

Looking to me, the Doctor says, "It may help you recover some memories to go back to your hometown. If you have been there in the time that is missing from your recollection, being in a familiar surrounding could be helpful. I wouldn't suggest you do this alone if possible."

Great.

So I need to go home to *maybe* remember something.

Guess those memories will be gone for the foreseeable future.

With my lip still curled at the casual way the doctor is formulating this plan, I say, "Can't afford a plane ticket home." The curtness of my tone is jarring even to my own ears.

With my belongings returned to me from our totaled SUV, my purse showed me how little I had in the way of finances. The card in my wallet had fifty dollars on it and there was no cash to speak of. I would have to pay that to get the totaled piece of shit out of the impound where it was being kept at some point and then my fifty bucks would be gone too.

The totality of what I currently own is this purse and duffel bag. I had some clothes and toiletries in the duffel bag since it seems that whatever I was doing in Colorado—there was a plan to be here. At least I could change out of this scratchy gown at some point soon. Other than that, I was basically homeless and hopeless with a hole in my memory large enough to make me vulnerable.

A woman with no support in a strange state where no one even sounded like me! My drawl made even more apparent, where it was common where I was from, everyone here sounded like dictionaries.

I hated it.

I hate all of this.

"It's okay," Mack assures me with gentle rubbing on my shoulder. "You don't have to make any decisions right now."

"I can't stay at this hospital forever," I snap.

Sensing the growing tension, Dr. Cresswell excuses herself. It's only Mack and me in the room now.

Somehow, this feels less stressful to me than with the doctor present.

He rolls in the chair next to me and the silence is a weighty thing that grows between us. I allow it to hang in the air and it's not lost on me that we have a lot to talk about.

But, I don't know what to say.

The only person I have to talk to about my care is a stranger who was in the accident with me. It's not right, but it's all I have.

He's all I have.

Even after all the testing confirmed I wasn't, I still feel broken. Nothing besides my brain obtained substantial injury. But isn't that significant?

Your memories, experiences, shape who you are.

Everything I know about myself is outdated.

I know it is and I can't obtain the information to update my sense of self.

My fingers gently run over the bandage on my head where it's still a little tender. "I don't know what I'm gonna do," I murmur.

Looking out the small window to the blue sky that mocks me with how clear it is, I wonder, not, for the first time why I came to Colorado. I've hardly seen any of it, but it's covered in snow and it's cold. I've never been somewhere that felt this way. Mack told me that it's not really as cold as it can get here.

Why would I ever leave Louisiana for this?

"If it's helpful at all…" Mack's voice cuts into my thoughts. "When they say you can be discharged, you can stay with me. I live about an hour from here and there's plenty of room." A warm smile greets me as I meet those aquatic blue eyes from the window. The color isn't too different looking from one to the other.

The man looking over my face is the only thing that has kept me grounded for the short time that I've known him.

He is a stranger. I shouldn't trust him.

He's a stranger and I still feel like I can trust him.

He's the first to distract me when my mood darkens.

Even after he was discharged, he's come to see me everyday.

Shares my meals with me and keeps me company.

I've come to need him.

I don't like it.

He gives me another small smile, "It works out for me, too, if you're thinking you'll be a burden to me." His head motions to the crutches against the wall. The statement lingers between us. "I'm gonna be on these crutches and my sister is on my ass about actually resting so that my leg can heal properly…"

There is no doubt in my mind about whether or not I want to go home with him.

Whether I *should* is a completely different problem.

I don't actually have many other options.

When I say "many other"… I have zero other options.

He continues, "I won't charge you rent or anything, but I will need some help recovering." He waits for me to look at him again when he adds with an eyebrow wiggle, "You scratch my back and I'll—"

"Ugh," I rub my forehead, wincing from the pain. "Don't make it weird."

His eyes sparkle with my response. "So, you will?"

"I don't really have a choice, now do I?" I stand and lie down in the bed, staring at the ceiling tiles. Mostly, resigning myself to the fact that I'm taking a leap of faith that I have no way of truly knowing if it will end in further disaster for me.

"Nope." He pops the P and I groan.

I guess I'm doing this.

I'm going to move in with a complete stranger and who knows what will happen. I'll only stay with him long enough to figure out how I can get back to Louisiana and get my memories back.

As I think that, a sense of foreboding crawls across my skin. I turn to face the presence now looming in the doorway. I sit up in the bed, looking at the man no one wants to show up unannounced when they're vulnerable.

His voice cracks into the space like thunder. "Good. You're up."

CHAPTER 4

Mack

"Good. You're up."

The deep voice cuts through the relief I briefly feel when she agrees to go home with me. She tenses next to me and I feel the entire energy of the room change. Looking to the doorway, I see a man who looks familiar to me, but I don't understand her reaction.

My instincts to protect are on high alert.

Blue Dupont leans against the doorway studying the two of us. He looks relaxed, though the intensity coming off of him says otherwise.

"Kathryn, do you know him?"

Her face still reflects the confusion of someone searching for something that they won't find. Maybe it's a specific memory but potentially not. Her hand clenches the blankets next to her like a vice. I rub the back of her little fist to release the grip for a moment as Blue remains silent, watching the two of us. Her fist is still nicked and cut from the accident, I guess. There are scabs that appear to be healing there, none big enough to need stitches.

Finally, she shakes her head slowly. I can't tell if that is an honest response or one that she feels comfortable saying in this intense situation.

"Oh... Well, that hurts, darlin'," Blue drawls, straightening from his casual position. He walks in and I meet him in the middle of the room on my crutches before he is able to make it to her.

He tilts his head to the side at me. He and his brother, Tony, are big men. Their stature is larger than mine, but not by much when I'm not using these crutches to support me. They could be confused for twins if it weren't for Blue's shoulder length locs that stand apart from Tony's much shorter hair. They both have dark brown skin and straight white teeth.

On first guess, you'd probably think that Tony was the more intimidating guy because he is quiet and more stern overall than his brother. But, I can recognize that the darkness in this man is sinister and I'd do well to remember that people aren't always how they appear on the outside.

I've known Tony for more than a decade and worked under him almost as long.

Tony is a solid guy, good. Blue, on the other hand, bad.

I've not been close to him and if it were up to me, I'd keep it that way. He blows into town every now and again to visit his brother, but the dead giveaway is how Tony acts around him. If Tony is on edge, I don't want to take any chances with him.

He looks me up and down, then grins. It's not a happy expression.

I stand my ground. "What are you doing here?"

He mirrors my stance and crosses his arms over his chest. "Here to visit, *Kathryn*." He has some strange intonation on her name. Like maybe that isn't her name. "I didn't realize that I needed to clear it with you first."

"Clear it with me? Nah." I look back to the woman in question and she's sat up more against the bed. She's looking the two of us over. I can't tell exactly what she's thinking.

Not that I should, but that pull to her hasn't gone away. I should call it something else with how bold it's made me in the face of a man I know I should have no business challenging.

And yet, here I am *challenging* him.

"I don't think it's best that you be here if she doesn't know who you are. I've never seen her react like this to anyone else. Any idea why she might *not* want you to be here?"

He looks around me to the woman and then, "Heard she can't remember nothin'." He tilts his head to the side again, sucking his teeth. "Just wanted to see if that's true. See, I knew *Kathryn...* well." *He knew her?* How could she have anything to do with this man?

My confusion registers on my face and he smirks. "Not like that. Not for the reasons anyone would guess. I'm sure of it. Have a... history of a kind."

"A history she doesn't remember fondly."

I hear her step down from the bed. I look over my shoulder at her and she places a hand on my shoulder blade. I soften the smallest bit at that contact, but put more emphasis in my words when I face Blue again.

"What do you want?" I bite out.

"Mack," I look down at her. Kathryn's hand is still at my back. Next to me, she still seems small and fragile. The bandage on her forehead indicates that she's lucky to be alive.

I can't let anything hurt her again.

Though she appears less unsettled now, her point of contact with me is firm. "It's okay. I remember who Blue is by reputation." That does nothing to comfort me. She asks, "What history do we have together?"

"Not important." He shrugs. "If any of those memories come back, you tell me first."

She crosses her arms over her chest, somehow managing to look down her nose at the much larger man—even with a bandage on her forehead. "How? My phone was smashed in the accident. I filed an insurance claim for a replacement, but who knows when it will come."

Blue leans over to the side table and writes his number on a tissue. "Call me if anythin' comes back to you."

She snatches the tissue from his hand and he chuffs at her. "Might not have your memories, but your attitude still fucking sucks. Thought some brain trauma would've helped you."

"Well, you thought wrong," she sneers, crossing her arms, more attitude that's much too large for her stature comes rolling off her tongue. "Somethin' else you're lookin' for?"

"Nah. I'll go." He doesn't wait for her reply when he leaves.

I flop into the wheelchair again, arms already done from being on my crutches so long today. "What was that?"

She had no fear. All determination and strength. It was sexy as all hell. Though my heart is still racing with adrenaline from the energy coming off of the both of them.

I had no way to really protect her if things went sideways. That fact sits sour in my stomach.

She sits back on the side of the bed and finally relaxes her posture. "Everyone knows who Blue Dupont is. He's king of green in the south and you don't cross him or show weakness." My jaw hangs open and she scoffs. "He's the boogeyman where I come from. But he won't make a scene to draw attention to himself. Especially this far from home where no one is on his payroll."

"Let's hope he doesn't remedy that."

"For what? I don't know why he'd bother to do any of that for me." She sits in the chair beside me again. "Maybe he and Ethan had dealins'. Not like I would know." The last of her thoughts comes out pointedly as she punches the armrest with the bottom of her fist.

"I don't know... It didn't seem like he was here for your friend." Her lips press into a tight line.

Silence lingers and I break it before someone or something interrupts us again. I want that feeling of relief I had before Blue came striding in here. I need to know that there is something I can do to keep her safe and comfortable until her time is up here. "So... You're coming home with me?"

"Is this somethin' I'm gonna regret?" Sharp eyes dare me to give her a reason to say no. If she thinks I will say anything to fuck this up, she's wrong. I want this for both of us. Badly.

"God, I hope not," I joke. "Do I seem like a bad roommate?"

"I don't think a hospital is the best place to make that kind of decision." It all comes out in a jumble, much faster than her usual cadence.

Her sticky sweet accent is at its fastest when she's nervous or unsure of an answer. I could listen to her talk all day. I basically have for the last few days. Dr. Ruby told me that keeping her mind working was going to be helpful for her. Light conversation and such.

Small talk? I'm an expert at.

Talking to someone who doesn't want to talk? Also an expert at that.

I could carry on a conversation with a brick wall and still end up laughing at the end.

Something I learned young is that if you aren't laughing, you're crying. And I'm no crier.

I don't think she's a crier either but laughing is not something that she does often enough—with good reason.

Kathryn might be a bit of a thorn, but who wouldn't be?

She's in a state she's never been in and she has no idea how she got here. After waking up, she found out her only friend in the world is gone and is reminded of how her family has all passed. I would probably be a little surly in that case too.

Hell, I was when I found myself in a similar situation. Grumpy as all hell when I found myself with nothing and no one. Maybe that was the liquor talking for me. The liquor was all I had to talk to and I wish I had someone by my side to sit or talk about nothing with.

But I can be that for her.

I can be whatever she needs me to be.

If she needs me, then I'll be needed.

It's far more likely that the accident was caused by her friend since they wouldn't be used to driving on snow and ice like I was. A small part of me wonders if I could be to blame as well. I was rushing to help Tony and Drea find her daughter, Mireya, after she went missing. Mireya is a sweet kid and I may have been a bit reckless myself in trying to get there as fast as I could.

But when a friend is in need and they call you for help, you show up.

They needed me and I was there.

Tried to be anyway.

And if Kathryn is nothing else, she's a friend. A new one who isn't quite aware of that fact yet.

We have the shared trauma of this car crash that is going to change our lives in more ways than we can even predict at this point.

I don't know when I'll be able to use my leg the way I once did again.

I don't know when I'll be able to ride my horse again, a thought I've been trying to avoid as much as I can.

I don't even know when my face will look anything like it's supposed to.

What I do know is that I can help someone who needs it.

My head tilts with nonchalance I don't feel . "How about this? I'll help you find somewhere to work so you can get back to Louisiana. Besides, where else are you going to go?"

She bites her lip, thinking over what I've suggested. "I don't know..."

"Should I provide references?"

"Wouldn't make any difference. Everyone you'd know is an unknown to me. Same is the same."

"So it's settled then." I try to give her a reassuring smile as I hold my hand out for her to shake. "We're gonna be roomies."

CHAPTER 5

Jeann

"Kathryn will take the front seat since it has the seat warmers," Mack asserts to the nurse when we're making our way to the main entrance of the hospital. I stifle another wince when he calls me by my Nana's name. At some point I'll have to correct him, not right now though.

I hold the duffel bag in front of me like a shield to the cold that assaults me when the bay doors open. Even in my coat, the temperature is uncomfortable and dry. I wrinkle my nose at the sensation.

Things I wasn't expecting to be a part of my new year... riding to someone's house when I barely know them—to live there indefinitely.

Well, maybe I did. I can't remember anything still and it's becoming more and more frustrating.

I suspect that the man beside me knows more than he's letting on, but I can't be sure.

He's so happy and...smiley. Always in a good mood.

It should be more creepy than it is, but it suits him so well that I can't get upset about his sunny disposition anymore. It does confuse me to no end where he finds all this joy. His face is still swollen and purple and his leg is in a cast from a car accident that he was definitely not at fault for. I would be pissed in his shoes. All I got away with was a few stitches and a botched memory.

His doctor insisted that Mack be rolled out in a wheelchair because of potential ice on the ground. It would be unsafe for him to take a fall on the concrete. He looks ready to jump out of his skin in the chair ,but is patiently waiting for the staff member to go so he can continue not listening to the information they provided him with for recovery.

I would think the guy would have been more polite and listened. It was obvious to me that he was zoned ou,t but I guess I was the only one to notice. After all, his resting face does make it seem like he is both intrigued and present with you. But, the papers were still on the chair when he moved to the wheelchair and he never reached to pick them up. He seems to be willfully ignoring the fact that he is going to need this information. Like when he gets home his leg or nose will no longer be broken.

We made a deal so when he wasn't listening, I was. I took the information the doctor gave him that now sits in my duffel bag with my own discharge paperwork.

The nurse turns to me when we reach the side of his sister's SUV as it's pulling up. "I've put all the information about his upcoming schedule and all the numbers to reach us should anything come up on the front page of his write up." She seems to think for a moment and then adds, "For you, as well. Though Dr. Cresswell isn't too concerned about you. If you are having any problems, prolonged headaches, vomiting, anything else concerning, please call us. Okay?"

I nod, only half paying attention because a light skinned Black woman hops out of the SUV to help Mack into the vehicle. She fusses with him while the nurse talks to me. I'm a little stunned at the sight. The nurse returns to the hospital and still I watch the two of them bicker.

"Hi, I'm Reese," she says to me once she's helped him sit in the back seat. "This one didn't give you too much trouble did he?"

I pick up my jaw and clutch my bag even tighter to me. "Hey," I murmur, looking her over and trying to remember if there was anything Mack told me about this woman. Remembering she asked a question, I add, "No."

She chuckles. "Oh, right." Shoving the hand she was holding out for me into the pocket of her coat, she rolls her eyes. Not at me but seemingly at Mack. "He didn't tell you that his sister is a tall Black woman. Expecting something a little different I suspect."

I grimace because she's right. "Just a lil'."

"Long story short, we grew up right next to each other from birth. In our small town, everybody knows that so it's been a while since I've had to do this disclaimer." She laughs at herself. "Well, no light hair for me anymore and I've never had blue eyes, but we're as close as siblings can be. Not the play kind, that end up actually dating or something." She sticks her tongue out, pretending to gag. Then she shows me the ring on her left hand. "I'm very happily married and Stewart men aren't really my thing anymore." She shivers but continues, "He's told me plenty about you though."

Chancing a glance toward the backseat, I can feel Mack's eyes on the two of us, but his gaze shifts to his lap, probably on his phone or something. "Oh really?"

"Yes," she smiles but there's sharpness there. "I couldn't get him to come home because he insisted on staying by your side." Those sharp eyes of hers claw into mine long enough to hook me. "Any reason in particular why my brother would feel it's necessary to put your recovery over his own?"

I shake my head once, snark rolling off my tongue. "I told him many times to go home. I don't even know him. I—"

Now, she's the one looking me up and down. "Yet, you're moving into his *nice* house to care for him when he's very *vulnerable* and susceptible to all kinds of... *manipulation?*"

My eyes narrow as I cross my arms more tightly over my bag still pressed to my chest. "It's not like that at all. He needs someone to look after him and I don't have anywhere to go. What he's offerin' is too generous and I've told him that."

"Reese, will you stop? I'm ready to go home." She turns on Mack, who has rolled his window down to snap at her. "You're like a dog with a bone. Let it go." I'm guessing they already had this conversation when he was telling her *all about me.*

"Calling me a bitch isn't winning you any favors, Maxwell," She huffs, but it comes out like a tease. "I'm sorry," she says to me. "He's been through a lot and I'm just... protective. You see?"

"Yea," I say. I do see that she was ready to fight me in front of this hospital if she thought I was taking advantage of her bro.

Well, at least I know someone does care for him.

She doesn't help me into the passenger seat, but I hop in fine on my own and we ride away from the hospital.

The drive to Alpenglow Ridge from Harmony Hill is stunning, like something out of a nature documentary. In all my years, I never thought I'd see something so beautiful as this. I've never seen mountains. I've never seen this much snow. It's piled up on the edges of the roads and frosting the mountain tops. The trees are fuzzy and white with it. Nothing in my memory could compare to how breathtaking the sight of it is.

I must have seen this all before. I guess I'm lucky that I'm getting to experience this for the first time, *twice.*

One of the only benefits of my current circumstances.

It looks peaceful and I wonder how something so delightful could have upended my life so drastically.

Mack and Reese talk about someone called Legend on the drive and about her kids. There's fondness in his voice when he talks about his nephews and nieces as he asks her follow up questions. Mack is the kind of guy who would be the fun uncle who lets his sister's kids climb all over him and gives them too many sweets when Reese isn't looking.

He never mentioned it, but I wonder now if he has any kids of his own. I decide he must not because he doesn't seem like the kind of guy who would stop talking about them if he did.

When we exit the highway, I don't know what I was expecting, but this town is even smaller than my home town. The numbered county road we drive along to get to Mack's house is only two lanes and it's a long stretch before I even see a single building for the expanse of white fields.

Finally we reach the half circle drive that has been cleared to lead back to a single lane. The garage is closed but could easily hold four trucks. His house is nice just as Reese said it was, but I wasn't expecting *this nice*. It sprawls across an expanse of land that goes back as far as I can see that is pristine and white from the fresh fallen snow.

Its charcoal-gray siding contrasts against the white landscape, while the dark roof holds a thick coating of snow. The covered front porch, framed by warm wooden beams looks inviting and how you would expect a welcoming home to be. I've never been in a house this big or luxurious.

Icicles hang from the edges, catching the winter sunlight. The surrounding hills and mountains are still visible because they are truly massive. The beauty of them stretches along the horizon, their curves accentuated by the way snow sits atop of them.

The entire scene embodies a quiet, peaceful charm. It's the kind of place where hot cocoa is waiting by the fire, and the stillness of the snow-covered countryside invites you to slow down and take it all in. It's more inviting that I could have imagined and entirely too picturesque to be real.

"Who shoveled this?" Mack asks when Reese parks in front of the garage door.

She's out of the SUV responding to him over the seat. "Cory paid CJ fifty bucks to shovel and then do the back porch too. Said he needed it for Valentine's Day."

Mack shakes his head. "Ha. That boy is wasting no time it seems. Has Mireya been by since?"

"Drea is keeping her locked down. But it's only a matter of time."

"I'm glad she's okay..."

I feel like a nosy Nelly still sitting in the car with them as they continue to catch up around me. Stepping out into the chilly day, I walk over to the edge to the driveway and put the tip of my boot into the fluffy white pile. It crunches under my shoe and it's pleasant to my ears. I make the shape of a bunny with the edges of my shoe and it keeps me busy while the two of them make their way out of the SUV.

"That's really good," Mack says over my shoulder. The warmth from his body is close to me and I feel the caress of his breathing across my cheek. *Too close.* He's too close. "You did that just now?"

I shrug, rubbing my hands together to warm them. "Yea. Are we goin' inside? It's freezin' out here."

He chuckles. "C'mon, the heat's already on."

I walk behind him into the house, nervous that he might still slip on the salted walkway. The house is even more fancy and we reach the front of it. I can see the lush interior decorating of the inside through two massive windows that bracket the front door. I'm stuck out on the front porch admiring it when I should be helping him. I rush to do that, but he's making his way inside without my help. The oversized heavy wood door slams behind us.

The first thing I notice is the fireplace and how it crackles. Reese stands next to it poking a metal stick into the stack of wood.

"I'm sure you're not used to this." She motions to the fireplace. "We haven't had a winter this cold or snowy in years."

"Lucky me," I grumble low, but Mack catches what I said and laughs under his breath on the way to the couch closest to the fire.

The doorbell rings and I startle, but since I'm the closest to it, I open the door and see who is there.

"You're not Mack..." An older lady with tan skin and red hair says as she peers around me. Spotting him, she moves around me into the house. "Oh sweet boy, you look like a train hit you. Sit down somewhere." She hooks an arm under his and he allows her to settle him on the couch he was already making his way to. She slides the coffee table over and puts a pillow down to prop his leg up. He smiles good-naturedly at her, but it's looking tight around the edges.

"Sammie, the boy just got home. Give him a break." An older Black woman with a pixie cut comes in, closing the door with her butt since her arms are full with a box that has several large paper bags in it. "I'll put these in the kitchen," she says and disappears down the hall.

"Okay the Aunts are here so I'm gonna head out. Give me a call if anything," Reese says, hugging her brother around the shoulders before hugging the red haired woman and giving me a little wave. She's out of the house and I'm still standing awkwardly by the front door. Sammie is fluffing the pillow under Mack's leg and has yet to acknowledge me so I figure I should probably allow them time to do whatever this is.

Something clunks around in my chest with the reminder that there is no one to fuss over me or care about how I'm adjusting to my new reality.

I have no one.

"Well," I start, clearing the emotion out of my throat. I need to have a moment to gather myself and it won't be in the corner of the room with these strangers. "I'll get out of your hair... Is there a room for me down that hall or..."

Mack hops up from the couch, disregarding all the fussing Sammie was previously doing to grab his crutches. "Wait a second," he says, coming to my side. He's far too perceptible and I need to figure out how to not be affected by that like I am. "Sammie, this is Kathryn. She'll be staying here for the time being. Kathryn, this is Sammie. She's my brother-in-law's aunt. The woman you saw going into the kitchen is her wife, Janet." He maneuvers into my line of sight, "They'll just be here for a little while. Is that okay?"

I blow out a breath. "It's your house," I say, squeezing my duffel a few times, "I just think I want to lay down maybe."

"Yea. That is probably best. C'mon," he starts down the hallway and I follow him, not taking note of anything on my path. Taking slow and deliberate breaths in through my nose and out through my mouth, it's easier to push down the swirl of overwhelming emotions rising.

The door that he reaches isn't closed so he pushes through with a shoulder to reveal a room that is sunny and open. I wonder how many rooms are in this house and how many people have such easy access to it. Mack sits on the bed and then pats the spot next to him.

"You don't have to stay here. *The aunts* came to check on you and—"

"Sit, Kathryn." He pats the spot again and I finally move over to the bed, let my bag fall in a graceless heap on the floor. "It's a lot. I'm sorry that there were so many people here all at once. I told Reese to let me get adjusted on my own, but this town is kind of like that. They can be warm and friendly and welcoming when they want to be. To be truthful, a lot of the warmth is a somewhat recent development towards me. I don't want to overwhelm you though."

What does that mean? He's literally sunshine personified. How could the warmth not follow him wherever he goes. "It's fine. I just... I'm not used to it." It comes out like a question because in the memories I can access it's only a few kind smiles that I can recall. "I don't know how to handle all this... concern."

Carefully, I lie down on the bed, fluffing a pillow under my head to hug it instead of reaching for the man next to me. *What a weird thing to want.*

He chuckles and his teeth gleam in the bright sun's reflection off the snow outside. "It is a lot." It takes him a minute to get up onto his crutches again, but he looks down at me, "I'll square things up with *the aunts* and then show you around. How's that sound?"

Burying my face into the pillow that smells like fresh linens and citrus, I breathe it in. The pull on my stitches at my temple from the pressure on the pillow makes me wince when I nod.

Mack pats my legs in a comforting manner, but doesn't linger. I hear the quiet snick of the door when he leaves.

Even without the welcoming party, this was going to be a huge adjustment. At the end of the day, I'm in a strange town—strange state—with a man I barely know and somehow, trust.

I've lost everything.

The last memories I have are of my best friend who is gone, gone, gone.

Everyone is gone.

Everything I know is gone.

The first tear isn't one I feel. The ones that follow soak the pillow and take all the starch out of my back. I fall into a dreamless sleep, bathed in white just like fresh falling snow.

CHAPTER 6

Jeann

IT'S DARK OUT WHEN I wake with this urge in my palms. It felt like a small thought in the back of my mind, but I couldn't let it go.

There's a lamp on the nightstand next to the bed I fell asleep on. I rub my eyes and flick it on.

I want paper and pencil.

Sitting in the bed with my head leaned back on the headboard, I stare at the ceiling. Moments pass before I get bored and then spend time looking over the inked drawings on my arms.

As a kid, I could remember drawing on myself. It brought me peace when I was in class, but I never thought I'd have this many tattoos. Not just on my arms, either. I've got them all over. I was clearly busy these past few years accumulating them. But these feel like mine. Like my work.

Somehow I know that I was the one to create these.

The crystals and ethereal lines on my forearms are identical on both my upper arms. There's a wagon full of bottles on the inside of my upper arm. So, so many butterflies all over. Some are sketchy, line work and others are full color and detailed. The sliding image of a clock melting down the back of my bicep. Many little animals that peer curiously back at me. A woman with flowers in her hair and a large lily over her mouth on the inside of my arm. She looks familiar and sad with tears pooling in her eyes. It could be me, but most likely it's *her*.

There's a knock at my door. I look toward it wondering why he's even bothering to knock. We're not in a hospital anymore and this is his house.

"You up?" Mack's voice comes in from outside the door and I sit up.

"Yea. Come in." I pull the blanket over myself, not ready to get out of this real bed yet. I'm at least wearing clothes but more as a courtesy to him. My preference would be to sleep naked after those days of scratchy hospital sheets when these feel so soft and inviting. It would likely be as inappropriate as I think it would be though.

I settled for something in the middle. At some point I changed into a large sleep shirt from my bag.

He looks dressed and ready for bed. His standard flannel and athletic shorts are replaced with a tee that highlights his shoulders and arms with "ARHS" over his chest and loose flannel pants that cover his cast.

It's the first time I've seen him in a short sleeve shirt. I never saw the tattoos on his arms before. There are a few small ones on his hands, but it never occurred to me that he would have more of them for some reason. His art starts right above his wrists and disappears under his shirt. All in black with no color, just shading and negative space making a bold statement. My eyes flick up to his when I realize I'm staring and checking him out. As usual, he has a smile on his face even with my perusal. Unabashed nor uncomfortable with my examination of him.

I still don't know why he has been so generous with me. We don't have any history together. *Strangers.* Absolute strangers and even if I had my memory, I know he wouldn't be there.

I would never forget a man like him.

Don't get me wrong, I'm grateful because there is nowhere for me to go. I've been apparently just floating from place to place or I guess being kept by Ethan all the while. It's hard to tell. Everything I owned waits for me in a box in his parents' garage. They paid a company to pack up his old place. I don't know if I could have even been a help in that process. Thinking about him for too long hurts. I can't imagine being surrounded by all his things when he's not here anymore.

Grief is a weird thing.

I miss him and I still feel like I don't really know him because of the time I've lost. I only have memories of us as twenty-three year olds and then loss and then nothing. His mom's words still ring in my ear from the hospital. We were good friends for as far as I know. Dating? That seems like a stretch after everything that happened with *her*. I don't get any romantic feelings when I think about him. I keep having these thoughts that there is something bigger missing that ties me to my late friend.

I know there is.

My memory evades me and I'm pissed all over again hitting that wall in my mind.

It isn't really like a wall. It's more like trying to remember the word for something and nothing comes. There's just nothing where there should be something.

"What are you thinking about?" Mack asks as he walks over to the bed, unceremoniously plopping down at the foot and leaning his crutches on the side of him. They slide all the way to the ground and he scoffs.

"I'll grab them for you," I offer.

"It's alright. I should probably figure out how to get around by myself anyway."

I frown. "Why? That's the whole reason I'm here and it's easy for me to do it."

He grins and looks my face over. My face heats though I don't really understand why... besides the obvious.

I mean, I can tell the man before me is attractive, even with the swelling still lingering from his broken nose. But attraction for me has always been about more than the physical for me. There's something about his aura. The energy around him is shimmery like the heat from the sun. Dangerous and inviting all in the same breath.

I don't feel like I'm in danger.

I know it.

He is the kind of guy who would want forever, promises, futures.

None of which I can give him.

I can't truthfully say I even have a present since I'm dwelling on wisps of what should be my past.

Empty and vast.

"I guess I'm grateful then," he says. "But I don't know how long you'll be here… or how long I'll need help." I don't respond, choosing to slide out of the bed and grab his crutches instead.

It's then that I realize I'm in my sleep shirt and panties. Not naked but also not decent. The cool air brushing across my bare thighs and stomach as my sleep shirt rides up.

Mack definitely notices.

I've never been a modest person. I don't expect that to have changed in the time I can't remember. I still feel the flutters of indecency as he tries not to acknowledge my exposed skin.

I'm teetering this line with Mack that makes me feel like it's better to err on the side of modesty.

Pulling my shirt back down to cover myself, I hand him the crutches. He clears his throat. "So, Sammie helped me finally get a shower and all ready for bed before they left, but we need to eat something… I don't suppose you know how to cook?"

"I do, actually."

Pulling some socks on, I pad out into the hallway and follow at Mack's pace to the kitchen. He settles into a chair at his dining table while I look into the fridge and pantry to see if he has anything I could use to make something quick for dinner. Something about it feels familiar. Likely because between Ethan and I, I was the only one who knew how to make anything edible. Couldn't trust him to boil water without nearly burning the place down.

It looks like Janet replaced the basics and cleared out anything that could have gone bad while he was at the hospital. I don't really want to get ahead of myself and decide on something he wouldn't want to eat since I'm using his food. I lean around the pantry door to check in with him.

He's doing something on his phone that makes him grimace, an expression I've only seen him make when he's in pain.

"How do you feel about breakfast for dinner?"

Looking up from the screen, his face changes from the grimace to something softer. "Eggs and bacon and toast?"

"I'll do you one better. Eggs, bacon and hot cakes."

"Careful, Kathryn. I might have to keep you."

That's exactly what I'm scared of.

I shiver under his proclamation and busy myself with preparing the ingredients. Not responding is better than saying the truth of my reaction.

Changing the subject entirely, I say, "Not many people called me Kathryn. It was my Nana's name." I lean my head to the side waving the spatula in the air. "Prefer Jeann more, it's my middle name."

A gash in my chest the size of the woman who I was named after stings as I recall the information. The memories of losing her are fuzzier. For that I'm grateful. We were close, more so than my parents. She was my everything and that doesn't come close to the true nature of our connection. She was in the room when I was born and the first person I told anything about my life.

He sets his phone down on the table and I hear it thunk against the wood. He doesn't say anything to what I've told him so I turn to see what his expression is saying.

Nothing could prepare me for the cheesy grin on his face. "Jeann..." He rolls my middle name around his mouth like he's tasting it, the smile never breaking once he's done. *He was waiting for me to look at him.* Would he have waited until I was done cooking to show me all his teeth like this?

"What?" I ask. "Somethin' wrong with Jeann?"

"It suits. It's perfectly you," He nods to himself, lips quirking to the side. "Not that there was anything wrong with Kathryn, but I imagine you are far more Jeann than her."

Despite myself, I laugh as his assertion. "I am more Jeann than Kathryn." I shrug. "I didn't see any need in correctin' the nurses since my name *is* Kathryn."

"But you didn't correct me until now…"

"Well, I didn't know you'd be takin' me to your house when we first met or when you were campin' out in my hospital room." I grumble.

Cracking five eggs into a bowl I've found, I busy myself with scrambling and adding seasonings to the mixture while I wait for the nonstick frying pan to get hot.

He allows me to finish cooking without questioning me further. He turns on a speaker to play music as he watches me moving around the kitchen. For some reason I was expecting Country music given his hat and boots, but soft rock that I recognize plays instead.

If it weren't for the gaping hole of information my brain can't access, I would think that I had just a little fender bender that was no big deal instead of a traumatic brain injury. My body is a little achy, but kind of like I haven't worked out in a long time and I need to again. My head isn't hurting too badly and I can do most things that I wouldn't have been doing before the accident.

Does that make me lucky or unlucky?

Maybe I picked up some sixth sense because I swear I can feel Mack's eyes on me whenever they stray from his phone or the rope he ties, unties and reties while he waits. He's surprisingly quick and I picture the types of activities he would need quick knots like that for.

Obviously, it's gotta be for cows or something like it. He's got the working hands that look like they've spent hours doing hard labor. Strong arms and forearms that are veiny enough to make my mouth water. I may have functioning eyes and a libido, that does not mean that it would be smart to do anything about these observations. He's letting me stay here for free which makes him right off limits in order to keep any lines from getting blurry.

But this girl has noticed that Mack is too damn sexy for his own good.

I find plates for the food and bring them over to where he sits. He thanks me and proceeds to finish his food like there is prize money at the end of this. I don't think he took one breath… or chewed?

"Have somewhere to be?" I ask, blinking slowly at him and his plate.

His eyebrow lifts. "Me? Not exactly mobile right now," he jokes.

"Any reason why you swallowed the plate whole?" I ask, gesturing to his empty plate. There's not even syrup from his hotcakes left.

"Habit," he admits. I raise an eyebrow back at him but continue eating my own food. I can't imagine what would make it a habit unless this man was in prison or something... which I guess he could have been, but I highly doubt that.

He offers no clarification but hedges instead. "So, I was thinking..." Pushing his plate aside, he leans onto the table top with crossed arms to get a better look at me. Or maybe steady himself, there's no telling, but I lean back to give him more space in either case. "I can't work with a bum leg. And they won't even let me do anything on Mason Ranch because I'm a liability all because Reese believes that 'I won't stay sitting and do what I am allowed to.' That leaves me with a lot of free time on my hands." He flashes a quick smile more at his expense than his genuine enjoyment of that realization. "So, I've been thinking about what you could do all day because as fun as I am to be around, I imagine that you don't want to watch my leg stitch itself back together for the next couple weeks."

I mirror how he has crossed his arms only I don't lean onto the table, maintaining the space between us. "You're right, I don't wanna do that."

"Well, I did say that I would help you find a job or something to help you get back home. I'm not completely useless on my own so you wouldn't be getting away with any responsibilities in our agreement if you worked part time somewhere. What did you do before now?"

If my empty bank account and wallet are anything to go by, "I didn't seem to have a job before now."

"Great," he blurts, but then thinks for a second and amends. "Well, not great, but you don't need experience to work at Tuft. My friend needs someone to fill in for her last receptionist. She's on maternity leave or something. You know, answer the phones and schedule clients? It can't be that hard... Maybe intense since her salon is the only good one in town."

My brows furrow, "Mack, you don't know what you're talkin' about. I worked at my mom's hair salon in high school. It is *a lot* of work. And if it's the only good one in town I'm sure it is busy as hell."

He ignores my observation entirely, choosing to focus on the part about me working in a salon before. "Perfect, so you do have experience. Settles that then, I'll let her know I've found someone."

Something in my chest flutters at his words. *I've found someone.* They don't mean what my stupid little heart thinks they mean, but my stupid heart doesn't care. And what the fuck is that? Stupid organ. Before I can object or process his words, he makes this call to his friend on my behalf. Even on the phone, he's charismatic.

I can't help that Mack's right though. If I expect to make it back to Louisiana, I need to start making some money. Declining his offer to buy me a ticket was probably not the best idea on my part, but I didn't want to owe him.

You're living in his house rent-free, you still *owe him.*

But that doesn't really count since I'll be helping him around here any-way. I continue to argue in my mind, wrecking my top lip with my teeth as he talks to his friend.

"She said you can come in Wednesday to do some quick training and start sometime after that. Will that work?"

"Yea," I respond, messing with the end of the braids I should probably take out if I'm going to be working at a hair salon. That is not how I would want to go to a job interview–with old braids that have literally been to hell and back. In my duffel bag, there are all the products I remember using on my natural hair before my memory loss so I could wash my hair as long as I'm careful to avoid scrubbing my stitches.

"Whatcha thinking about?" As usual, Mack is too perceptive.

"Hair," I say simply.

He tilts his head, "What about hair?"

"Umm... I was thinkin' I'd take my braids down so I can make a good impression."

His eyes go wide, "That's a lot of braids... Do you need help?"

"You?" I ask, "You'd help me take my braids down?"

I pick up our plates from the table and take them to the sink to rinse and put into his shiny stainless steel dishwasher. "Yea... There's hundreds, you'll never get any sleep tonight if you do it by yourself."

With a hand on my hip, I turn to face him again. "But I also don't have time to fix any disasters that could come from you tanglin' my hair into oblivion..."

He scoffs, "With the number of times I've had to help Reese take hers down, I should put it on my resume. She used to get those all the time and they were always so damn long."

I had almost forgotten that his sister's Black and she does have super thick hair from what I saw. "Okay, I guess we should get started then."

He puts on a movie that starred Michael B. Jordan for us to watch on his cozy leather couch. It surprisingly wasn't overstuffed and stiff, but soft and warm like a hug, like the man. I wonder if he had any say in how this house is designed. It isn't a bachelor pad, it's thoughtfully decorated in neutrals ranging from dark brown to cream. Photos of what I'm guessing is his family and friends are on the walls along with some art that doesn't fit what I imagined he'd pick for himself. Though the house is large, it still has a cozy and homey feel.

I started out sitting on the side of him since my braids were pretty long and it would be more comfortable for both of us. Eventually, I ended up laying on a pillow in his lap when the left side was done. It takes us two and a half hours to finish. I couldn't believe that we both unbraided about the same amount.

People say that there is something intimate about having someone play with your hair, but having Mack do it...

I'm only human.

I'm only so strong.

I am beyond proud of myself for not being a puddle on the ground or with my legs spread wide.

I was awkward when I stood, my hair crimped and loose from the style it had just been in. I had to press my thighs together, desperate for a shower to take care of feelings that I had no business having simply because his fingers were in my hair.

His olympic eyes, as impossibly blue as they are, couldn't hide the affection he has for me.

At what point he stopped watching the movie to watch me, I don't know.

All I know is that I don't deserve the care he's shown me, *is* showing me now. Only a saint would volunteer to take someone's hair down. Especially if they're not getting anything out of it.

He needed to curb that, honestly, because someone like me would capitalize on it.

I don't know where that thought came from but I had to forget about it when I discovered all the showers had detachable nozzles.

CHAPTER 7

Mack

"I WAS THINKING I'D go over to the Ranch today. Maybe you want to come with me?"

I'm sick of sitting in this house doing nothing and it's only been two days. In the hospital it was different. I knew there was an end to the stay there. I had something to look forward to. Now the waiting is still ten weeks of being patient and I want to scratch my eyeballs out. I grimace down at my casted leg while I wait for Jeann to look up from the notebook she's drawing in.

She cocks her head to the side, the large curly bun she put her hair into losing a few of the strands in the process. I track the fall of her hair around her pretty bare face and swallow thickly.

She is stunning with the soft morning light shining on her and the sweatshirt I gave her. It hangs off of one of her dainty shoulders where the small infinity arrow tattoo peeks out.

Sure, I'm attracted to her.

Not only *attracted*, but I care about her.

I've learned her moods and her faces. Of which, there are many. She is so expressive without having to say a word. I like how exactly what it seems is exactly what I get with her.

That feeling I had about her in the hospital of being drawn and needing to reassure myself that she was safe is mellow when I have her in my house. I worry about what it will be like when she'll have to go to the salon for work soon.

I miss her already and she hasn't left yet.

"What would I do there?" Jeann puts the notebook down and sets the charcoal next to it. I'm so grateful that online delivery is not lacking in our small town. She said she wanted to draw and the next day everything showed up at the front door. It's consumed most of her attention and, frankly, most of mine whenever I get a chance to watch her work.

"You don't have to do anything. I work there—worked? I don't know. To be honest, I miss my babies."

"B-babies?" She chokes out, hesitation in her eyes.

"Oh," I laugh. "Not human ones. My horses. I have a couple that I call mine though only one actually is. It's almost been three weeks and I'm starting to itch. I'm in a bad way when I don't get to see them for a long time," I admit.

"Umm... I don't know." She bites her top lip. "Wouldn't that be... I don't know. You can't just bring me to work."

"Why not? I won't actually be working. I can't do much for at least a couple more weeks. Even with a boot after the plaster, it will be hard to do anything I would usually do there. Why can't I bring a friend?"

She shrugs, twisting the end of a curl around her finger and tucking it into her bun. "It just seems strange. I mean, all of this is strange." She gestures around her in an agitated movement. "You've already done so much for me when it's basically my fault, you're..." She doesn't finish the thought. We both know what she's referring to.

"It was an *accident*, Jeann. You were in the passenger seat. I can't just go around blaming the world for my bad luck. It was that way long before you came into the picture."

"What does that mean?"

"One day, I'll tell you." I think that thought over a bit, adding, "I'll tell you when I think you won't bolt."

There's skepticism in her brows when she asks, "Why would I bolt?"

My lips twist to the side while I think about what I should tell her. But then, I decide that less is probably best for the reason I've already stated. "Eh. It's not you. It's just the usual reaction for me, I guess."

"For people to run when you share your truth?" Now her confusion plays out in all the features of her face, her eyes are tight, nose scrunched and lip curling. She's offended on my behalf instead of being leery...

Did I mention that I like this woman?

"Maybe not my truth but my weight..." *Weight.* That is probably not giving enough context. "The deeper the layers you uncover about why I had to fight hard to be the person you see standing before you today is heavy for a Tuesday morning, don't you think?"

She doesn't respond to my question and I don't add anything else. Leaning against this doorway is not the most comfortable, but I don't want her to feel like I'm shutting her out by leaving. Or for her to feel more comfortable prying by sitting on the bed. There'll be plenty of time for her to leave and I don't want it to be now.

The silence is a tangible thing, but she rises from her spot on the bed, closing the distance between us and hugs me.

I wouldn't expect it from her, but relief washes over me as I accept her comforting without hesitation. She may not know why she's doing it, but she senses enough of my unease to make the choice to do something about it.

Her arms around my neck.

My arms around her waist.

Much too heavy for a Tuesday morning.

But I'm still grateful for her presence in the *weight* anyway.

She breaks her hold on my neck, but I don't let go of her waist. Allowing the small space between our bodies, my hands hold her secure, even as I use the door jamb for support. My eyes take in all the details of her face. How close the color of her eyes are to copper. How curly and long her eyelashes are. How soft her lips look...

"Well, I guess I should get ready then..." she says with her eyes on my lips as well. "I don't have any boots or anythin' though."

"I—don't worry about that. I'm sure there's some here. Give me a sec." I finally release her and turn in the opposite direction down the hall.

"Mack," she calls after me since I'm already on my crutches and headed down the hall. I don't stop and she follows me through the house. "It's fine. I've got—Where are you goin'?"

I duck into a different room, on a mission.

"You're an eight. Right?" I ask from where I sit on the floor of the walk-in closet.

"Huh?"

"These are an eight. She never really wore them so they might be a little stiff. Try 'em out." I hold a pair of black cowboy boots up toward her from where I'm sitting.

"I will if you promise to slow down. I think you're overestimatin' how much you can do on your own," she snarks.

"I'm fine." I roll my eyes at her precautions, but I enjoy the concern she has for me.

She gives me a look and sits on the bed to slide her foot into the boot. "It fits pretty well," she says, sliding the other one on.

"Great."

"Um, whose boots are these?" She asks, looking over the stitch work.

"My mom's," I respond knowing there's more coming from her as she frowns.

She starts taking a boot off, but I stop her with a hand over hers. "She left these knowing I'd either donate or throw them away. She doesn't care about any of the stuff in this house anymore. Including me apparently." I didn't want to get into anything heavy, but this is the truth. As sad as it is. Reese came when I was in the hospital, not my mom. She hasn't even called.

"Mack, that's—" she starts, but I cut her off.

With a smile I don't truly feel, I tell her, "Too heavy for a Tuesday morning. How about around five we'll head over?"

Hours later, she's in a long sleeved black crop top and black jeans with the cowboy boots I gave her. A jacket is thrown over her arm for when we will soon be out in this Colorado cold again. In the days I've known her, I've never seen her outside of the baggy hospital gown except for the glimpse I got the other day in her sleep shirt.

But man... her body looks incredible in this tight outfit. She's curvy with full, high tits, a slim waist and hips that flare and beg for my hands. My neck heats and my hands twitch, wanting to do just that. I do my best not to stare and make her uncomfortable, instead. I'm gonna be thinking about the curve of her ass all night and maybe forever.

With her following behind me again, we walk to the garage on the other side of the house. There's a row of hooks for all the vehicles parked here minus one that I never replaced since my truck rests in pieces. "You have another ride?"

"I've got two more actually. Since my right leg is completely fine, I can drive or... you can if you'd like to try."

She looks at the two cars and the ATV in the room. "What kind of cowboy drives a compact car?"

"It's not the vehicle that makes the cowboy, trust me on that." I wink and walk to the driver side of the small car she was just referring to.

"Whatever." Scoffing, she hustles to cut me off and stop me from opening the driver's side door. "I might have had my head knocked around a bit, but I still think I'm the better option between the two of us."

"Alright," I agree easily and she helps me over to the passenger side unnecessarily, gathering my crutches for us to leave.

"We'll have to stop by the main house before we go out to the stables. Chandie is probably making dinner by now so the house will be full."

"Okay..."

"The Masons are a big family and all of them are big personalities. I know you don't... love people so..."

She parks the car and is about to get out when I stop her with a hand on her forearm. Jeann looks back at me and I say, "It's probably best that you just let them fawn over you than to resist it."

"Who? Why would they fawn over me?" She asks. I give her a second to put the pieces together. "Oh, yea. Well I'm perfectly fine. They should be fawnin' over you. If anyone is the damsel here, it's you."

I chuckle at her assessment. "That may be true, but I'm sticking with the advice I've given you."

"So what exactly does that mean?"

"Exactly what I said."

Jeann shakes her head at me and then helps me out of the car and the noise from inside is already spilling out before we get to the front door.

"We'll just be here for a little while or you can eat too. It's completely up to you."

"Mack, I'm not gonna make a scene or somethin' because there are a lot of people here. I am house-trained, you know." She smirks at the tease I can feel coming. "I'm already with Reese on one thing. Callin' me a bitch is winnin' you no favors."

The heat crawls up my neck and I bluster, "I—I never said–" I don't get a chance to finish that thought because Jeann opens the door and all my family sets upon us at once.

CHAPTER 8

Mack

I MUST HAVE REPEATED myself at least a dozen times. Dinner goes just how I thought it would. Something in me wanted Jeann to be uninterested in sitting down for a meal. Faced with a choice of cooking or eating, I'm sure the choice would be obvious for anyone though. Especially if it's Reese's Mom, Chandie, who's doing the cooking.

Chandie forced Jeann to sit and be taken care of. Plates of food come and go, and Chandie or Sammie asked her question after question about everything that happened—that she could remember—and then packed her two containers of the leftovers. The only plus side was that Chandie made extra of her lemon poppyseed cookies to send us home with. I'm obsessed with those things.

I sat back, observing how Jeann was handling all the attention. From what I can tell, she doesn't have much family to speak of. Her and I are alike in that way, except the Masons took me under their wing without prompting. It looks like they'll do that for Jeann, too. Even Reese is comfortable around her and that woman is territorial as all hell with her family. Now that she has her own kids, she's even more fierce about protecting the people she loves. I think Reese and Jeann would be good friends if Jeann let her in.

"So the puppy got a new owner," Cory says to me when a spot opens up next to me on the couch. My sister's husband is about the same build as me but deceivingly soft. To hear him call me puppy is laughable at best. Reese has Cory so wrapped up it's not even funny.

Laughing at him, I attest, "I couldn't say that I know what you're talking about."

"Your eyes haven't left her, man. You think anything could happen to her at the crib?"

"It's not that."

"Then what is it?" He eyes me for a while before his attention is taken by his son asking him something as he flops onto the couch with us.

"I don't want her to be uncomfortable."

The kids are watching something on the TV now that dinner is over. Reese, Chandie, Sammie, Janet, and a couple of their friends I don't re-member the names of are all sitting at the table still. Danny, Reese's Dad, is talking with Tommy Lewis and Peter McKenzie on the opposite end. The women are at the table talking about who knows what, but Jeann doesn't seem to be out of place. She does a lot more listening and watching than I would expect given how quick she is to pop off at me.

The thing is, I feel like I know her so much more than I do. I have no right to have *expectations* of what she will or will not be like. It's been almost three weeks since I met her. And meeting her was not a casual affair like we were just grabbing drinks or something. Heavy machinery colliding the way ours did is not casual. Maybe that's why I don't feel like she's simply some woman that will come and go from my life.

Though I should treat her like the stranger she is.

I can't make my mind think of her like that.

She's not just some woman.

Cory makes a sound that shows me he doesn't believe what I am saying. "And you think she would be? Here?"

I shrug. "I don't know. She doesn't like small talk and all that."

"She looks like she's doing just fine. Maybe you should loosen the reins on her."

My eyes narrow on my friend. "Maybe you should let me be."

"Damn." He shakes his head. "You're down bad,, but I like it on you. Happy puppy is better than sad puppy."

I laugh with him. "Shut up." It takes me a minute but I get up off the couch and make my way over to the table where Jeann is still listening intently. Ten sets of eyes look back at me when I approach.

Placing a hand on the back of Jeann's chair, I address the group. "All right, we're gonna go to the stables." Jeann gives me a knowing look, but grabs the large tote bag with the food up.

"Good night and thank you for the meal. It was so good," she tells Chandie with more manners than I managed just then.

Chandie stands with her to hug her goodbye. The woman is always decked out in all kinds of custom jewelry that she designs herself. It manages to catch the light no matter where she is and it's like she's sparkling when she moves in any way. Holding her by the elbows, Chandie says, "Don't be a stranger. There's always enough to share here and we're right across the way."

Jeann looks over to me, but I keep my face neutral, not wanting to affect her response. I'm genuinely curious about what she's thinking. "That would be nice," She settles on, noncommittal but pleasant. I'm shocked.

Chandie hugs her once more for good measure and then comes to hug me. In a low tone, she tells me, "She's a good one. Do right by her. Rebecca would agree."

That's the crux of it all. My mom would not agree because nothing is ever good enough for her. I settle with just telling her, "Okay."

"Wait! Let me grab you some arnica for that face. Honey, you're still all green under the eyes." She flits off to grab the cream then Jeann puts the food in the car before we head over to the building to the west of the main house.

The walk to the stables isn't far, but by the time we reach the staff entrance, I'm tired and my armpits hurt from balancing on the gravel. Jeann spots the chair Tony usually sits in by the door and unfolds it for me.

"Are you sure you don't just want to go home?" She questions. Though it's freezing outside, I wipe the sweat from my brow. "You've done a lot already."

"I'm close to agreeing with you," I admit. "But, I'm near them now and I just want to see 'em if only for a short while." Desperation laces my words and I do nothing to hide it.

Through everything I've been through over the years, they were my constants. I always had a horse to rely on when I was feeling low. My spirits lifted by being close to the animals that always fascinated me. Even as a young boy, I knew I wanted to work with horses when I grew up—much to my dad's dismay.

Then again, everything I wanted was to his dismay.

"Fine. But, we're gonna sit here until you cool down at least." She crosses her arms and I know she means it. I won't fight her on it because I really am winded.

"C'mere," I say, not a command, since I'm still a little breathless from the walk over. She doesn't uncross her arms, but walks closer to me from where she stood by the door. She does that quite a lot. Stand on the edge, not joining what's going on. Even at the table, she didn't add anything to the conversation, just sort of let it happen around her. I want to help her change that. I don't want her to feel like an outsider with me or my family. If there is something that makes her uncomfortable, I want to change it.

I need her to be comfortable with me even if I can't quite place where that need is coming from.

She steps close enough for me to reach out and touch her. I reach for her, my hand tugging at her jacket once then twice before she closes the distance between us. Jeann's careful when she stands between my open legs. "That's better."

As far back as I can remember, I've been a hands-on kind of guy. A pat on the shoulder, squeezing someone's hand, scratching a horse's neck. Reese would always tell me how I'm too huggy or touchy-feely when we were kids and that not everybody likes it. I was the kid who was not good with personal space. My friends had gotten used to it, but I've forgotten how to preface that fact about myself because everyone in Alpenglow Ridge knows this about me.

I didn't even think about it when Jeann and I were in the hospital. I never hesitated to try and be there for her in any way that I knew how. She never pulled away. She leaned into it, even though she would snark the whole time about everything else. Probably another reason why I feel like I know her far better than I do.

My hands hold her close to me on the back of her thighs. It's proprietary and probably inappropriate. I pause since this was exactly what I've been fighting not to do all night.

There's no push back from her. Her arms are still crossed as she looks down at me, "You're doin' too much. Still huffin' and puffin'. You put me in charge of helpin' you and I feel like I'm just lettin' you get away with murder."

A laugh bubbles up out of me. "Murder? It's not even a quarter mile from here to the house. I bet it's not even five hundred feet from the Mason's house to the barn. There was nothing in the doctor's orders that said I couldn't move around."

"A quarter mile?! Mack have you lost your whole mind? I'm not lettin' you walk this far on crutches anymore. You're about to sweat through your jacket."

I rest my forehead against her stomach, fully laughing at her assessment of the situation. She smells like a flower I don't know the name of and lemons. I'm too close if I can smell her. It's gonna haunt me, I know it.

She pats my head. "Yep. There goes the last of your marbles across the wood chips." I laugh harder and Jeann grumbles. "It's not funny. You should be restin'. Healin'.'"

I wipe the tears from my eyes and regain my composure. A stupid smile on my face by the time I look up at her. Her lips twitch like she'll smile back at me, but she puts a finger to my chest making me back up more so she can properly look down her nose at me. "You will take what the doctor said seriously, Mack. Say it."

"I will take what Dr. Kathryn Jeann Barker says seriously," I respond with my eyebrow raised. She shakes her head at me, but allows me to rest my forehead on her again. Maybe it's magnolia? What could that flower be?

"Let's go see my babies." I say after a time of cooling down. My arms still ache, but I'm at least not as hot as I was before.

I'm satisfied by how empty the stables are. I walk us over to my favorite part of the building, about grab the things I need from the tack room, but remember that I'm not going to be riding anytime soon. Muscle memory took me here and now I just stand looking at the hooks that are for my things with longing that feels too heavy to hold.

Jeann places a hand on my back, "Horses are over here," she prompts. I nod, swallowing the lump in my throat.

We take the right out of the tack room where most of the horses are resting for the night.

Artemis and Legend talk to each other over the low gate of their stables. There's lots of room for them to move around or even lay down, but they both probably got up when they heard someone in the building.

I hope they missed me as much as I missed them.

"Which of you are gonna help me cope, huh?" I swear, they deliberate amongst each other and Artemis walks over to lie on the straw stacked up for her.

"Oh, it's like that Arte? I'll remember that when the carrots come out."

She huffs, sending straw flying around, but doesn't get up.

"Alright. Legend, I want you to meet someone." His big tan head rests on my shoulder and I hug his neck. My crutches land with a thunk against the gate. She catches them before they slide to the ground and sets them more strategically so they don't fall. "You're my buddy," I say, scratching him all over.

"He's beautiful," Jeann says. "He looks just like that horse from the Barbie movies."

My lips tilt at the corner thinking of her watching one. "A fan of the Barbie movies, are you?"

"Shut up. I was a little kid once, you know?"

"He's a Halfinger and would probably prefer that you didn't call him a Barbie horse." I snort a laugh. "Give 'em a rub." With my eyebrows dancing on my forehead, I add, "He loves the ladies. Right, buddy?"

She holds a hand out toward him with tentative fingers. Legend looks at me and I nod my head in her direction, telling him *go on*. He puts his big head against her hand, sniffing her fingers. "That tickles," she remarks.

There's wonder in her voice in between the Southern drawl of her words.

She steps closer to him to scratch the side of his neck. He drops his head gently on top of her shoulder and she looks at me, eyes wide. "Is he… huggin' me?"

I smile back at her, "It's awfully one sided…" She catches my meaning and hugs my horse back.

As I lean against this gate taking in the sight before me, something squeezes in my chest. I wish I could take a picture of this moment so I could keep it forever.

Jeann with her eyes closed, a small smile on her lips. She's completely relaxed with her arms around his neck. Legend, to his credit, is a good horse. He's steadfast and loving. The calm of his energy is only surpassed by the confidence he has when we ride out to get work done. I missed being around him. If Artemis wasn't in a mood from me being gone, I'd love for her to properly meet Jeann, too.

She is someone worth meeting.

Someone worth making time for.

Someone worth keeping.

The woman finally opens her eyes. The dark depths glimmer with emotion, but she's quick to collect herself. "What are you starin' at?"

"Perfection."

CHAPTER 9

Jeann, Then

"Just breathe, Lauren. Breathe, baby. You got this." Ethan told Jeann's sister as she gripped the side of the bed until her knuckles turned white.

He stood beside her holding a cup of ice chips, mimicking the way they were supposed to be breathing.

The way the doula showed them over the past few months they had been preparing.

Jeann couldn't for the life of her figure out why they had a doula in the first place when they still ended up at the stale hospital. It smelled like chemicals and lavender so strongly, her stomach churned to think about the sweet little life Lauren was making having to endure it.

Lauren's blue papery gown was crinkling and sharp looking against her round belly. Her sister barely looked like herself. Her nose and face had gained water weight which in Jeann's mind was a clear indication that she was ready for her new role. Lauren had changed and she was going to be a mom. Her entire body went through a metamorphosis. *She barely looked like Jeann.* She was a butterfly and it was beautiful.

Jeann's mom had the girls back to back. They were what people called Irish twins, but they looked so similar people assumed they shared a womb. Though they weren't that far apart in age, Jeann was always the big sister who had her back. Even though the kids were cruel and mean to Jeann, she would never let that slide for her sister. She was willing to put anyone in their place when it came to Lauren.

Jeann protected her from everything and anything. She took that role seriously.

Ethan was constantly getting kicked out from his house and staying at their place since they were sixteen. He basically slept on the couch until they graduated and he got his own place. The guy didn't know how to stay out of trouble, but he wasn't a bad guy. Jeann and Ethan were the town weirdos that no one understood. A little too alternative, not cool enough, not personable, but they had become friends in elementary school and had been inseparable.

Lauren was their opposite. She was the goodness between the two of them. She was friendly and open. Lauren could make the grumpiest grump change their tune. Like Jeann or Ethan.

When Lauren came to Jeann and admitted that her and Ethan were together and had been for months, Jeann was furious. All that lying and sneaking around! Ethan wasn't the man that Jeann would have picked for her sister but somehow, they made each other happy. That was all Jeann wanted for Lauren—and Ethan.

They could have just told her though.

Ethan was terrified that Jeann would beat his ass for *defiling* her sister. They were adults though. Jeann couldn't stop them from making decisions that they stood behind. She loved them both and after a few weeks of initial weirdness, Jeann knew she needed to just accept that they were actually a sweet couple.

Looking at the two of them bringing a whole new life into the world was incredible. He will get his shit together for this baby, so help her God or Jeann would skin him like a cat.

Jeann was gonna be an aunt.

The little squish was going to be so beautiful. They didn't know the baby's sex yet. Lauren wanted it to be a surprise.

With her hooked up to all these machines, Lauren could barely move on the bed and each contraction hit her like an earthquake she was bracing for. Ethan "hee, hoo'd" to her over and over. Sometimes, she listened and followed along with him, sometimes Jeann was afraid Lauren would crack a molar from how tight her jaw was.

"Lauren, you're gonna pop a blood vessel," Jeann said just to agitate Lauren who was normally pleasant and bright.

"If you're not gonna be helpful, how about you leave?" Lauren snapped at her.

"Ooh, so testy. You'd think she was pushin' a human out or somethin'," she said to Ethan.

He gave Jeann an exasperated look. "I know you love to tease my girlfriend, but maybe..."

"Fine, I'll go," Jeann said. Before she left, she pressed a kiss to Lauren's damp forehead, saying, "Next time I see you will be with auntie's squish." She waved me away and continued crunching ice. "I love you, Lo."

Jeann fell asleep in the waiting area, and woke to Ethan shaking her. "J-Jeann. Jeann you need to wake up."

Her best friend's panicked face came into focus, his eyes were bloodshot and he looked rough. Jeann rubbed the sleep out of her own eyes. "She's back there and I don't know what's goin' on," Ethan says.

"Who's back there? Where's the baby?"

He paced in the short space in front of Jeann. "I-I, I don't know. Jeann, my babies are back there and they won't let me stay in the room."

"What? Why not?" Jeann sat up more alert. "Start from the beginning. They kicked you out?"

"The machine started beepin'. It was beepin' so loud and-and the nurses rushed in and started talkin' to each other real fast. I didn't know what was goin' on. They-they they said somethin' was abnormal and that I needed to wait out here."

"Okay. They're workin' on it. We're in a hospital, they are gonna figure out what's wrong. It'll be fine."

Jeann tried to soothe her friend, but she was in a panic, herself. Her sister was only twenty-two. She would make it out with her healthy baby and it would all be fine.

"I CAN'T DO THIS anymore," Ethan shook his head. "We can't do this anymore."

The bottle fell from Jeann's hand with a dull thud and she squinted at the swirling figure in front of her. "Isss fine," she slurred. "Another round!" she shouted.

"We left the bar hours ago, Jeann. We're not even in Baton Rouge."

That startled Jeann for a moment. Ethan stood outside of the car with his arms crossed. *When did Jeann get into a car?* It was a lesson in balance as she tried to sit up in the car and face him. She situated her clothes with agitation like she had any right to be indignant.

"It's not fine. You can't keep drinkin' like this. You lost your job and now, I've had to pick you up from Baton three times." His stern face made her gut drop. Or maybe it was the liquor. "We both miss her, Jeann. I lost a loved one too. Fuck! I lost two! My fuckin' girls are gone. You don't think I'm hurtin' too!" He held her face to look at him and his three faces merged into one, "I refuse to lose you, too."

"Ethan, I—"

"Nope. It's done. I've been strong for the both of us and I'm puttin' my foot down, dammit." He helped her to the condo and fished for the key in his back pocket while she leaned against the wall for stability. "We're gettin' out of Louisiana. I'm gonna find a way." Jeann murmured something, but he shushed her. Probably because it was late and her Nana was trying to sleep. She'd never been good with volume control when she was drunk. Either too loud or too quiet.

Jeann almost forgot that she had moved in with her Nana. It was too painful for her to be in the apartment that her and her sister had lived in.

He got the door open and helped her to the couch. At some point, her bottle had disappeared again. Then she remembered the conversation they just had. Ethan had taken her bottle. Overwhelming emotions bubbled up and she felt like she was gonna puke. Pressing her face to the cool leather of her Nana's couch, she started to feel more stable.

Then Ethan was in her face, loud whispering. "Get up. Get up. UP!"

"What's goin' on? I'll get in the bed later. I'm good right here."

"No," he snatched the pillow from under her head. "That's not—Dammit. Just get up!" He was still whispering, but she sat up.

The lights were off now. He was looking out the back window and closing the curtains all around.

"Oh, God." Ethan backed away from the window, pulling her along with him. "We need to go."

Jeann's legs were concrete pillars under her body. "Imma comin'."

The world was still tilting at odd angles then she registered the pain down her side as she tripped off the curb. "Ow."

The damp grass was torn between her fingers from trying to catch herself and mud was all down her arm. It was too damp for her comfort so she tried to swipe it off, but more grass got stuck in the mud than she was getting off her arm.

He was back to help her get the mud off and she swatted at his hands, frustrated that he'd done it so quickly.

"J, I'm not kiddin'. We have to go now." His shoulder was under hers, hoisting her to stand again. "I hope like hell that you don't remember any of this."

"Memberrr whaaa?" Her body slumped into the backseat and blackness consumed her.

CHAPTER 10

Jeann

LAUREN. THE BABY. ETHAN.

Dream after dream.

No.

Memory after memory.

Too much pain all at once.

I felt that hole within me, remembered that I had a scar, but I didn't remember it *this vividly*. It was like I was experiencing it all at once. The loss of my sister and her child. *How broken I was.* We truly had no one but each other.

My parents passed when I was eighteen from a gas leak that the three of us didn't get exposed to because we were young and dumb and snuck out for my birthday. Coming home to that was enough to change someone's life.

But then, taking my sister and her baby.

If I could just figure out what the hell happened to me in this time I've lost. I could just...

Fuck.

It would only hurt worse. I'm so alone and lost and—

Fuck.

I slam the dresser drawer closed and slide down the front until my butt hits the ground.

With my head in my hands, all I can hear is the disapproval in Ethan's voice and all I can see is the sadness in his eyes outside the car.

I was so selfish and he deserved better.

He wanted to get out of Louisiana and I didn't blame him. He deserved more and now he's gone.

It should have been me who—

"Jeann?"

His panicked voice reaches me from outside the closet. I squeeze my forehead tighter, 'til there's white behind my eyes with the heels of my palms pressing in.

I don't want to cry.

A soft knock, "Jeann? Are you... I'm coming in."

"Don't."

I hear a soft thud against the door and then his muffled voice. He must have his forehead pressed against it. "Are you okay?"

No. I'm not. "Don't ask me that," I snap.

He sighs and it turns my stomach.

God, I'm so messed up.

Why does upsetting him upset me?

"Can I come in?"

A moment passes where I think to lash out more, but I'm too tired to think of anything clever. I need—

"Please," he says moments before the door opens outward toward him. The morning sun shines behind him. He waits for what I'll do or say next. The lines deepen across his forehead as he takes me in on the ground. I feel my puffy eyes from a restless sleep and the itchiness I have under his scrutiny.

He's gotten under my skin and I can't take it right now.

I drop my head into my hands again.

Mack says nothing as he slides down to the ground with me, his crutches clattering together just outside the door frame.

The warmth from his body envelops me slowly. First one arm around my shoulders, then the other until I crumple into his chest and his grass and leather smell engulfs my senses.

"What happened?"

Shaking my head slowly against his chest, I clutch his shirt tighter in my fist. "I'm alone. They're all gone."

"Who's gone?"

I just want him to keep talking. The feeling of the words rumbling in his chest feels good to me and I need more of it.

I shake my head again.

I'm so frustrated that all I can remember is the hurt and the pain.

I want to know something else about myself.

Anything else.

Something good.

Did I recover? Did I ever move past this part of my life when everything was shit?

"I know how you feel," he says as we sit on the floor in this closet together.

That makes me stop.

I stop moving, breathing, seething.

"What?" I finally pull away from him to look into his eyes and see the truth of what he's said.

"I know how it feels to be alone. To feel like they're all gone."

"Don't play with me, Mack. You have all these people in your life who love you. Who came to you when you needed them most. I saw."

"It wasn't always like that." The blue burns in his eyes. I sit on my hands to resist the urge to pull him close to me again.

I blink my stinging eyes. "What was it like?"

"There's a lot you don't know about me or this town. I don't think now is the time to get into all that."

My fingers run over the ribbing on my sock stretched along my ankle, each column of stitches something I focus on as I think about his words. "Give me somethin'," I ask, but it comes out more like a demand.

"Okay, bossy." He looks to the ceiling for a moment, thinking. "I'll share something... if you share something." He meets my eyes and raises an eyebrow, daring me to object. I nod once and he settles against the dresser.

He does something that I don't understand at first. He places his hand, palm up on his knee. Pointedly, he looks at his waiting hand. Waiting for me.

An invitation.

I place my hand in his and he lets it sit for only a few seconds before he's rubbing the back of my hand with his thumb.

"I was married once."

Nope. That is completely not what I expected him to say.

"How *old* are you?" I question.

"I got married young." He chuckles and the smile brings light back to his face for a moment. Brushing his other hand over his mouth, he says, "I've been divorced for almost five years. I'm thirty-one."

"Wow. How—" I pause to decide if I do really want to know more about this and I do. "How long were you married?"

"Three years, but we started dating in high school, so we were together about six years."

"Oh... wow." I don't know what else to say. I've never been in a relationship even close to that long. I don't even know what it's like to *want* to be in a relationship with anyone for that long. But looking at the man next to me, I can't actually imagine how anyone *wouldn't* want to be in one with him for that long.

"No follow up?" He chuffs in a self deprecating way that makes me feel like no one does ask the follow up questions.

"Just one." He leans his head to one side to let me know that he's listening. "Who was she?"

He takes a hearty intake of breath. "Well, that is where it gets complicated."

"Okay?"

"She is Reese's best friend."

"Okay, that's not too bad. Adults can be adults..."

He grimaces, "And was my best friend's girlfriend..."

I twist my lips to the side... "Okay we're gettin' a little spicier here..."

His nose scrunches into the previous grimace, "And now, new wife."

"Well, damn." I throw my hands up and they flop down into my lap. "There is no savin' that."

"Exactly." His head bobs from side to side, thinking for a moment I guess. "In a town this size, everyone knows everyone and their business. There aren't that many options as far as dating goes. Except somehow our divorce wasn't well known so they speculated about any details they didn't know. She was the sweetheart and when she left me, they all sided with her. They thought I must have really been a piece of shit to lose someone so precious. I must have messed up big time in losing her. Believed it myself for a time too."

I blink, stunned and upset on his behalf. "Did you really mess up?"

"Nah, that's enough from and about me. It's your turn." At some point, he retrieved my hand again. His thumb returning to stroking over my knuckles. It's soothing in the extreme.

I huff out a breath and stall as long as I can, inhaling again. "I dreamed a memory last night... well, a couple. I didn't really get any rest." The words run together like if I can get them out fast enough, they won't register as painfully as they are.

"That's good," he says, but looks me over and then frowns. *I hate the frown.* "They were bad memories." I nod instead of responding. "That's not how it works. I shared..."

"Who's bossy now?" He gives a look and I sigh. "Fine. They were horrible memories. My sister passed away and she was Ethan's girlfriend. We were both at the hospital when it happened and I sort of spiraled after."

"Sort of?"

"I was drunk for probably the entire month after buryin' her. Ethan picked me up from a bar and brought me home. I was so lit that I didn't know I had left the bar or remember the two hour drive home. He basically made me get my shit together after that... I think."

Mack squeezes my hand before deciding that it's not enough and embraces me instead. "I'm sorry you lost them both. I'm sorry you had to go through that twice."

"I'll always miss my sister," I tell his chest. "We were damn near twins. But the disappointment in Ethan's eyes that night broke me. He lost the love of his life. I wasn't there for him even though he was there for me. And now he's gone too."

"None of that is your fault, Jeann. You're as much a victim of these losses as either of them. It changes you when you lose someone, no matter how they go."

Shaking my head, I sit up, folding my legs under me. "You don't get it. Ethan was the troublemaker. Loved the guy, but he was a fuck up. I always had his back though. Coverin' for him, lettin' him sleep on my couch when he got kicked out, whatever. I held him down. That was my *best friend*. He's gone now and I don't know for sure that it wasn't my fault. Did I do everythin' I could to protect him?"

"You're not superwoman, Jeann. Car accidents happen all the time. You weren't even driving."

"Let's drop it for now. I shared my one thing. I should get up off the floor and get ready for this job."

There's a beat of silence before he gives my hand another squeeze. I look over at him and truly meet his eyes. His voice is steady when he says, "We're not responsible for the choices others make. We can only process the consequences as best as we can moving forward." He seems reluctant to do so, but I need the space to get ready.

Splashing cold water on my face and then using a bit of product to re-shape my curls behind the twisted crown gelled into place. Quick makeup, enough to cover the circles under my eyes, but there is no hiding the stitches that are very visible at my temple. Maybe I should have left my hair completely down so I didn't look like Frankenstein's monster.

Too late for that now, changing it will only make me late. I step into the living room to where Mack is waiting in a tan canvas jacket and thick brown sweatpants that are large enough to cover his cast.

I brush a hand over my skinny jeans and distressed sweater. Everything I have is distressed, oversized or leaning toward edgy in some way. It's an... edgy mix of pieces, but the only that seemed to match in my duffel bag to be interviewed in. Chunky jewelry and ankle boots that have managed to keep the snow off my feet complete the look. Nothing in the bag they took from the SUV gives me any clue as to what exactly my purpose in Colorado was, but I'm sure working at a hair salon wasn't it.

Mack bites his lip as he looks me over before asking, "Ready?"

"As I'll ever be," I respond drolly.

CHAPTER 11

Jeann

THE ROADS ARE STILL clear from snow and, to my shock, the salon is less than fifteen minutes from Mack's house. He gave me three directions, two lefts and a right. When we park in front of the building, I notice that the sign that says TUFT is over a sign for QB's Sports Bar.

He notices me looking this over when I help him from the car. "Second thoughts?"

"No, just... nothin'." I fidget with my sweater and smooth a hand over my hair one final time before I follow him into the building and to the elevator in the back of the sports bar where a few people are already drinking though it's only eleven. A few of them give Mack a wave, but he's focused on getting to the elevator and waits for me.

Upon opening, the bright open space of the hair salon greatly contrasts the bar downstairs. It's modern and sleek with the feeling of welcome greeting you. The scent of expensive hair products and burning hair from a nearby flat iron clings to the air, mixing with the faint, lingering notes of citrus-scented cleaning spray. It's familiar and fond memories of growing up in a salon like this one come to mind. My mom was a manager for as long as I could remember so I feel much more at ease in this building than any other I've been to in the last couple weeks. Not that being at Mack's house is uncomfortable. It's just new.

The sleek, white counters gleam under bright vanity lights, each station meticulously arranged with shears, combs, and an array of spray bottles. On the wall opposite of the elevator entrance, floor-to-ceiling mirrors reflect every inch of the space—and every insecurity I didn't realize I had before stepping in here. I fluff my curls in the back to make certain that my hair isn't too lopsided from the short drive here.

The few stylists, all effortlessly put-together with perfectly styled hair and perfectly arched brows, float around the salon like they belong here. Which, of course, they do. *Unlike me.* There are few places that I do belong. I shift in place, my fingers tightening around the strap of my purse as I force myself not to bolt. This is just a salon, not a battlefield. I've worked in places like this before. A salon is a salon, is a salon.

A cushy-looking lounge area sits in the corner, all muted pastels and plush chairs, where a couple of clients sip coffee from a complimentary bar behind them like they have nowhere else to be. I exhale slowly, steadying myself. I need this job if I expect to get back home.

I can handle this.

Probably.

A sleek, black reception desk sits up front, manned by a Black woman who somehow makes answering the phone look like a high-fashion event. Her dark skin gleams in the overhead lighting with a swinging bob that moves with each of her animated responses to whoever is on the line. After a few moments she waves to us and ends the call. "You must be Kathryn Barker! Hey, I'm the Chloe Bridges you have heard about." She flicks the sleek black hair on her head with a flourish and steps from behind the counter.

She's dressed in a fuzzy bottle green sweater and light green slacks that contrast her lime green booties. It would likely be ridiculous on someone who didn't have as much confidence to pull it off as this woman clearly has. But "the Chloe Bridges" has personality in spades, that much is obvious.

I look over to Mack who is stifling laughter as Chloe holds out a hand for me to shake. "It's Jeann, actually. I go by Jeann—" My words are cut off as she uses my handshake to pull me in for a hug.

"Oh, I'm a hugger. I'm so sorry about what you've been through." Releasing me she tells Mack, "Get going unless you're gonna stick around to cut all that damn hair on your head! You're overdue. I'll just show her around today. I'm sure Quincy has a pint for you downstairs." Mack gives me a little wave from where he holds onto a crutch before leaving to get back onto the elevator.

"Now, *Jeann*, what kind of experience do you have?"

"I spent a lot of time in my mom's salon before I started workin' as a receptionist in high school. I did that for about three years before I graduated."

"Oh, that is perfect!" She leans over to whisper conspiratorially, "You've already got the job, it's really not too difficult and since you have experience it will be easy, honey! Between you and me, I just wanted to give Quincy time to get on Mack. He hasn't been by in a while." She pauses, lips twisted to the side, "Before the accident, of course. He's moving around pretty well in spite of that though."

"Really?" I ask because it doesn't seem like there is anything else to do in this town besides be at a sports bar.

"I suspect it has something to do with how they all tease each other. Men! They have no idea when enough is enough."

"What do you mean?"

"Well..." She looks around now that we've gotten to her station at the back of the salon. "People talk and all that business with him and my brother, Ty, was messy. Hell is still a little messy though everyone pretends that it's not. To be fair, it has gotten better, but if you ask me, I think they should just scrap the whole thing. How could you be friends after all that, you know?"

I don't know, actually. There is a lot of information she's throwing at me. I can only put some of it together to make any sense. What questions could I ask to get any idea of what it all means? "Who is Ty?"

She laughs and presses a hand to her chest. "I forgot just that quickly that you're not from around here. Ty is my brother. He and Mack used to be thick as thieves until my bestie came floating in. Men lose their minds over women, I swear."

Oh.

"Anyways, enough gossip! Let me show you where everything is and what you'll be expected to do. It's not much, but you will want to keep up because this place is deceptively small. There are far more nooks and crannies than you could imagine. I like to keep us well stocked, but I don't need clients to see all that clutter, you know?"

I simply nod as she shows me around. The salon sells most of the products that they use and those are stored in an alcove that is opposite of the bathroom. Then she has an entire room with extensions of all sorts, from hair pieces, to wigs, to wefts and braiding hair galore. And finally the two break rooms are in the far right corner. One is for food, because she said she hates to smell food when she isn't eating. The other has plush chairs and plenty of charging cables as well as a couple of cubbies that the staff can store their things in. It really is a nice salon. Much nicer than the chain location my mom managed.

After the tour she introduces me to the stylists that were there, Francesca, Misty, Jesse and April. Then the software that they used to book everyone out. It was quick and easy to pick up on. Though I will admit that the receptionist, Tania, had a system of symbols on how to handle each of the clients based on their attitudes. That was more than I was expecting. There was a note on the desktop with red triangles for the more difficult clients. One triangle for "difficult to book" and two for "difficult to handle" which I figured would come in handy for me. There were more, but with the time I had to look everything over, I'd just have to learn on the job once I clocked in.

"So, how many days do you think you can be here? We're closed Mondays. Weekends are a must, but we have Belinda who works Tuesday, Thursday and Saturday mornings."

"I guess I can work on whatever days the other girl doesn't. I don't have any other place to be."

"Great! We'll see you here on Friday morning then." She sits at the desk when I grab my bag and head for the door. "Let Mack know that I went easy on you. I don't want him barking at me like he's been doing to everyone else."

I nod, but I also don't know what that means either.

He's been barking at people? About me?

For what?

By the time the elevator dings on the first floor, I'm greeted with the smell of fried food and beer. Such a difference from the salon.

I feel Mack's gaze on me before I see exactly where he is at the bar. He holds a glass of something, but waves me over. He must have been waiting for me to come down.

I sit on the stool next to him and plop my bag down in front of me.

"So how did it go?"

"It was... a lot." He looks back toward the elevator with malice before turning back to me. "But I'll be fine. It's better than the salon I grew up in."

"She was helpful?"

I think over the question. She gave me more information to think over and a lot to process, but the jury is still out on how helpful the tidbits of gossip were to me. "She's the boss. She was informative and I think I like her."

"Good." He spins the glass between his palms. He looks agitated and I don't really know why.

"She said to tell you that she went easy on me."

He chuffs. "Did she?"

"Yea... Somethin' about you barkin' at people."

To my surprise, he just rolls his eyes. "Cory and Chloe gossip like hens."

My brows pinch. "Your brother-in-law? Gossips?"

"Oh, yea. Last night he called me a—Never mind. Are you hungry? I ordered a bunch of stuff and I don't know if I'll be able to eat it all."

"I could eat," I tell him even though I don't want to stop exploring what he's said about Cory. There are a lot of things between the people in this town that don't sit right with me. Some of them are fine, but the way they treat Mack... there is definitely something strange about it. It's both patronizing and critical. But maybe that's just my own bias coming into play since most people give me the ick.

A blonde woman with a towel over her shoulder comes over to the two of us to ask what I'd like to drink. I eye her to see if she tries anything with Mack, feeling overall suspicious.

"I'll have what he's havin'," I say.

She gives me a soft smile and I hate it. "Sweet or unsweetened?"

Thoughts of what the conversation was like between the two of them before I showed up is playing in my mind. Was she flirting with him? She looks like the kind of bartender who would. Small town girl charm just wafting off of her. Then my brain realizes that she asked me a question. "What?"

Her smile falters a bit as my eyes narrow on her, but she clarifies, "He's having tea. Usually half and half of both as of late."

I look at Mack and back to the bartender. "I guess I'll have it half and half too."

She nods before walking off to pour my drink and I turn to Mack. He wears a goofy smile which shouldn't be a surprise, but it is, given how he looked just a moment ago.

"What's with your face?"

"Oh, nothing. But... I'm surprised Sarah Anne still has one. You ever turn the laser eyes off?"

"I don't have laser eyes."

He's smug and feeling pleased with himself. "I know jealousy when I see it."

"Me? I'm not jealous. And of her? *Please.* Besides, we're roommates. Not really even that, because I'm squattin' in your house for free."

His lip curls up on one side. "I don't love that imagery."

"Well it's the truth. I'm not jealous because we," I point at the space between us, "aren't a thing."

"It's only a matter of time and place," he says. At some point he took hold of my hand and I wasn't aware or just didn't care because it's been happening too much. I'm completely desensitized to it.

I shake my hand loose. "Will you listen to me?"

"I am listening. If you don't want to... then, I respect that. I'm sorry."

His puppy dog eyes cut into my chest.

"I never said that." *Why am I saying that?* I clear my throat. "I just—We should not cross that line. You're doin' me a favor and I don't want to take advantage."

He starts to say more but I hold up a hand. "Nope. We're leavin' this here. Let's just watch these football players get knocked around and eat some dinner I don't have to cook."

CHAPTER 12

Mack

 "A̲ᴿᴱ ʏᴏᴜ ꜱᴜʀᴇ ᴛʜᴀᴛ you should be handlin' fire?" Jeann asks.

"If not, then I'd better let Danny know right away. He taught me when I was young and no one has gotten hurt in the process since."

Snow is starting to fall outside and it looks like another storm is gearing up. From the forecast on the news earlier, it should last all night and into tomorrow, too.

Her face twists up, something I notice she does when she feels confused by something. "Who is Danny again?"

It's been about two weeks since I invited Jeann to stay with me at the house and it has been the best idea for so many reasons and the worst for one very big one.

The woman is staying with me.

Self control is not my strong suit, but being around her all the time is really testing me. The days where she's at the salon are the only reprieve I get from my mind telling me to *get close, hold on, don't let g o.*

"You only met him when we were at the Mason's for dinner. There were a lot of people there. Reese's Dad is Danny. The one that looks just like her, but you know... A dude."

"Oh," she says, "The mean one. He did have a big smile for Chandie though. I think I like her." A *rare thing*. Especially off the bat like that.

Jeann, doesn't like or trust anyone. It's a guilty until proven innocent sentiment that she has for everyone. She has more snark than sweetness and I like that she questions all the details of something before she will accept it.

She bites on her top lip, something she does when she's not sure if what she'll say is appropriate. She usually asks or says it anyway. I wait for her to say whatever it is she's thinking about now. "So, are Danny and Chandie like... your parents, too?"

A chuckle escapes me for a moment, but then I think about it. "Probably in a way... There were many times where I wished they were. I spent a lot of time across the fence at Mason Ranch when I was younger. If my leg were better I'd still be there now, so I guess I still spend a lot of time there." I could forget at times that I wasn't able to move around how I wanted to since we crashed into each other.

"You miss it," she acknowledges. "You miss them."

"I do miss it. I love the horses. Riding is my happy place. The people are good, too. It's the closest I've ever gotten to real family, being on that Ranch."

"I'm not a very good replacement," she says, crossing her arms.

The ends of her braids get caught under them and I think back to watching her do all these minuscule braids herself. She spent a full day sitting and watching TV with me while she transformed her curly dark brown hair into skinny single braids. Both of us locked into our spots on my bed, her watching TV and me watching her. Spending hours with her is easy, comfortable, like I've been doing it my whole life as opposed to the time it has truly been.

These braids are different from the ones she had when I first saw her. There are a few in different colors like pink and blue and green randomly throughout the golden blonde ones. Some have little metal cuffs on them in gold and silver. She looks like a mad goddess as she purses her lips at me.

"No, you're not," I say, releasing one of the braids from under her crossed arms. She huffs in annoyance, but I continue, "You're something else entirely. A category all your own."

"A weirdo who doesn't fit in anywhere. Yea, yea, I know." She gestures to herself and it makes me upset to hear her talk about herself like this. It's off handed and untrue all in the same breath.

I know she thinks much more highly about me than I deserve. "No more weird than I am."

Her scoff is a bitter thing. "Come off it."

"You don't see there being anything weird about me being the only White guy in my family?" She raises an eyebrow. "Alright, in my *chosen* family. But, I had to learn exactly how different and how similar everyone was to me."

"Fine, that could be weird... I guess. Not unheard of though. But you have a family. I see their pictures are still up in this house."

My smile falters. I should have taken down those pictures years ago. Something feels worse about having empty walls there instead. "You see the images, but none of the stories behind them. I've had it better than most. Trust me, I know that. My actual parents are both the worst kind of people though. I think I knew that even when I was younger."

"What stories?"

I sigh. "They just shouldn't have been parents. My mom tended to use me to manipulate my dad and my dad only cared about me in two cases—when I was ruining his public image or if he could use my presence to get back at my mom for something. They are horrible people and the things they've done... especially, my dad..." I pop my jaw, trying hard to release the tension I feel whenever I think about him. "Let's just say the Mason's house was always warmer than this one and they didn't mind me soaking up some of that warmth for myself."

"Oh," she says more quietly. She goes back to biting that lip again, but now she fiddles with the blanket on her lap.

I lift her chin so she'll look at me. "Just ask what's on your mind."

"If you moved here after your divorce, then why aren't they here now?"

"I'll tell you anything. I promise. I have nothing that I want to keep from you. But, not that right now. I want to keep the light just a little while longer."

"The light?"

"Yea," I brush the braids behind her shoulder, using it as an excuse to touch her because that's all I want to do and it's killing me not to. "We have light here between us. I don't want their darkness to spoil a good thing."

She shakes her head. "I'm not the light between us. It's you. Just bein' near you is like standin' near the sun." She grimaces down at her hands. "You're a good thing and you're wastin' it on me."

I consider her words before I speak again. "Shouldn't I get to decide who I want to give my light to?"

"If you do, I'm not givin' it back. If it's mine, I'm keepin' it." Her eyes snap to mine, the joking from before absent from her declaration.

Her words wrap around the broken soul in my chest and embrace it in a way I've always longed for.

Keep me. Have me. Keep me, I'm yours, it says.

So, I don't think twice when I lean down to kiss her.

Her eyes are wide when our lips touch. The warm brown depths of them hold me while she processes.

Her surprise changes to something else when her hands find my shirt and pull me into her. It's not long before she's the one controlling this kiss.

Her mouth demands and seeks what I'm willing to give her.

She pushes me back on the couch until her body hovers over mine. Golden braids creating a curtain of privacy for just us two.

I don't know what my hands are doing, but I need to figure it out quickly.

The decision comes to me by way of holding her hips and then her firm ass in these leggings that only highlight how blessed I am to be able to have these curves in my hands finally.

Her tongue explores mine, and I'm lost in the energy that surrounds us for a moment of our own making.

She wants control.

I want to see what she'll do next.

She nips at my lips and I allow her to consume every bit of my attention.

She wants more.

Her warm hand holds my face to hers while the other hand is on my chest. It searches for something and pauses when she finds it. My heart beats at a rapid pace beneath her hand and she sighs into my mouth.

Our eyes meet with my lips between her teeth.

She dares me to object to her possession of me and I can't.

Whatever she wants, whatever she needs, I'm more than willing to supply.

It feels good to be wanted by her.

No, *good* isn't adequate. Being wanted by her isn't just *half-bad*.

Being wanted by her is swell, sublime, fucking superior.

I hope that this is as good for her as it is for me. The thought of not being able to feel this with her again already clouds my judgement. I sit up abruptly, pulling her down onto me.

Both her hands cup my face and I see the fire reprimanding me with just her eyes alone. Jeann uses her new position to nip and kiss along my jaw and down my neck. She moves the neckline of my collar aside and continues her assault to the tops of my shoulders before huffing in frustration.

"Take this off," she demands, pulling my shirt up before I've even agreed to do it. She's careful around my face since my nose is still tender from the accident.

It's then that I realize she was doing all she could to avoid bumping into my nose in the first place when she laid me down before.

Fuck.

I'm lost.

Lost in her.

Lost in sensation.

Lost in this moment.

She wastes no time, hesitation unheard of, as she kisses me again. Her mouth both obliging and yielding with mine. "You have a ton of tattoos," she comments in between kisses.

Her hands roam my shoulders and ribs down to the plane of my stomach and sides. Demanding fingertips that memorize every bit of the shading and lines on my tattooed skin. When she's satisfied, little sounds of approval vibrate against my lips when her little nails scrape over my front. The sharp point catches my nipple and I whimper into her mouth and freeze.

She stops immediately, breaking the kiss.

I don't know what to say so I press my lips together. Hoping this will pass and we can forget that I'm—

"Did you just whimper and then panic?"

"Huh? What? No?" I feel the heat crawling up my neck and to my ears. I've never been more thankful for how my hair covers the tips of them right now. Not covering my face from showing my nerves though.

"You did." She scrutinizes my face in a way that doesn't give away any of her feelings on the subject.

"Okay. I did... but I haven't been with anyone in a really long time and you're so fucking sexy and I just—"

She puts a finger to my lips to stop what was likely going to be the longest ramble of rambles. Thank God she put a stop to it. "I want your whimpers and all the sounds you make. I stopped because I thought I hurt you. What I don't want is to hurt you."

"No. Definitely not hurt. I—I liked it. Like all of what you're doing." I close my eyes and press my palms together in front of my face in a praying gesture. "Please tell me that I didn't fuck this all up and you're going to stop doing it..."

Mischief plays in the line of her smile when I chance a peek at her. "You want this?"

"Baby, you know I do."

She gets off my lap and for a second I start to think that I'll be the butt of some kind of cruel joke. Instead, she takes her shirt and bra off, returning to where she was before. Her body, even half exposed, is a canvas of artwork with all her tattoos on display. We're similar in that way. So much ink, pain and stories etched deep.

Her light brown nipples sit just inches from my lips. I don't hesitate to pull her into me so I can get a mouth full of her perfect tits. The weight of one against my tongue and the other in my hand has me rock hard and throbbing in my boxer briefs to the point of almost pain.

She adjusts me over my clothes, against my thigh, so that she can use the stiff ridge to get herself off while she's making out with me again. She moans into my mouth and I help her along with my hands on her ass as she grinds her hot little core over me.

I don't think I've had anything as sexy as this. This woman is using me just how she wants for her own pleasure. It's heady to be treated like this and as she shudders over me, tits brushing and pressing against my chest. I come, too. Not much surprise there though. Jeann does it for me like no one has before.

I have the urge to apologize once the sparks die down, but when I look at Jeann I keep my mouth shut. She's softly smiling, completely pleased on the couch next to me. Her nails are scraping lightly in my hair as we're both spent, with her head on my chest.

My boxers full of cum and her panties likely are too, but neither of us seem to care.

I know she's listening to my heart because her fingers are moving in time with it in my hair.

A guarantee that I can make with all certainty is that I have never met a woman quite like this one daring me to change everything I know about what I want.

And fuck if I don't want her to change it.

CHAPTER 13

Jeann

I'M STARTING TO SEE why people dislike the snow... outside of the obvious.

The obvious being that it will literally wreck your life.

Besides that, yesterday was a day of nothing but snowfall, so nothing is open and I'm off when I should be working. I wonder if this is a sign of some sort.

"We should go outside," Mack suggests.

"I really don't want to be outside in this. It's the worst of all the precipitations."

He reclines on the couch. I don't lift my gaze from the shading I'm meticulously adding to Legend's fair features. Mack did not care for the comparison I had for how similar his beautiful baby was to Barbie's horse. But the likeness is uncanny.

Yea... Mack treats Legend like he's his kid. It's sweet, but also it's kind of... fascinating. Maybe it's a cowboy thing. I wouldn't know. I've only dated gamers and losers in the past, I think.

Ugh, I still don't know what I was up to for the past few years besides getting tattoos. I mean, seriously, I look like the scary version of my own memories of myself. Like *Jeann... in dark mode*. I think I discover a new tattoo every day but no new memories.

But this guy, despite the ever present cowboy hat and his one-cowboy boot, did not strike me for an *animal guy*. He's like two coos away from baby-talking them.

And it's... endearing.

I'm *endeared* and I should not be.

I use the fine point of the charcoal to create details as I'm lost in thoughts of Legend and Mack. Those huge, round eyes looking back at me from the paper. I have to get them just right. Animal person or not, this one is special to me.

They're kind of similar.

Mack and Legend.

Like siblings maybe.

They seem to banter back and forth and I've seen up close how dramatic he is.

The horse, I mean... Or the man. To be honest, Mack does have a way about him that is more playful than petty.

"Is that Legend?" Mack's head leans over the pad I'm sketching on. The mess of his sandy hair tickling my fingers where I hold the paper still at the top.

I pull it in close to my chest and meet his stunning blue eyes. They sparkle with mirth. He's just so happy. I have to figure out just how I can stop smiling back at him.

"No," I respond, trying not to smile and failing. I am concentrating, not smiling like some shy schoolgirl.

I'm... Jeann in dark mode.

But that can't be right. If it is, then so is Mack and that doesn't suit because of the light that radiates from him.

He has his own weather system.

Like the sun.

It's not the first time I've thought it.

If he's the sun then how can I function outside of his orbit? How can I survive without his energy?

He laughs, hard. His head thrown back with the strong column of his neck exposed. "You know it's my leg that's broken, not my eyes. I know my horse when I see him."

Fresh from the shower, he's in athletic shorts and nothing else it seems. I change the subject, "You have a hell of a lot of tattoos, Mack. So much more than me, even." It's crazy how much of his skin was actually covered with his collared shirts. Ink drips from his neck down over his chest, down his chiseled stomach and even below to where I can see with only his shorts on. His arms are covered. Little peeks of his tan skin show through the artwork that is all blackwork. No color in any of his pieces. The art is both deeply sad and full of history that I know is meaningful to him.

It's somewhat reminiscent of how I like to work with my charcoals. I prefer black and shading only.

I don't remember getting any of the tattoos on my own skin, but I know they are painful to get. The emotion in the art is present even without the memory.

When he's done laughing his flushed cheeks are noticeable and he brushes a hand carelessly down the front of his body. "Yea... I'm covered. It's... kind of addicting. I went with Cory once and I couldn't stop. Just have that kind of personality, I guess.

"You don't do anythin' by half measures do you?"

"Don't think so." He thinks for a minute. Concentration sobering his otherwise cheerful face. Then he smirks and catches my eyes. "Maybe with laundry?" he guesses.

I roll my eyes. "Well I'm sure there are plenty of stories here." He leans further back into the couch. Unashamed of his ink or my perusal. His skin is warm as I trace the lines of the winged piece over his left peck that has a date under it. "What about this one?"

"Wow." The mood in the room changes. "How do you do that?"

Pulling my hand away, I sit back on the couch. "Do what?"

"You pull the darkest parts of me to the front. Of all the ink on me, you pick this one to start?" He's not hostile but definitely upset. The incredulous look in his eyes tells me more than his words.

In all truth, I don't know what drew me to choose this one. "You don't have to talk about it if you don't want to. I'll just pick a different one."

"It's fine. I—" He stops abruptly and sits up. I mirror him, setting my pad to the side and straightening. "Look, I don't know how to talk about him without there being the need for everyone to give me pity. It's a rough situation and I don't know how to say it other than bluntly."

"Okay... I really want to know now."

"Of course you do." He sighs. "His name was Callan. My baby boy. We lost him."

I'm caught off guard and all I can do is inhale sharply. I blink at the wings for several moments. "I-I'm so sorry. You don't have to tell me more. I didn't—"

"You didn't know. My ex-wife and I split the day she found out we lost him." He flexes his fingers over the back of the couch, making his chest muscles flex. His jaw ticks in agitation or something else I don't know how to place. "We didn't split. She left. Few people know about him and all of the people who do are more her friends than mine. I guess my sister and Cory are there for me too, but it's..."

"Hard. That's so incredibly hard." I reach over to his flexing hand and get a better look at the piece on the back. So many times I'd seen it before. In the clouds are his son's name. I thought Callan meant something else, but the design takes new life with this knowledge. He lets me inspect him again, saying nothing. "How many?" I ask.

"Five."

I think for a second about what he's told me of his past marriage. "For every year?"

He nods. "There's not a day that goes by where I don't think about him. What would he have looked like? Would he be like me? Or like her?" His head tilts from one side to the next, "I lost everything when I lost him. It hurt to know that she was gone, but it hurts the most to know that Callan will never be. That's when Jack and I became real good friends again."

"Jack?"

"Daniels. I was drunk more times than not. Hell, I only have a handle on it now because I couldn't ride anymore. At my eighteen birthday party, Mel and I got into a huge fight because of how much I drank that night, among other things. I sobered up for her. Then she was gone and so was Callan. Could not take that fact. I'd be so shit faced, I couldn't sit up straight. I was tired of missing everything. The whole town has an opinion of me because they all think my ex has some big, fucked up reason for leaving me."

"I know what that's like."

His face scrunches up. "I guess you do. The liquor doesn't solve the problem, but it sure does feel good to be numb while it lasts."

"The only thing that lasts is the solitude. Keep drinkin' long enough and then there'll be no one left."

Emotion flickers in his eyes. The blue depths of them becoming murky with the recognition that I do know what it's like. It's there and then gone just as quickly.

"Yea, well. Something must be wrong with me. I've been dry for two years and single as can be. I'm not exactly trying anymore. Other than you, I really only talk to the horses."

"And Reese. And Cory..."

"Sure."

"That's not a real answer."

"Why not? Works, doesn't it?"

"Not for me. If you're gonna talk to me—I want you to talk. 'Sure' could mean anythin'. You feel like the horses are the only beings that you can be honest with. Who is that helpin'? Why not leave? You're a good guy. You could make a new life anywhere you want."

"I don't want to leave. I shouldn't have to. What more could I get any-where else?"

His eyes are sad and I hate it. I hate this sadness and everything that's put it there. I hold his face so he can't look away from mine. "You could be happy."

He stares at me for several moments as my words linger in the air between us. I could be completely over stepping. I don't care. All I know is that I can see how his hurt has defined him in all the wrong ways. The man that I've seen is not the same as the one he's been portrayed to be.

"Mack, I shouldn't have—" There are smudges from my fingers on his face that I try to wipe away with my clean hand, but he stops my fussing and holds my hand in place.

"No, you're right. I could be happy. I could leave all this behind me and then what? Wipe my mind of who I am and what I've been through. What they think about me is wrong, but their actions don't lie. I failed my sister. I wasn't enough for my wife. My parents are gone and aren't coming back. I moved out and came back when they didn't. Barely changed a thing and it's a constant reminder of how things don't change. What do I have to offer someone? What am I missing? I'd go to a new place and it would be the same story with a new setting."

I know from experience that wiping who you are from your mind doesn't solve anything.

I want my memories, but something tells me that I'm better off without them.

Nothing about that sounds like a solution for Mack. He needs family, community. He thrives with his family around him. His glow made brighter by their presence. I know he needs more than I can give him but I want to give as much as I can anyway.

I'm on my knees on the couch by him. The stubble from the day scratches against my palms with my hand back on his face. His eyes are shut tight, eyebrows scrunched, "Open your eyes." He resists, but I wait.

Finally the blue pools blink open.

I soak up his vulnerability and take it within me.

"You have so much to give. Do you know how I know that?" He doesn't say anything, but I keep going. "Because there is so much I want to take. So much I don't dare hope to claim. You deserve happiness which is why I don't dare seek what's in front of me now."

"But you could." That unabashed hope shines in his stunning eyes. "Don't tell me that what happened here yesterday was an accident."

"No, but it shouldn't have happened when I know you need more than I can offer."

"I don't want you to give me anything." He leans forward, his nose almost brushing mine. "You can have whatever you want. If you ask, it's yours. I'm—"

I put a finger to his lips before he can finish that declaration. Thinking quickly I say, "C'mon, let's go build a snowman. I've never done that before."

Mack lets me end the discussion. It only takes him a moment to fix his composure while I hunt down a plastic trash bag to wrap his cast in.

I tie it tight enough to be secure around his leg and he watches me with careful eyes.

"First rule about snow," he says, but I'm still making a trail in my boots through the freshly fallen layer. "Beware of snowballs."

"Beware of—" The cold registers before the realization does. Snow slides down the side of my head and into the neck of my coat. I blink at the man looking both guilty and like he's seconds from toppling over with his mirth.

I frantically shake the snow off me, but it seems to permeate my warm layers anyway.

I'm not able to gather my wits before another thud against my side causes me to slip right into the side of the walkway with snow piled up high next to it. I land with an "oof" as more snow covers me.

The burst of Mack's cackles are loud over my flailing and crunching while I make unintentional snow angels on the ground. I'm shivering and stuck, having dug myself into a slippery little mold. The laugh pours out of me and I just lay there soaking up the utter ridiculousness of my circumstances.

We're both laughing and the sound of the two of them together makes something click into place that probably shouldn't be.

I really like the sound of us happy together.

His head peeks over the hood of my coat which thankfully remained up in my fall. There's joy all over his face when he starts tamping down some of the higher sides of my snow angel with a crutch so I can move.

Sitting up, I give him a look.

"Hey, it's a hard learned lesson that everyone has to have at some point." He snickers into his shoulder, but I get up and face the grinning fool.

"Ah, I see." I say. "What lesson is this then?" He's too busy looking at my face to notice the clump of snow that I have in my hands. I've got it down the front of his sweater quick enough to retreat as he hops up and down to get the crumbling snow ball out of his top.

I laugh until my sides hurt and he catches up to me. He hugs me around his crutches. We share warmth and this moment of levity after so much of the opposite.

He makes me laugh. *I make him laugh.*

He makes me happy. *I make him happy.*

What am I supposed to do about that?

CHAPTER 14

Mack

"WHAT HAPPENED?" HER VOICE cracks into the barn.

Ellis, Taylor and Josh all "ooo" at the sight of Jeann standing in the doorway with disappointment in the lines her arms make, crossed at her chest.

I look at the ranch hands present and frown. "Which one of you ratted on me?"

None of them say anything like the jerks they are. I hear the wood chips crunch under the steps of someone and turn to see my sister striding in. "I did." She gives me a stern look, to Jeann she says, "Thank you for coming. I'm hoping he'll listen to you since he won't listen to me."

"I was just fine."

Reese gives me a disapproving look. "Mack, you fell on your ass and nearly took the feed shelf down with you."

"You what?!" Jeann exclaims. "It's only been weeks since the accident. You know you shouldn't be doin' anythin' let alone playin' cowboy over here."

"It was barely anything." My face flames with embarrassment about the whole situation. My ass is in pain from landing on some spare wood chips in the room and I hit my forearm on the way down. My balance was just a little off kilter with the weight of the bag on my shoulder and how unexpectedly slippery the boot is in comparison to my work boot.

"Those horse supplement bags are fifty pounds." Reese supplies.

Thanks for nothing!

Jeann is seething. "Get in the car, Mack," she barks. I glare at my sister the whole way out of the building, but she doesn't flinch under my glare.

Jeann fusses over and at me the whole way home from the Ranch. I don't like that Reese told on me, but I enjoy getting Jeann in a tizzy. The three-minute drive making the twenty-minute walk I took look like an easy feat when it's not a twenty-minute ribbing.

"Did you forget that you have a pin in your bone! You might not have to use the crutches anymore, but they just let you have this boot yesterday," she says as she helps me into the house unnecessarily.

"And like I said, I'm just fine."

"What would the doctors say?"

I slide a seat from under the dining table. "My *one doctor* would also say that I'm fine and that I need to show up for physical therapy tomorrow on time."

She taps the table to get my attention. "We had an agreement."

"We do have an agreement." I say, grabbing ahold of the hand she was just tapping the table with. She arches an eyebrow, but allows me to pull her into me anyway.

Ever since that kiss on the couch, Jeann has kept her distance. No more snarky than usual, but avoiding any situations where we would be too close to each other. Not for lack of me trying. I've done everything besides just saying that I want her to ride me in plain English.

I'm tempted to do it, but I know that won't help her open up to the idea again.

She taps my chest, "You're not holdin' up your side."

I feign offense, holding her hand still on my heart. "How am I not doing that?"

"You're supposed to let me help you get better. Let you rest and not do too much. Haulin' fifty pound bags around the Ranch is not restin' or not doin' too much."

I smirk a little to myself, "You weren't supposed to find out about that."

"Mack!" She pushes lightly against my chest.

"What? I thought you were going to be at work for at least another two hours. I was bored."

Her eyes sharpen to points on my face. "I *was* gonna be at work for another two hours until Reese called me to tell me you had a bad fall."

"And you came running."

"And I came runnin'," she repeats drolly.

My ass hurts even now just sitting in the hard dining chair or else I'd put her in my lap. Instead, I guide her to sit on the table in front of us.

She sits with a huff. "You scared me."

I look up into her eyes. "I'm. Fine." My smile spreads with my arms asking her to see my body missing the grievous injury everyone is acting like I earned today.

My hand finds her thigh and she presses her hand over it. "You scared me and I don't like feelin' that way. I already feel guilty about someone else who I couldn't save. If somethin' worse happens to you while I'm here... I could not take that."

While she's here.

Does she still plan on leaving?

"Was he your man?"

"No," she says quickly. Shaking her head, "I don't know. God, I hope not. I don't know."

I consider pulling my hand away. I don't like that answer, but she holds it in place. "Ethan was as much a brother to me as you are to Reese. We went through a lot together. I don't know what happened after we both lost my baby sister. That time is completely gone for me. I don't want to lie to you. I don't want to make you believe somethin' I can't confirm either."

"Okay." I resist the urge to grind my teeth in frustration over a man who lost his life just one month ago. He has lost more than I have. I can be reasonable. *I hope.* "Is that why you think you can't be mine?"

She catches my eyes, nodding slowly. "Among other things."

I blink several times. *This isn't rejection.* Not completely though it feels like it.

I have lived for years knowing that any person in my life could be gone in the swift blinks I'm performing right now. All of it could go up in the smoke of *could have been* with just the change of someone's mind.

I know the feeling of losing someone, quickly and slowly. Of having something so sure in your hands only to look down and see it's all slipped through my fingers.

Jeann is not like any of those cases. She is just as I've noticed before.

Something wholly her own.

I want to show her that she can give in to this... This attraction, pull, desire between us because I am a sure thing. I'm not going anywhere until she wants me to.

And even then I'll have to be heavily convinced.

I hope like hell that whatever is in that time that she can't remember, doesn't tear us apart. I don't care if there was someone before. *There is always someone before.*

How do I show her that though?

How do I show her that I'm ready to give her whatever she wants as long as she stays?

This isn't rejection.

"Tell me something then." We've danced around, talking in riddles around it. "If you can't be mine, can I be yours?" I want to know that this is more than just some over-the-pants action.

I don't do half measures.

If I'm going to give her *something*, I'm going to give her *everything*.

Hesitation is thick in her voice as she asks, "What?"

"I like you. Look I know people are scared to say how they feel and all that, but I've never been dishonest about that. I like you, Jeann. I invited you to my house because I wanted you to be safe and cared for. I invited you here because I see something in you that I only want to get closer to and understand in a way that no one else can. I have been plain about my intentions. I want you. If you don't want anything from me, with me, I'm going to learn to be okay with that. You can stay here as long as you need to get back on your feet. No strings attached. But know that I will keep trying for a space in here," I place my hand over her heart and her breath catches slightly with the pressure, "until you tell me I need to stop. Do you get me?"

Her body leans closer to mine and she states, "I told you that once somethin' is mine, I'm keepin' it." My eyes trace her features down to her lips as she tells me what I want to hear. "There is no goin' back. If I take you, Mack, you're goin' to be mine and I'm not havin' this conversation again. I don't believe in sharin' or anythin' like it."

"No half measures," I say to her lips.

"Kiss me," she commands.

I close the distance between us, pulling her even closer to me on the edge of the table. Her soft lips are like water to my dehydrated soul. It's been too long since I felt her lips on mine, but I want to drink in more and more of her.

I want to drown in everything that is this woman.

Her socked feet land on the sides of my hips before she crosses them behind my back. My hands seek skin and find it. Her back is smooth and soft under my touch, but her pants have that elastic back that make it easy for me to trace a finger under her thong.

Jeann's fingers are in my hair. My hat is barely hanging on, but she takes care to remove it and place it on the table beside her.

The low dip of her silk blouse calls my attention with just the sliver of cleavage I can see from how she leans over me on the table.

I'm half hard and desperate.

She sees me shift in the chair to adjust myself and watches me with fascination.

Her little toes trace the edge of my length. I only get harder under her attention.

The wicked smirk she wears is down right devious as she takes note.

I kiss her again, more fiercely than before. My hands travel up her back to her bra strap. I pop it against her skin and she gasps into my mouth.

"Help me out of this top."

Another command and another direction I obey.

The pearlescent, buttons are just small enough to make me concentrate on my task instead of how hard I am right now. A very difficult task because each button I work through the hole, is another addition to the picture that is a topless Jeann in my dining room.

We're both breathing hard.

Her lips kiss-swollen and perfect.

Our eyes hold as I unclip the bra behind her. She shrugs out of it with careful movements.

I don't allow her tits to even bounce from the bra coming off before I replace that support with my hands. They're soft and supple in my grip.

Her gaze follows me as I put my mouth over her dusky nipples. Kissing softly before, biting them. *My girl likes pain.* Someone with this many tattoos must.

I'm glad I trusted my instincts. Her grip tightens in my hair as she moans with the increase in pressure of my bite.

I take my sweet time showing attention to each until her breaths are coming faster. Her pulse thumps at a rapid pace in my hands.

"I need to take these off."

"Yes, you do."

She works the pants down and I help her get them over her hips and thighs till they pool in my lap, teasing my hard-on, before sliding to the ground. I like her casual clothes. They're cool and unique, often saying *don't fuck with me* before she has to. But I like what she's gotten to wear to the salon. Everything is flowy and soft while still saying *don't fuck with me* but this time professionally. And underneath either is always mouth-watering lace.

She wears lace the color of wine today.

I don't even like wine, but suddenly I'm thirsty.

Dehydrated.

I need to quench my thirst.

Her thighs on my shoulders flex, but she doesn't stop my face from getting closer to her center.

Sliding the lace to the side, I chuckle.

She leans up on her elbows, "Are you laughin'?"

I wipe a hand over my face to quell the sound, as my mouth waters for a taste of her so close to me. "These are a bit on the nose, huh?"

She looks down at the two strawberries inked on her skin just on the inside of her thigh crease that look ripe and juicy as they drip.

A smirk is all she wears beside this lace that barely covers her now that I've moved them to the side. "You tell me," she says.

I run my thumb over her lips and they bloom open for me. *Perfect.*

I don't understand what I did to be so close to heaven, but I'm sinking into this moment.

Taking a deep inhale, I commit her smell to memory.

My blood pumps through my veins as I get the first taste of her dripping wet pussy from my thumb. It's like I'm floating on a high because fresh strawberries couldn't compare to how juicy my girl's taste is.

"Does that feel good?" I hum into her folds.

Swollen and ready for more of my touch.

"Give me more, Mack," she moans.

"More," I purr into her core, my lips on hers, just barely touching. "How much more? Do you want my tongue on this wet cunt?"

She pulls me into her with the hold she has on my hair—I might never cut it again. My nose in the soft hair and my tongue spearing right into her opening.

Fuck me, I'm not leaving this spot until she drags me off of her.

CHAPTER 15

Jeann

"WON'T THIS BE AWKWARD?"

Mack gives me a look of genuine confusion. "Why would it be awkward?"

"I'm squattin' in your house right now. I shouldn't be meetin' your friends."

"You're not squatting in my house." He shakes his head, laughing. "That really is a gross saying. I wish you wouldn't keep saying it."

"You're missing the point." I check myself in the pull down mirror another time now that we're here. After getting some clothes from my favorite thrift shop online, I feel like myself in a heavily distressed cropped sweater and black wide leg jeans. A few oversized chains hang from one belt loop to the next and I've even got chunky silver jewelry to match. My eye makeup is graphic is heavy and graphic, but I kept my lips relatively simply with just a gloss. It matches the feel of my outfit and really... my personality.

I'm in this parking lot all the time for work now, but I've not actually been into QB's to drink. Chloe's husband, Quincy, I've met a few times, but there was never a reason to go to the bar. Ever since I had that memory of Lauren's passing, I have been even less inclined to drink. "Bringin' someone to this kind of thing has... implications."

"Does it?" He asks casually, grabbing a beanie from the back seat of his car.

He's adjusting it on his head, but I snatch it off. "Mack, I need you to hear what I'm sayin'."

"I am hearing you." He looks into my eyes and I know he's feeling the energy rolling off of me. His hand is on mine holding the hat tightly. He rubs his thumb over the fist like he does and I release the knitted fabric. "You're nervous, but there's no reason for it."

I splutter. "I'm not—Why would you—"

"Is it because we hooked up?"

"Ugh. Are we goin' to talk about this now?"

"As opposed to?"

"Never."

He settles into the chair with his hands behind his head. "Fat chance. All I can think about is how between your legs is heaven. That's a cloud I won't be stepping down from."

I roll my eyes at him. "How about we put it in a box and not touch that box because it's actually at the bottom of the Atlantic?"

He considers my words and I expect a different response from what he actually suggests. "How about we have a word you can say if you feel uncomfortable and we can leave?"

"Like what?"

"I don't know..." He thinks for a moment. "What about gummy bear?"

My face scrunches up around the word. "Gummy bear? That is so random."

"Then it's perfect. And I could actually go for some gummy bears right now so that makes it a plausible reason to go as well."

"What? Mack—"

"Do you trust me?"

"I..."

His sparkling blues hold me. "Would I ever put you in a bad situation?"

"No... It's not you that I don't trust."

"Then what? My friends might give me shit, but they'd never be rude to you."

"You don't know that."

He turns fully to me and waits. I turn fully to face him as well. When I look down he's holding his hand palm up on his thigh. I rest my hand in his and he holds it there. Instantly, I feel better.

"Tell me what's wrong."

I don't want to tell him the ways that I feel insecure even though I know he wouldn't judge me for it. "I'm... weird."

"Okay?" He looks at me with open eyes. "And...?"

"You're charismatic and charmin'... and people like you. I'm not like that. I was never well liked at school. I only had one friend and my sister and that never really changed. I will make it awkward or say the wrong thing, probably rudely." It's pretty uncomfortable to be introduced to a group of long standing friends even if you aren't... me. But these are all couples which is even worse.

He squeezes my hand lightly. "This isn't school. It's just some friends. They aren't like that. You've already met Reese and her husband. Chloe and her husband. There's just some other people you haven't met and it will be fine. Everyone's cool."

I raise a skeptical eyebrow. "Gummy bear?"

He nods, "And we'll leave."

I look at myself in the mirror again then look back at the man who seems miles more comfortable than I do right now. "Okay."

* * *

THERE'S A PITCHER OF something Quincy called Third Ringer at the table when we get there. It's a bubbly cocktail that is way too easy to drink. Maybe downing a pint of this was a bad idea. I've already abandoned the plan I had in my head to *not* drink.

I originally thought it was some sort of beer. I'm already feeling warm and fuzzy on the inside. The high top table we sit at is probably a hazard for how wobbly I'm feeling. At least the edge is a little softer now that I've had it though.

Mack is to my left and he sits closest to the wall. His arm is around the back of my chair. I was sitting ramrod straight when we first got here, but as I've gotten more tipsy, I have melted into the security of his touch at my back. He lazily traces some shape on my shoulder that Reese definitely clocked but said nothing about.

Instead of getting wrapped up in what I should or should not say, I do what I do best. Observe. Clothing is one of my favorite things to account for if animals aren't around.

His sister is on my right in a jean jumpsuit that's over a frilly red sweater underneath. She looks like country royalty with her hair slicked back into a severe high ponytail. Her husband is in a sweater that is, unbelievably, the same color as hers with light wash jeans. He's not stopped looking at her since they sat down. He makes conversation, but it's like his eyes are only for her. It's sweet and something I noticed the first time I met him.

Chloe is fully in her husband's lap. They fit together so seamlessly that it doesn't look awkward as he talks over the top of her head with everyone gathered. She wears another signature bright outfit that I've gotten used to. It's a fluorescent purple and pink patterned sweater dress with bright pink tights to match. Her husband by contrast has a sporty bomber jacket on with what I'm guessing is a sports team's patch sewn on the chest and dark jeans.

The conversation is easy when I'm finally relaxed enough to have it with everyone. I'm actually enjoying myself. Mack seems to be at ease with everyone laughing and joking sometimes at his expense, but they all seem to tease each other.

I observe from the outside and it makes me more aware of who this man is as a person. I love that he is full of warmth when it comes to me. I love even more that I've been able to receive that glow of his. These people couldn't possibly know what they take for granted.

All of a sudden, Chloe hops from her husband's lap to go hug a tall Black man in a black cowboy hat. She squeezes him tight until he removes her from him. Then she's hugging a much shorter Black woman who was more or less completely behind the man before now. Two other men talk among each other before Chloe's arms are around their necks as well. The one with intricate cornrows lifts her in a twirling hug that she laughs through. The White man with the sides of his head shaved and several visible tattoos on his neck just kisses her cheek when cornrows finally sets her down.

They walk over to the table and Reese hugs the two men as well before hugging the smaller woman. Cory daps up the man with the cowboy hat, but when he goes to hug the woman he steps in front of her saying, "You're still good on that."

Cory laughs it off, shaking the hands of cornrows and shaved sides, and the table joins in on the laughs.

It's... odd to me, but what do I know about these people? There's a lot of teasing going around.

I was never a cool girl or someone who had many friends. It was just me and Ethan, neither of which people liked. Mack and his friends seemed like the type who were popular in school. Easygoing and confident. A closeness that came from knowing someone for years hung in the air here. It was clear since there never was a lull in their conversation.

My sister would have probably gotten along with all of them. I don't really know what it's like to have so many good looking and amicable people around me. The last thing I wanted was to stick out like a sore thumb and ruin this night for Mack by showing just how unused to this I was.

Cory then whispers in Reese's ear and she giggles, smacking the man in his chest lightly. I look away from the two of them suspecting that something private is happening there.

Chloe starts talking to the new woman animatedly as she pours her a drink from the pitcher. Then she blinks and stops talking. "Oh, you haven't met Jeann yet." She turns to me. "Jeann, this is Melody and my brother, Ty. This is Zeke and Robert, they're a part of the band too." Zeke, the one with cornrows, has a tight henley on with ripped black skinny jeans and combat boots. Robert, on the other hand, has an oversized cream colored long sleeved tee and tan cargos.

I'm no country music fan, but I recognize the man in front of me now that the shadows from his hat aren't so severe. I had no idea that Chloe's brother was Tyson Abrams. It's kind of hard to escape between the headlines of what went down with him and Jordan Hurst and now how big his career has gotten. I'm surprised there isn't security here for him and the band or something.

Now, it makes a lot more sense why his music plays all the time in the salon.

I feel Mack tense slightly behind me, clearly gripping my chair.

"Hey," I say, not bothering to get up and hug or any of that business everyone else did for them.

"How was the flight back, Ty?" Mack asks the man now that he's relaxed again. I get the feeling that he was unsure of how I would respond to this group of stragglers, but short and sweet was the safest bet in my mind. It makes me uneasy with so many unknown people talking around me regardless. I pour another glass of the cocktail, asking him if he wants any, but he's sticking with tea.

"Not too bad. We got delayed in Ohio. The turbulence is always rough this time of year but otherwise smooth." Ty responds. The woman, Melody tucks tighter into his side, sipping her drink and listening to Chloe and Reese talking. Every so often, she sneaks a glance over toward us.

I look up at Mack and his jaw is tight. There's an emotion I haven't seen him use in public before. This uncomfortable anguish. This man is happy and always smiling whenever we're out. The only time I've seen him look like this is...

Oh...

Oh. Fuck.

Reese's best friend.

My best friend's girlfriend... Now, new wife.

My brain is slow, but it all connects in my mind.

This is Mack's ex wife. The mother of his child that passed.

My stomach lurches. The alcohol sitting like a lead weight.

Not for the first time, I curse his ex-wife.

It's unfounded in origin because Mack and I aren't anything serious. *Mack and I aren't anything.* Roommates who had a couple slip ups.

But this woman— don't like her.

The conversation between the guys is stilted, but they still keep the pretense of joking from before. There is no missing that he's different with her around. I can see the sadness in his eyes when he looks at her. It's not longing. More like the kind of look you give someone when you feel guilty.

I don't know what he could feel guilty about. I'm also terrified to ask about the look because I don't know if I'll like the answer.

Every now and then, she gives him a similar look.

They both feel badly about *whatever* happened.

With how closely she clings to her husband, I know it's not that she longs for him either.

Taking a moment to really look her over I decide that Melody is pretty. Pixie-like. Ethereal. She has the kind of face from fairy tales. Big, wide eyes, pert little nose, full lips. Her delicate cream sweater contrasts her medium brown skin perfectly and she looks like the kind of woman who is always put together and who would be married to a celebrity. The ring glints on her finger as she drinks from the glass. Tyson's black bandana and black, thick cabled zip-up makes him look as monied as he likely is. Her husband is famous and acclaimed and watches her like a hawk, shifting whenever she does and casually checking in with her every now and again.

She has everything.

Why would Mack look at her like she's hurting or like he hurt her? I can't tell which.

Grinding my molars in restraint with the need to know what really happened, but I know that will have to wait for another time. I'm not sure my tipsy ass could handle whatever it is right now. Or that anyone at this table deserves what's on my mind. So, I seethe quietly instead.

When I lie in bed thinking of the empty place next to me, I wonder if he's also lying in bed thinking of that empty place next to him.

Maybe he's wishing it was her there.

She seems like the kind of woman that men dream about.

The kind that can make promises and smiles all the time and get invited to things. All her friends rallying to her side and showing up for her.

She probably—

Mack tips my chin up to look at him, taking the lip from between my teeth.

He's warm again.

The sun and all his rays.

My hand finds the wrist of the arm holding on to me. "Are you feeling hungry?" He asks me, eyes flicking over my face to assess me.

"Huh?" Is all I manage because I have been spiraling down into my own thoughts. I'm not really sure what was going on outside of it.

"My sweet tooth is getting out of hand..." he prompts and I stare at him for a moment. My—let's call a thing, a thing—drunken thoughts aren't piecing what he is prompting me towards fast enough. Plus it's hard to think when those storm cloud blues are assessing my face. The temperature of my body is rising and I don't know what to do. Do I keep looking at the welcoming depth of his gaze or his plush lips that are smirking with my attraction leaking from my pores like pheromones.

Touch me.

Kiss me.

Take me home.

"I—" can't get any words out. Somehow I know that I should respond, but I don't know what to say. He asked me something. It's taking all my effort not to voice the thoughts in my head right now.

"We've got a couple apps coming to the table," Chloe says, breaking me from whatever lusty haze I've fallen subject to in this bar.

Mack releases my face, but satisfaction has replaced the otherwise guilty look he was sporting before. I have moved closer to his body though I should still remember that anything between us should be locked away in that box in the Atlantic right now.

His display has made it very clear that something more is going on to the people at this table. The people closest to him. They still talk to each other, but I felt their eyes on me to see what we would do next.

Maybe another woman would shrink from the scrutiny. Maybe a better woman would be embarrassed about any assumptions that I'm sleeping with Mack since I'm staying at his house on a favor instead of rent.

Beats me on why, but I suddenly don't care when I see those exact thoughts playing out with concern on his ex's face.

I rest my hand on his thigh under the table, but there is no mistaking where my hand is. *This is mine*, it says.

"I could go for some gummy bears," I tell Mack.

He winks and says, "Let's go then, sugar."

Chapter 16

Mack

"Who would have thought that this miniature grocery store could have this many options for candy?" Jeann's voice is a little too loud for indoors. If it were one of my nieces, I'd ask her to use her inside voice. However, I don't think that will go over well with Jeann.

Instead, I use a whisper, hoping she'll catch on. "I think it's a supply and demand kind of thing. The convenience store at the gas station doesn't have this much."

"Why are you whisperin'?" she basically blares down the aisle.

"Well, it's almost eleven at night and we're indoors... so..."

She blinks and then her face scrunches. "I am no good with volume control when I drink. Ethan would always tell me that too."

"We won't be here long. I just don't want anyone to start gossiping about you, too."

"From a grocery store? Who does that?"

"Well, it's happened to my sister a few times and to her friend, Drea. This is a hot spot for old ladies and hot goss."

"Hot goss? Nope. Don't say that anymore," she giggles, again much too loudly.

I smile at her silly mood. "Why not?"

"What kind of cowboy says hot goss? Aren't you supposed to be rugged and rough?"

"Oh, yea?" I raise an eyebrow. "What else?"

She swipes a bag of gummy bears, but also some sour strips from the rack as she thinks it over. "I don't know. Probably grumpy."

"Sorry to disappoint, but I'd rather not be."

She looks my face over to what end? I don't know, but she finds it and decides, "I don't want that. I think I'm enough for the two of us."

"You're not grumpy..." She just looks at me with a bland face. "Okay, a little but not all the time."

"Sure," she says.

I step around her, holding an arm out in front of me to stop her. "That's not a real answer."

"You can't use my own line on me!" The stickiness of her accent carrying, again. I wince and her eyes flicker with recognition. "Why do you care if these people gossip about me? Who gives a *fuck* what they think?" She says more loudly, making sure that people can hear her. With a lower tone she asks, "For real. Why do you care?"

"I... don't. Not really. Not anymore."

"You do. You think they'll say somethin' about me. Maybe about us."

"Jeann—"

Her voice carries and I wince at the fact that she's just getting louder. "Fuck that. Fuck them! Who cares if they say somethin' about me? They don't know anythin' about me! Hell, I barely know anythin' about me."

I pull her to the side, whispering again. "That's why I want to protect you from it. They'll just make things up to fit their idea of you."

With narrowed eyes that hold me in place, she interrogates me with a finger punctuating each question on my chest. "So what? So what if they do? What does that matter at all? *I know the truth. You know the truth.* How could you give them power to hurt you? Manipulate your emotions just because they have nothin' better to talk about." I let her words simmer in my mind as I guide her over to the checkout line.

One of the best improvements they made to this store is the self-service checkout line. I get a couple looks from people who are still waiting in line despite how empty these aisles are. They would rather stick to what they know, waiting, instead of doing something new like checking out their own things. I guess they have nothing better to do or just like things the way they always have been. That speaks to me more than what Jeann has pointed out. I pay for the candy while she scowls at a woman who is visibly turning her nose up at her.

When she sees I've finished paying, Jeann opens the grocery store door for me and it's then that I decide to respond. "I never thought of it like that. Not once."

It's a short walk to where she parked before and she's already in the muscle memory of helping me into the passenger seat before getting into her own side.

She throws the candy into the back and turns on me. "I will never let them hurt you like that again. Do you hear me? I know the truth of you. I know who you are. There will never be a time that they could spread lies about you or speculation that I will let stand in your head. I'll tell them all to fuck off. You're a good man. You are special and valuable and worth more than any garbage they could ever spread about you. Just the fact that I'm here is proof of that."

"Jeann—"

"No! Tell me that you believe that. All night you let your friends get on your ass and laughed at their jokes *at your expense.* That's one thing. But these randoms... these no-life havin' anons say things about you and you take them to heart. No! Absolutely not."

"I don't—"

"You do and I hate it. Tell me that you know you're *good* and worth more than those rumors they spread about you."

The copper in her eyes shine bright at the demand and I can't stop the draw that attracts me like a magnet to her.

My hand slides behind her neck and I pull her close to me. It's the closest I've been since we were at the bar. It took everything in me not to kiss her in front of everyone. The only reason I didn't is because Jeann doesn't want people to think she's taking advantage of me by staying at my house.

How ridiculous is that sentiment?

More than anything, I'm the bastard who lured her to my home to be close to her. To know her more because I couldn't bear the thought of letting go of what I felt between us in the hospital.

Even now, that draw to her is strong. We can't ignore the fact that there is something more to us. There is a reason that we crossed paths. Or better yet, why she crashed right into my life. She's changed it more than she can see.

A little tipsy and a lot passionate, she demands more of me.

Not just sexually, though there's plenty of that with the way her lips possess me and she takes everything I have to give—but my soul, my heart could be hers too.

She reaches across the seat and finds the release for my chair. I'm suddenly sprawled backward. I start to say something, but my mouth won't work as quickly as she is.

My jeans are unzipped and my boxers are down before my cock stands at attention between us. Her grip is just as possessive as she looks into my eyes, stroking me slowly.

"Prove it. Show me that you don't care what they think about you with your cock in my mouth in this parkin' lot."

The challenge in her tone and her eyes sends shivers down my spine as I try my best not to blow my load right here with her looking at me and my cock like this.

Like she longed to taste me.

Like she was memorizing every vein and shade.

Shiiit.

I couldn't say no even if I wanted to.

Her face is inches from my tip. Eyes on mine, pupils blown wide enough that there is barely any of the copper left.

The moment the soft give of her lips allows my head between, I suck in a breath.

They say to think of something else to keep from going off too soon. The worst advice. What a fool? An idiot. I would never be able to think of anything else besides my cock sliding into Jeann's mouth for as long as I live.

I'm not missing a moment of this.

The warm, wet pressure of her tongue on the underside of my dick while her lips wrap around, does me in.

I'm not fucking her face. I'm not fucking—

She takes the full length of me, not stopping when I hit the back of her throat. She keeps that up and though I'm not fucking her face, she's doing a damn good job of it herself.

Tears start to track down her face and I'm careful to remove them. She smirks around me. "You like having my cock in your mouth, huh?"

She nods, picking up the pace. I hold her braids around my fist out of her face so I can see how her rose lips make my cock disappear like it's her favorite snack.

"Fuck that feels like heaven, god damn," I pant.

Her tongue flicks along the underside of my shaft, each pass making my balls tighten. If she keeps this up, I'm gonna bust... and soon.

I push my hips into her mouth deeper and the tip touches the back of her throat, she gags and I'm pulling out. Fuck, I said I wasn't going to fuck her face, but her nails dig into my thighs, throat squeezing the tip again. It all adds to how good she feels on me.

She's bobbing more furiously now, demanding what I've been carefully avoiding with all the strength I have as a man.

Fuck it.

I'll give her what she wants.

"Yes, sugar, take all of me in that pretty mouth. Let me slip into your throat."

I'm slow at first, but she rushes me. I'm moving faster, pushing deeper and she hums around me.

In and out, she looks at me with those flames burning in her eyes as I keep pumping into her.

I'm close, so goddamn close.

Black spots dance in my vision as I reach that point. Her hand swivels and pumps, making sure every last drop of cum I have to give is hers.

I collapse back into the seat, spent and mind blown.

Looking over at Jeann, she is also sitting back. She wipes her mouth with the back of her hand. "You showed me," she laughs. "I think ol' biddy got an eyeful before she left."

My face burns as I sit up looking in the parking lot to see if anyone is still there watching. There is no one, but who knows what was happening while my cock was inside her mouth. I wipe my sweaty forehead. "That's not funny," I say. But I can't help the smile at the thought of one of those holier-than-thou gossipers catching that sight.

"Admit it..." her head falls back with laughter still. "It's pretty damn funny."

"You're gonna get me in trouble. Just a bad influence."

"Eh," she shrugs, "Worth it. Now, let's go home."

I don't correct her or point out that she called my place home. Maybe soon, she'll slip up and call me hers too.

Chapter 17

Jeann, Then

"Again."

Jeann's fists hit the bag, first one at head level and the other at stomach level.

"Again."

She switched stances and hands. The impact of her hit radiated up her arm. She grit her teeth against the pain.

"Kick."

Her left leg reached the top of the bag and then she parried away.

"Other leg."

She switched feet and kicked with the opposite leg on the opposite side of the bag.

"Very good. Let's take a break." Redd suggested.

"Okay." She drank from the water so deeply she needed to catch her breath for a bit after.

"How's your grapple?" He asked.

"It's better." She huffed out. "Better than last time."

"Let's see it." He looked around the gym space, finally landing on the person he was searching for. "Ethan, get over here."

"He's much heavier than me," Jeann balked, but mostly because she knew she was a better grappler than her friend and didn't want to embarrass him in front of the people gathered. Even with the size difference.

"Good. Show me what you've improved," Redd barked.

"I'm not gonna hurt you," Ethan tried to reassure her.

Redd clapped and pointed to the ring. "Fuck that. Don't take it easy on her! Show me!"

The moment the two friends squared off, the tension between them was thick and curling in the space between their bodies. He smirked, confident as ever, rolling his broader shoulders and neck. He had been training hard and put on more muscle than Jeann had ever seen him have. She knew he felt confident and strong because of this. But Ethan, like most men, underestimated her simply because she was a woman.

She adjusted her stance, weight evenly distributed, muscles coiled and ready though exhaustion would likely take her after this bout. She had already trained hard today.

"Sure you can handle this?" he teased, circling her slowly. "You could concede now."

"Why don't you come find out?" Jeann shot back, eyes locked onto his movements. "I've improved. Save your pride before I crush it."

He lunged first, aiming to close the distance, but she sidestepped him, quick and controlled. Her smaller stature gave her the advantage of speed.

His reach gave him the advantage, and he used it to feint a grab, forcing her to react. When she did, he hooked an arm around her waist, using his strength to sweep her feet out from under her. They hit the mat, her back slamming against it with a muffled thud. Fuck.

For a second, he had control. Pinning her wrists down, his weight pressing into her uncomfortably, she wasn't flustered. She used the moment to analyze his positioning, searching for an opening.

Then, she found it. *Done deal.*

Shifting her hips, she bucked hard, unbalancing him just enough to free one hand. With precision, she slipped an arm under his throat as she twisted her body, wrapping her legs around his waist and locking them in tight. His body stiffened as realization set in—she was setting up a rear naked choke.

He fought it, gripping her arm that would surely bruise to pry it away, but she had the leverage. Her forearm pressed deeper against his windpipe, cutting off his air. His breathing grew labored, movements more frantic as he tried to roll out, but her legs cinched tighter, her control unshakable.

"Tap," She murmured, voice low.

His fingers twitched, hesitated.

"Tap. Out." She told him. She knew he couldn't breathe with the hold she had under his neck. He could try to roll us, but she was far too deep into this hold. Her arm was under his chin securely.

He was going to pass out.

"Tap out, dammit!"

He patted her arm finally, moments from passing out.

She released him and went for her water bottle again. Ethan laid sprawled on his back on the mat for a while, trying to get control of himself again.

"I warned you," Jeann said, heading for the showers.

"Definitely better! Good work," Redd said to her back, but she just threw up a hand ready to get clean and take a damn nap.

***

Bang. Bang. Bang.

Bang. Bang. Bang.

"You are a scary individual," Ethan told her.

She took her electronic ear muffs off and placed them on the hook to the left divider wall. "No scarier than you."

He shook his head. "Did you miss at all?"

They called the targets forward to see what the damage was. Three shots to the head—one to each eye and the other center forehead. Two shots to the torso, one in the chest.

"You know the answer to that," Jeann responded. It's not an option to be anything less than ready for anything.

"I'll take that as a no," he cackled with his goofy laugh and shook his head again. It wasn't often that Jeann heard him laugh like that. He put his baseball hat back on, sunglasses hiding a black eye that was no longer purple but a sickly yellow color. "He'll be pleased."

Rolling up the hole-filled paper, she tossed it into the big recycling bin on the way out. "I hope so. I know I'm ready for this." The big braid she put her smaller braids into was restrictive now that she was no longer shooting. She let it down and grabbed her bag.

The two of them exited the building, checking to see if anyone waited for them outside. She touched the side of her purse to ensure that she could grab her piece quickly if it came to it. You never knew in their hometown.

"It'll be nothin like a shootin' range," Ethan remarked before they were getting into the SUV. He didn't put his seatbelt on, but he never did . She didn't bother telling him to do it for the millionth time. The man was reckless even with his own life.

He reversed out of the parking lot. The windows were down and the humid Louisiana air blew in making the hairs prickle on her skin with the contrast of cool air from the A/C. "I know, but that's good. I could be useful. I could be his weapon."

At the red light, Ethan looked at her and asked, "And what would that gain you?"

She returned his bland look, "You know and I know that bein' useful is better than bein' dispensable. I'll be vital."

"You'll be a target, J."

Scoffing at his assessment, she sucked her teeth at him. "Why? Because I'm a woman."

"*Because* you'll be indispensable."

She crossed her arms over her chest. "There's worse things to be."

"How's it healin'?" Ethan asked her.

"So good. You can barely tell. I'm lucky it was a clean cut. You can't see the scar at all."

"I can," Ethan added unhelpfully before stuffing fries into his mouth. The diner was not far from the warehouse, but if they didn't eat now, there was nothing for a couple miles out. They may not be able to eat or have an appetite until much later tonight.

"Whatever, I'll just cover it." Jeann flipped the small notebook she kept in her bag open. The page she was looking for had been a quick sketch she did while watching the Faye place to see if Kev was actually going to run or not. For his sake, it's a good thing he didn't.

She recalled when Paul tried it and that's how she got the new pink scar Ethan just asked her about. She didn't take her gun out unless she truly intended to use it. He had a shitty little switchblade and caught her.

She took him down anyway.

He wore her blood to the warehouse and got the venom treatment regardless.

"That's fuckin' dope, J." Ethan took the notebook from her hands to look the design over more closely.

The crystals all shot from one that laid across the bottom. The geometric shapes were different from her usual softer style. Her art had taken on a new edge in addition to the frequency that she found herself in the tattoo chair.

"When are you gonna sit for it?"

"Ack. We've got a run so probably when we get back. The skin will be hard enough to take ink." The new responsibility was a good sign. If they kept them up and they were successful, they'd rise up the ranks faster than they thought.

"You're gonna have more than me pretty soon."

"I've got more than you now. Just because I don't have any on my neck—"

He slid a hand over the roses creeping down the side of his neck. "Man, chill. They love the roses."

"You look like an off brand rapper." She chuckled and took a bite from her burger.

He laughed with her. "You'd buy my mixtape."

"To bootleg? Sure."

CHAPTER 18

Mack

I STARE AT THE bottle on my dining table.

It stares back at me.

The infuriating note tied to the neck, taunting me just as much as the liquor does.

Piece of shit.

Angrily, I loosen the knot in the rope I'm working with and tie another just as angrily.

I curse the day that they allowed him to walk away more and more.

He has managed to taint the very gratifying memory I just had on this very table with his malice.

Not just that, but make a mockery of my sobriety. On and off for years, trying to stay dry, be clean. All the work I've done... He never gave a shit anyway. He enabled my drinking long before it should have even been a thought. I couldn't help that I had an addictive personality. It was easy for anything to become an issue for me. But nothing good had ever come from me drinking.

I stare and stare at it.

Don't know why I didn't throw it out when it came in the mail. I should have. It's only sat like a headache at the front of my head since I received it.

I should just throw it out, but I can't. He'd never know if I drank it or if I tossed it.

Tossing it would mean that I'm still affected by the man when he deserves less than a passing thought. *But I am thinking about it.*

The soft sound of feet pattering into the kitchen breaks my reverie for a moment. Jeann grabs a glass from the cabinet and fills it with water, drinking deeply. Her back heaves up and down as she leans over the sink with both hands braced at the edge of the counter. I think she might throw up, but I stay quiet and let her have her moment.

I'm having one of my own.

She turns to leave and practically jumps out of her skin. "Oh, shit!" She places a hand over her chest. "You scared me."

My roommate reaches for a light switch to turn the light on in the kitchen. I was sitting with only the moon to illuminate the room and now my eyes sting with the brightness, but I embrace it instead of covering them.

She looks me over for a moment or two. She takes in the bags under my eyes or maybe the set of my jaw. *Does the hatred I feel reflect on my face for her to see it?*

As she looks me over, I do the same to her. "We're a gnarly looking bunch. Why are you up?"

"I had a dream."

"What was it about?"

She blinks a few times as she recalls, "I'm not sure that it was just a dream. It was so real that I think it might have been memories."

I get to my feet and hold out my hand for her. "Do you want to talk about it?" She sets her glass down and takes the offering. She shakes her head.

There's little resistance when I pull her with me to the recliner and into my lap. I sigh in relief when she rests her head on my shoulder. We sit like that in the wee hours of the morning. My arms wrapped around her, her hand on my chest and our breathing syncing up.

I think that maybe she's falling asleep until she asks, "Why were you up?" The tension I had started to feel dissipate, resurfaces. My hold on her instinctively tightens. "What's with that bottle of D'usse?"

"It was my dad's drink of choice," I grit out.

"Okay..." When I don't elaborate, Jeann pushes out of my hold. I let her go with as much reluctance as I can. I don't want to let her go. I don't want to let this moment of peace with her go. "Tell me." Jeann does a lot of commanding and it's always without any sort of reservations. She pushes and pushes until you push back. Then she'll reassess.

She's not reassessing.

The longer she looks at me, the more determination sets into her features.

"He sent this bottle of cognac to me with some dumb ass note hoping for a swift recovery. What the shit is that? Six weeks I've been out of the hospital. And D'usse? What kind of pretentious, pompous asshat sends his son who broke his leg a bottle of liquor weeks after he's left the hospital? And to a recovering alcoholic at that!"

Her confusion is palpable as she chews on her lip through my outburst. "Did he know?"

"Fuck if I know. Reese knew which means Chandie knew. And if Chandie knew then Sammie knew and that pair are almost as bad as Chloe when it comes to spreading news through the Ridge. He had to have known."

"Are you sure about that?"

"I really don't care if he did or not. He's dead to me. A bottle of liquor doesn't make me more inclined to forgive him. Not after what he did."

She sits up fully in my lap. She holds my chin tight to look at her and I don't know why I like it. Her concern is plain as day. I know if I don't start sharing something then she'll start fussing at me. Normally, I'd push her to do it, but I can't. Not about this.

"He's not here—he can't be here because of the restraining order that is permanent. If he doesn't know what's going on in AR then that's how it should be."

Her eyes widen. "You have a PRO on your dad? What the fuck happened?"

"I don't. My sister does."

Her jaw drops. "Nope. You have got to give me more than that. Are we in danger?" She begins to scramble off of me, but my arms lock her into place.

"No, you're not in danger." My lip curls. "I really don't want to give you any more than that though."

"You don't have a choice, Mack. I need to know why you're so strung out about this." She traces the bags under my eyes with gentle pressure. I only keep one hand on her since I have a hard time not touching her in some way.

I can't help it, but I'm thankful that she hasn't pushed me away entirely or passed judgement before I can tell her the full story.

Even though I don't want to tell her the full story.

I heave a heavy sigh and tell her as condensed of a version as I can of what happened to the best of my knowledge. "For years Reese and Alex, my dad, apparently had a secret thing together. The Stewart's are a sod monopoly. My family has been growing sod for generations and this is just one of the properties that we own. It paid for him to go to school and make a 'name for himself'. He left my mom to manage it and she resented him for it while he lived this fancy life in the city.

"No one knew that he had taken a liking to Reese. He lured her in with his money and the acclaim he got from working as a corporate lawyer in Denver, separate from us, for years. It was fucked up and only got worse the longer they were together. She was obsessed with the lifestyle she saw celebs leading and I remember her always going on about how she would have D'usse every night when she 'made it'. He gifted it to her one year. I never knew it was from him because they just hid everything. He made time to abuse my friend, when I barely saw him once a month when this was all going on. Not that I wanted to see him, since all he did was talk shit about how I wanted to be a hick and he couldn't 'make me see reason.'"

I scoff and find myself talking to a pink braid I've started rolling around my finger. "A few years back, everything about their relationship got leaked, including the fact that he was abusing her since she was seventeen from a different girlfriend. He went ballistic. The only thing he cares about is his reputation and he was convinced Reese was the one who ruined it by exposing the true nature of their... relationship." I shudder. "He almost killed her, but she got away with a shot in the arm and Cory found her. He called for help."

"Fuck. I don't know what I thought you would tell me, but it wasn't that." She shakes her head. "That is... God, that is beyond fucked up. That's what happens on the Ridge, huh? How is he not in prison?"

"I wish he were there too. My sister didn't press charges. She didn't want some drawn out thing. A permanent restraining order and a year in jail was as much as he got. And some bullshit fines that he had no problem paying. Now the piece of shit is living in Mexico, likely *being* a piece of shit." I grind my molars. "It kills me. It *kills me* that I never knew and that I didn't help her. He used our closeness to get to her. I didn't protect her. If Cory wasn't there, I—" I hang my head. The same cyclical thought running through my mind like it always does.

I tug at my hair to the point of pain, eyes stinging. "My head is full of all these shitty choices I've made. I lost my wife and my baby in the same year that I almost lost Danny and Reese. I couldn't do *anything* to save *anyone*. I barely sobered up for any of it. The last thing I want is a bottle of fucking alcohol from that man."

"Don't blame you for that." She shifts. "We'll pour it out and smash the bottle." Then her shoulders kiss her ears. "Fuck him."

A disbelieving sound comes from my mouth as I really meet her eyes. She has nothing, but righteous indignation directed at the situation instead of at me. "I don't want you to think any differently about me. Knowing about him. I like how you look at me now."

Her face scrunches up like it suddenly smells bad here now. "Why would I think any differently about you?"

The bitter laugh that escapes me is foul in my mouth, but I can't contain the memories affecting me. "You know everything that happened with Alex now. I must be a carbon copy, right?" I look away, eyes focusing on the moon still shining in through the bay window.

"No... Not right." She holds my chin to face her again. "Why would I? Who told you that?"

"Doesn't matter. It is what it is. The Ridge will form an opinion and then stick to it unless something serious changes their minds. First, I was the hoe of the town. Then I was Mel's husband. I was sober for her because she couldn't stand when I drank. I couldn't blame her for that either. And now, I'm Alex's son, *no wonder I lost my wife*. Never mind I haven't done anything that could possibly make me like him."

"Exactly! What happened with your dad is not your fault. We already had this—You told me that you knew you were more than what those rumors are about you." I attempt to interject, but she holds a hand up. "He is responsible for his own actions. You were a kid just like her, your sister. It was not your job to protect her in this way. All that went down was fuckin' horrible. I won't deny that. That was not okay. But you had nothin' to do with it."

"The apple doesn't fall far from the tree."

Incredulity is heavy in her brows when she asks, "Who is sayin' that? Was it your ex? Is that why she left?"

"No. I don't think so... No." I scratch my neck. "It's a completely different story and her and I are on good terms. As good as they can be. She's happy. They both are and I'm happy for them."

She crosses her arms, rolling her eyes. "What a canned response. Are you a greetin' card now?"

"What do you want me to say, Jeann? Turns out she was not happy being married to me. If leaving me made her happier, then kudos on her finding it. She's the lucky one."

"I don't think I like this woman very much."

"We were young and we both made mistakes."

Her eyes pierce through the very center of me when she asks. "Do you still love her?"

Sliding my fingers into her braids, I relish how she rests her head in my hands. "I'll always have love in my heart for her but no, I'm not in love with her. We were both broken by the time I met her. I had to deal with the fact that my dad preferred his teenage son to be drunk and out of his hair over actually fixing his marriage or letting his wife go. My mom hated herself and tried to smother me with her 'love' for me, but Alex didn't care. She blamed my sister for her failing marriage and tried to drive a wedge between us by always making little digs at her or spreading rumors about her. It was too much.

"Melody lost her mom young and then her dad while we were together. Both hit her hard. I learned to smile through my pain, pretend like none of it was happening and that's not what she needed. Melody had her own struggles with mental health, but at the base of everything was supposed to be our friendship. She shut me out though. I couldn't help her and I *wanted* to. I think I made it worse and she shut me out more. I was in our marriage alone by the time she left, but I was blindsided nonetheless." I sigh. "She put me through too much, made me suffer through too much. Mostly by myself."

"I definitely don't like *Melody*," she grumbles and scoffs. "Or your parents. If I ever see them... You deserve better than all this. I don't know if a blowie can fix that though."

A laugh from deep in my stomach bubbles up after she delivers that line and it feels good. "I hate to say it, but I don't think a blowie will fix it either."

She made me feel good though she's outrageous but still painfully honest. I've laid so many heavy things at her feet tonight.

And Jeann simply holds it and she's still here.

Jeann is still here.

With a smile on my face, I ask, "Would you want a grilled cheese sandwich if I made one?"

She looks at me with piqued interest, "I think I would..."

"Good. Sit tight and I'll be right back."

It takes me no time to whip up a couple sandwiches and we watch some TV in my room, falling asleep for the night with her in my arms.

I sleep more soundly than I have in years.

CHAPTER 19

Jeann

I WAKE WITH A start and hop off the bed.

Not my bed down the hall in the guest room, but Mack's bed.

Then, grilled cheese and all the conversations from last night come back to me. My heart is instantly heavy with the truth that Mack shared.

He told me once that he thought I might bolt after hearing it. What a fucked up way to feel? And what's worse is that he probably believes this from experience. Everyone in his life has given him reason to believe that if he's not the sunshine guy, then they won't stick around.

His ex, who I hate with absolute certainty now, used him for his light and left when that wasn't enough to save herself.

His friends sided with her after they separated, and still he has remained friends with them. And now I don't think he really knows what a true friend is. Believing in forgiveness is one thing, but I have not forgiven them, even if he has. Taking one for the team, so they can be comfortable while this man was struggling on his own...

I don't like it for him.

I don't like it at all.

No wonder he needs his horses as much as he does.

His dad, *oh him,* he deserves a smack upside the head and more. I get sneaking a beer or trying some things when you're young. Teenagers have been doing it... probably from the beginning of time. But encouraging your own underaged son to drink so that he's easier to deal with or whatever the fuck was the reasoning—he should be in prison. The pervert should have been prosecuted to the fullest extent of the fucking law. *Goddamn.* His poor sister. It couldn't have been me. I would have pressed for life.

His mom is not one I'd want him around either. I don't know what her deal is. Driving a wedge between your son and his best friend... and for what? That sorry sack of shit, Alex, or whatever? Disgusting behavior.

I hope I never meet her or his dad.

All of it makes me want to scream and rage and hurt someone on his behalf. Looking down at the man who is still sleeping peacefully in bed, I brush some of his overgrown hair out of his face. He looks so happy even in sleep.

Bless, he deserved better.

Last night would have been the perfect opportunity to tell him about the memories that I've been recovering. I should have told him. After all, they are parts of me. I don't know for sure how much is true because sometimes our memories can be distorted by perception. What I perceive from them at this point is that I was training for something. Training hard. I was becoming someone to fear. Fighting, shooting, stake outs? I was someone's weapon. The thought should scare me, but it doesn't. Why should I be scared of something that is true about me?

I'm *more* nervous of what Mack will think of me. That scares me the most.

I shouldn't care at all.

I watch him for a few moments before returning to my room and getting ready for the day. When I'm back out into the hallway, Mack is already dressed and waiting for me.

"PT today. You ready?" His smile is bright and he looks so rested. Maybe sharing a bit of his life's burdens lifted the weight he would normally be carrying.

I'm still here. I didn't bolt like he thought I might.

"I'll just be sittin' around. Are you ready?"

He wiggles the boot in front of him. "Been ready."

A TALL WHITE WOMAN in sweats walks up to the desk at the Physical Therapy center Mack will be going to for the next few months. She's pretty with her brown hair pulled into a ponytail that highlights her killer cheekbones and green eyes. She smiles at him while he fills out the paperwork that she handed him and my fist clenches. Stepping around the counter she asks us to follow her back into the facility.

I hope she trips.

I'm less irritated when a big, strong Asian man sits down at the bench and begins talking through the plan he has for Mack's recovery.

The first session of PT is always the hardest. I don't know from personal experience, but because of the poster that's hanging on the wall of the room we're in. It's rife with motivational quotes and images that I guess are supposed to be inspiring for the clients.

It's going to be a long hour and I regret not bringing anything to do in the meantime. I cross my arms prepared to settle in. With the sweater I'm wearing, my arm becomes exposed just enough to see the tattoo. I may have dreamt the memory of planning this tattoo, but it's still so strange to learn the reason why I got it and exactly what it's covering. The crystals' design is large enough to cover the slightly jagged edges of the scar and it's almost undetectable under my finger.

I don't know why I didn't tell Mack the whole truth last night. I'm almost certain that it was a memory and not a dream. Everything about it feels that way. And I know in my heart that this is something that happened to me.

I know how to fight. Spar and grapple. At some point I learned and I got good at it.

How to hold a gun. I know how to shoot a gun. How to aim and fire with precision.

Ethan was there the whole time. He knew this about me and was training just like me.

I'm not intentionally trying to keep things from Mack. I mean, it's cool as fuck to be a total badass, but something in my gut is telling me not to tell him anything until I know the full picture.

Why get him all worked up for what could be nothing?

Maybe they are just dreams.

I'm kind of hoping they are.

Trying to distract myself, I look up some recipes online and make a list of things I'll need to grab on the way home.

Home.

To Mack's house, I correct myself. Louisiana is home and I'd be smart to remember that.

His session goes smoothly, but Mack is pretty tired as we drive home from the clinic in Harmony Hill. I'm still grateful that it hasn't snowed since the other night and driving is easy again. We had to pass the spot where the accident happened to get here. He held my hand. I don't know if it was for him or for me, but it was a comfort to have him there to experience it with me.

I expected that maybe a heap of memories would come back just being in that spot again, but they didn't. Should I feel more let down by that? Probably. But I find relief in not having to process more memories that complicate my current life.

"I'm going to take a shower," Mack announces from his room while I pile ingredients for dinner on the counter.

"Okay," I respond off-handedly.

I chop fresh spinach, sun-dried tomatoes, and a couple of chicken breasts while the water boils in a pot on the stove. The sauce is easy with heavy cream and some cheese I didn't bother to grate, but instead bought shredded already. I lose myself to the process of preparing this meal because I don't want to keep thinking about that dream. I can't.

I'm making a quick casserole so I can shower too. I combine everything how I'm supposed to and set the oven timer. I have work again in the morning and I want to eat and go to sleep… and hopefully not recover any more memories to plague my waking thoughts with.

"If you're gonna spoil me like this, you better be prepared to keep it up. My stomach is scraping my spine. I've been trying to be patient." Mack says when I pad back to the kitchen in my sleep shirt and on bare feet.

I tilt my head at him. With the braids piled on top of my head from my shower, the quick bun I had them in unravels around me. It was not my intention, but his eyes track the sprawl of my hair around me now. The hunger in his eyes is not just for the delicious food I made before we both washed the day off.

"Ah-ah," I say, tapping him on the nose. "Only good boys who wait get a treat."

He barks like a dog, charging me fast enough to grab me. I'm laughing in his arms completely caught off guard by his silliness.

Mack kisses my forehead right over the faint scar there from the accident. It tingles with his lips over it in a way that it doesn't when my own fingers touch it.

The oven timer goes off and he releases me to pull the dinner out of the oven. It smells so good that I hate I'll have to wait a few more minutes to dig in.

With the food on the table, we fall into easy conversation over our meal. Mack talks animatedly about what he's looking forward to being back to work, even in a small capacity. The physical therapist decided that some light activities were fine as long as he wasn't lifting heavy or spending too much time on his feet. He goes into a tangent about the overlook he can get to on horseback that has the most amazing view of Alpenglow Ridge. "I'm going to take you one day."

"Are you askin' me on a date?" I ask.

"Does it seem like I'm asking you on a date?"

"Yea…"

"Well, then. Yes. Will you go on a date with me to the overlook?"

"Umm," I scratch my shoulder, choosing not to think about the ink underneath or why it suddenly itches. "I think we're kind of past that, don't you?"

"Past what?"

"Datin'."

"You don't get past dating." His eyebrows show confusion where his mouth still smiles. He's enjoying this and I don't understand why.

"Yes you do! You date and then you're in a relationship and then you're just together."

"Sugar, you've got it all wrong."

Sugar.

SUGAR!

"Then explain us. Because nothing about anything between us is how it's supposed to go."

He stabs at the penne noodles on his plate with the fork. "Who am I to argue with fate?" He stuffs the food into his mouth, chewing while maintaining the smug expression on his face.

"Fate?" I guffaw, the unhinged sound coming deep from my stomach. "You think this," I motion to him, then me and then his house, "was fated?"

"Some things about it are extremely unfortunate, but I never would have met you otherwise. I'd have never had the opportunity to invite you to stay here. We never would have had that first... whatever happened over there. And now, we're talking about future plans."

Forever, promises, futures.

I drop my fork, the grief hitting me like a freight train.

All things that Mack wants to give me while Ethan will never have those things again. Lauren never will.

The warmth of his hand on mine pulls me to the present and out of the encroaching melancholic thoughts. "Hey, I didn't mean—You don't have to ignore that pain or the loss with me. It wasn't your fault and you don't have to punish yourself for wanting to live or move forward."

"How is that fair to him? To them?" I ask, emotion thick in my throat.

His eyes soften when I meet his blue, blue gaze. "How is it fair to them for you to be in a standstill, taking for granted what you've been given? A second chance at life."

I nod and he releases my hand. He's right, but not in the way that he might think. *I have been given a second chance.* With Mack, maybe I can leave behind the malice of my past. Whatever Ethan and I were doing in the last few years, I don't think it was good or honorable. With Mack, I can live an honest life. A soft one in a small town where nothing truly bad happens.

We both finish our dinners, thinking over what has been said, and he takes the plates to the kitchen. We don't go to the living room. Instead, he takes me with him to his bed. He pulls back the covers and we both get under them.

He holds me and time ticks by as I soak up the warmth of his embrace and the smell of soap that lingers on his skin. The silence between us isn't tense or weighted—it's comfort and understanding. Just being close to him feels right even if there are so many unknowns in the air.

Mack is the first to break the silence when he declares, "Out there, nothing has to change. But when you're in my arms, in my bed, in my mind—you're mine. I don't need a label. We don't have to call this what we both know it is. I'm not dumb enough to tell you that I lo—" I put a hand over his mouth.

"There's two words that I want to hear from you. If it's not those two, then I just need you to show me that you like what we're doin' together."

He rolls over me, mouth meeting mine in a kiss that I could only classify as passionate. His lips are insistent, sweet and I need all of it. I catch one in-between my teeth and he moans into my mouth. My nails find his waist pulling him on top of me, wanting to feel the full weight of his body on mine.

My legs have a mind of their own, wrapping themselves around his back and we start this rocking that builds the intensity of heat growing hotter and hotter at my core.

He leans back, but I refuse to let his body go with my legs. He rips his shirt over his head and helps me take my sleep shirt off. I'm left in just my thin cotton boyshorts.

He kisses my body with a kind of reverence that makes my heart squeeze too tightly.

I've been in his bed more times than I can count at this point. We've spent time here talking or watching TV and, after last night, sleeping.

But I've never been naked in his room.

The strength of his arms as he holds himself over me is a marvel. It's sexual even though he still wears his pants and all I can see are his tattoos rippling over his chest and arms as he is still kissing me.

Soft lips amidst the scruffy stubble.

Rough hands but gentle touches.

I don't feel when the last scrap of clothing I had on is suddenly gone.

"Tell me, Mack." I demand.

"I'm yours," he responds from between my legs. My head falls back to the pillow with the first kiss he places over the most sensitive part of me.

How he knew that was what I wanted him to say, is beyond me. It's not even worth pondering because the fact of the matter is that *he is mine.*

I don't care about anything else.

Mack is mine and I'm going to keep him because I want to. Even if I don't deserve to.

His kisses are soft against my pussy. His focus solely on making me feel good.

And I do.

I feel so damn good under his attention.

"Suck me into your mouth," I moan. His eyes flick to mine, alight with something too intimate when he does as I asked. "Yea, just like that."

My head tilts back, the sensation building in my core. His finger plays at my entrance before he enters me. My walls squeeze at him, desperate for more, but all too happy at being filled in some way.

He laps at me with reckless movements. There is no politeness in the vigor that he works me up. The longer hair at the top of his head tickles my thighs. I brush it out of the way so I can look into his eyes when I say, "I love seein' me all over your face. Make me drip down your chin."

Mack makes a sound too close to a whimper that vibrates my clit, sending sparks down to my toes. I will never get enough of the sounds he makes. Like he's desperate to please me and that pleases him.

Fuuuck, this good boy is definitely getting a treat.

I come hard and cry out his name, his fingers still inside me stroking that spot until I'm boneless on the mattress.

My body goes cold as he scrounges around for something before coming back to the bed and rolling a condom over himself.

Then, I hear the tell-tale sound of the Velcro on his boot. He was told that every step he takes needs a boot. The fact that he's putting it on now, means he's about to get down to business. He moves deliberately but efficiently to get his leg secured.

His cock bobs long and hard just out of reach when he's finally done with his task.

For some reason, I've caught my second wind. On my knees, I crawl my way over to him. He holds himself in one hand and my chin in the other. "Do I get to be inside you now?"

I bite my lip, loving how he talks to me in this bed. "Do you want to see it from the front or the back?"

"Lie back," he says, pressing a hand to my chest. I allow him to guide me and he gives my nipple a pinch. I hiss, but he's there soothing the sting with his mouth. I barely notice that he's lifting my ass onto a pillow. I help him adjust it and then he kisses me again. The taste of me still lingering on his lips. "I want to see the look in your eyes when you take all of me for the first time."

Okay. Daddy Mack has officially joined us. Legs wrapping themselves around his waist again, I hold myself up on my elbows to get as clear a view of him as I can from my back.

He's still hot as fuck. His body is very much so the result of whatever work he does on the Ranch. Every cut, crevice and crease will need to be licked just as soon as I feel how his hard, long and veiny dick feels inside me. I'm throbbing with the need and every moment that passes is unbearable.

I should have climbed on top of him.

The hot head slides through my wetness and I sigh with relief at the first push inside me.

The slide is tight as he gives me more and more of him.

He doesn't watch where his cock enters me. His eyes remain on my face, taking in every change of my expression while he fills me.

It's too much, I think. Too intimate. He pauses, though I haven't said a word.

Sweat beads on his brow, but he asks, "You okay, sugar?"

Sugar.

SUGAR.

I'm whimpering and writhing to take all of him with just one silly little name that's not even my own.

He rolls us to our sides and cups my face. My leg lifts over his hip and he drives into me. It's a thrust that makes my tits bounce, but he kisses me deeply, thrusting and pumping his hips.

The intimacy of the sex between us has not been lost on me and for all I know it's been years since any man has touched me this way.

The way we held hands before was platonic, comfort. But the way we hold hands now is private and personal, vulnerable.

This is not a slip up between roommates.

This is so much more.

Nothing could compare to how his care surrounds me and I clench him inside me.

"Mack, I'm goin' to—"

"Not yet," he says, gritting his teeth as he moves me again to be on top of him.

Strong, calloused fingers trail over my skin until he holds a breast in each hand, "Show me how much you like what we're doing," he smirks, repeating what I've said and I do.

Fuck, I love being on top.

It's a slow bounce up and down his length for show until he tilts his hips and each slide up and down hits that spot inside me that makes me pant and keen.

"Mack," I cry. "I'm goin' to come."

"Yea, you are. I feel how tight you are on me." *Thrust.* "Show me. Show me how you come on my cock."

Then... I break.

Little pieces of me shattering and popping like hot glass or fireworks. It's too big for just my body. The feeling is so massive as I fall apart. I want to keep all my pieces, but I know he's keeping some of them for himself.

I should be worried about that.

I should not have fucked my roommate.

I definitely should not have fallen asleep in his room, in his arms as he's made it a place to call my own.

CHAPTER 20

Mack

THE SUN BREAKS THROUGH the gaps of my curtains, waking me.

Consciousness comes slowly to me next. And then I register the weight on my chest.

Golden braids spread all over me, her face hidden, but *it's her*.

Jeann stayed the night in bed with me.

I half expected her to sneak out at some point in the night, but she didn't. After we had sex for the first time, I didn't know how things would change between us. I hoped that they would only change for the better. Getting used to waking up next to this woman is something I'd like to do.

I couldn't have prepared for us to have sex twice more and end up passed out between my sheets.

There was only the one condom and to be honest, I don't even remember when or why I had it.

My desire to pursue another woman after my wife left me seemed like an impossibility. No woman in town would try and I didn't want to take my chances with a one night stand. That is not the kind of guy I am.

I lie as still as I can so that I don't jostle the woman sleeping on me. Her arms are wrapped around me like I'm her favorite pillow. *I'd like to be her favorite anything.* I don't care what. She made me feel things I haven't in… that I hadn't before.

If she let me call her my girlfriend to no one else, I don't think I'd care. As long as I got to have her just like this. As long as she'll let me keep her. This wild spirit.

Years ago, Danny told me that I shouldn't chase the mares that couldn't be tamed. His version of the birds and the bees conversation had come a couple years too late, but I think about the wisdom he shared with me growing up more fondly than anything my own dad ever told me. He meant to warn me about trying to pursue Reese.

It was a natural thing. You see two young kids spending all their time together and you suspect that there is a "young love" brewing. It's never been that way. Reese has always been a sister to me and nothing else. But his words still resonate.

I couldn't keep my ex because her heart belonged to someone else and I was too stubborn to accept it. So hellbent on proving to her, on proving to myself, that I deserved for someone to love me.

Maybe because I was missing it from my own family and found it for myself. I thought I could find it and make it work for me.

But I was so wrong. We were both wrong, my ex and I.

But this free spirit, strong and passionate, is my calling. Her spirit called to me as soon as I woke up in the hospital bed and got my senses back. When I was able, I searched for her. I didn't know what I would find, but when I did, my own spirit calmed.

I might not know what that means, but I know how it feels to be without her and I don't want to feel that ever again.

I smooth back the hair from her face and a slight grimace forms there as the sun shines down on her. She burrows closer to me, taking a big inhale of the shirt I'm wearing before settling again.

My chest tightens and I vow to be the safe space that she needs.

After a while she wakes probably because I've begun to trace some of the designs on her body.

I've been trying to take note of all of them. I'm pretty sure that she was the one to draw each of the animals, people and concepts here. I'm constantly in awe of her talent.

"Mack, what are you doin'?" Her sleepy voice is barely above a whisper.

"Looking at your ink," I respond. She turns in my arms. There are some creases from where her face was pressed against my shirt and she looks adorably rumpled this morning. I smirk to myself and she frowns. "Why are you smirkin' at me?"

"Nothing, nothing," I can't help how my smile stretches to its full width now. "Just thinking about how someone wore you out last night."

She rolls her eyes, "Someone did."

"Do I know him by chance?"

Now she's the one to smirk. "Not as well as I do."

A laugh rips out of me. "Nah, I guess not," I say, squeezing her closer to me. I don't want to let her go from this moment in my bed. I want to keep her with me just like this.

Jeann sits up and her perfect tits are exposed for a moment before she pulls the covers up with a shiver. "Since you're doin' inventory, what did you find?"

Looking up at her from where I lie on my pillow, I think about what exactly I can tell her. I don't want to come off like a creep even though I likely could with the information I have gathered about her. I start slowly, "I've counted and there's more butterflies on you than anything else."

"I noticed that too..."

I have my own ideas about why, but maybe they were there before her memory loss and she knows more. "Why?"

She frowns. "I don't really know." At her discomfort I set my hand face up in her lap. There's no hesitation when she puts hers in mine. I take notice of how smooth her knuckles and hands are now from the first time that I did it when my thumb runs over them.

"I remember thinkin' that my sister was like a butterfly when she was pregnant. Changin' and beautiful. But really, she was always entrancin' and beautiful like one."

I tilt my head, running a finger over the one on her hip. "Maybe they're supposed to remind you of Lauren then."

"It does. We were so different," she recalls. Her eyes take on a dreamy quality as she looks out the window.

"In what ways?"

"She was the nice one. Always had a smile for people. Understandin' and patient. People were drawn to her." She looks down at our hands. "She loved me harder even when I couldn't love myself."

I think for a long while, tying and untying the words she said. There are many things I know about Jeann and so much I still want to learn. I think that she is too hard on herself, putting value on things that don't need her concern. Finally I say, "Maybe you're more like a butterfly than you think."

The crease in her eyebrow deepens. "Doubt it. A moth? Maybe. Those are cool."

The one on her neck that looks like it's just landed there to whisper in her ear is the one I've been looking at all morning. I reach over to trace it and she shivers. Sitting up to meet her eyes, I blurt the thoughts that I've had about these tattoos. "Nah. Butterflies remind us how fleeting beauty can be. They make us appreciate how special it is to be in their presence. You never know when you'll see one or for how long. But every time, it's meaningful. You could catch them, keep them, but they need to be free to have a full life. And you want that for them. You want them to be beautiful and free because that's what makes them special."

Her nose scrunches up and I smooth it away. Her copper eyes shimmer in the early light of my bedroom. "That's what you think of me?"

"I do," I respond simply. Placing my palm up on my leg this time, I need to be touching her again. She obliges with her hand lying in mine so I can intertwine our fingers. "You can find a way to keep a butterfly though. Make them a sanctuary. A soft place to land so that they want for nothing. And you can marvel at them at your leisure."

She allows me to pull her in close to me and I'm thankful that I can talk to the hair on her head instead of her face. The lump in my throat distorts my words a bit anyway. "They migrate south in the warmer months."

We're both quiet with that truth looming over us. She doesn't agree to what I've said, but she doesn't dispel what I'm not saying here either.

I want her to say that she is thinking about staying. That I've made a sanctuary for her to feel safe and taken care of in. Wanting to keep her and to marvel at her is possibly the most selfish thing I've thought in a long time. But how am I supposed to let her go when she fits too perfectly here, with me?

It's not about what I want though. I knew that this had to be temporary when I asked her to stay here. I knew that she would leave eventually.

I knew.

But I've still fallen for her and there is nothing I can do about it.

At the end of this all, I have to find a way to be okay with letting her fly away.

⸻◆◆◆⸻

"What are you drawing now?"

Pulling her top lip into her mouth. "I think the mountains behind your house," she responds.

I brush the corner of her mouth with my thumb. "You think?"

She releases her lip and sets her pad down. "Yea... I didn't know what I was goin' to draw, but I've never sketched mountains before. These look like somethin' from a postcard. The snowcaps and how the sky still seems so wide above them." Her shoulder hikes up. "I don't usually like drawin' landscapes. Well as far as I know, I don't. Colorado has made me do a lot of things I never thought I would. But these... they feel like a presence. A bein' all on their own."

This piece looks so detailed already. No doubt they are the peaks behind the house though. "I get it. How could something so massive feel so tangible."

"Exactly. I'd never thought that I could be the kind of person to admire that kind of thing. Snow, in my mind, is still so abstract even though I've seen my fair share of it now."

I laugh at her contemplations. "How could something seem abstract when it's right in front of you?"

"Easy," she shrugs.

"How?" I insist.

"Like people."

"What? That makes even less sense."

"Doesn't it though? You can be around someone for their whole life, everyday and still have a different picture, a whole different idea, about who they are than what they consider about themselves. Does it get more abstract than that? One subject, completely different pictures. I could draw you one way and you could look at it and say I've got it all wrong. But both of us would be right. That's the beauty of art and what makes abstract art so compellin'. I prefer realism, but still snow only exists as an intangible idea. It represents many different ideas in my mind."

"Like what?"

Sitting back on the couch, she sighs as she thinks. I sit beside her, pulling her legs up onto mine. "It represents peace from what I remember readin' about it online and even now I can see how someone would come to that conclusion."

"Of course."

She bites her lip again. "It also represents the cause of a major loss in my life. I'll probably never see snow without thinkin' about what I lost."

"Your memories. Your friend."

"My life as I knew it." She drops the charcoal pencil and fiddles with the nail on her index finger. "I may not have the memories of what I wanted my life to look like, but I know this isn't it."

"Same... same." Looking over the page again, I see there are a few geese and cattle. She never leaves a page without an animal of some sort. "Is that such a bad thing?"

"It's not *anythin'*. Plans change for a reason. Without the snow, I wouldn't have you."

The way she brings up what we talked about over dinner in her own way is music to my ears. She may not completely agree, but I think we were fated. "And you do. You have me now and I think that is a gift that the snow gave me."

"That's because you're soft."

My eyebrows rise. "I haven't had any complaints..."

"Oh, stop," she laughs, launching herself at me. Her arms wrap around my neck and we fall back onto the couch together. Her above me, just the way I like.

"How about you get dressed and I take you out of this house for a change?"

She frowns. "Take me where?"

"Can it be a surprise?" I hope that my eyes are showing her that she can trust me as hers flick between them. "I haven't had a Valentine's date in years." I widen my eyes as big as I can, pleading with her. If she doesn't agree, I guess I just have to deal with it, but I hope that my planning will amount to a really nice evening for the two of us.

"Aw... nooo. Don't put the puppy dog eyes on me. It's just not fair."

I poke my lip out for effect. "So...?"

"Fine. Give me some time and I'll be ready."

CHAPTER 21

Mack

I PARK IN THE back when we arrive and not without having to drive around a few times before. The Senior Center is all decked out for the event and I'm grateful Chandie was in charge this year. She and Chloe rival each other on who can throw a party better. But if either are on the committee, you're probably in good hands.

Red streamers and heart balloons assault us when we walk into the building. The cost for admission is based on donations to the center. It's how they afford to keep the elderly residents of Alpenglow Ridge entertained and such. Many come just to see friends, but there is a wide range of classes and programs they offer here outside of the parties they occasionally throw. There's a donation table with a bowl to collect paper donations, but I scan the QR code to leave them something instead.

"Wow, you keep the gramps in style in AR," Jeann remarks as she walks down the heavily decorated hall.

I've never heard her refer to Alpenglow Ridge as AR before... That is such a local thing to do. Maybe my home is feeling more like her home than she realizes. I could point it out, but instead I just respond to the comment she's made. "They do have a pretty good time. Being here is a little bit nostalgic for me." I walk with her into the gym area that looks a little like prom night.

She gives me a curious look. "Were you lying about being thirty-one?"

"No," I chuckle. "Just after I graduated, I spent a lot of time here volunteering with the shuttle service they offer. It was an easy way to make extra money in the summer and there really weren't many jobs in town. Driving them to and from their classes was basically just Uber for the elderly. Let me tell you, it wasn't always an easy task, but I liked it. Sometimes I miss when my life was that easy."

"Always being a good guy," she scoffs, but follows me to the gymnasium that has been transformed for the evening.

There are older couples here, but there are plenty of people my age too. With few options for dinner or a nice night out when you can't be too far from your kids or just don't want to fight the crowd in town, *Forever Young: A Sweetheart Soiree* is not a bad option. The banner with the name hangs proudly from the small stage at the back of the room.

I spot Chandie and Danny as soon as they spot me. She waves to me and I pat Jeann's hand that's looped through my arm.

We meet them over by the table and I congratulate Chandie on the beautiful event. She immediately dives into telling me about all she's been up to today. I keep Jeann's hand in mine as she looks around at all the room has to offer until she gives me a squeeze to let her look around. When I turn to see where she has wandered off to, she's dancing with Danny.

Somehow the grumpy man is making conversation with my girl. She looks amazing in a charcoal cable knit sweater dress that hugs her every curve and red heels. Half of her golden hair is piled on top of her head so the colorful braids on the bottom mixed with the gold cascade down her back.

"Mack," Chandie says.

"Huh?" She looks so at peace dancing with the only man I'd ever recognize as a father figure. Danny tried his best to be there for me and open his home when he could. He had a heart scare a few years back during the time Melody and I had first split. It's what brought my sister back home, but more than that, it was the start of a wakeup call I needed. Without the Masons I may not have been in a position to receive my snow gift.

Since I had the thought, I haven't gotten it out of my mind. Jeann is the gift that the snow gave me.

"My goodness you are smitten. Did you hear what I said?"

Turning back to Chandie with a hand to my chest rubbing the spot, I apologize. "I'm sorry, Chandie. Tell me again."

She chuckles. "I suppose it doesn't matter. I see why you paid the big bills for the snow carriage ride."

I feel my face heat, "Do you think she'll like it?"

"I do, honey." She pats the hand on my chest, bringing awareness to the fact that I haven't stopped rubbing the spot. "Go get her before my husband gives her some of his 'trade wisdom' about you," she says with a wink.

A romantic acoustic melody begins to play and I make my way over to the woman who has taken over my life in the best way possible.

"Do you mind if I cut in?" I ask when I get closer to her and Danny.

"Not at all. I was getting tired anyway," he says, giving my date a rare smile.

"I wasn't asking you but okay," I respond blandly, handing him his cane.

He leaves us on a chuckle and I hold out my hand for Jeann.

She takes it. "So, this is a date?"

"This is a date." I pull her close to me. "Though, I'm spoiling you tonight. All of them won't be this... grand."

Jeann looks up at me with contrition in her eyes. My hands find her waist and she allows me to direct us around the dance floor.

"If I ask, will you tell me what's wrong?"

"It's nothin'. Just thoughts." She blinks and her face returns to one that is missing the regret she was once holding. "You have so much love in your life, Mack. You should appreciate that more."

"I do." My brows pinch. "What did he say to you?" I turn my head to try and find the man in the crowd, but she cups my face gently to bring my attention back to her.

"Nothin' I didn't already know." Her smile is tight before her hands press to my chest. "This is very special. I'm glad you brought me here."

I'm not settled with the disquiet I feel under the surface of her words, but I simply respond, "Just a little small town magic."

We dance for a time. The glittering red ambiance, shimmering into the background with Jeann in my arms. It feels like it's just us two here tonight.

That was until, "Mack?" I turn to see the teenager who tapped my shoulder. "Your carriage is waiting."

They normally have carriage rides for the major holidays where the town is all lit up and decorated. The one main street where we have shops put up lights for Christmas will have the carriage rides all week until New Year's Eve. But for Valentine's Day, they alternate the lights to red and white for the night and it's a vision with the red banners billowing on theme.

I guide us to the front of the building where the carriage sits decorated along the same red and white theme as everything else tonight.

Glaring at Patrick when he tries to take Jeann's hand, he returns to the bench seat behind the four horses. *Damn straight.*

I take care to help her into the back bench. She swats at my hand. I may or may not have gotten a feel of her ass in that dress with her on the top rung of the steps.

She sits and I pay extra attention getting onto the carriage myself. Between the residual snow and the size of my boot, it's a tricky task. These things can tip over with how top heavy they are and I'm not exactly a small fella.

Finally, we sit on the bench that's illuminated by the street lights. It is a moody, romantic feel with how the red tints her face. The night has grown colder so I'm glad we grabbed our coats on the way out. Still, I grab the fur blanket from the basket underneath the bench and situate it over our legs.

She settles easily under my arm. Her cheek is already cold, pressed against my chest and she shivers a bit as I trace little hearts over her shoulder. Though I know it's not from the cold.

Jeann looks up at me asking, "So how long is this ride?" The rhythmic crunch, crunch, crunch of the salted pavement fills the otherwise quiet street. Either people are in their homes by now or in the city for a lavish evening. I'm glad it's just the two of us out here...

I need to remember Patrick is here so I don't do anything *too un-gentlemanly* on this ride.

"Well, I bought the whole night so I'm guessing until the horses get tired."

She looks at me with incredulous eyes. "You did what?"

"Arranged a romantic carriage ride with my girlfriend."

"I'm not your—"

"Ah-ah. You already agreed in bed and we sealed it with cock."

She guffaws, a rich and hearty sound. I love that I can make her laugh like that. "Sealed with cock? That is so crude, oh my god. What am I supposed to do with that?"

"Nothing. It's done," I wink. "Now look, we're getting off of the main road. The stars are bright already and it's not that late yet."

"They're shinin' just for you," she says offhandedly, like a joke. But it doesn't feel that way. The cloud cover has made them difficult to see for a while. I know because I had been making sure they'd shine *for her* tonight.

Whether Jeann and I had this date or not, I was always going to try and get her here, in this carriage with me. As soon as Chandie told me, I snapped up every slot they hoped to sell for the evening.

"Not me," I say, holding her face in my hand. Her inky eyes draw me in. The depths begging me to drown within them. "It's just for you."

She reaches for me as I pull her in, capturing her mouth, tasting the strawberry of her lipgloss as she opens for me.

I'm unhurried in the way I devour her. She's soft and warm in my arms.

I suddenly wish that there was no carriage ride and we were already at home so that there was nothing between us. Not coats and sweaters and jeans and... Patrick.

Her body is my every desperate desire.

Now that I've been with her. Felt her grip me while she takes her pleasure, I don't think I could have another motivation in life if it doesn't end with her moaning my name or telling me how much harder and deeper she wants me to go.

The first feeling of her cold fingertips on my side under my sweater makes me flinch, but it's not long before they're warm and trailing down my body.

She's kissing my neck and leaving what I know will be marks of her hold on me. I don't care. Let everyone know that I have a woman who wants to claim me.

I'd like nothing better.

I'm desperate for that too.

She cups my length, growing hard in my jeans like it belongs to her.

And let's be honest. At this point—it does.

She could tell me to get on my knees and bark and *woof* WOOF. I'm obedient.

"You better be quiet or I'll have to stop," she warns in a low tone and I bite my lip. "Can you be quiet for me?" she whispers.

I nod as quickly as I can because I don't want any of this to stop.

Under the blanket, there would be no way to tell how she's carefully unzipping me to give her more room to work my dick.

She holds my gaze steady all while stroking me in her capable hand. I'm caught, spinning at the edge of her hook.

Each slide of her warm palm over me is like a tick in many ticks, leading to the countdown of ruining this blanket. I'm going to be liable for it and I've just accepted that I'll be taking this home with me too. Fuck it, I'll earn it like a trophy and display it on my couch for the memories.

Her blown out pupils glitter in the light of the lanterns hanging from the corners of the carriage. Now that we're on the gravel under the trees in the woods, it really feels nostalgic.

A dry handy on back roads is not a foreign concept for me, but it feels wholly new with my pleasure in Jeann's hands.

She commands my body and I want her to have it all.

I *trust her.*

I know she will take me where I want to go. Even if I didn't know where exactly that was.

The destination is heaven all the same.

CHAPTER 22

Jeann

FROM THE MOMENT WE got back to his house, I haven't been able to keep my hands off of him. Actually, it was from the moment I found out that he planned a romantic carriage ride like I was some kind of Disney princess. It was not something that I ever expected would happen to me in my lifetime. Who could have thought that would be a possibility?

Mack.

Mack thought of it and planned all of it without me even knowing.

Making him come on said carriage ride was the only way I could begin to show him how much I liked what he did for me. His red cheeks were pleasure enough when he had to explain to Patrick why he would be reimbursing them for the blanket that he marked as his with my help.

That wasn't enough for him. With the doors closed and an entire house at our disposal, he walks us over to the kitchen.

"Oh, I like where your mind is goin'," I say, lifting my dress over my hips and climbing onto the counter.

"You knew I got chocolate covered strawberries from Drip and Whip?" He holds up a green box and opens it to show me the largest strawberries I've ever seen all dressed in chocolate and glitter. They don't even look real. Much too pretty to eat.

"No, I..." My voice trails off as he takes a bite out of one, letting out a sound that tightens my lower belly so much that I have to press my thighs together.

"This might actually be the kind of strawberries that would rival yours," he taunts.

His smirk is lethal when he holds the fruit up to my mouth for me to take a bite as well.

I fully planned to say something sharp back to him, but when I taste the dessert, I make the same sound he did.

"What the hell is in that? Fuck, I'm goin' to eat the whole box."

Mack licks his lips, lowering to his knees and spreading mine, "I was thinking the same thing." He kisses my strawberry tattoo, making sure to trace all around it with his tongue. It's close, but not close enough and I feel myself dripping onto the counter. He licks up the mess, trailing his wet tongue through my lips. My legs shake in anticipation.

I don't know what he'll do next.

But I'm eager to find out.

He licks me clean, taking his time between my thighs.

We end up on the dining table, and I ride him.

Taking.

Using.

I can't get enough.

How could I when he treats me *like this* and the night is still young?

* * *

"WHAT TIME IS IT?" His breaths are short from exertion, hands gripping my sides, keeping me in place.

"I don't know," I pant back at him.

He reaches a long arm down to the ground beside the bed and lifts up my dress at first. Then, with a few more awkward reaches trying not to disrupt the rocking of my hips, he finds his pants.

His phone casts an eerie glow on his face as he smiles wickedly. "It's twelve-forty two."

"Why are you smilin' like that?"

He flips us so that I'm able to look up at him, careful not to break our connection. I'm caged in by his strong arms and my legs are wrapped around him.

I have to keep him close to me.

"Happy birthday," he says simply.

"What?" I try to buck and get him off of me, but it's no use. He is much stronger than I am. Mack kisses my neck and I'm utterly infuriated by the fact that I'm powerless under him right now.

"I knew you wouldn't let me celebrate you." *True.* "It worked out that the Ridge seems to *love* love and I got to celebrate your birthday yesterday into today."

I buck again. "Yea, because you tricked me!"

"And it worked perfectly!" His smug grin over me is infectious. *I hate it.* "Now you can't give me shit for anything we do today because technically, we're already celebrating and you agreed."

I scowl at him. "Oh, I can definitely still give you shit."

"Fine. I'm sure you could. But you're not." I scoff, but he's undeterred. "You want to know why?"

Crossing my arms, I glare at him for having the upper hand. "Do tell."

"Because you like me."

My mouth hangs open. *He's got me there.* It's so true and it's embarrassing. How the fuck am I falling for this man?

"It's okay. I know and you don't have to say anything. Just let me spend this day with you."

Agreeing to whatever it is that he has in store for me isn't as difficult as I thought it would be... especially when he puts me to sleep satisfied and boneless.

The next morning he gets out of bed to start getting ready and I lie there debating just how much deeper I'm getting. Way too deep into a relationship that I should not be entertaining in the first place.

I know I shouldn't, but I can't make myself stop. The water is still running in the shower by the time I'm finally walking over to the steamy room.

Water sluices and rolls over his body. Tight with muscle he's earned from long days on the Ranch. This man is sexy as fuck and I feel a little bit bad for watching him shower.

Okay...

I don't.

And I don't know if he can see or sense me watching him.

That feels even naughtier.

He lathers up with a towel and starts washing the remnants of our sex off his body. *I'm a little sad to see it go.* This vision of him is making me want to dirty him up all over again.

His hands slide over his body and his head tips back with the water running into his face as his hand works his dick.

How could he still be horny?

"That better not be my orgasm you're tryin' to take." I say, stepping into the bathroom fully so there's no mistaking that I can see what he's doing.

I drop the sheet I had over me and step into the shower stall with him. He's still under the spray, but now it trickles over his shoulders, rinsing the last of the soap away.

His cock is hard and jutting upward towards me, closing the space between us.

"I thought we decided that you were mine. That means all your cum too." Careful not to touch him, my finger trails up the center ridge of his abs to his chest. *"That's mine."*

"I was just trying to get clean..." he says with a smirk.

"Oh, I bet you were." I stroke him once and the pleasure of it registers on his face. Eyebrows pulling down, mouth slightly agape. "And if you just happened to come... you wouldn't mind. Would you?"

His eyes meet mine, sparkling and blue as ever. "No," he says and I stroke him two more times.

With my other hand, I take the handful of his balls, carefully rolling them. He hisses and reaches for me, but I step out of his grasp. "So you wanted to be bad?"

He shakes his head, trying hard not to thrust into my hand. Stepping closer to him, I force Mack to step on the other side of the spray so the water is fully on me now. "I mean, I wasn't—"

"Shh, I know you were trying to be good." My arms wrap around his neck and he instinctively knows to pick me up. He uses the shower wall to support most of my weight as he pushes inside me.

We're both moaning and coming in the shower before the water runs cold, shocking us out of the lusty haze.

We can't keep our hands to ourselves and neither of us wants to stop.

I can't think of a better way to start off the day I dread the most than by coming until my pussy is worn out.

❖❖❖

"SO WHY THE BIG stink about today?" Mack asks me as we eat some food after our long shower.

"It was my birthday that my parents passed. My birthday is now the anniversary of their deaths. That's why I don't like celebratin'. Just felt wrong."

"Fuck. I'm sorry. I didn't know it was... Fuck, sugar." He holds me in his embrace and I soak up all the warmth he's giving me. Taking all the comfort I can get from his genuine concern. "We don't have to do anything. We can just stay here and—"

"No, this is good. I want to see what you've got."

He scratches the back of his neck, pulling at the collar of his tee. "Well... there is kind of pressure now."

"Why?"

"It's not all that..."

"It is as much what it is, more than what it's not." I see the doubts he's struggling through all flashing through the tumbling sea of his gaze. "Stop,"

I hold his cheek in my hand, looking up into his eyes. "Whatever you've done is more than I've ever had before." He takes me in, appraising each detail of my face in his way. "Will you show me?"

Mack nods and there is no discernible difference between him and Legend as he nuzzles my hand. A giggle tears from me, just for him in this moment. He scoops me up, "Comfortable shoes are a requirement."

I raise an eyebrow at him. "Are we goin' for a marathon?"

"Of sorts..."

"That's not cryptic."

"Do you trust me?"

"Yes," I respond without hesitation. "More than most." He blinks and I amend, "More than anyone."

Kisses warm my neck and shoulders, "Then grab your shoes and let's go," he says into the curve of my skin there.

CHAPTER 23

Jeann

"When you asked if I trusted you, I was thinkin' bungee jumpin' or paraglidin'... Why would I need to trust you for a museum?"

He grins and hops out of the car to open my door. "We haven't gotten to the part that you need to trust me for." He's driven me to Denver, another place I've never been, and parked in a garage that is connected to a massive building. From the outside, I suspected it was a professional building of some sort until I read the sign.

I hold his hand and walk into the building. Its impossibly tall white walls hold frosty temperatures and bright lights. Rolling piano music plays softly into the space and it beckons me. There is a small congregation of people waiting for their tickets, but Mack leads us to a desk that is off to the side of the admission area.

He introduces himself to the man there and they begin talking so I take a look around. One large wall has a screen that flips from event to event. I take note of some of the exhibits. The first is one of sculptures with bright colors and intricate patterns. Their pictures are striking and I'd like to see them up close. The second one is tapestries and weaving from an early 1900's community from the area. Before the third exhibit is revealed, Mack says my name.

"Are you ready?"

"Yea," I hug his arm closer to me, trying to soak up more warmth from the man who is the embodiment of it. "What are we doin'?"

"I'm going to be taking you on a guided tour of our newest collections. The first features some of the greatest female artists from America." The man in a black sweater vest and black slacks does a bow in our direction, "I'm Randy. I'll be your tour guide today. If you have any questions about the work, I'm happy to answer."

I look up at Mack who has a reserved little smile on his face, then back to Randy.

I'm speechless.

"You don't have to say it. Your face says it all," Mack whispers into my ear. I shiver at the way his voice licks across my ear.

"You will pay for this," I bite out just as quietly while we follow the guide to the elevator. "I was prepared for mediocre and I was goin' to have to fake appreciation."

"Oh, sugar. I'll never make you fake it." He kisses my forehead and the scar tingles where his lips linger. "I'll make your toes curl, I promise."

I smack his arm. "You better stop before we have to ditch Randy and this sweet gift."

The elevator door opens and Randy steps inside. I'm about to follow right after him, but Mack steps in front of him. His big body blocks the door for me. I stop just before running right into him. "I'll be good," he says, tilting my chin up to look at him. He doubles down, adding, "For you, I'll always be good."

There is more he's saying than the words he's giving me. His joking from earlier still lingers, but there is the seriousness of his commitment that hangs heavier.

I can't be upset with him for being hopeful that one day I will accept the true meaning behind his words. That I won't run from this life that he wants to offer me. But I know that letting him settle for me is not in his best interest.

Telling him that right now is not an option. Neither is denying to myself that I want the life he can offer me either.

From what I can remember, there is no indication that I could be the wholesome and sweet woman that Mack *should* be with. I couldn't possibly be the demure and prim person that he actually needs.

It's one reason why I don't really want to gain any more of the memories I've lost.

I don't want to know just how big that divide is between us... how much more he deserves. If I stay here a little longer, then I can pretend like a fling is enough for the both of us.

A *pit stop.*

Not *a destination.*

"Don't," it comes out like a plea more than a command. I squeeze my eyes closed. "We shouldn't keep Randy waitin.'"

Understanding and patience gleam in his eyes before he kisses my lips softly. The pillowy feel of them against mine, a balm to my darkening mood. "C'mon."

We finally make our way into the elevator and the doors open to the unobstructed space. It's more quiet than the lobby downstairs. There aren't many people from what I can see, but the partitions and exit walls are just as tall as the walls on the lower floor and I can only see as far as they allow.

Mack is a consistent presence behind me as we listen to the guide tell us about each artist and their journey to gain acclaim for their works. His hand on my waist and his chest at my shoulder. It's not restrictive or overbearing. Our bodies move in sync.

There is no one that I would rather experience this with.

Each woman's work inspires me more and more. Whether it's their bold strokes or the use of space on a canvas or the emotion they're able to evoke in their subjects' eyes. I am in awe of the sheer amount of talent on this floor.

I've never felt like I fit in anywhere. Always on a thin tether but nothing solid to hold me in place. In this room, I don't feel that tentative connection. The way I find nostalgia for places I've never been through each artist's given medium makes me feel more in my body that I have in a long time. If I had a dream, it would be to create an experience for others with my art like these women have done for me.

I look over my shoulder to Mack.

I shouldn't be shocked that he is looking down at me already. Who knows if he has seen any of the pieces? But I know he's seen every reaction that I've had to them. My gut tightens with that realization.

My emotions are too big here. I could mess up and say something I can't follow up on.

Forever, promises, futures.

I can't tell him how deep my appreciation for him actually runs.

I can't tell him that I've never felt care for someone outside of my family like I feel for him.

How could I?

He spent time on this. He planned this for me.

My birthday has never been this special.

Maybe when I was young and everything felt fantastical and new. But never as an adult has someone seen me like he sees me. Or does what they think will make me happy just because.

He's happiest in the stables with the horses. Or riding out on the pasture as fast as Legend will carry him. He belongs outside in the sunshine and with the clouds puffy and light behind him. With his sky colored eyes and sun-kissed cheeks.

I'm lost in my own thoughts of how he would and should look on paper. He's too big for anything smaller than an extra large canvas. To draw him without the fullness of Colorado's beauty around him would be a travesty.

I could never do him justice on paper.

By the time we reach the end of the tour of this room I tune back into what Randy is saying. "And in this section, we have a few works from local artists. Each piece has been submitted by someone who felt their work should be in this exhibition. It rotates every week. We live in a time where art is more accessible than ever and our curators felt it was important to allow as many aspiring women to envision themselves amongst the many incredible female artists of our lifetime."

Paying attention to each of these up and coming artists' work, I make a mental note of the names I see. Maybe I'm the first to see who will be the next greats in this country. On the back wall three pieces stop me in my tracks.

I double take, my neck straining with the action. I squeeze the muscle, blinking tears from my eyes. My fingers can't catch the tears before they roll down my cheek. "Mack."

He stops the next tears with his thumb, careful not to smudge my makeup. "Yes, butterfly?"

"How did you—What is this?"

"Not just me." He shrugs, holding me in his arms.

I shake my head, "Yes. Just you."

Three of my sketches that I had created are spotlighted.

The first is a vast winter landscape, stretching across the page in shades of black and silver, the snowy world coming alive through delicate strokes of charcoal and subtle hints of white pastel. No vibrant color, just shading. I can feel the cold just by looking at it. The elk, proud and steady, crossing through the snow. A fox, barely noticeable at first glance, its tail a streak of motion against the white drifts. I wanted the animals to be more than background and I felt so proud of this piece when I finally finished and showed Mack.

The one on the far right is a night forest scene, the page awash in darkness but alive with depth. I played with a darker palette and focused on highlighting with negative space. Towering firs stretch toward a sky full of stars, the twinkling effect of them streaking across the heavens like a river of silver dust. The details are sharp in the bark, leaves, the shimmer of moonlight on a quiet creek winding through the underbrush. And just at the edge of the path a sneaking coyote makes an appearance.

Finally, I take in the middle piece. Memories of that night come rushing in as I look at Legend, proud and majestic on page. His expression is fierce, almost defiant, with deep eyes that seem to stare right into my soul. I still love the ways I was able to capture how he's not just a graceful creature built for speed. He can be stubborn. Strong. Wild, even though he lives a pampered life. I wanted this one to look like he might be ready to come right through the page and hug you even though he should be working. To me, this one refused to just be a drawing. It's so much more.

More than anything, I know that Mack can feel that too from what I've been creating in the time that I've been here. My throat works over the lump in it.

"You are so good to me," I whisper because my throat is so full of emotion I can't make my voice work. "Take me right now." I start heading for the restrooms, not waiting to see if he will follow behind.

"We still have more to see after this one, guys," the guide calls after us.

I hear Mack scoff. "Don't mess this up for me, Randy." He's behind me again, taking my hand.

There is no way I can tell him those three words that he wants to hear and I can't let him say them to me.

But, I can ask, "Two words?"

"I'm yours," he answers without hesitation.

This, I can give him. I take his mouth and express as much gratitude as I can in the family restroom stall.

CHAPTER 24

Jeann, Then

HIS VOICE WAS COLD when he said, "The first shot is the hardest."

Jeann looked up at the face that changed everything she knew about her life.

Blue Dupont.

"Pull the trigger." A command. One she could not ignore.

Could Jeann do this?

She had to. She had come too far to second guess his command. This man on his knees was responsible for covering up those two murders that upended her life. She would not be here if it weren't for this careless Faye dummy. Her life no longer belonged to what she wanted. It belonged to the Duponts.

Bang. Bang.

One through the chest and the other through his eye.

Gone.

Definitely gone.

Jeann's hands shook though her shot was accurate.

She could never go back from this.

"Tighten up. We're movin' out," Blue said when three people she barely recognized came to grab the body and haul it away. She hadn't moved yet and that was a problem. They were moving out.

"You good?" Ethan asked her under his breath so the others couldn't hear him.

No.

But she had to be.

<hr>

"SOMEBODY BETTER TELL ME what the fuck happened this week!" Blue's voice boomed through the open warehouse. His hunting knife gripped tight in his hands. The tip glistened with venom he's known for now.

Jeann stepped forward from the row and offered the information she knew. "Thane and I went to run the drop, just like you asked. The package was light." They were a day late returning to Clayton Terrace but not short.

Blue turned slowly to face her. He kicked the bag in front of him. "These weighed in at excess. What. Happened."

Ethan stepped up next to her, but she talked over him. "He had somethin' to say about my methods." *Men always did.* They didn't expect her to be a threat which was always their first mistake. Jeann couldn't count the number of times a mark would address Ethan before they would talk to her. Their assumption that he was running the show cost them. Sometimes a black eye. Depending on how egregious, their limb.

Her boss had a light in his eye, fully expecting the extent to which Jeann would show her methods. "What did you tell them?"

"I didn't say anythin'." Blue's jaw ticks. He opened his mouth to probably command her to elaborate, but she saved him the trouble. "I broke his leg."

Blue laughed, the hand that was positioned at his waist, where the sheath for his massive bowie knife waited, dropped off to squeeze her shoulder. "See. You men need to take a lesson. The Dupont name means everythin'. If we lose our edge—if they don't fear what it means to talk out the sides of their necks—then we don't stand a chance in these streets. Be discreet, but handle the problem. Heard?"

"Heard," came the response from the men and women in the building.

"Alright, if you're not one of us, top tier, get back to your shit." People filed out of the big room and she watched them go.

The same man who trained her on the mats and saw her potential stood from his chair. Redd clapped her on the shoulder, "You did good, Kitty. He's gonna move you up no doubt."

Kitty.

Kitty.

Kitty.

CHAPTER 25

Mack

MY BED IS COLD beside me when I wake up from a loud noise outside the room.

It's been a few weeks since I've been cleared to go without that annoying boot and try to get back to my normal routine. Physical therapy is brutal, but I've been seeing improvements steadily. I feel strong and, as long as nothing drastic happens, I can say I'm in the clear.

Now that I really don't need anyone to help me get around, and that is the doctor's words, there is this lingering thought that maybe Jeann will leave.

She'll realize that there's nothing keeping her here. She's been working long enough to afford a plane ticket.

She could go.

But every morning I wake to find her still here, I count my blessings. Twice.

The banging from my kitchen says that she hasn't left and something is paying the price for it.

I rub my eyes as I walk over to the source of all the racket.

The skillet clangs onto the stove top. I look over and see her beating the ever-loving shit out of a couple of eggs in a bowl beside it.

She violently shakes seasonings into the bowl and lets the spice cabinet close with another bang.

Next, she slams a sheet pan onto the counter, ripping the package of bacon and cursing as she lays the strips onto the metal surface.

"You know? You don't have to make breakfast today. I can help."

"No, I'm already doin' it," she snaps.

"But you seem…" Her fierce eyes meet mine and I take a step forward, slow and deliberate, but not quick enough to upset her further… *I hope.*

"I'm fine," comes her quick response as she continues to whisk.

I look to the stovetop that holds the source of her angry music. "I think the pans would beg to differ."

She blinks and then sighs loud and long. "Sorry."

I put a hand over hers and she finally stops whisking. Setting the bowl down, she frowns at my hand. "What's really going on, butterfly?"

Her eyes soften with the new name I've called her and she huffs in exasperation. "Nothin'. I'm just—a little shaken from a dream I had last night."

"A memory?" She nods slowly. "Have you been having more dreams like this?"

"I don't know. I guess." Her tone is clipped and I wonder what she was dreaming about, but I could tell she wasn't ready to tell me more about it. She doesn't seek permission to say anything that's on her mind. If she wanted to tell me then she would.

"I was thinking about it anyway, but maybe you should just move into the room. You know? Have your stuff there so it feels more like you…" She avoids my eyes, picking the bowl of eggs back up to whisk. Undeterred, I add, "Plus you'll have me every night. I'll keep your bad dreams away."

That causes her to pause her furious cooking. "In your room?"

"Yea, why not?"

Her lips twist to the side. "That's probably not a good idea."

"You don't think I'm scary enough?" She laughs big and loud. I should probably be offended. Her laughter sparks something hot and thick in my blood so I could never be offended by the presence of it.

"That is a good one," she pats my arm. "You're plenty scary, but that's not why I think it's a bad idea."

"Then why not?" Am I always begging this woman to get closer to me? Yes. And do I see myself stopping anytime soon? No.

I back away only so she can open the oven to put the bacon inside.

"If we're stayin' in the same room, we'll probably start havin' sex a lot more than we already do."

I nod my head from side to side as I consider what she's saying, then shrug. "I'm failing to see a downside."

Her look is droll before she pours the beaten eggs into the skillet. She stirs them around with practiced movements. I let her focus on her task instead of pushing my agenda further. We'll have time to talk about it in the future.

She's distracted when breakfast is ready, not carrying on any kind of conversation and I wonder what she was dreaming about that has her so consumed.

Before she told me that she thought they were memories. It has been a while since she actually told me what happened in them.

That... is probably something I should be more curious about. Asking her about it when she hasn't offered on her own feels like prying. She always says what's on her mind so I should let her work through this.

I wish that she would include me in it though.

But I won't push.

She'll share when she's ready.

"It's pretty nice out today," I try for conversation again.

"Yea," she says down into her plate.

"We should go for a ride."

Her eyes meet mine finally. "Right now?"

"Why not? It's Thursday and we're both off. I'll probably start my regular hours at work again so I don't know how long I'll have the full day off in the middle of the week like this again."

"C'MON, LEGEND. LET'S SHOW her a good time."

My horse takes off and Jeann holds on to me as tight as she can.

We make it through the pastures quickly and to the more wooded area leading to the riding trails. The midday sun filters through the trees, dappling the trail in shifting patches of light and shadow. The air is warm with spring coming up fast. The smell of damp earth, wildflowers, and the smallest bit of new fir tree needles surrounds us. Birds chatter in the trees, and somewhere in the distance, the creek murmurs over smooth stones. It's the kind of day that makes you want to ride forever, no destination, no worries at all. Just the rhythm of hoofbeats and Colorado putting on a show.

I glance over my shoulder at Jeann, to see if she's catching all that I'm seeing as well. I would love to see this scene through her eyes. She notices far more than I do.

The wind blows through her braids, and she brushes them back impatiently, unaware of how damn good she looks with the sun kissing her golden brown skin.

"You doing okay?" I ask, when she squeezes me a little tighter as the trail gets a little more bumpy.

She huffs, rolling her shoulders and loosening her hold on me just a bit. "I'm fine. As long as Legend doesn't suddenly decide to throw me off the back."

I chuckle. "Legend is more likely to show off with you on his back than throw you off." I meant it. I think he likes her more than me.

Jeann shakes her head, but there's a small smile playing on her lips, and damn, I love seeing it. She might like my horse more than she likes me, too. The thought makes me happy paired with how she looks lighter. Free of whatever was weighing her down earlier.

My plan is working.

We ride in easy silence, the trail winding through a grove of aspens, their bright green leaves shimmering. It's a hell of a sight, but I find myself trying to catch glimpses of her over my shoulder more than the landscape before me.

"You ever think about staying?" I ask, keeping my voice casual. Hoping that I'm not putting my foot in my mouth and ruining our ride.

Her fingers tighten slightly against my middle, and she doesn't answer right away. "Sometimes," she admits, so soft I almost don't hear it. I pull on Legend's reins and he stops so I can turn and face her fully in this moment.

It's not a promise.

Not even close.

But it's something more than I had before.

A warm breeze rustles the trees, and a few petals from a nearby flowering bush drift past. Some rush past my face and I bat them away. Then I see that one catches in a braid that whips past me, and before I can think better of it, I reach over, brushing it away. My fingers graze her cheek, and for a moment, she doesn't move, her copper brown eyes locked on mine. There's something unspoken there, something fragile and uncertain, but real.

I could kiss her. Hell, I want to.

Instead, I let my fingers linger just a little longer than necessary before dropping my hand back to the reins.

"You hungry?" I ask, breaking the moment before she can run from it. I don't know quite where we stand after our earlier conversation. Maybe it's too soon to actually ask her to move in with me for any reason other than helping a friend out.

She blinks, like I pulled her from some deep thought. "I could eat."

"Good. I brought something." I nod toward my saddlebag. "We'll stop by the creek, stretch our legs."

She eyes me, like she knows exactly what I'm doing—giving her space, letting her breathe. She doesn't fight it.

And as we ride toward the water, past more blooming trees, I think maybe showing her more of what my hometown has to offer could only help me. Alpenglow really is putting on a show with how beautiful it is today.

I'm careful as I hop down from my horse, still putting most of the pressure on my right leg. Once I'm steady on my feet, I help her get down as well.

Legend fakes like he'll trot off when I approach him again to get my bag. I suck my teeth at him because I could've fallen right on my face if I didn't see what he was trying to pull. *This boy is trying to make me look like a fool in front of my girl.* The small giggle from behind me is unmistakable.

She's close enough that I could feel her warmth against my back. "You are a mischievous thing, aren't you," she tells my horse as she scratches right next to his mount. "I like it."

Legend preens with her praise, pushing his head into her hand more. We've been by to see the horses plenty, but taking her for a ride without having anyone help us was a big step for me.

I don't need Jeann to stick around to help me anymore either. The fact of that is a blaring warning sign in my mind, but my heart doesn't listen. As I pull things out of the bag and lay them out, she meanders through the nearby trees inspecting new leaves and flowers. Legend ambles behind her as she explores our surroundings. The sight is too beautiful not to stare at her and him in their peaceful exploration.

This woman makes me happy. Happier than I've been in a long time. I want to hold onto this moment and create more for us to look back on fondly.

She must sense my attention after a while and finds her way back to the spot I've picked for us. I spend some time tying Legend to the tree closest to the spot and he uses the lead to settle as close to our girl anyway.

"It would be too easy to get roped on the Ridge," she comments, having watched the whole exchange between us. She's almost wistful as she looks at Legend looking all too comfortable. Now, Jeann lies on the blanket I brought and looks over the burbling water as it glides lazily along pebbles and furry green rocks.

"Hmm," is all I say, taking the spot next to her on the blanket.

"You planned this didn't you?"

"Me?" I rear back, falling over and holding my chest. "I've never had a plan in my life."

She rolls her eyes, but rolls over with me so we're both on our backs. I scoot closer to her and she lifts her head to allow my arm around her shoulder. She ends up with her head on my chest as we watch the petals float on the breeze and the sun play in the leaves while the ambient sounds of the creek play behind us.

Lunch can wait.

Being here with her is worth slowing down for.

Chapter 26

Mack

By the time we get home, the peace still lingers between us. It's tentative, I know, but I'm not ready to go into the house yet.

I park the car in front of the garage without pulling in.

She reaches over to open the garage door with the remote on my visor.

My hand stops hers and I pull it into my lap instead. "Indulge me?" It's a request that I kind of expected her to give me push back on. Instead, she eyes me curiously without saying anything. I get out of the car and come around to open her door.

"I'm not ready to go inside just yet."

Jeann looks around. "So, what are we doin'?"

"Something a little country..." I pull her close to me.

Her eyes narrow. "You know I'm from the country, too, right?"

"And how many times have you done this?"

"Considerin' I don't know what *this* is," She bites her top lip, admitting, "None."

"Perfect." I let her go, only to pick a song from my playlist and slide my phone into my back pocket. After putting the headlights on high, there's just enough room in front of my garage to do what I'm thinking.

The music starts up slowly. I don't know how she'll react, but we could both use this.

"Come here," I tell her, holding my hands out for her. She comes to me and I'm just as pleased by her willingness to join me as I always am.

We sway to the music for a bit before she says. "You know I'm not a big country music fan?"

"Whose parking lot party is this? Yours or mine?" It's been so long since I wanted to listen to country anyway. Ty had ruined it for me. I was sick of listening to him sing about my ex-wife. I wouldn't take that chance to be exposed to it.

She reels back. "Is it a party if it's just the two of us?"

"The two of us can be whatever we want the two of us to be." Her little face scrunches up. "We can be a party or we don't have to be. As long as the two of us are a 'we', I don't care." She scoffs, but I say, "Either way, I'm in control of the music so deal with it."

The rain starts as a soft drizzle, warm and weightless as it kisses my skin. It trickles down at first, enough to be annoying to look through. It's cold and startling. I keep us in time with the music, unaffected.

Jeann holds a flat hand over her eyes to protect them as she looks up at me. "You don't feel that?"

"Is he poking you? Can't help it," I shrug.

"No, not that! *It's startin' to rain.* We should go inside."

"Do you know how often it rains in Colorado?"

Confusion twists up her face. "No…"

"We get over three hundred days of sunshine here. On the days it's not sunny, it's usually snow. Rain is far less common." I continue swaying us as both our clothes get soaked through. Our shirts are already sticking to our shoulders.

"Kind of like you," she says. "You are the sunshine around here."

"If I'm sunshine then you must be my moonlight."

The shining amber of her eyes is not only enticing, but they are alight. "Moonlight?

"Mysterious, misunderstood, mythic…"

"I'm only mysterious because I don't even know who I am anymore."

"You are who you are. And I want more of you. Every little bit of you makes me want to know even more. The closer I get to you, the farther away you seem." I intertwine our fingers, locking us together. "Then, it's morning and you've receded again. How can I hold onto you if you're always leaving?" My eyes close, letting the rain fall over my face in soft patters. She holds onto my hand, but I can't look at her.

Her words drawl over to me in the accent I've become obsessed with hearing. It caresses my ears when she says, "The moon is always there. When day breaks, and the sun rises givin' off its warm glow, the moon is still there waitin' to cross the sun's path." When I blink my eyes open, she's looking at me with an open expression.

I wish she was saying what I want to hear more clearly. I want to know if the feelings I have are reciprocated in any way. That there is more to us than physical attraction.

Then she goes and says something like this and my heart opens wider to make more space for her.

Whether she wants a place there or not, I've made one for her.

If there's any part of her that I can have, I'll take it.

It will have to be enough for me.

Her body presses to mine, soft and warm despite the cool rain. Her tank and shorts cling to her curves, soaked through, teasing me with glimpses of the shape I already know so well, but can't get enough of. My hands slide down her waist. Fingertips tracing the dip of her spine down her waist to her ass. She shivers, but not from the cold.

Our lips clash in the rain like thunder or lightning though neither are present in this storm.

She is both when she's with me.

Energy buzzing from the two of us holding each other like there is no beginning or end to what we have here. Just a continuous loop of her need and mine going round and round.

The car sits behind us, headlights glowing soft in the mist, illuminating the droplets clinging to her lashes. She kisses me again and nips my lip hard enough to make my dick kick against her, waiting for the opportunity.

Earlier today, it seemed like she didn't want to have sex as much as we have been. Like maybe that upset her. Or maybe she thought I was only wanting her close for that reason. Do I enjoy fucking her? Duh. What idiot wouldn't? But that's not the only reason I like being with her, spending time with her. The way she kisses me is really testing my resolve to give her space.

"You're trouble," I murmur against her ear.

She looks up at me, her breath warm against my jaw. "And you like it," she says before dragging her teeth along the spot.

Damn right, I do.

I don't overthink it. I don't hesitate. I just take her face in my hands and kiss her again. If she wants this, wants me, then I'll give her exactly what she's asking for.

She gasps, but it turns into a sigh against my lips, her body molding to mine like she was always meant to be here. The rain slicks our skin, our clothes clinging, but all I feel is heat burning through every touch, every shift, every press of her against me.

I lift her easily, her legs wrapping around my waist as I turn, setting her down on the hood of the car. The metal is warm from the earlier sun, now cooled by the storm, but she's fire beneath my hands, heat against my lips.

She fists my shirt, pulling me closer, her knees tightening at my hips as she kisses me like she needs me more than air.

Maybe she does.

Maybe I do too.

I trace my hands up her thighs, fingers teasing the hem of her top, feeling the damp, soft skin beneath. She tilts her head back as my lips move down her throat, her pulse racing beneath them.

"Mack..." she breathes, and damn if my name has ever sounded better than it does like that. "Don't tease me," she pants, hips already working against me.

I drag my hands up her sides, appreciating every curve and every shiver.

It's more of an awkward wiggle to get her shorts off with how wet the fabric is, but I'm prepared to rip them if I need to. Her lace thong doesn't stand a chance when I see it's the last layer separating us. The satisfying sound of the fabric tearing is the last of the barriers between her and I.

She reaches for me, quickly opening my fly and finding me hard and ready for her. I'm leaning over her on my hood, watching her work like she knows my body better than anyone. And maybe she does.

She collects some of her arousal that's already hot and dripping from her onto the tip of my cock, but I don't let her sink down onto me like she wants. I hold us in that moment just before, teasing her with how close she was to being filled by me.

"Tell me that you want me. I need to hear it." I know she won't say the words I truly want, but she can give this to me. Fuck, I don't want to need the reassurance, but I do.

I need that and more.

Her eyes meet mine. The bossy little retort moments from escaping her lips, but she pauses too. The heat softens to something too heartbreakingly close to love in the depths of them.

She doesn't say what I've asked.

"If ever anyone could need someone as much as I need you, Mack, I'd seriously worry for them. But I'm not worried because I know that you've got me. I don't only want you. I need you. Can't you see that?"

"Maybe I just see what I want to," I admit. "Did I push too much in asking you to move into the room with me? Am I asking for too much?"

"No, I'm—Movin' into the room with you is just a big deal."

Water drips down my face and between my brows as they furrow. "Are we not there?"

She looks between my eyes and then to my mouth. Her gaze feels like a brand, but it also feels like the time she's taking to respond is answer enough.

I pull away, but she pulls me in deeper, her fingers threading through my hair, her body arching into mine, taking me right to my base. I'm snug inside her. Her tight muscles gripping me as her fingers pull on my hair to look at her.

"You are mine." She says, not moving an inch as I try to think straight with her tight and warm around me. "I wanted to give you the chance to understand what that means. It's not a joke."

I pull out of her slowly and thrust into her once, holding her gaze, and tell her, "I'm. Yours. I wanted to show you that I'm serious."

"It's settled then," she responds, tugging on my hair again.

The rain comes down more heavily at that. The storm is raging around us, but right now, she's the only thing I want to get lost in.

And I'm lost as each time our hips meet, she slides up the hood just a little bit more. She releases her hold on my head and I'm able to grab onto her hips more easily, keeping her right where I want her.

Fuck, I could come at the sight of her pinching her nipples through the soaking wet top and mewling my name, all while I pound into her. I could, but I'm not. I want to make this moment last.

If on the trail was peace, then on the hood of my car is nirvana.

I have no plans to let her come quickly or easily.

I flip her over to get a better look at the rainwater trailing the deep arch and curve of her back down to her juicy ass. Holding her braids out of the way with them wrapped around one hand, she's pressed to the hood on her tiptoes to keep my dick right where she wants it.

"You couldn't know how beautiful you look bent over my car like this," I pant, taking every opportunity to bounce off her ass with each thrust.

"Show. Me. Then," Jeann manages. "Fuck, I'm gonna—"

My fingers beg for purchase at her hips, but we're both slippery and I'm close to nutting, myself.

"That's it, butterfly. That's it. That's—" She's squeezing me so tight as she flutters around my cock. I can't help, but tumble there after her.

There we lay with my back pressed to her front as each stream of cum pulses out of me inside her.

Goddamn it feels good to slide into her bareback, but I really need to start wearing a glove.

When I finally soften and slide out of her, a mixture of our releases trickles down the water already streaming down her thick thighs.

I bite my lip at the sight. "What are you starin' at?" Jeann asks.

"Perfection."

CHAPTER 27

Jeann

THERE ARE MANY THINGS that feel foreign to me in this town.

One that I've come face to face with is that everyone knows everyone's business.

You hear about this phenomenon, hell I've experienced it in Clayton Terrace, but my small town could eat like three or four of Alpenglow Ridge.

Nobody knows this much about my life where I grew up.

Case in point: a woman, who I recognize as Cory's aunt with bright red hair and a smile too big, damn near cornered me during the intermission of this Spring recital Mack dragged me to.

And I do mean drag.

I don't dislike dancing or even little kids. I actually enjoy both.

But it's his ex-wife's recital. As in, her choreography being taught to little kids to perform. Two of which are his nieces, so he had to be here to support them. Obviously, I get that and I don't want to keep him from supporting his nieces. But it's *her* I don't want to support. I've been itching to leave.

Am I jealous?

FUCK YES!

Even after she hurt him, he is still supporting her. Not really... but you know what I mean.

In his shoes, I'd ask for the video playback instead.

But I'm not him.

I'm Kitty.

Those thoughts have been on a constant swirl through my mind. Each memory I've recovered so far has made it clearer and clearer that I should keep Mack at a distance. Not allow him to get close to me. To fall for me.

I can't help the feelings that are growing stronger inside me though.

He meets me where I'm at, resisting the urge to push for more though we both know he deserves it. He's patient, testing consistently to see what more I'm willing to give him. I'm too close to doing that.

But these memories... I don't like the picture they are painting about me. I don't like the person that I had become.

Am I even that person?

Capable of wrestling a full grown man to submit, excellent marksman with blood on my hands.

I don't have to find out. I don't have to answer any of the whys or hows of my choices. None of my past has come to haunt me besides in my dreams.

I'm just Jeann here in Alpenglow Ridge. I'm just the awkwardly rude chick living at Mack's place who can draw pretty pictures.

That's all I have to be here.

Jeann, not Kitty.

I just know that if someone were to find out that I was Kitty, it would not be long before everyone would know it as well. Small town fodder that juicy would spread like wildfire with how dry it is here.

Shielding Mack from finding that out is my number one priority.

Back to this woman, Sammy, who is saying, "...it would be just beautiful. Mack showed me that landscape that you drew from behind his house. We would love to have something similar, but much larger. We could put it over the dining table. Do you do color work at all?"

I focus back on the words the woman is saying and I fight back the smile about the fact that Mack has sung my high praise and is even selling my work for me.

Silly man.

Fine.

I'm not jealous of little miss pixie, but I still don't want to be here.

"I can do color pieces. I actually haven't in a while though."

Despite how I didn't want to set up roots here, I make plans to work on this commission for the woman.

I'm not growing roots, I'm creating a fund to move.

A *moving fund.*

Not growing roots.

Mack returns to my side with a glass of wine and thankfully takes over the conversation with the older woman so I don't have to.

His arm is around my waist and the calm washes over me, warm and heavy like a weighted blanket.

I trust this man, even if he does share my business to anyone and everyone when it pertains to art.

It's not long before her wife, Janet, ushers her back into the audience to continue watching the second half of the show.

We don't have a seat with the rest of his family and Reese's friends to see Kelsie and Kyra. Our seats are several rows back from them. I don't know if he did that for me or if he usually sits apart from them in public. I get the sense that Mack, despite the sunny way he is around me, still carries the stigma of what he once was. I watch him more than I watch the show and commit all of his micro expressions to memory.

I've wanted to draw him for so long, but it was difficult to choose what I should depict.

I love his smile and how it's perfectly imperfect. I love how it lights me up from the inside out.

Another appealing expression would be his smirk. So different from the smile. It might be the most honest look he has. It's playful and light. But fleeting.

But I respect his sadness and his desperation. That expression that he has when he wants more than he's been given. I can relate to it. I can understand it.

How does someone who is like the sun ever get that same energy back? What does the sun receive in return for giving life to everything it touches?

How he perceives himself is so flawed, I want to show him what I see.

One day I will draw him.

It will be the first of many.

Just as soon as I get the courage to do it.

The weather in April here is not what I could ever remember it being like back home. It's still cool and breezy. Some days, it still snows, but it doesn't stick like it once did. For the event, I wear cat eyeliner thick and deep navy to match the dress I chose and a dark lip. This long sleeved dress has thick bands that overlap and criss-cross around my body. In the shade of a large tree, I shiver by the car while Mack goes to grab the jackets we forgot at the coat closet. I could have gone in with him, but I wanted to go back in there with the crowd like I wanted to pluck out all my eyelashes individually.

"Hi," the high pitched voice comes from the left of me. I turn to look at the shorter woman who walks over to where I stand. His ex-wife seems far too comfortable approaching me and *she should not.*

As I told Mack, I didn't know if I'd be capable of kind words for this lady. She hurt Mack.

In my book, that's cause enough to resist the notion of behaving nicely to her. "What do you want?"

She looks affronted at first, but then she nods slowly. "So, I'm sure he's told you all about me."

The slicked back bun and small arrangement of flowers in her hair makes her look every bit the ballerina and dance teacher. Sweet and prim. She wears a pastel floral blouse and tan trousers that makes the light makeup she wears look even more velvety smooth.

The woman couldn't be more different than I am.

I glare because I don't want her to feel like I A) want to have this conversation or B) hear her out.

"I'll take that as a yes. I won't take up your time, but I just wanted to let you know that he and I are just friends. We're trying to make amends. I am, anyway. I know that we had a rough break—"

"Ha! A rough break." I sneer. "Must be nice to sugarcoat devastatin' someone's life and then turnin' everyone he loved against him."

Shock registers on her face. I'm sure no one talks to this prim little woman with unfiltered honesty since she seems as sturdy as a champagne flute.

She gathers herself and rushes out, "That's not what happened nor was it my intention. He was grumpy and sullen and pushed everyone away when I asked for a divorce. *For weeks until Reese came home.* I knew he was hurting, but so was I. I couldn't be what he needed because I could hardly breathe from under my depression after losing Callan." Melody smooths down the front of her blouse. A nervous tell if I ever saw one.

I hope she is uncomfortable. Mack deserved better.

She looks truly sincere when she meets my stare. "I am not the person I once was and I've extended the olive branch. I just wanted to extend one to you, as well. I am his friend even if he doesn't want to be mine anymore."

There is no way that I would think he was grumpy or sullen.

Does she know him at all?

If ever he was not his true self, something was deeply wrong. He was hurting and earned the right to be sullen. That is no excuse for him to be abandoned.

"Don't want to be friends. And I don't want you upsettin' him, either. Divorced people are divorced for a reason. He's happy. You should let him have his happiness and you have yours," I point back toward the building we both came from, "somewhere else."

She fiddles with the hem of her top now, thinking over my words. "You're here to stay then?" Her gaze is severe as she looks me over. I don't care what she thinks about me. This woman clearly doesn't know a good thing when she sees it anyway.

"That is none of your business," I dismiss her. "Your husband is probably lookin' for you. Wouldn't want him to cause a scene if you were to go missin'."

Her eyes narrow ever so slightly on me. "Are you threatening me?"

I sigh, stifling my urge to roll my eyes. "You picked the right one today. These are just words, but I'd be happy to show you actions."

She takes a step back. "I-I..."

I put my hands up, not to hurt her, but in a placating gesture. I wasn't kidding. But I do feel like this small woman will cause more problems for me than she's worth if I don't try to smooth this over. "I'm just lettin' you know that I don't want your friendship or whatever it is that you came over here for. This is me bein' tolerant for Mack's sake because I know he wouldn't like me to say what's really on my mind."

"Ohh... and you haven't been?" She shakes her head and holds a hand up before I can respond. "I'm leaving, but I know what it's like to be a villain in someone's story. I'm sure you do too."

What does that mean?

She doesn't know me.

I spot Mack walking over to the car and the look of concern on his face. I know he saw his ex leaving from here. The parking lot isn't that big and most people are still inside. He doesn't stop to talk to her. Instead, he meets me by the car and holds my jacket open for me to slide my arms into it.

Our drive home is quiet outside of his soft rock. I nibble at my top lip knowing that I might have overstepped with the way I talked to Melody.

When he goes to his room and I don't follow, he doubles back to grab me. The second his hands are on me, I don't resist the pull into his orbit.

He takes me into his arms on the bed. "What happened when I left?"

"Nothin'," I respond.

Lies, lies, lies.

"Are you sure?"

I nod my head, unwilling to tell another lie.

I feel his lips curl against my neck. "Just so you know, there is already a group message in place so I know what happened."

Damn small towns.

I try to make a break for it, but Mack tightens his hold. Holding on to me like a koala so I can't go anywhere. I laugh at how ridiculous the position is and when I finally catch my breath I answer.

"I just had a conversation with *Melody.* That's all."

He lets me go so that we can both sit on the bed. I note that he takes the spot closer to the door. "What did you talk about?"

"You said there was a group chat. You already know what we talked about."

His head bobs to one side and then the other. "True enough, but I want to hear it from you."

I let out a frustrated sound. "Blah, blah." I do a rolling motion with my hands like I'm filling it with conversation." So on and so on. I told her I didn't want to be friends and that she should leave you alone."

"Ah." Is all he says. He looks my face over for a while, but I don't back down. I stand behind what I said even though I don't want him to think I overstepped.

"Well?" I ask when the silence stretches for too long.

"Well, is that what you want?" He holds his hand how he always does when he wants me to take it. I do, because it's us. "Melody relayed it a little differently, but the meaning overall was the same."

Now, I'm curious. "What did she say?"

"She said that you were wary of her and that she didn't want to get in between whatever I was trying to make work."

Damn her for making me sound more palatable than I am. I basically threatened her. *I did threaten her.* The entire conversation was meant to be an attack.

"Yea... so?"

His grin spans the width of his face. "So, admit it."

I look down my nose at him. "Admit what?"

He laughs. "You really can't, can you?"

"I can't what?"

Mack is so smug it rolls off of him. I'm hit in the face with the satisfaction that he has with himself. "You tried to scare Melody off because you want to be with me."

"That's not what it was at all." I shake my head. "I just like when we fuck and I didn't want her interferin'."

"Nah."

I shake my head more fiercely, trying a different lie. "Your horse is sweet and I'm usin' you to spend more time with him."

"Nope." He crosses his arms, smug grin still looking back at me.

"I... like your house."

"Uh-uh." He's pulling me into his arms again.

"Don't," I say even though I'm melting into his embrace already.

"You're my girlfriend."

I put a hand on his chest though it does nothing to actually create space between us. "Am not. I'm just squattin' in your house."

His goofy grin is too much to take and I look away. He holds my chin between his thumb and forefinger, enunciating every word so there is no mistaking his words. "You're my girlfriend and you *are* making sure other women know that."

"I did not. That's not what happened..." I trail off because his other hand is roaming over my curves, leaving fire in its wake. His touch is distracting and I can't even remember where I was going in that sentence.

"Take this off." He pulls the sleeve of my dress down so my shoulder is exposed. A light kiss over the skin there sends shivers down my spine. His lips make me feel like I've really been set alight.

Maybe it is a little too hot in this dress...

He finds the zipper at my back easily and the once tight dress slumps forward, off my body. The strapless bra I'm wearing is not enough to save me from the warmth of his appraisal. I slide my arm out of the sleeves and stop taking the dress off. It sits around my hips in a heap, but Mack is still on a mission to cover my body with kisses.

"Mack," I try, but fail to resist him. He pauses only briefly to take his own shirt off. Who am I kidding? After today, I want to fall into him.

I don't want to think about anything else besides how good his hands feel on me or the sounds he makes when he's got me in his grasp.

This man makes me feel like I could be Jeann, his girlfriend.

I could be good for him.

"Tell me," I pant when I'm wiggling his slacks off him.

"I'm yours," he says and it's all I want to hear.

He guides my hips onto his cock that is already hard and weeping for me. Fingers digging into my ass as he slowly enters me. Our eyes lock in an intimate battle of wills. I'm not going to look away from the stormy blue of his gaze. The way his brows furrows and his cheeks begin to flush with his pleasure.

He's the first to break when his head tips back the moment I feel his balls meeting my ass. He's all the way inside me and I swivel my hips just a bit to bring his attention back to me.

With my arms around his neck and his hands still gripping onto me, we start moving together.

"God, you're so deep inside me, I don't know if I'll be able to hold off." I admit. He kisses me hungrily, taking all the moans from my mouth with his tongue brushing across mine.

He starts to push up into me harder and faster, chasing his high alongside me.

"Jeann," he calls out. "I want to come with you." I don't respond fast enough and he holds the back of my neck, forcing my attention on him. "I'm coming with you."

"God, baby, yes. Come with me. I wanna feel you inside me." I'm playing with fire. *I know it, but I keep going.* "I want to feel you drippin' out of me, baby, please stuff me full."

"I'm gonna bust with you talking to me like that, butterfly." I reach behind me to cup his balls as I bounce faster and faster.

"Oh fuck," he says, "I'm—"

He doesn't get a chance to finish those words as my muscles grip onto him and I'm coming with all the strength in my body. He's not long behind me, cussing and stroking into me with fast, jerky movements. Our sticky bodies are still clinging to one another. Our eyes never leave the others'.

"No, don't get up. Lean back." I tell him and he listens though he's confused. "I just want to lay like this for a little while.

His eyes sparkle, "You wanna lay with your boyfriend." A statement, not a question.

I ignore his taunts and brush away some of the hair that sticks to his forehead. "How long are you gonna let your hair grow?" In all the pictures around the house, it's always cut short. It was maybe a little longer than that when I first saw him in the hospital and it's gotten a lot longer.

"Don't know... There's too many benefits to keeping it longer at the moment."

I raise an eyebrow at him. "Benefits?" My fingers curl into the length and gently pull. He hums and I do it again.

"Yea." He closes his eyes as I continue pulling his hair. The warmth of our releases runs between us, but he doesn't seem affected by that at all. "I'm keeping it long so you can keep pulling it just like this. I could fall asleep right now."

With his eyes closed, I can look at him undeterred. Pure bliss is written into his features and I want to keep that look right where it is.

I can't stay here. I can't be with him forever.

But I can give him this.

CHAPTER 28

Mack

APRIL IS THE TIME of year when Colorado starts to look like it does in all the promotions. It's the *Colorful Colorado* that it's known to be. Flowers are blooming in all different shades. The weather is comfortably warm but not too hot. The grass is coming in with all different vibrant shades of green. Not to mention the longer days.

And with all these blooms and warmth, come a handful of butterflies. One passes by me as I'm loading up some hay on the back of the truck with Taylor.

Most of the herd is in the south field where the largest part of the stream that runs along the back of Mason Ranch is wide enough for them to stand in. We're not moving them, but there isn't enough grass just yet for them all to graze happily. These bales will give them all an opportunity to eat good.

"Gotta say it's good to have you back out in the fields," Taylor says on the way to the herd.

"Ellis finally annoyed you to the point of no return?" I joke.

"Funny that you mention him," they say.

I look over to the ranch hand sitting in the passenger seat. Taylor and Ellis are good friends and are usually inseparable. Ellis, however, left town with his girlfriend and we don't know if or when he'll be back. Roseangela is a pretty girl but not a very nice one. But who am I to judge? The two of them seem to be happy.

"What's funny about it?" I ask.

"Nothing really." They shrug. "Just wondering when you're gonna let go of that grudge."

My hand tightens on the steering wheel. "Me?"

"Yes, you. It's been years since that happened. And you're all cozied up with Chloe's receptionist. Don't you think you could let it go?"

The "that" they're referring to is when Ellis took it upon himself to try and push up on Melody a month or two after our divorce. I mean. What the fuck? My wife that I had been with for years and years, that he knew was my high school sweetheart.

I thought that was my boy, that we were cool. When I showed up to Reese's welcome home party, only to see that he was flirting with her openly, I saw red.

The only thing I could do was knock his ass out. My fist flew before I could comprehend what I was doing.

How could my own friend—someone who I thought was my friend—go after my ex like that? I felt so betrayed and undermined. Piece of fucking shit.

It was the first time that I got kicked out of QB's and it wasn't the last.

My drinking was at its worst and I had no reason to change it. All I wanted was to hurt him like he hurt me. I haven't really talked to Ellis other than briefly at work ever since. It's made working with him tenuous and thankfully there are enough of us that I don't have to be paired up with him often.

"I'll take that as a no..." Taylor hedges. And they're right. They should take it as a no.

Even though, "I know that Melody was not right for me. It's the principle of the thing. How could my supposed friend do that to me?"

"Look, I'm not saying that he was right for doing it. I'm just saying that maybe you could talk it out. Let bygones be bygones."

I consider their words for a moment more. "Nah. I'm good."

"C'mon, Mack. What could it hurt? You've moved on. He's moved on. Melody's moved on." How far away are these damn cattle? It already feels like I've been driving an hour.

I glare at them, completely over this conversation. "Exactly, what is the point in talking it out? When people show you their ass, you take a picture and move on. There's no need to watch the recording."

"Uhh... I don't love the analogy, but I get it. I don't know what I would do in your situation, but there aren't that many of us working here. Y'all were friends. It has to be exhausting to be the one awkward one with your sister and her friends. Wouldn't you want to hang out with your friends who don't have to pick sides?"

I pause as confusion and frustration overtake me. "They don't—"

"Pick sides? Yes, they do. I know because I'm there. It's not often that Ty and Mel are there when you are. Sometimes friends... Sometimes keeping the peace... How many times are you left out because they want Ty there more?"

I wince.

"Look, I'm not trying to make you feel bad, but I just think you're choosing something that isn't choosing you. Ellis, Josh and I have get-togethers and we'd love to have you. But I don't want to be mediating an all out brawl if you and Ellis can't be civil."

Finally, I start seeing the cattle dotting the pasture. I maneuver the truck over to an open part of the field and park. Hopping out, I climb the side of the truck and kick the first bale out.

Taylor is there cutting the wrap off and breaking the bale up to spread it out just enough.

The cows are already moseying over to start eating. I throw a couple of potatoes from the huge sack I brought too, so the ones who aren't as impatient can find little treats along the way.

Taylor takes the truck over to the next spot and it gives me time to think over what they've said.

It's not far-fetched. That night I had shown up to Reese's welcome home party *uninvited*. It wasn't that my sister didn't want me there. It was the fact that Melody planned the party for her and her friends. That technically didn't include me anymore.

Our divorce was fresh and I was still nursing a bottle of Jack just to get to sleep. Reese had come to see me when she was back in town. The only person for weeks who had come to check on me after the divorce. We had a talk about me coming back to work, more like a lecture to get my shit together. I remember getting dressed to surprise Reese. There were a couple of story posts of her friends having drinks at QB's. No one called me, of course, to come out so I just thought they were drinking. I could definitely do that. So what? It might be a little awkward to see my ex, but I wanted to show up for my sister, my friend.

Instead, I was completely blindsided by someone, who I thought was my friend, stabbing me in the back.

It was a shitty night and even though I've moved on, grown, from that situation, making amends with Ellis is as high up on my list of priorities as making amends with Tyson. I don't need either of their "friendships", but I'll be civil. That's where my effort starts and ends.

Taylor is a good buddy. If they invite me, I'll show up, but I'm bringing Jeann. She just makes any and all of these interactions better.

Breaking and spreading the hay more and cows come over, I notice one of them is lame as it limps over the hay. It doesn't look like she's trying to put any weight on the left hind leg. *I know what that's like, girl.*

There could be something wrong with her hoof and if so, we should check it out before it gets out of hand.

Slowly, I make my way over to her and crouch down to get a better look at her hoof. It's not the best idea, but I don't have any of the materials with me right now to help her out. Josh does the hoof trimming, but these cows are all coming up on time for a trim pretty soon. I need to still assess the situation to figure out what to do next.

She holds that foot up off the ground to keep the pressure off. I can basically see the entire sole, but it's caked and mud and grass too thick to judge.

Putting my gloves on, and with as little pressure as I can manage, I brush the mud away.

I've messed up.

She's much more sensitive than I accounted for and putting pressure on her lateral claw makes her moo and kick.

The next thing I know, a cow hoof is coming right for my chest and I'm falling, more like flying, backward into the grass.

CHAPTER 29

Jeann

"SOOO," MY BOSS HEDGES, "You and Mack." She stands in front of the reception desk, trying to act coy.

I finish adding the notes I need to on the appointment I just took on the phone. I'm stalling on purpose, but I did really need to finish setting up this appointment. "Me and Mack what?"

"Oh come on... You and he..." She makes a smashing motion with her hands, pressing the palms together and twisting. "Tell me! I'm like a vault. I won't even tell anyone."

"Chloe, you are the opposite of a vault. Kinda like a revolvin' door."

She laughs. "That's not true. There are things that even *the Chloe Bridges* has not shared with you."

"Like what?"

She opens her mouth to tell me and then she smiles, pointing a long nail at me. "Oh, you're good! But not that good. I'm keeping many truths behind these lips and you'll never know."

"Great." I start relaying notices of the appointments into the respective stylists' notes section of the scheduling app.

"Jeann, come on. I promise I won't tell. I have my suspicions, so my imagination could suffice... But I would be much happier to have confirmation."

"Trust me, there is nothin' to confirm. I'm stayin' at his house. That's it."

"Bullshit! Chandie told me that he rented all the carriage rides last month for a special date. They were able to meet and exceed their fundraising goals because of his generous donation." She throws her arms into the air. "Might I remind you that I'm also in the group chat and I know how you approached Melody about him." Her eyebrow raises, but I keep my mouth shut.

Generous donation? I knew he paid for the carriage, but...

My first thought is to correct her statement about me approaching Melody, but that would only give her more fuel. I don't want her to spread anything about my relationship. Real or not. I know my time here is still temporary.

Mack could probably be with someone better than me. If he could see himself the way I do, I'm sure he would be no slouch when it came to getting female attention. A part of me knows that he should be doing just that.

A bigger part of me wants to keep him to myself.

Even as her stare gets more intense, I don't say anything. My scheduling task is all of a sudden much more intensive and needs my full attention. I squint at my computer screen like it's giving me trouble.

"Now, she's an actor. Here's your Emmy!" She leans closer to the desk with her voice low enough that no one could overhear her. "I think you're good for him. He needs someone to keep him in line."

I give her a tight lipped smile. "That would be a very sweet thing to say... if we were together."

She scoffs. "When you need your braiding hair again just know I'm charging you two more dollars per pack." That kind of hurts.

I recently changed my braids to a deep eggplant-purple color. I was able to get a much better deal buying the hair directly from the salon with her wholesale discount than I could have at a shop online. This state has the most expensive hair products in comparison to what I remember from the south.

"I'd expect nothin' less from the Chloe Bridges ™!" I retort with a smirk.

"Don't play! I will trademark it!" She winks back at me and thankfully the doorbell rings when her next client comes into the salon.

"You again?" Estelle comes up to the desk, putting her gaudy purse on the counter, moving around the business card display, a few of the product samples and nearly tipping the vase of cut flowers onto my computer.

I grab it and glare at her. "Yep. I work here."

"For now." She looks down her nose at me. "When is Tania going to be back?"

"Couldn't tell ya."

She tsks. "Surely her and the baby are fine by now."

"She'll be back when she's ready to be back." I stand from my chair and motion behind me. "Chloe is ready for you now though."

"Good. Talking to you is such a delight," sarcasm dripping in her tone.

I roll my eyes at the back of her head as she passes me to Chloe's station. "She's someone's grandmother. She's someone's grandmother…" I repeat under my breath. "Even if she is a dick."

"Don't worry about her." Francesca says. She leans on the side of the counter trying to rearrange the things Estelle purposefully knocked astray. "Her kids don't even talk to her anymore. It must be hard for her to have no one to antagonize."

"I feel bad for 'em. She is the worst."

"Tell me about it. I've never been more happy to not be her repeat stylist. Whenever Chloe is out of town, I end up having to take her. Ninety minutes of her negativity is too much for me. Takes a whole bottle of wine to recover," she jokes. "The woman is the definition of a Negative Nelly."

"You're givin' Nelly a bad name just makin' that comparison."

"Stop," she laughs. "Oh! Did you see Tania's baby pictures?" I don't get a chance to respond before she already has them pulled up on her phone. "Of course. You didn't. Why aren't you in the salon chat? Look! He is the most handsome thing! I've never seen a more perfect baby."

I look at the cherubic little bundle on her screen. His round cheeks are lifted in a gummy expression of joy. I don't think I've ever seen a baby so adorable.

As quickly as the happiness of the picture lifts me up, the memories of preparing for my niece's arrival assault me. Lauren was manic in gathering all the resources that she could about pregnancy and newborns.

She never got to become a mother.

She never got to hold her baby.

The cold graveyard where my sister's body was laid to rest, icy and still. The chill of loss makes me shiver in recollection of how her life was over all too soon. The frown that drags my face down, is riddled with pain.

I don't know how long I stood there after everyone else had gone. She was loved by so many and I never knew what that kind of admiration was like. Even in grief, I was an outcast. No one could have cared if I was there or not. They consoled my Nana and Ethan, I just stood and watched that dirt pile up and mark her new resting place. Ate nothing at the wake and the silence of everyone avoiding me grew louder and louder until I eventually ended up in bed.

Forever changed.

Forever hollow.

I jump when the press of Francesca's hand startles me out of my reverie. "Are you alright, Jeann?"

"I—Yea." I sit in my chair and drink from my water bottle desperate to clear the dryness there. If I don't do something I might start hyperventilating.

The door chimes again and Willie Mastiff walks in. "Oh, good." Francesca looks over to me, still slow breathing and drinking from my bottle. "I'll take you back now. Come on, Willie. Tell me all about how those chickens are doing." She gives me one last look as he walks over to her station, and I give her a soggy thumbs up. She seems satisfied enough with my answer and follows Willie.

God, the grief never ends.

It hits me out of nowhere and now I have another two hours of work left.

My cell rings in my purse and I snatch it up immediately. The only people who have my number are Mack and his sister for emergencies. He should still be working until after I'm done here, so I answer the call seeing that it's him.

"What happened?" I ask into the line before he is able to say anything.

He sounds out of breath when he huffs out, "Wanted to tell you. Before my sister... tattled on me."

"Mack, what happened? Where are you?" I'm already packing up my purse before he responds. My heart rate has spiked at his labored breathing and the mention of his sister calling me.

"It's not. A big deal," he says though I don't think it's to me. Then there is some shuffling and a voice I don't recognize is on the phone.

"Hi, I'm taking Mack back to the main house. He got kicked by one of the cows and it knocked him out for a bit. He's definitely done for the day."

"Kicked by a cow?!" I exclaim.

"Yea. Dummy was messing with her hoof because she was lame and he must have hit a pressure spot. She kicked back and got him right in the diaphragm, he went flying across the field!"

I gasp at the image and rub my chest, trying hard not to imagine what it would feel like to have an animal that big kicking me.

There are more shuffling noises and Mack is back on the line. "I'm okay. I just got the wind... Knocked out of me. They're making. A big deal. Out of nothing."

He can barely breathe.

"I'm on my way." I wave over to Chloe, mouthing *emergency* and she gives me a concerned nod. The door chimes behind me as I hurry down the stairs as carefully as I can.

"Butterfly, I don't—"

"Shut up. I'm gettin' in the car right now."

"Take me. To my house," Mack huffs to the other person before he tells me, "Don't let Chloe. Know why you're leaving. The last thing. I need is. This to go around town. And get blown out of. Proportion." He huffs again. "How many. Cowboys get knocked around. Like this?"

He's trying to make jokes, but all I can think about is how close his chest is to his head. What would have happened if he got hit there instead? Or worse. He can barely catch his breath right now.

"A lot, I'm sure. I'm on my way," is all I can say before I hang up.

My mind swims with the possibilities of what I could be walking into.

Mack is prone to downplay his pain. He's willing to give up his own comfort for the comfort of others. I hate and love that about him.

Love.

Fuck, no.

Not love.

Because if I love him, then I should tell him the truth.

That I'm not the woman he thinks I am.

That he should stay far, far away from me.

That I love him.

Fuck. No.

If I were a decent person then I should tell him all these things minus the last. A decent person would pack up her shit and leave right away. Knowing what I know, and even him finding out might put him in danger.

I pull up to the house and they are already there. I see a dirty old pickup truck in the driveway and rush inside to check on Mack.

Despite everything I've been thinking, I can't lose him.

I just need to get my eyes on him and see for myself.

Someone stops me as I'm making a beeline to the bedroom.

"Hi, I'm Taylor. Pronouns are they, them. We talked on the phone earlier..."

I'm sending daggers with my eyeballs at the person standing in my way to the man I care about.

"What exactly is your purpose?" Taylor seems shocked by my words. I slow down my next question since they don't seem to be comprehending my previous question. "Why are you still here?"

"Oh, yes. Well, I'm just supposed to stall you so that Mack could clean up. He said, and I quote, 'If she sees me covered in shit, she'll probably not touch me'. And I thought it was a fair point so—"

"You should leave." I blink a few times and take a deep breath. "I mean, thank you for bringin' him here, but it would be best if you left now."

"Yep, you don't gotta tell me twice, I am on my way out." They grab something from the side table at the door and add, "If you two are free next weekend, we're gonna have a little thing at my house. Nothing serious just—"

"Please go." My temper is through the roof with this person keeping me from seeing my man. I'm about to come out of my skin with the anticipation to see what condition Mack is in.

I hear the door close by the time I'm in the master suite. The shower is still running and I step inside the bathroom.

Mack turns with the thud of my purse on the tiles.

I gasp at the sight. Not because he's wet and naked though there is never a time that a naked Mack is not a sight. There's a large bruise already beginning to form in the center of his chest.

He covers it with his hand and turns the water off. He knots a towel around his waist and with soft eyes he comes to me, shushing me though I didn't know that sound was coming from me.

His gentle strokes across my cheeks brush the wetness away.

Am I crying?

"It looks worse than it is." I look up at his face through my watery eyes. "I promise."

Why am I still crying?

"Do you see me standing here? There is nothing to worry about."

I shake my head and drop my head to his shoulder. In my head, I was spun up. I'm still spinning up. "I've lost so many people."

He holds my chin, looking over my face. Blues eyes flicking between my watery ones. "You're not losing me."

"You don't understand. Everyone—

"It will take more than a stray hoof to keep me from you. I'm not going anywhere, butterfly. You can count on that."

Butterfly.

I blink, another fat tear rolling down my cheek. "I can't count on anythin."

"Jeann," he kisses my lips so tenderly, though it bruises my conflicted heart. "You can always count on me."

That was never the problem.

It's me who can't be counted on, who shouldn't be able to stand here with him.

I don't deserve him and knowing what I know... It will break him when he finds out that he put his trust and all of this care for someone like me.

CHAPTER 30

Jeann, Then

JEANN WOKE UP AND her head was killing her.

Her first thought was to grab another bottle of something strong.

You couldn't be hung over if you were still drunk, she thought to herself.

Then Ethan's voice came into her room... Actually, his room. "I hope you slept better than I did. My couch is shit."

"Nah. I feel like shit." She messed with the hair on her head. Fixing the haphazard nest of a bun on the top of her head. "What happened last night?"

"We need to talk about that," he said. His expression was grim and Jeann could only expect the worst.

"First, I need some food. Greasy and hot." Jeann raided the fridge, moving aside old take out containers and, likely expired, condiments to find anything that she could possibly make for breakfast. She checked the clock on her phone, make that brunch, for the two of them.

Ethan was also on his phone, swiping around while she mixed up a just-add-water pancake mix.

"Fuck", he said. She looked up from her task and Ethan set his phone down in front of her on the counter.

There was a video playing. A man with perfectly coiffed hair and a suit was reporting from their local news station. "A house party gone wrong. Madison Fredricks is outside of the duplex where neighbors reported hearing gunshots fired. Deidre Previn, says that she called police multiple times about the noise levels and no one came to break up the rowdy event. Later when she heard gunshots, she called local police again. Two of her neighbors were fatally wounded from stray bullets that pierced the thin walls separating the properties." Two images popped up and Jeann dropped the bowl and batter to the counter where it covered Ethan's phone though the audio was still clear. "Kathryn Barker and Lewis Blundell were found dead. Authorities are still reviewing potential suspects, but there are no leads so far. Neighbors believe that it might be gang related as the owner of the house has been connected to many known members."

"Jeann, there is no time for this." Ethan grabbed his phone, cleaned the screen off and tucked it away somewhere. "Can you hear me?"

Jeann couldn't hear him. There was ringing in her ears and a fire in her heart burning too hotly.

"We got there after everyone scattered. I saw Redd's car out back and got us out of there. I didn't know..."

Suddenly, her eyes snapped to his. "You didn't know my Nana was dead. Shot from a stray bullet." Jeann threw the whisk into the sink and stalked to the room to grab her things. Her head was throbbing, but her heart was broken.

Another loss.

How much more could one woman endure?

The two of them drove to the morgue to identify her grandmother's body and make preparations for her service.

Another service.

The anger in her heart was turning her blood cold and black. Ethan did most of the talking as Jeann struggled not to scream at everyone around her.

At their incompetence and lack of consideration.

At their blasé attitudes.

At their bullshit pandering.

"Jeann."

She blinked and they were back at Ethan's house again.

"I want to talk to them." She sat on his couch and crossed her arms.

He looked confused at her declaration. "Talk to who?"

She simply said, "The Duponts."

Ethan's ears went pink and he blustered. "F-For what? We don't know that this is because of them."

"We don't know that they aren't! I want to know who killed my Nana."

The anger simmered and rose to a boil. If she weren't already trying to recover from losing another family member then maybe… Maybe, she could have been there to do something. She could—

"Chill. We have to think rationally." Ethan was shaking her, trying to get her to focus on him.

"*You* have to think rationally! I have nothin' to lose! There is nothin' left of me." Her voice broke on the last statement and she was sure that there was nothing left of her heart. She was burying everything good about her. It was all gone.

"Stop talkin' like that. You still have me. Just take a second."

She stood from the couch. Her mind was already made. "NO! I'm takin' no more seconds. I'm goin' to the Duponts. Are you comin' or not?"

CHAPTER 31

Mack

"I'M HEADED OVER. ARE you home?" With my phone on speaker, I'm already headed to my sister's house. I say, "I'll be there in five minutes at this point."

Jeann was back at work and I—I was not. Of course, everyone made a big deal about the hoof incident and I've been made to take the rest of the week off.

Reese is always prone to over reacting. I didn't expect Jeann to agree with her, but I guess I should have seen that coming.

"Why is it that you can never stay home and rest when I tell you?" My sister questions.

"Because I need to talk to you."

Pulling into her driveway, I'm already parking when she says, "I'm the only one who gets to demand conversation and it's a role I take very seriously. I think I'm losing my touch. No one takes me seriously as an annoying little sister type anymore and that has to change."

She's standing in the doorway, probably having been alerted by her security system that I was on her property. "Oh, I take it very seriously. You're still plenty annoying," I tease, hugging Reese then she moves out of the way to let me in.

"You don't—You... You're having lady troubles! It's written all over your face. What is it now, Mack? Who am I fighting?"

"You're not fighting anyone. I'm not having lady troubles." I give her a half-hearted smile. "I only have the one trouble."

"Mmmh. I could tell you were gonna get lost in this one at the hospital." She sighs and grabs water from her fridge and we go sit at her patio table.

Though she spends a lot of time at the ranch house where her parents still live, she doesn't live on Mason Ranch anymore. The house Cory bought is not too far, as most things aren't too far in the Ridge, but it felt like I was driving for an hour to get here when it was only fifteen minutes.

My mind was so caught up in thoughts of the woman I know is pulling away. I can't figure out why though.

She looked like she was coming to a funeral when I saw her standing in the bathroom last night. We slept together, I woke up with her in my arms but... something is changing. I don't know what exactly though.

My sister kicks her bare feet up onto the bench beside her and situates herself. "Alright. Tell me about her," she encourages. "Help me understand what's going on."

I lean into her on the bench. Her dark hair blows in the breeze around her and it makes me think about when we were young together on the Ranch. I had many friends back then, but Reese was always more than that.

Chandie had thought it was the cutest thing when I started calling her my sister. "Is my sister in the stables?" Or more often, "Has my sister woken up yet?" I'd walk across the property early in the morning and spend most of the day at the Mason's so often that I likely could say I lived there. My father never cared and my mom was... well she is who she is and how I wanted to spend my days didn't change that. It was likely easier for her to cope without me around all the time.

Neither of my parents considered what it was like to grow up in the middle of their bullshit. If I didn't have the Mason's I'd probably be half feral and strung out on a street corner.

I scratch the back of my head. "Umm, I don't know where to begin."

She takes one look at me and suggests, "How about the beginning?"

'The beginning… Reese, I—" I cut myself off thinking about how it would be great to actually share what I'm feeling with someone and see if I am out of my mind or maybe what I'm feeling has some merit to it.

She gives me an encouraging look, waiting to hear what I have to say. I try again. "Remember how Danny sat me down to talk about how horses belong to no one? And that it would take a lot to convince a free spirit like you to stay in my pasture?"

She grimaces. "Yes. I do remember this harrowing scenario. He was still under the impression that we liked each other at fifteen. That still shocks me. He was off his rocker, I tell you."

"Maybe not…" I pick at a callous on my hand and think a little more.

Reese lets out a long sigh. "You know I'm married right? To one of your good friends, no less."

"Oh, shut up. I don't want you." I shove her lightly and she dramatically jerks to the left with a gasp. "I'm being serious. He might have been wrong about the person, but that conversation has stuck with me for much longer than I thought it would. What Danny could see, I've learned, is much more than I could. I am drawn to these free spirited women who I can't grasp long enough to tame."

Reese scoffs. "You can't tame a woman. Very misogynistic of you to think you could."

"Dammit, Reese. Are you gonna let me talk or are you gonna keep swan diving into your own conclusions?"

She laughs, "Listen, I have to make sure we're on the same page. If you start comparing women to horses like they're only meant to be ridden and kept on your land, I need to know exactly how hard to smack you."

I glare at her before laughing myself. "That is obviously not what I think. What I'm trying to say is that Jeann is like that. She's a free spirit. She's also an amazing artist. She can draw, like really draw. The other day she made the most heartbreakingly realist drawing of Legend from memory alone. She captured the personality in his eyes and the detail…" I run a hand through my hair. "It was incredible. Less than a few hours and she was able to see him so clearly. I wonder. What it would be like if she…" I trail off again. I hadn't talked to anyone much about my roommate. *My girl.* I had only thought these things until now.

Reese picks up on my train of thought even though I didn't finish. "If she sees you just as clearly." She nods a few times and I go back to looking at my hands. "What if she *does* see you and she *stays*? Then, what?"

"She wouldn't stay. I have no misconceptions about the fact that Alpenglow is just a rest stop. But being a part of her recovery is no problem for me. I can be that for her." That's the worst part. She could leave at any point now. Each day is a ticking time bomb. She has no reason to stay anymore. She's worked long enough to go where she wants.

"You can also be more if you want, brother. You can be anything. But you'll never get something you don't ask for. How will you know what's possible?"

"Ask her?" I reel back. "Are you trying to get me to scare her away? I'm basically bad luck wrapped in a dark omen. Everything I touch turns to shit."

She looks over at me with compassion I don't deserve. "I know you think you're the worst thing walking after all that you've been through. And I also know that people are too hard on themselves when it comes to their flaws." She pats my arm and waits for me to look her in the eye before she continues. "But your big heart is not a defect. She likely sees that you are special and feels what you're feeling. Whether she wants to do something about it is yet to be seen. You'll only know if you..." She grabs my hand and waits.

"Ask," I complete her thought.

Just then, the pattering of feet on the concrete is followed by giggling as Reese's twins do their best to now sneak up on me.

One of them pops out to the side of the table, asking, "Uncle Mack, why are you looking sad?"

I waste no time standing, scooping her up and throwing her over one shoulder. I'm a little sore from the hit I took, but not too much where I can't play with my nieces. Kyra giggles from over my shoulder and I poke her side to make her squirm even more. "I'm not sad, Kyra baby. I'm just thinking real hard about something."

Suddenly, Kelsie is on the other side of me, trying to find a weak spot to distract me and help her sister. Looking up at me, Kelsie says, "Mommy has on her serious face. Are you in trouble?" Then she whispers, not as quietly as she thinks, into my ear, "I can help you hide it. Whatever you broked."

The two of them are even more chaos than my nephews ever were.

"Okay... enough of that," I say and grab the other twin to throw over my shoulder. I run them around and they giggle even more.

With the commotion, we've alerted Cory to their whereabouts. He stands in the patio doorway looking as stern as this lovesick man can muster.

"Oops," the twins say in unison. I don't know what they've been caught doing, but he does not look happy about it.

"I told you two to tell Mommy that it was bath time..."

I set the two of them down and they hug my legs before rushing into the house to the side of the imposing man.

"Well, that's my cue," Reese stands from her table and before she reaches her husband, she turns to me again. "Think about what I said. Your sis knows best."

"Yea, yea," I smile at her even though I'm waving her away. The two of them kiss, and kiss for a much longer time than I feel comfortable observing. I head over to the gate expecting Cory to follow his wife inside, but he holds up a hand, breaking their kiss.

"Not so fast," he says, still using his dad voice. My sister slips inside the house and he walks over to me. "What's she talking about?"

"Just that I should confess my undying affection for Jeann... and effectively run her off."

He nods, not picking up on my sarcasm. "It works," he says, voice full of conviction. "If that's what she said, I stand behind it too. Women aren't mind readers. She's never gonna leap if you don't hold out your arms to catch her."

"Wow. That was..." I look at my friend, truly look at him. "Kinda profound."

"I know," he claps me on the back. "You'll see that the time is right when she's ready. Not a second before then though."

Reese was right. He is one of my best friends. And knowing that, I'd kept him at a distance because I feared being burnt again by the fickleness of adult friendships.

After losing everything—my wife, my baby, my friends, my parents—I truly trusted nothing to be permanent.

Everything can go up in smoke just as quickly as it brought you warmth. I want to bask in the glow that is inside Jeann. I want to show her that I can be the oxygen that stokes her flame. I'd never want to dull it.

"Everything you're thinking right now—bring that to her. It'll do no good to tell me." Then he smiles big and toothy, "But when it works, tell me all about it."

CHAPTER 32

Mack

I'M GONNA FOLLOW CORY'S advice.

He was right. All I have right now is speculation and hearsay. *And not even that.* We've both been dancing around what we really mean to each other and that is not fair to either of us. I can't expect her to know what is on my mind either.

A lot has changed since I first nearly blurted out that I loved her. And if anything, that love has grown stronger and stronger the more that I got to spend time with her. I know that I can't be feeling all these things on my own. I know that she feels it too. Even if it's not the same as I do, it's close enough that I can wait for her to meet me where I'm at.

So here I stand, in front of a literal fire, trying to set the scene for the first step into our real future together.

"It's finally warm enough for me to grill again," I say when I hear the woman in question coming out of the patio door. Jeann joins me in the back yard with a big pad of paper under her left arm and a quilt underneath the other.

She's setting up a comfy spot for herself on the grass. She's in cutoff jean shorts with black and white paint splatters on them and a tight cropped white tank. It's got a few holes in it that show her pink lace bra underneath.

Her braids are a dark purple color that look black until they're in the sun like they are now. She looks good enough to eat.

I'm gonna tell her exactly how I feel. Not about her looking good enough to eat... Well, that too. But, about what's in my heart.

It's been months since we first had that conversation where she said she couldn't be mine. If anything, I've proven that she can. *She's here now.* We haven't even talked about flights to Louisiana. For all intents and purposes, this woman is mine.

What's in a label? Nothing of substance, but I want one anyway. I was only lying to myself before. Behind closed doors is not enough. When I see her, I want to tell the world that this is my person. And I want to be her person in return.

The moment has to be perfect though. I'm pulling out all the stops.

From where Jeann sits, her arm is already moving across the paper, creating something. "I was beginnin' to wonder if you did know how to cook anythin' beside grilled cheese," she says sarcastically, never looking up from what she's doing.

"Ha. Ha." I take the foil off of the pan where I was marinating the steaks. The two big ribeyes sizzle on the grill before I close the lid and let them cook for a bit. "Everyone knows that it's best to work smarter, not harder. I have one of the best cooks in my house. And if not, then I've got second best just across the way. I don't even have to do dishes at Chandie's."

"Keep it up and you're gonna be doin' dishes today, too," she snarks.

"When you taste my meat, that is the last thing you're gonna be thinking."

Her hand pauses and her brows pinch though she still hasn't looked at me. "What?"

"My meat is big and juicy," I hedge.

She looks at me finally, making a face. "Oh, God."

I keep going, adding a little pump to my hips now that I've got her attention. "Doesn't even need a sauce. Rich flavor."

Her lips quirk into a smile. "Stop, please."

I smirk back at her. "Goes down nice and smooth like butter."

"You're a fool," she laughs

"Not just any fool. Your fool," I say, snapping the tongs at her and she just rolls her eyes, back to drawing whatever she was before.

Time passes quickly while I work on what I'm going to say to her next and still manage to cook this food perfectly. It takes over all my attention and I don't notice when she walks up behind me to peer into the grill.

"This looks real good," she says and I flinch when her words reach me.

"I hope it tastes that way too." Grabbing the steaks to rest on the chopping block, I start bringing in the rest of the food to the kitchen.

I even made mocktails since that seems like serious dinner protocol.

Jeann takes a seat at the table, watching me move around like I usually do to her. I set her drink down in front of her saying, "So, I was thinking about you all day today."

She blinks, owlishly. "You spent your whole day off, thinkin' about me?" I set her plate in front her next and then my own across from her

"Yea, but I think about you at work too. It's not *only* an off day task." I sit as well, but I wait for Jeann to eat first.

"Do you?" she asks, a little smile on her face as she cuts into her perfectly medium steak.

"I do." Cutting into my own steak, I stop and watch her face when I say the next bit. "You've been here almost five months. I can't believe time has passed so quickly."

There is a little bend in her brows. "Five months," she repeats.

Her face twists up, but I keep going, already full steam ahead on my speech. "Yea. And—"

I don't get a chance to finish because she rushes out of the dining room. Cannot recall a time where she's moved this fast to do anything.

Not a good sign.

When I hear the sound of her vomiting, I rush over to the bathroom. The door is closed, but I give the handle a jiggle anyway. "Jeann."

No answer.

"You okay. Can I get you anything?"

"No," she responds quickly. "I'll be out in a bit."

Helplessness claws at me like this is somehow my fault. The night has already gone bad, but I do my best to lighten the mood anyway. "Are you sure? Was it my meat?" I hear her huff a laugh and that makes me feel a little better.

It's been a while since I cooked a steak, but I didn't think I could have fucked it up that much. Can you get sick from a steak like that?

Water rushes on the other side of the door and Jeann says, "I'm gonna take a shower, I feel... I'll be quick. Okay?"

"'Kay." *Damn.* I guess I did fuck that up.

I start cleaning up the table and toss the food while I wait for her to clean herself up. I'll probably be sick soon too.

She comes out of our room in one of my shirts and sweatpants with her hair piled up on top of her head. "I'm so tired. Can we just watch somethin' in bed?"

I agree and she picks out a movie that I barely watch any of because my mind is wheeling.

Well, now is definitely not the time to tell her how much I care about her after I just probably gave her food poisoning.

"Will you hold me?"

I hold my arms open for her and she snuggles into them on the bed. "Yea." I kiss her forehead over the scar from her stitches. It's almost invisible now. "Of course."

Chapter 33

Mack

"Mack. What are you doing here?" Tony, my manager looks at me confused. At that moment, Jeann comes from around the half door to stand beside me. His face turns to granite with her arrival. "And you brought someone... to work?"

"This is Jeann. We won't be in your way, I just wanted to say hi to the horses since it's been a while that she had the chance to."

"Let me talk to you for a second," Tony says low in my ear.

I watch Jeann as she walks over to the horses who are already loving on her after how long she's been gone. For a while there, she would come with me on Thursdays to ride the horses and it's kind of been our thing. If the horses couldn't win her over, then I don't know what could.

It's a good sign that the two of them are comfortable and not cautious around her when I'm not there. Horses are so perceptive and sometimes downright fickle. If there was a litmus test for how good a person is—this would be it. I'm a firm believer in that.

I follow Tony to the other side of the barn so I can still see her from where I stand with him. The other people working right now mill about on their duties, not paying us or Jeann any mind.

"What's up, T?" I ask. After she was sick the other day, I want to stay close just in case whatever it is comes back. I didn't end up getting sick so I don't think it was my food after all. So it's gotta be something else that's affecting her.

He looks my face over for a couple of moments and I feel like there is something important that he has to say. Tony is not a particularly talkative guy and I get the impression that he would rather not talk at all—to any-one—besides his wife, if I'm honest. But since he is the ranch manager and my boss, I've talked to him plenty. However curt that may be. "You know this woman?" He finally asks.

An eyebrow rises on my face at his question, but I answer anyway. "Umm, yea. It's kind of a long story, but she's actually my girlfriend." I smile to myself at that. *Girlfriend.* My girlfriend. "She's been staying at my house. I would've introduced you sooner, but with everything it's just been busy."

He frowns. "She's staying?"

"Yea."

"At your house?"

I shrug. "Yea."

His arms cross over his chest. "You don't even know her."

Even more confused by this aside, I ask him, "What is your problem? You know her or something?" They're both from Louisiana and since his brother clearly knew her for some bizarre reason, it wouldn't be the *weirdest* thing if Tony knew her too.

He continues to scrutinize my face. "You don't know who that is do you?"

What the hell is he on about? "I do." Crossing my arms over my chest, I feel the full force of his scrutiny, but don't budge. "What's got your boxers in a bunch?"

"My boxers aren't—" He shakes his head at me and I feel like a chastised child. "This woman is not who you think she is."

Now, I'm the one frowning. "Come again?"

"Not even a few months ago, this woman held a gun to my chest. Threatening both me and Drea's lives when we were trying to rescue Mireya. Her and her guy took Colton and are in bad business with my brother."

Around Christmas time, I did know that there was a lot that happened with his wife, Drea, but I didn't really know all the details. Reese called me to say they needed help to find Mireya and I got into my truck to help right away. No second thoughts. I never did make it there because I had the accident with Ethan on my way there.

My life completely changed after.

It occurs to me that it has been a while since I actually talked to Tony. His life has been just as crazy with his new wife, Drea. And from what I hear they are crazy happy together. Besides passing at work or him assigning a task to me, I haven't been spending a lot of time with the rest of Reese's friends in general outside of who I see here at the Ranch.

"You're mistaken," I say with conviction laced deep in my tone. I don't know what he's talking about, but he doesn't know Jeann. At times she can be a little adverse to being friendly, but she's not dangerous. She would never be holding a gun up to anyone. Threatening someone's life? Definitely not.

"I'm not. I remember everything about that day. It was the longest and worst day of my life. Had no idea where Mireya was and I had no leads other than the cabin she was last at. Would never forget the face of someone who threatened my life and put my daughter's life in danger."

I shake my head. "Tony, you—"

"Listen to me, Mack. You do not know this woman or what she's capable of. She beat Colton's ass with very little effort. I saw that with my own two eyes. If that's not enough, then Colton told me himself what happened. I don't know why she's here, but I don't have a good feeling about it." Colton is Drea's ex and Mireya's birth father. He's also a cop. Not just a cop but a sheriff. What business would a Colorado sheriff have with a woman from Louisiana?

Better yet, how could Jeann have beat him up?

Ridiculous.

"Well, I appreciate your concern, but it's misplaced. Jeann is not that woman." *She can't be.* She might be a little sharp around the edges, but she wouldn't have put Mireya's life in danger... Or held a gun to a sheriff. "Show some respect for my girl. Excuse me." I brush past my boss to go check on my horses and my woman.

"Everythin' okay?" Jeann asks when I return to where she's brushing Legend. He leans into her touch, nearly bowling her over in his quest to be close to her. *Same, buddy. Same.* The feeling is there even as the words Tony has said make me doubt myself.

I nod and then find the stool we keep nearby to sit and watch the woman with my favorite guy. Satisfied with my response, she returns to her affections.

Like the first time I saw the two of them together, I can't get enough of this feeling. The feeling that something is just right, perfect.

So perfect.

I couldn't ask for more than this.

A good judge of character, I am not. Not off my own merit. Not to say that I have ever missed a red flag before.

But if I like someone it is likely the wrong person. I attach myself to women that are so unavailable, I may as well not bother.

Not anymore.

She could be the one.

A big chunk of her memory is still gone, but that doesn't make her any less likely to be a person who could last in my life. There's a place for her here.

The space that she's taken is likely hers no matter whether I finally tell her about my feelings or not.

It's not long before I decide simply looking at her is not enough and I'm walking over to where she talks to my horse like a person.

It's very clear that she had a love for animals from how they frequent her drawings. If she's creating anything, they pop up.

I wanted her to love what I do. Love the life I could provide for her. And she fits into it so well.

My hands find her hips, but she doesn't startle. She continues telling Legend about how handsome he is and that he is the one she loves the most. About how much he loves her is going to stress daddy out.

The sound of *daddy* from her lips is too good.

Dangerous for her, really.

I want her to stay.

Yea, I want her to choose to stay here.

Talking to her about a future with us together is not something that needs to happen right this second or today. But it will happen. And when we do, I'll be there to catch her just like Cory said.

"How about a ride?" She turns to look at me over her shoulder. "I promise to go slow."

Jeann nods and I start prepping Legend for a ride.

With the wind whipping Legend's hair and Jeann's arms wrapped around me, I'm certain that a future with her here with me is imminent.

CHAPTER 34

Jeann

EVER SINCE THAT LAST memory that came back, I've been on edge.

Thankfully, not to Mack because he's done nothing to deserve my ire but at work, it's getting to the point that I am resorting to head nods and thumbs up to avoid going off on everyone. I'm just so much more irritable.

Spending time with Legend and Mack made me happier than I've been at work. But that is the effect that Mack has on me. I think that Legend is becoming a very close second though.

But then, I've noticed that my body feels different in a way that I couldn't explain. Unexplained nausea and the irritability. I had my suspicions.

I didn't want to be right.

After work, I drove straight to the store in Harmony Hill before I could second guess myself. It's been a while since I was here, but it has the closest big store. And hopefully, I'll be far enough away from the small town nosies.

Mack called me right as I parked and asked where I was. I knew it was from a place of concern so I picked up the call and told him where I was. "I just want to get a little shoppin' done." The lie tastes bitter and foul in my mouth.

"Okay, butterfly. Will you bring home some candy? I'm missing something sweet already."

Normally, I would give into his playful flirting, but my mind is too distracted with my task. "Sure, yea." He lets me go and I sit in the car for a second before I finally get out.

It's jarring to be around so many people after months of the small stores and online shopping I've gotten used to. With the memories trickling in, and only giving back what is probably the most triggering of memories that I've had the past three years, I feel like it's been years since I've been to a store like this.

I find the aisle I'm looking for and grab the box I saw online as quickly as possible.

I'm thankful for the self checkout line because I don't want to have any small talk about what I'm purchasing. If I think about it too much longer, I might scream. The possibilities are killing me and I need an answer.

I rush over to the restroom in the store and rip into the box like a scavenging raccoon. It would have been easier for me to use the perforated tab but dammit! I'm impatient.

Relieving myself, I cross my fingers like that will do anything. Hoping and praying that my suspicions are wrong.

I put the blue cap onto the stick and wash my hands.

Time moves much too slowly and eventually the results begin to show on the little window.

"I'm pregnant," I say aloud into the room. I stare at the stick for moments on moments.

A small smile looks back at me in the mirror when I finally look up again. I look back down to the test in my hands. The number of lines are clear as day. If that wasn't enough of a confirmation, the all-caps letters that spell out PREGNANT couldn't be mistaken.

I know it's unexpected and it's kind of horrifying, but I'm smiling all the same.

They say that pregnancy is a miracle.

A *miracle.*

Could being pregnant with Mack's baby be a miracle?

Is that even something he would want? After everything he's been through...

I can't remember ever wanting to have kids, but the idea of a little baby with Mack isn't the worst thing I could picture for myself.

It's the most complicated scenario that I could find myself in though.

And the smile remains on my face when I do picture it.

I can picture the joy on his face already in my mind.

After Callan, I want to tell him in some special way. Maybe have some kind of reveal or something. I don't know. Maybe I'm making too big of a deal out of this.

There doesn't need to be some big song and dance. I can just go up to him and say, "Hey, I'm havin' your baby."

Okay... maybe a little more pomp than that.

Dammit. Why am I getting excited about this?

There's a small voice that's growing larger in my mind warning me that I should not be happy about this.

What an unconventional path this life has taken me on.

I don't know how I ended up here.

There is so much that I'm keeping from him. Too much that I need answers about from my past. Telling him anything now would be partial and not a complete explanation. Though any way I spin this, I'm keeping my truth from him. I haven't been honest about what I've been dreaming or the fact that those memories are coming back to me.

And I should have already.

I'm beyond frustrated that even months later there are glaring holes in what I can recall. I only seem to remember the worst parts of myself and that is a big problem.

Then that small voice tells me that there are only bad parts because that's all there is to me.

How am I supposed to come clean to Mack when I don't even know what I'm going to say?

By the way, I've been known to break people's legs for threatening the crime family I worked for as some sort of henchman or muscle.

That will go over real well.

Not.

None of the appropriate follow up questions have answers. We would both be scrambling for what they could be.

Worse yet, what if I tell him and he condemns me for all the shit I've gotten myself into.

With those memories, it's like I'm remembering a past life.

Kitty and Jeann are not the same person.

Kitty no longer exists and I'm just Jeann Barker now.

No matter how much I wish for that to be true, it's not.

I could be putting him in danger by just being around him at all. I have no idea.

His association with me could mean there's a target on his back.

There was nothing I could do to protect him either. Kitty knew how to fight, shoot, and spar. Jeann doesn't know how to do any of those things. If he was in danger, we would both be fucked. Royally. And it would be my fault.

I can't do this to Mack.

I can't do this to Mack.

The whole reason that I came here was to save up enough money to get back to Louisiana. Not fall for a man who reminds me of the sun and smiles even when he's hurting. I definitely should not have gotten so comfortable in his house or in his heart.

It looks like that needs to be put back into my main priorities. I have to leave and go back to where I came from.

I don't want to.

I don't want to uncover more worse parts of me, but I owe it to myself to learn the truth.

I know it will hurt him, but I need to know for sure that I can keep him safe.

His safety is more important than either of our feelings for each other.

Potentially life and death.

I know what I have to do.

Rushing back to Mack's place, I barely have a chance to be grateful that he's not here. I'm running to my room. The room I used to stay in before I started sleeping in his room like it was my own.

God. I knew that was a bad idea.

But I was weak for him. *I'm still weak for him.*

I have to shove down those feelings.

All of them.

Every single one needs to be pushed out of the way.

I have a different goal now.

Searching through the duffel I first brought from the hospital, I find the napkin with Blue's number on it.

I stare at the number for several minutes until it goes blurry in my hand. My eyes fill up with tears. Angrily, I brush them away with my forearm.

I don't want to call Blue and I really don't want back in to whatever life I had before.

What I've built here with Mack is the best my life has ever looked. I'd be willing to bet my life on that even with the chunks of my memory gone.

That makes this decision even harder for me. I hate myself for considering staying and letting the chips just fall where they may.

It's selfish to take this amazing life from him. Or the possibility of one.

I can't do that.

I dial the numbers one at a time and wait for that deep voice to register on the other side.

"Kitty. Been too long." Flickers of the memories I have flash like a montage with his voice. Each act of violence clangs in my mind like a death knell.

"I know," I respond, voice flat.

Straight to business, Blue asks, "When are you reportin'?"

"I'm not. Not exactly."

"Two weeks," he says. I scoff. He continues, "I've been both generous and patient while you play house in Colorado. Two weeks, then I'm bringin' you back one way or another."

He ends the call and I drop to my knees.

Two weeks and then this dream will blow away in the breeze.

CHAPTER 35

Jeann

NEVER THOUGHT I'D BE back here again.

Harmony Hill Hospital looks extremely different when it's not covered in snow. It's clean and clinical like you would expect, though just as daunting as I knew it would be.

I stand just outside of the car looking at the massive building in front of me like it might bite me.

Need to take that step...

One step...

When I called a couple of days ago to make this appointment, I was grateful that they would be able to see me so soon. I was hoping that maybe they would be slammed. It was just my luck that there was a cancellation and I was able to take their spot.

I sigh. I'll have to go in at some point and it's better if I'm not late.

Hurrying into the obstetrics ward, I'm assaulted with how pastel and dreamy the area is in contrast to the part of the hospital I was in all those months ago. The assistant at the desk smiles at me and hands me a clipboard with all types of forms to fill out. Most of it is supposed to be about my history, but seeing as though I still don't know a lot of that information, I make broad assumptions based off of what I do remember and what it's been like since I woke up here.

"What day is it?" I ask the nurse as I sign the last line on the page.

She looks up from the computer she's typing diligently on to respond, "May twentieth."

"Oh," I mumble and sign the bottom of the paperwork before sliding it across to her again.

I can't believe it's been so long.

Five months.

Mack pointed that out to me a couple of weeks ago when the first of what I now know was morning sickness hit me. Though, it doesn't stick to mornings. I've at least had the grace of not having to upchuck when he's home. Don't know how long that will last though.

I have been feeling like shit. I'm nauseous all damn day and *tired*. I've never been so tired in my life. It's shocking that Mack hasn't put the pieces together.

Right now, I'm thankful for it.

I wait in the lobby until they call me back and before I know it the whooping thumping of a heartbeat fills the room.

"Your baby is looking good and healthy, mama," the obstetrician says. "I'm going to just get some pictures really quick and get the measurements."

I just nod and watch as she clicks and presses buttons on the machine.

This is real.

This baby is real.

I'm pregnant.

I'm pregnant with Mack's baby.

"From the looks of it, you're about fourteen weeks along." She clicks some more. "Baby is looking very healthy." She looks over the chart and reads for a moment. "Do you want a few copies to share with family and friends?"

Family and friends?

I don't have any of those.

"One copy is fine," I manage.

She smiles and collects my one roll of ultrasound photos. "Let us know if you have any questions or concerns at all. Even if you think it might be silly. We have a twenty-four hour phone line that can handle the basics, but they will be able to contact me to relay any urgent matters. It's just on the back of my card there." She points to the card in my hand with a smile.

I can only nod and mumble a "Thank you," before she leaves.

Taking my time to clean up all the goo she rubbed on my belly, I make sure none of it got in places I didn't notice. My stomach is still relatively flat even though I have a whole life growing in there.

I look at it in the mirror and try to imagine what it will look like to grow rounder at the middle. I'm reminded of what my sister looked like.

Will we look like twins again?

Mack has taken to calling me butterfly and in a way... I have become one.

I'm becoming the beautiful being that Lauren once was.

Quickly dressing, I take care of what I'm supposed to at the front desk and race over to the car.

My phone vibrates in my purse as soon as I get the gear in reverse to leave the parking lot.

It's Mack.

I answer it though I likely shouldn't with all these conflicting emotions swirling around in my mind at present.

"Hey, are you at the salon?" His voice does everything to calm me.

"Umm. I came to Harmony Hill. I was cravin' Greek food." *Dammit why did I say craving? Dammit.*

Now, I do actually want some Greek food.

The smile on his face bleeds into his voice. "Oh, hell yes! Will you bring me some too?"

"Sure. Text me your order." The roll of sonogram photos falls from my bag and I grab them up from the floor before I forget.

"You're so good to me. How'd I get such an amazing woman in my life?" If I were there he'd probably play it off like a joke, but the sincerity in his voice is unmistakable. *Mack loves with his whole heart.* Though I have managed to keep him from saying it, I know he wants to. He shows me in so many ways.

All of them I don't deserve.

All of them are more heartbreaking than the last because this man is worthy of a woman who is better than me.

Why is he so perfect?

Why did I do this to us?

I change the subject entirely. "I'm gonna be workin' on a piece all weekend. Will you have somethin' to keep yourself busy?"

"Yes," he responds simply.

We're both quiet as I wait for him to explain, but he doesn't say anything more.

"What are you gonna do?"

"I'm gonna watch the games and my girl creating a masterpiece."

My girl.

I need him out of the house so I can pack before whoever Blue is sending will pick me up.

"Maybe you and Cory should spend some time together. I'm sure he'd like that." I try to lighten the mood with a chuckle, but it's stilted and sounds fake to my ears. I wince and truck on anyway, "I feel like I'm always takin' all your time."

"Have you met this man? He likes to be firmly underneath my sister, literally and figuratively. That is not something I think he wants."

"He might want some company since you haven't been around. Mack, please."

There's another pause and then he says, "I'll find something to do. If you want some alone time, you can just tell me. You know that right?"

God this hurts. He's such a good man. "Yea, I do."

I need to get off of the phone.

I need to get off the phone now before I come clean.

Can not afford to do that.

Clearing my throat of the rising emotion, I say, "Let me order this food and I'll see you later, okay?"

"Okay, butterfly. I'll see you later."
Butterfly.
Butterfly.
I hang up and rest my head on the steering wheel.
How the hell am I going to do this?

CHAPTER 36

Mack

"I'M GLAD YOU CALLED me," Cory says.

We're in the greenhouse he had built a couple of years back. His obsession with flowers has taken on new heights. As the owner of Whitfield Landscaping, he had gotten tired of having to drive to another town to get the plants he needed every time he had a new project. Now, he has his own place and the business has gotten big enough that he has staff who specifically work this part of it without him needing to be present.

He also works part of my family's business with growing and selling sod. What started as a few contracts became a partnership that has been profitable for both of us over the years.

Basically, Cory has a huge green thumb and has become synonymous with landscaping in Alpenglow Ridge and a few of the surrounding areas. The building is large enough to house a family of three, but instead of furniture and pictures, there's wall to wall, row upon row of botanics. Each room has a different temperature control and setting. It's fancy as hell for stuff that grows in dirt, in my opinion.

He's walked me through all the rooms before and though I haven't retained enough information to call myself an expert, I recognize a few of the plants. The room we're in now is warm and humid. Hanging ferns and large tropical leaves make it feel like a jungle though there are pops of bright colors from some flowers on the tables within.

The large sealing door closes behind us as he leads me to an open area outside that is a shock to go from humid to our own drier weather. Several alpine blooms, smaller firs and what I guess are hydrangeas are growing in rows on benches that line the outside perimeter. More flowers I can't name are in some of the pots, as well. The biggest feature is a fountain at the middle that he said keeps it from being too dry out here.

Finally, we enter another room on the other side and I find a chair to sit in. The one we're currently in has the most comfortable of the environments he's artificially created. I'm thankful I'm not sweating my ass off since it is more mild here than the dry weather Colorado has to offer outside. This is where he has what I'm guessing makes up most of his famous bouquets. Roses, peonies and dahlias are the ones I can name though there are many, many more.

"I'm surprised you picked up," I say, careful to step over some cords and irrigation that cross over the narrow walkway.

"Ha. I bet." He opens a refrigerator in the far corner to get us some drinks. "But, nah. I needed something to do. Mrs. said I was hovering."

"Jeann said the same." I cheers my pop bottle to his beer. "What were you hovering over?"

"Mireya and CJ are 'friends' again, but we both know that boy is in love. Deep. Can't believe he almost blew it."

I chuckle. "That's a common thing. It's always us blowing it."

He tilts his head and raises a thick eyebrow. "Speak for yourself."

I give him a bland look. When he and my sister were just at the beginning of their relationship, I had to be the one to tell him, in plain English, about Reese and Alex. It wasn't my favorite memory between the two of us. But when I look back, that was the moment when I knew we could be friends. And his reaction upon hearing the truth showed me exactly what kind of man he was.

One worthy of my sister and of being a part of this family.

"Aye, I was young," he balks.

"Not that young," I snort into my bottle.

"Young enough to still not know when I'm putting my foot in my own mouth. Guess I have you to thank for that."

"You guess?" I blurt. "You guess, when I saved you from yourself?"

"Being a lightweight is a medical condition. And one I still suffer from."

I laugh at my brother. "You are something else. What are we even doing in here?"

"I'm still gonna try to help my son not look like a fool." He gestures to the wooden table on the other side of the room that has what looks like the materials he'll need to wrap a bouquet. The kraft paper, ribbons, tape, cards, pens, etc. "Even a small bouquet will be better than his dry hands."

"That boy does need some lotion."

We both laugh. "Help me with this," Cory says, holding a small basket out to me as he grabs some kind of scissors to cut the flowers. I take the basket following him around as he tells me about what the kids have been up to. I've missed a fair bit since I've been trying to spend all my free time with Jeann recently.

Maybe she was right in wanting a little alone time today. I've been in her lap since we'd come back from the hospital.

By the time he's finished telling me about how his middle child is on the track team this year and that the twins are learning to read too quickly for his liking, the basket I'm carrying is chock full of flowers that mostly have dark hues.

Cory takes the basket from me and places the few light colored flowers and sprigs into a small bundle on twine and sets a rectangle of cardstock into the knot he tied. "I'll let him pick what to say. He might not say much, but I think CJ probably feels the deepest out of all of us. Gets that from his pops honest."

I cross my arms. "You mean he's a lovesick sap? Yea. He gets that real honest."

Cory points the scissors at me. "Shut up or I'm not helping you."

"Helping me?"

He nods and takes some of the flowers out of the basket. "Yea. With your woman problems."

"I don't have woman problems ."

He's still busy stripping the stems of the flowers he holds of leaves and such. "Did you at least tell her what I said? If you did and this whole time you've buried the lead, I'm gonna be pissed."

"You gossip more than Chloe."

"She's much better at conversation than you," he comments, but doesn't deny my claims.

"How so?"

"She at least offers information back. I've gotten nothing short of grunts from you today. Something is on your mind. What happened when you told her?"

"Well... I haven't yet." I scratch the stubble coming in on my jaw. "There hasn't been a good time to." Which is true since I don't know what happened the other night. It's been over two weeks and I haven't tried again. Not because I don't want to, but because I want it to be perfect. This might make or break our relationship.

"A... Good... Time... To?" He questions with wide eyes.

"Yea. I made this dinner before. You know? Grilled some steaks, potatoes. Even make a cocktail without the alcohol." I shake my head. "It was pretty romantic."

"That's a perfect time. You set the scene. Okay. Then, what happened?"

I think back to the night. "She got sick. Barely got to enjoy the dinner before she was in the bathroom. We ended up just cuddling and watching *Space Jam* until she passed out. We kind of both did."

"She got sick?" He taps his chin in thought. "Sick how?"

"What do you mean, sick how? She was throwing up in the bathroom. Wouldn't even let me help her."

"Hmm," is all he says.

"Hmm what?"

His eyes flick between mine, searching for something. "You said she barely ate, but she was throwing up all night?"

"Yea, that's what I said."

"Hmm," he repeats himself. "And after, you said she was tired?"

I throw my hands to the side of me, not understanding his line of questioning. "Are you listening to me, Cory?"

"Oh, I've heard every word." He takes me by the shoulders and moves me over to the fold out chair to sit. "What's between y'all is between y'all, but... Have you, at any point, forgotten the glove?"

My eyebrows slam down. "No!" He tilts his head to the side and gives me a dubious look. "Okay, maybe a few times we've gone without. So what?"

He sighs, "You've done this before..." He rolls his hands in front of himself urging me to make whatever conclusion he has also made. "Am I going to have the birds and the bees conversation with you?"

I give him a droll look. "Get to the point, bro."

Undeterred, he continues to spell out the birds and bees talk. "Well, when a boy and a girl love each other..." His words trail off and he just stands there, looking at me with his hands rolling in front of him again. Why would he be having *the talk* with me when I know—

"Pregnant?" I exclaim. "No way. We—"

"Yes, way. She didn't eat, but she threw up. She was tired. Y'all have probably been doing the nasty all over that damn house. I wish I was getting it like that. We've got way too many kids around the house to be—"

"Ugh. Keep that shit to yourself." I complain, not wanting any more details about what he and Reese get up to. "If Jeann were pregnant, she'd tell me."

He tilts his head. "Why would she?"

"What the fuck does that mean?" I cross my arms again.

"It's her body. Why does she have to tell you she's pregnant?"

"Cory."

"Mack."

"She would tell me."

"I think you should maybe think about this woman some more. Imagine how she feels. You said that you haven't even told her how you feel. And she's just gonna tell you that she's carrying your baby? That's a big deal. It's not like getting ice cream before coming home or painting the hallway a different color. It's a whole person and she's a single woman as far as she knows in a place that is not her home."

"She's not single."

"But she doesn't know you'll catch her. She's carrying your baby."

"We don't know that."

He gives me a droll look now. "I've done this a few times, Mack. The woman is pregnant."

I'm quiet for a while, thinking about what he's said. Cory goes back to arranging the dark flowers he's cut into another bundle, but this time he wraps them in the Kraft paper before tying them.

"Look, you could be right and she's not pregnant. But if there's the slightest chance that she is... The right time has already passed. You need to tell her your feelings for her as soon as possible."

Shame coats the back of my throat, thick and gloopy.

If she is and I haven't been there for her, it'll kill me. I can't let her think that she is doing this alone.

I'd never do that to her.

"I'll figure it out. I'll text you," I tell him as I make my way out of the greenhouse.

• • •

THE ENERGY OF THE house is all wrong when I walk back in.

There is no music playing how I would expect. She hates working in silence.

It's utterly quiet in here.

She's not in the dining room and none of her materials are there either. I toss the flowers on the table and set out to look for her. Maybe she just has her headphones on or something.

Looking in the bedroom, I don't see her on the bed or in the shower.

Maybe she's outside since it's been nice out today.

I pop my head out of the door and it's empty too. The sun is setting since I've been gone all day. I begin to panic that something very wrong has happened. The uneasy feeling in my gut persists after I've done a lap around the yard to make sure she hasn't set up somewhere obscure that I couldn't see from the patio.

It's been weeks, maybe months now since she's slept in the guest room. But something draws me in that direction. I walk over there just to see if maybe she's working or sleeping in there. I'm no artist, I don't know how inspiration hits and all that. I push the door open and it's glaringly obvious.

It's empty.

Her duffel bag is gone. None of her stuff is in the dressers. The closet is barren as all hell.

No.

No, no.

No, *no, no.*

My brain gives me the conclusion to all my findings and yet I refuse to believe it.

I run back to my room to see if any of her things were there. I frown at what I find there instead. *Nothing.* All her clothes from my drawers and closet are gone. Even the dirty clothes hamper is missing all her stuff.

The bathroom that I checked before is where I'm really gutted and everything sinks in. All, and I mean all the bottles and jars, of her skin and hair products are no longer there.

She's gone and there is no trace of her here anymore.

Like I dreamed the past five months and a half.

I slide down the shower wall and sit there on the cold tiles. A couple hours pass as I think back through everything that she's said.

What did I miss?

Her.

I already miss her.

There are no clues as to where she could be in the house, so I go out to my car that she's been driving to see if anything is there. There must be something that can help me find my girl. My legs and back ache from sitting on the shower floor for so long. It takes a minute for the pins and needles sensation to abate enough for me to move around again.

When I get outside, I notice that the car still smells like her. One clue that I haven't gone crazy. She was real. I didn't just dream her into existence. I know she was real, but my mind is jumbling over so many details while I try not to spiral over what's missing now.

The seat is pushed all the way up to accommodate her smaller size. If she's gone, I might as well put the car back into the garage. I can't drive two cars, after all.

I roll the seat back so I can fit behind the wheel again and there's a picture or something underneath. I snatch it up, prepared to just throw it away, but when I flip it over, it's a sonogram.

The name and date look back at me in bold, black font.

Kathryn Barker, May 20th.

Confirmation of what Cory suspected and I was too dubious to believe.

But here is all the proof I need. The black and white splotches of the small human growing inside my girl.

Jeann's pregnant.

Jeann's pregnant with my baby.

She's pregnant with my baby and *she's gone.*

CHAPTER 37

Mack

It was Thursday night and I had no one in tow with me.

My horse was *pissed* about it.

Legend stamped his feet and bucked his head. More agitated than I'd seen him be in a while.

This was the second Thursday that we'd been without our girl. Jeann had been feeling tired before and wasn't up for our usual visit to see him. He was throwing the world's worst temper tantrum and I couldn't blame him.

I wanted to do the same.

"Jeann is gone, buddy. Can't I be enough?"

He huffs and walks off to the back of the stall. With his head pressed to the corner wall, it was clear that I was not enough. He wanted Jeann and I couldn't give her to him.

I could go prep any of the other horses for a ride.

He didn't want to run with me. *Fine.*

Artemis was poking her head over the gate up front when I was coming out of the stall. She was the most hesitant of Jeann. Even after all the weeks of Jeann trying with her, they had just gotten to a point where she was comfortable with her. I approached her, my hand raised to give her a scratch, but she also retreated when she saw no one was with me.

It didn't seem like I was going to catch any breaks around here. I didn't want to ride another horse. I kicked at the wood chips on the ground, thankful that no one was here this late to see how both of my usual horses rebuffed me.

I didn't want to accept that Jeann was just gone.

But I had to.

If I learned anything from my relationship with Melody, then it was to read the goddamn room. If a woman wants something else then let her have it.

Fighting harder for Melody was not the answer. She hated it. My attempts were completely unwarranted. In the end, I hated myself for the effort I put into a losing battle. I can see how much happier she is without me.

Whether she still wants to be friends is just the worst. Being honest with myself, I didn't want her olive branch. I didn't truly want to repair any relationship with her or my old friend. But I held it all back because I didn't want to make a fuss and be difficult. I couldn't lose what little semblance of the life I had the possibility of gaining again. It was my only choice because in either choice, making amends or going my own way, I was the asshole. The dummy.

Jeann showed me that I deserve to be something more than what everyone needed me to be. She needed me, but she wanted me just as much as I wanted her.

It was about more than being a decent person.

It was about giving and receiving the same care.

She never wanted to tell me that she loved me, but I saw it in all the ways she defended me, supported my choices, and got on my ass when she knew I was making wrong ones. Coming home to her after a long day at work was like stepping on to a cloud. Like laying your head on cool memory foam fit just for you.

And that's the fucking worst.

Jeann was my memory foam. She was exactly what I needed to support me and keep me honest.

In my head and my heart, I knew that Melody and Jeann were completely different people. Nothing about the relationships were the same. But here I am, standing like an asshole with my empty hands. Both of them took what they needed from me and left me with nothing.

Boy, do I know how to pick 'em?

Despite the pregnancy Mel and I lost, I wanted to try again. Everything in me wants the future that I thought I could make with Jeann. She was carrying my baby. There is no doubt that the baby is mine. Whatever she decides to do, will be her decision. I, at least, wanted to talk about it.

How was she feeling?

Was she excited? Scared?

Did she know that I would be there for her no matter what she chose to do?

God, how am I in the same position again?

All signs point to the fact that it's me.

I'm the one who doesn't deserve the happiness Jeann said I could have.

What else did she say though? She told me that I couldn't have her. To not tell her my feelings. To have only what was in front of us. And now what? None of that matters. She's gone like she told me she would be. I should have known. Should have been better prepared for it.

I pack up all my stuff and walk to the long drive where I parked this morning for work. The lights are on in the main house. I could go and have dinner with Danny and Chandie. Reese's truck isn't here, but the kids might be there tonight.

I decide to just get into my truck and drive back to my house. No one deserves my bad mood. I couldn't fake it, if I tried. Being honest with myself, the horses probably sensed that and that's why they weren't trying to be near me either.

Couldn't blame them.

I'm out of the shower and looking through the fridge for something to eat. I settle on some leftovers that I don't bother to heat up.

Leaning against the counter, I try not to think about how I had my tongue through her lips dripping onto this countertop, kissing that little tattoo that only I know about. Or how I had her ass in my hands, with my cock buried deep inside her in this very spot not that long ago. I definitely don't think about how easily she would fall into my arms for a hug in this room.

Whenever she was upset, this was the first place she would come to hate-cook something. And though she was upset, it would still be more delicious than I could ever aspire to. She made beauty in this house and the fact that I was able to bear witness to it, guts me like a fish.

Memories continue to assault me as I eat my cold barbecue, when the brown bottle winks at me from on top of the fridge.

I hate Alex.

I should have thrown away this fucking bottle when he sent it. I should have destroyed it like Jeann suggested.

But I didn't.

A little too late to be thinking rationally now.

The top twists off easily and that whiff of pungent alcohol burns my nostrils, giving me a preview of what it will be like to throw two years of sobriety out the window.

The first sip goes down smooth. I know I'm in trouble and I don't plan on stopping.

My phone rings in my sweatpants' pocket and I pick it up without checking to see who it is. "Yea?"

"What are you doing?" My sister's voice is clear on the other line. I was just at the Ranch with her today. She didn't say much to me though I knew she was brimming with all kinds of ideas on how to be nosy and overbearing. Guess my time is up on her being patient.

"Nothing. Eating dinner. What's up?"

"Put the bottle down."

I look around to see if she's peeking in on me through a window. "Are you watching me?"

"No, I'm not." There is some shuffling before I hear the sound of her truck engine turning over. "Chloe told me that Jeann resigned the other day. And considering you're still here and she isn't... I figured you'd be grabbing for a bottle."

So, Jeann told Chloe she was leaving but not me? *Love hearing that.* I take a long swig from the bottle.

"And if I am?"

"I'm on my way."

"Save yourself the gas. It's just a nightcap."

"Nightcap, my ass. Mack, put the bottle down. I'll be there in ten." She hangs up and I toss my food container onto the counter.

I don't want to talk to her about what I'm going through right now. Turning some music on, I resign myself to whatever pep talk Reese is coming in with.

I've finished a third of the bottle by the time she comes charging in.

"Come on in, why don't you," I snark as she slams my door behind her.

"Thanks, I—" She stops her snarky remark and listens to the music I'm playing. "Oh God, is this Matchbox Twenty? Are you there already?"

"Oh, we're there," I say. "And up next is some Lady A."

"Ty's old stuff would probably be more your speed at this point."

I scowl at her and take another drink from my bottle before setting it on the table. "Do you want me to kick you out?"

"I want you to throw that bottle out." She stands and looks at the bottle in question on the table. I think to grab for it, but I'm too late. She already has it and darts out the door. By the time I'm up to chase after her, she's already poured it down the sink.

"Goddamn it. Get out, Reese. I'm not in the mood."

"Neither am I. We already had this conversation."

"Pretty sure we didn't."

"When I first came back, you told me that looking at me was like looking in a mirror. You and I were both broken. That was true. *We were.* But now, I've healed. I want you to look into that mirror again and both of us be healed."

I squeeze my eyes shut. "Sorry to disappoint, but it seems I've broken in a different way this time."

"C'mon," she tugs me by the shirt to my room. "You're gonna sleep this off and try again tomorrow."

"No, I'm not. I'm going to go to sleep and wake up to an empty house again and it will be just as bad as today."

"You know I can't let you come back to work drunk anymore. Promise me that you're going to at least get a handle on this."

I plop onto the bed like a fish and pull the blanket over me. "Maybe I won't come back to work. Those gossips. Have nothing but shit to talk about me. I'm calling out sick."

She sighs, "Mack, you're not sick."

"Maybe I'm not, but my heart is."

Patting my back, she says, "The horses keep you sane. You've got to come back for them at least."

"I don't. Neither of mine even want to fuck with me since I don't have Jeann anymore."

There's a pause that extends long into the space. "That will pass…"

"Sure," I start to expand my answer since Jeann never liked *sure* as a response, but I don't. She's not here. Reese will have to deal.

My sister stands from the bed and walks over to the bedroom door. "So, you'll be at work tomorrow?"

"I wouldn't count on it."

CHAPTER 38

Jeann, Then

JEANN COULDN'T RECOGNIZE HERSELF. She was becoming someone she didn't want to be.

Ethan knew it too.

This had run its course and she was done seeking revenge. *She needed to heal and move on.* She couldn't hold onto her anger anymore. She couldn't replace the love she had for them with any more violence.

Jeann didn't want to be Kitty anymore. Ethan didn't want to be Thane.

But there was no leaving the Dupont family. Not quietly. The only people she saw leave were into the afterlife or disappearing entirely.

She didn't know if she liked either option.

The two of them sat in the SUV and waited to see what Colton would do next. He was clever and it couldn't be that difficult for him to find a way out of his cabin again.

It was almost forty degrees colder in Colorado than it was in Louisiana when they left. And Louisiana was unseasonably cooler than usual for this time of year.

"We'll just have to be smarter. I know exactly how."

"What are you gonna do?"

"Why?" He asked incredulously, like she was the dummy for wanting to be clued in on whatever he was cooking. There were still blood splatters on him from where he just shot Colton. Not only was he our boss, higher ranked than either of us in this operation, but he was also a sheriff in this county.

In trouble was an understatement.

They didn't have very many options moving forward.

Jeann was too far into this world and there was no way out for her. Ethan could have made it on his own because he wasn't indispensable. Jeann wasn't even sure if Blue knew his real name. They had spent time and resources to hone Jeann into becoming their secret weapon. The unassuming woman.

Running was their only option now if they intended to leave together. Especially after today had gone so spectacularly wrong.

They had run into Blue's estranged brother, Tony, in the cabin. Though Jeann knew that Blue told his men that Tony was as good as dead to protect his small town life, there was always a tightness around his eyes that Jeann knew meant his feelings were more complicated than they had been led to believe.

She wondered if the two of them were actually close and that was why he didn't want him to be mixed up with his business. There was a deep regret she was already feeling because she had to hold him at gunpoint today. Jeann really hoped that by leaving him unharmed, that could be a point in her favor with Blue if word ever got back to him about what really went down today.

"I hate that guy," Ethan remarked, all but spitting at the sheriff again. Jeann shared the same sentiment, but she understood hierarchies and intended to work within it to their common goal of getting out of this life. There was little disappointment at the opportunity to rough him up a little to deter him from coming after them.

However, Ethan and Colton were always at each other's necks. He was slimy and condescending when he talked to Ethan, showing him little respect. "Besides, we don't need him anymore. Everythin' he was doin', we can do better. I'll be protected by Blue if we can just find someone to replace us."

There were more cars that began to show up at the cabin and it was better for them not to be recognized near the scene of the crimes. Most of them were probably here to look for Colton's daughter. Jeann was not going to get caught up in that fanfare.

She glared at him. "And what about me? Were you gonna clue me in at any point?"

"Kitty."

"Don't *Kitty* me. There is no one around. My name is Jeann."

She sat up a little straighter to see how he was driving in this snow. Getting up here was nerve wracking enough. She should be back down south where it was still getting up to sixty degrees everyday, even though that was still too cold for her liking. She shivered again with how cold it was there and folded her arms in around herself.

"You know Blue will come after you... He's gonna come after me. You aren't gonna get away with this. You're not nearly as slick as you think you are. We should have talked this over first."

"I'm more slick than Colton. I'll just explain how Colton is unnecessary. We'll do what he's been doin' here for a while. Just until we get our bread up. We can put money aside and then disappear. I've got us. I've already been stashin' a little bit for our getaway. Blue will never know. If he did, he would have caught on by now."

Cutting her eyes at him, she found that this man was going to cause her more stress than she was prepared for. He was so short sighted and Jeann didn't know if she would be able to clean up his mess. That cruel sense of foreboding itching up the back of her neck. "What makes you think he hasn't?"

"Look at where we are. Once I get my hand on his delivery and I'm movin' it, these boys will know I'm good for it. I can cut him out and we'll be a new unit entirely. We never needed Colton."

She took her pistol out of her waistband and tossed it into the lockbox in her lap. She glared at Ethan, yet again, and wondered just how stupid he could be. Everything they had been working for, down the drain. Blue chose Colton for a reason. Neither of them knew why and that was never their job to know. Underestimating the literal king of green was a mistake they could never expect the true extent of.

Did she want to be a runner forever?

No.

She had dreams, plans of her own.

With the haze of grief and sorrow becoming a benign thing that she could tuck away instead of waving it around everyday like a red flag, she wanted more from her life.

She knew that Blue could be reasonable, if he wanted to be. Maybe he would let them leave... She just needed to talk to him. She didn't know what would happen, but she had to try.

Setting the lock box on the dashboard, she closed the lock on it and reset it.

Ethan took his eyes off the road for a second to look at her and ask, "Is this the life you think Lauren wanted for us?"

Then she had the nauseous feeling of weightlessness as the SUV slid across the road they were on.

Immediately, her eyes found her friend beside her. He was panicked, moving the steering wheel to try and correct himself, but it was too late as they skidded out of control. "Ethan," she gasped as they crashed into the truck on the opposite side of the road. Fear over took her and all she could do was panic as things were happening too fast.

The other driver was calm and their eyes connected in the weird moment of silence of the unknown. She couldn't imagine how someone could not be freaking out in this situation.

Suddenly, Ethan's body lurched forward. Nothing keeping him restrained, his head hit the windshield. Then, there was the sickening crunch of their vehicle wrapping around a tree on the edge of the road.

The lockbox rushed toward Jeann's face when she was stunned by the image in front of her. The pain of metal meeting her skull, ringing like an alarm, before they tilted and the tree gave and rolled on top of them.

CHAPTER 39

Jeann

I WAKE IN THE hotel room in complete darkness. Tears are tracking down my face and a cold sweat makes my flushed skin even more uncomfortable to live in right now.

In those final moments before I lost everything all over again, I saw Mack.

He had resigned himself to whatever was coming for him. Even then, he probably thought he deserved what was happening.

I can't just go around blaming the world for my bad luck.

And he didn't. Even when it was Ethan's fault. It only took a second for his carelessness to cause this much destruction.

But if I thought about it, the whole day had been a downhill dive from the moment we found Colton's cabin.

Thankful that I had saved enough to get a hotel while I was in town, I showered and got ready for another day of trying to pursue what continues to evade me.

My memories.

Taking the car that Blue is letting me use while I'm here, I make a trip into town. I had been to every place that I could think of to try and spark some sense of familiarity. The hair salon my mom worked at, my parent's old house, the craft store that I used to go to when I was younger, the tattoo shop, the diner that I had remembered and even Ethan's old apartment. Nothing had done the trick until I reached my Nana's old condo.

Memories didn't flash back at me, but I remembered her face more clearly. The day I showed up to stay with her after Lauren's service. One box to my name and the weight of the whole world on my shoulders. She opened her door nice and wide to let me in with my one box. In life, she was very similar to me. A little bit grumpy and a lot sassy. But she always had a smile for me. *Her namesake.* We were peas in a pod and I thought that I'd have forever with her.

The grief hit me two fold because you're never prepared to lose someone you love so much, who meant the world to you. But losing her and missing those final moments because you were being a drunkard at a club, couldn't hurt anymore than a serrated knife twisting into your gut.

I sit on the curb out front, unable to stand any longer.

Then I realize that someone is pulling up the driveway, clearly having moved into the condo since it's been years since she passed.

I quickly dust my pants off and walk over to the car before the new tenants call the cops on my trespassing.

Once in the car, I let the tears fall. And the only thing I want is the embrace of someone who I know I broke.

For several days, his calls were coming in and the voicemails were gut wrenching. After listening to the first, I had to start deleting them.

The texts were worse.

What was I supposed to do?

There was nothing.

I couldn't make him feel better. I couldn't even come to terms with what I had been doing myself. And though it doesn't feel like it, it was my lived experience.

Could I expect him to forgive me of my sins, my wrong doings?

No.

I couldn't even count how many there were.

I didn't deserve to be absolved of my misery because Mack loved me regardless.

He shouldn't forgive me. He shouldn't be by my side. I'm no good for him and if he were smart, he would have heeded my warning long ago.

But neither of us were smart.

I had fallen for him just as hard.

In this car, parked in a place I barely remember, I let all my tears fall until my face is sore and my throat croaks from overuse. If feeling better was the goal, I'm nowhere near it.

Driving back to my hotel and climbing into bed is the only thing I can manage for the rest of the day. Tomorrow, I will worry about moving forward.

Tonight, I just want to be alone.

⋘◆◆◆⋙

I DON'T RECOGNIZE THE woman who stops me before I can follow Hector. "We've got to search the bag." I give her a nasty look and hold my bag tighter to my body. There is nothing dangerous here, but it's the principle of listening to what this woman has to say that makes me behave so pettily. "You've been here a week. We have no idea what you could have in here. Boss is priority number one."

"Whatever," I say, purposefully dropping my bag onto her feet. I may not remember exactly who Kitty was, but I have a feeling that she wouldn't take shit from someone so low in rank. Blue could have told everyone or no one about my memory loss. I'm not taking any chances if he hasn't.

She glares at me, but pulls it through a scan that rivals TSA. I roll my eyes when she returns my bag to me, finding nothing. Snatching it from her hands, I follow Hector again into the small room that holds the man I couldn't forget because his reputation precedes him.

"Welcome back," Blue drawls.

I plop down into the chair at a table full of others all talking strategy or debriefing, it's hard to tell and I'm not sure I would be able to even with my memory. "Can we talk?" I ask, looking directly at the man in charge.

He nods. "Everybody out." There's shuffling and a few of them pat my back or shoulder in greeting on their way out. I don't recognize any of them, but I return their gestures with a close lipped, tight smile and nod. I'm truly in a foreign place.

When everyone is out, I set my bag on the table and sit back in my chair. "I remembered some things. But not all of it is clear to me. I don't know how I ended up..." The words tumble out and trail off.

"Workin' for me?" He laughs. "I asked myself that a few times. But I knew I was makin' a good decision. I never regretted it. Until I did."

Cryptic. Okay... "Tell me," I demand.

He raises an eyebrow at my demand, but doesn't comment on the apparent disrespect. "You showed up at my house. Not here but at my family home. You had fire in your eyes. I figured you were high or somethin'. Nobody talks to me like that and lives." His eyes narrow in a way that suggests he sees that is still the case. "But it turns out that you and I had mutual goals."

My eyes widen, completely taken back. I should have had some idea, but I never thought it was me who initiated all this. I brought all this upon myself. This is no time for speculation though. He's been the only person that could share the truth with me. "What were our mutual goals?"

"Revenge."

"Revenge?"

He nods. "Both wanted revenge. The night you lost your Nana was the night I lost a good friend and a valuable soldier. The Lafayettes set up Lewis, Redd's brother."

I don't know who Lewis is nor does the name ring a bell. But Redd is unforgettable now that I've seen him more than once in my memories. "And that's how I ended up workin' for you?"

"In a way. We're still beefin' with the Fayes. You said you wanted in and Thane came too. Trained hard. Rose quick. Ran green for me until one day the green didn't come back. Thought you were stealin' from me. You beat Colton down pretty bad up there and then I find out you were in a hospital and remember nothin'. Luckily, I found my shit and you weren't blabbin' to the cops. I didn't wanna deal with that… complication."

Knowing something and suspecting something are different feelings entirely. Hearing about Colton from Blue is chilling. I swallow thickly. The most recent memory showed me that I was ready for a change. I wanted to leave this life and now I need to know if all that has gone to shit. "And what about Ethan?"

"Yea. Knew he was takin' some off the top. He was the type. Problem resolved itself, didn't it?"

I flinch at his lack of concern for my dead friend. There is likely no good way to ask what I want to. So I suggest, "I've been gone for months now. What if—What if I don't come back at all?"

"Why would you do that?" He seems genuinely confused. "You made good money. Earned that respect around here. What could be better than that?"

To this man, that is likely all there is in life. He couldn't understand wanting something different. If I lay things out plainly, maybe he will see where I'm coming from and allow me to make the best decision for myself. "Well… I'm expectin' a baby… in November. I want out. Need it." He looks down at my flat stomach. "I wanted out before the accident. I just didn't know how…"

He looks at my stomach more pointedly which doesn't give much away even now that there is a little more of a swell there than before. Shrugging, he says, "Eh. I believe in equal opportunity employment and all that. You can work until you need maternity leave and then come back after."

I shake my head. "I'm really not the same soldier you knew before. You don't understand, I am not the same asset I once was. What motivated me then, it doesn't anymore."

With hard eyes, he regards me anew. "Convenient that you forget all about the reason you were in this to begin with."

"Yea… those are the only memories I do have." Quick flickers of every loss reels in my mind and I shudder. "So much loss and I just want out."

His head tilts to the side. "Comes at a price."

"What price is that?"

"Twenty large."

My jaw drops. "I—I don't have that kind of money!"

He rolls his eyes. "You have a gamblin' problem?"

"No..."

"Bought a house recently?"

"No."

"So, where is all the money I *paid* you?"

I blink a few times, and try to make sense of what he's asking me. "What?"

"You thought you worked for free? Don't spit in my face. Twenty is chump change."

My body slumps in the seat, another loss. "I don't remember where any of that money would be."

"Tough." His phone slides across the table as it vibrates from a call. "I'm givin' you a pretty solid deal. I've lost one of my best and it doesn't sound like I'll be gettin' her back any time soon."

He picks up that phone announcing, "This Redd." I nod, like it will matter if I want him to take the call or not. To my surprise he puts the phone on speaker. *Maybe that's how it always was with us.*

There's heavy breathing, but Redd's voice is clear, "I got 'em. They're comin' for you."

Blue stands, "The fuck?"

"That bitch finally showed his face and I took the shot. Blood for blood," Redd replies.

My old boss's jaw worked as he struggled to gain composure. "Told you to stand down. Let us handle it."

"I've been waitin' over a year for this, Blue. Lew had more life to live. I couldn't let it stand no more. He made a mistake gettin' comfortable in Clayton again."

"Fuck," Blue scrolls on his phone and I see he's pulling up different views of the warehouse we're in. "You fuckin' idiot! They were waitin' for your dumb ass."

Twenty people rush into the room and stand guard around the table.

Looking back at his phone, there are nine cars all pulling up to the front of the property.

"Blue," Redd pants. "They're takin' me."

"Who? What the fuck? Who is takin' you?"

"The cops found me," Redd says and the blaring sirens start up in the background.

"That's not a problem. Did anyone see you?" Blue asks.

Silence.

"Redd, did anyone see you?"

"A few folks maybe."

"Maybe? What the fuck?! Tell me you aren't this dumb." He huffs a long suffering sigh. "You're on your own for now. I have to deal with whatever Faye Senior wants here. Go with them and say nothing until I come to get you out."

"Heard." The line clicks and Blue grabs the knife that is always on his hip.

"With me," he says to me when I'm still sitting as he makes his way through the guards to the door.

I instinctively put a hand over my stomach. "What are you doin'?"

"Goin' to have a chat with Lafayette Senior to see if we can't come to a deal."

Chapter 40

Mack

"Lucky me," a voice says. "I get to be the one to find you in the same predicament you found me in all those years ago."

The cowboy hat I slapped onto my head keeps the lights from over the bar out of my eyes. It isn't a replacement for a shower to get my greasy hair into any sort of shape. It's too long and I don't feel like going to Chloe to cut it or any of that shit.

Who am I looking good for anyway?

My house is empty just like my heart.

"Oh no," I turn on the stool. Cory looks concerned and not smug as he should be. He warned me that this would happen if I wasn't honest. But since she's gone, I don't know what the true reason for her leaving could have been. "It was me finding you in the preli-predica—In the same place I was in."

Cory takes the stool next to me, pointedly ordering a tea from Sarah Anne behind the bar.

"Traitor," I sneer at her when she leaves. I know it was her who called him. Can't a man drink in peace?

"Well, either way the tables have turned yet again. Look at you, man." He gestures to what I'm wearing and I look down at myself. It's not great. I swipe a hand over my tee and tug my hat down a little tighter.

"Yea, well what did you expect?" I finish off the double I ordered and slide it to the back of the bar top.

Cory slides his card under the glass before the bartender can pick it up. "Close the tab," he says to her and then gives me a hard look. "Better. I expected better. You're not this guy anymore."

"Aren't I?" I take his tea and drink from it. I need something to do with my hands and it's not like he needs this anyway. "Lost everything all over again... Look at it go poof and I have no idea it's gone—Until I'm standing there like an asshole with my empty ass hands."

He slaps my back, "Awe, man. There has got to be more to it than that. Always is."

"What more could there be? I'm not worth sticking around. Jeann saw that and flew the coop."

"She's not a prized chicken, Mack. She had to have her reasons."

"Oh yea. Care to share what you know that I don't?"

"No, but I would." My sister's voice is now on the other side of me. I hang my head, squeezing my eyes shut. "You promised me Mack."

"Nope. I actually didn't." She thought I was joking last night and that was her problem not mine.

Reese spins me in the chair to face her, finger digging into my chest with her accusation. "Yes, you did. You're shit faced at noon on a weekday. Didn't even bother to get someone to come in for you."

"I'm sorry to disappoint. Been doing that a lot apparently," I respond with the only attitude I can muster.

My sister shakes her head, asking "Will you cut the pity party bullshit?"

I shrug and spin back to the bar. "I like this party quite a bit, actually. This party comes with easy sleep and few memories. Except there's like seven too many people crashing it." I respond pointedly when I see that the rest of the group is headed this way.

Did they have some talk outside before coming in here?

Reese and Cory are joined by Chloe, Quincy, Cammie, Drea and Tony who are sitting at the high top table just behind me. I don't know what this is, but I'm not in the mood for one of Reese's speeches right now.

"Drunk Mack is a dick." Cory says to his wife.

"Yea, he is." Reese agrees.

"Drunk Mack can still hear you."

This time Reese spins me back around by the shoulders. "I'm sorry that Jeann left the way she did, but you don't have to do this because you're hurting. There are better ways of coping."

The room spins as I shake my head. "She fooled me," I say. "I'm a goddamn fool."

Patting my back pocket to make sure my wallet is still there, I stand to walk out of QB's and to the liquor store and then home. Since they're all ganging up on me and Cory came in to cut me off, I can at least go have another in peace at the house.

At some point, the pain of losing a woman I was picturing a future with will blur into nothing. I know I will get there soon enough.

I don't get far because someone is standing in my way.

"She didn't fool you. You knew exactly who she was and you loved her anyway." Drea says. "There's nothing wrong with believing in someone." I ignore her earnest eyes. Drea and I were never close, but I've known her for years. Of all Reese's friends, I knew the least about her so it surprises and irritates me that she thinks there is anything she could say to make me feel better.

"Who else is here?" I scowl. "Did you bring the whole Ridge here with you?" I turn glare at Reese. "What is this?"

When I was down before, I couldn't throw a rock and find another soul, but now I can't get away from everyone without someone there to stop me.

I take a sharp left to walk around Drea, but her husband is there really blocking my path. If Tony were a smaller man, I'd shoulder past him. Seeing as though I don't want to end up on my ass and my stability is even less due to my drinking, I don't even attempt it. I'd just end up looking even more like a fool than I probably already do.

"My wife is right. Only knew her for one thing. You knew her much better than we ever did. With all the ways our meeting could have gone wrong, it didn't." Tony claps my back and continues, "she was just doing what she was told to. None of us were harmed."

I try to focus on his face. "So what? Now you fully support the relationship since it's over?"

He shakes his head once, jaw set. "No. But I think that you should still know what you were getting into. If my brother trusted her to do what they were doing here in Colorado, then she was an important part of his operation."

"Operation? What are you talking about?"

"Come with me," Tony says, damn near dragging me out of the bar by my arm. When we get to the side of the building he finally stops. It's daylight so it's not like people couldn't see us if they wanted to, but it's also not exactly in plain sight.

I lean against the side of the building, adjusting my hat to keep the sun out of my bloodshot eyes. "Are you gonna beat some sense into me over here?"

He looks me up and down, seeing the sorry state of me. "Is that what you need? Because you look down pretty low already."

"Will you just tell me about Jeann?" If Tony knows anything about where she was I need to know. I need to breathe her scent and if she wasn't ready to talk to me yet, that was fine too. Just knowing she's safe and well is enough for me.

"Well first of all, she's known as Kitty with the Duponts. She's what you would call *the muscle*. Kinda like a bodyguard or something close to it."

I give him a skeptical look because it sounds just as feasible as the nonsense he said in the barn the other day. "And she was guarding what?"

"The shipment of marijuana that my brother was going to distribute in Louisiana. The story is long, but just know that she was sent to make sure that happened without a hitch or use force if necessary."

"Okay..."

"And there was... a hitch this last time. I ended up having to help clean up the mess because your girl was in the hospital and the other guy was dead. The fact that she is alive at all is a miracle."

I shift restlessly from foot to foot. "Why are you telling me this?" I already knew that there was more to Jeann than I could have imagined. I sensed it and it didn't matter either way. I loved her. You don't have to know every nook and cranny of someone's life to fall for them. I barely needed any of that when it came down to it.

My butterfly was mysterious, misunderstood and mythic. That's why I loved her. Even now, learning this information makes me just want to be closer to her.

He sighs. "I don't think that she is the person you think she is, but also don't think she is the person I thought she was. Not anymore. She didn't seem like the Kitty I knew, but she is. Fuck. I don't know how to explain it. But I know where she is and I think if you really cared about this woman, Kitty, Jeann, or whoever then you should try to make it right."

I blink. "You know where she is?"

"Yes," he responds with no discernible emotion.

Pushing off of the wall, I'm in his face, "What the fuck? Why didn't you start with that?"

He puts a hand to my chest, creating the space between us instead of responding to my drunken overzealousness. Again, I should be more cautious but when it comes to Jeann, I have no sense of chill. "Because you needed to—"

"Where. Is. She?"

CHAPTER 41

Mack

SEVEN HOURS, ONE STOP and two rideshares later, I arrive in Clayton Ridge, Louisiana. I've been out of Colorado before, but never to the South. I must look as out of place as I feel when I check in the hotel that Tony recommended I stay in. I packed to stay as long as it could take to find Jeann. There is a small hope that finding her will be easy, but I'm prepared to spend as much time as necessary.

Clayton Terrace is nothing like Alpenglow Ridge. I couldn't just go to a shop and ask about her and that person automatically know who I was talking about like it was in the Ridge. It's a far larger town with a larger population to match. She must have felt completely stifled in my home with how small it is in comparison.

I hope that I don't have to be here for long.

But I'm willing to search high and low just to talk to her.

Just to have a talk.

I have so many questions. The least I could do was try to find out what I could.

I sit in my rental car now on a long dusty road that reminds me a lot of being back home. Nothing but fields on either side of the two lane road. Dialing the number, I wait until Tony answers with a, "What?"

"Were you trying to just get me off my ass or what?" I ask while the dust settles around outside. Desolate and empty all around me.

"You did need to get off your ass," he chuckles. "But, trust. It's far and you won't know that you're close until you're close."

"Okayyy..." That doesn't make me feel any more assured.

"Look, my wife just got home so I'm gonna let you go. Call me if you still can't find it."

"I—"

"Don't call me though. *My wife just got home.*" Tony hangs up and I throw the phone to the passenger seat.

The sonogram photo is sitting there too. I snatch it up and look at the grey blob on the image. I'm parked in the middle of this road, walking into who knows what. I'm in no danger of anything happening since there is not another car for maybe miles in either direction. I can barely see the highway from here... or any buildings for that matter.

"I'm coming to find you," I tell my baby in the photo.

I continue driving and driving and driving until finally a large warehouse appears. It's truly massive and I wonder even more how and why Jeann would be here. Maybe I should have asked more questions of Tony while I was in Colorado.

There are more cars than I can count around the back that is visible from where I pull up.

No signs point me to where I should park. There is definitely no visitor parking, so I just pick a spot up front. Surely, I'll be able to move it before they decide whether or not to tow it. I'll just ask if they know where Jeann is or where I could find her. If they don't know anything, I'll have to start trying plan B.

When I get out of the car, I realize that I've left my phone in the passenger seat. Leaning back into my car, I grab my phone and–

A bag is over my head and two people are holding my arms. Restraints are tied around my wrists as I kick and question, "Hey! What is this? Why are you doing this?" To no avail. They're carrying me inside of the building and I still don't have my phone.

We walk for a long while and my feet never touch the ground. That alone lets me know that whoever took me is strong and I would not be able to take on both of them if I try to resist or fight them off.

We pass through several rooms because I hear the doors unlock and slamming closed behind me. I'm far, far into this building now and there is a chill to the room that makes me shiver. The concrete floor is cold beneath my knees, but I barely notice. I'm too busy trying to see what can be done about the zip ties that bite into my wrists. My head throbs from a hangover that is long overdue, but I haven't touched another drink since Tony told me where I could find my girl. I needed to be clear headed to find Jeann.

If it had been rope binding me, I'd be able to get out of it easily. But zip ties are another story. I have no idea how I'll get out of these without hurting myself in a way that would hinder me. Something tells me that I will need every advantage I can take.

The door whooshes open and heavy booted footsteps approach me. Suddenly, the bag is ripped off my head. It's utterly empty in here, save a drain at the center and a tool box that presses against the far wall. A Black man with light brown skin stands in front of me, arms crossed, his expression carefully neutral.

"You're wasting time," I grind out, flexing my hands to keep circulation going. "I don't know anything." And truly... I don't know what the fuck is going on right now.

The man kneels in front of me, his dark eyes unreadable. "See, that's where I think you're wrong."

I grit my teeth. "I was looking for Jeann. Nothing more than that."

"That much we knew already." He tilts his head slightly, holding up his phone that has a picture of Jeann and I in Colorado together. My heart hammers in my chest. The need to protect my girl, strong in my veins. "Been a while since we knew anybody to call her that... But you didn't just happen to show up here at the same time everythin' went to hell. That's too much coincidence for my taste."

I exhale sharply through my nose, trying not to panic. "Maybe you don't get this, but when someone tells you the truth, you take it. My girl is missing and I just want to find her."

Something flickers across his face, but it's gone before I can place it. "Very touchin'," he says flatly. "But Jeann isn't in any trouble here, so I don't buy it."

The other man—the one who's been watching silently—steps forward. He's older, his presence heavier, darker. He leans down slightly, voice gruff like he's been smoking cigarettes every hour on the hour since birth. "I got this, Vert." The first man, Vert, steps back. "Tell 'em we'll be there in just a second."

"Go easy on him, G."

I don't feel reassured by Vert's words, but I don't flinch. "I just want to talk to Jeann and then I'll be on my way. I don't want any trouble."

He studies me like he's peeling back layers, searching for something deeper. "Yet, you show up here at the... wrong time, I guess."

"I was looking for Jeann."

He looks me over, disgust in his demeanor, then he barks out, "You were keepin' her from us, weren't you?"

I exhale sharply, keeping my voice steady. "That's my girlfriend. We've been living together for months. Are you stupid or something?"

A sharp crack echoes through the warehouse as he backhands me across the face. My jaw jerks sideways, pain shooting up my temple. Blood coats my tongue, but I don't let my expression change. I spit to the side of me and accept that nothing will change his mind.

Jeann could handle this. Hell, she's probably handled worse. Tony said she was a part of this life. She's clearly important to them. The muscle, she was likely doling out these punishments. If I want to find her—if I want to deserve her—I can't break.

G waits, like he's expecting me to cave, but I meet his gaze head-on.

"I. Didn't. Keep her."

Silence stretches between us. The door opens and Vert steps through with two other men before G huffs, standing back up. "Put him with the others."

Vert's eyes became slits as he saw the angry handprint on my face. "Geno. I said go easy. What the fuck is this?!"

Geno's jaw ticks before he asks, "Do you know how much green we lost because Kitty was playin' house with this man?"

"That wasn't your call to make," Vert bites out.

"Can't take it back now," Geno shrugs. "He's lucky it wasn't my piece."

Vert looks like he will argue more, but he doesn't. Instead, he nods to the men and they yank me up, and drag me through the heavy door.

The room we step into is dimly lit, reeking of sweat and piss. My gaze sweeps over the group inside. Men hunched on crates, some pacing, all looking like they've been here longer than they want to be.

These are the actual suspects. Of what? I couldn't say. But they're all dressed like they were ready for a fight.

Vert shoves me forward before closing the door behind him. I roll my shoulders, forcing myself to relax as the men size me up. They don't say anything, but the tension is thick enough to cut with a knife.

I lift my chin, steadying my breath. Jeann could thrive in a world like this. She's strong enough, sharp enough. And if I'm going to be in her life, I have to find a way to be the same until I can at least talk to her again.

I square my shoulders and step deeper into the room.

Whatever happens next, I won't break.

⊰•••⊱

SEVERAL PEOPLE COME INTO the room and rouse the group to follow them into a different room deeper into the cold warehouse. We're forced to our knees to wait for whatever is going to happen next.

"What is this? Why are you doing this?"

No one answers me, but someone else speaks. "Have anymore men comin' to lay down their lives for your stupid decisions?" Is that... Blue?

Lay down my life? *What the hell.*

"Actually—" I start, but a gunshot goes off in the small room and I flinch away.

"No one is talkin' to you." Blue says, "All you Fayes are going to die if someone doesn't tell me what you're doin' here."

A different voice far in front of me says, "We only brought the men who came with us. Got the go ahead when your second popped his son."

Popped his son?

I am not in the right place right now. I have to do something so that I'm not held accountable for whatever this murder was.

Fucking murder!

Slowly, I start inching in the opposite direction of where the voices were coming from when someone stops me. I can barely see the other men in front of me who are in a kneeling position with their hands fastened tightly behind their backs as well. It's so dim in this room that I can barely make out how large it even is. The corners are dark, but I sense that there are far more people here than just the men on their knees.

The man on his knees who was speaking before looks confused when he sees me even in this dark light. "The fuck is that?"

Yeah, join the club because I don't know who you are either.

Someone shines a flashlight around. I wince when the light hits me in the face and then Blue charges over towards me and pulls me to stand by the arm. "Mack? What are you doin' here?"

"Mack?"

I would recognize that voice anywhere.

It's been taunting me in my dreams and I've been so desperate to get back to it.

The shock written on her face quickly turns to anger as she hurries over to me. Shadows playing over her face as she gets closer and closer. She looks good even now with so much rage directed toward me. Though I can see she hasn't been getting sleep from the puffy look around her eyes. I wonder if she's been missing sleep because of her decision to leave without a word.

In this moment, I don't care. Something settles in my chest, having eyes on her. I can finally breathe again.

I bite my lip. "Hi, butterfly."

She ignores my greeting and barks at the man standing behind me. By the look of him, he was likely one of the guys who grabbed me out front. "Loose him. Now."

Her growling tones send a shiver down my spine. The woman is normally bossy, but seeing her command a man who could easily be double my size and he obey is...

We'll come back to that thought.

The man cuts my ties and I rub my wrists that are already angry and red. I almost reach for her, but decide against it. Though not touching her, is killing me a little inside now that she is within touching distance.

"What are you doing here?" She bites out. I open my mouth to speak, but that's when I notice that the room is full of strangers. It's probably best that I don't just go into the full reasoning of why I'm here in front of them.

Blue clears his throat loudly, "You mind takin' your lover's spat somewhere else? I'm tryin' to get biz done in here?"

She flips him the bird and ushers me out into a corridor just outside of the room. The door closes with a thudding finality that makes me wonder what exactly will happen next in there.

"Talk. Now." She demands while looking down her nose at me. Her arms are crossed, but all I want to do is hug her. To squeeze her tight to me and kiss her forehead.

"You left," is all I can manage out of my overwhelming rise of emotions bubbling to the surface.

Her forehead creases and she looks only marginally softer when she says, "Mack, you should not be here. How did you find me?"

"I—" The look in her eyes is more than frustration. She looks... nervous or more likely scared... *for me?* "Why didn't you want me to find you?"

"I really can't answer that question here." She looks down the hall when a group of very intimidating people approach from behind me. They acknowledge her with respect that they don't show me at all and enter the room we just came from.

We walk a little farther down to a door that leads to an empty room. A single long table with chairs around makes it seem like this is some kind of conference room. She closes the door behind us and my curiosity is really piqued now.

So many secrets.

Everything that Tony said to me feels more plausible now that I see her outside of my home and my town. Maybe she could be the woman that Tony thought she was.

I blurt, "*Who are you?*"

She blinks, taken aback by my question. Her lips form a tight line, but I wait.

I need some answers.

"That is a complicated thing to explain." She grimaces. "I'm not sure that I could tell you that in full."

"Well, you've gotta tell me something. My brain is going to explode from the questions I have and the things I want to assume. A man bitch slapped me today just for wanting to talk to you. The least I deserve is some details."

Her grimace is fierce when she turns toward the door, but she turns back to me. "Sit down."

She presses my shoulder down until I finally take the seat she's pulled out. "I am the woman you know. Probably more than I am the woman that they know." She throws a hand up in the direction of where we came from. "I worked for Blue. All that time I lost, all the things I couldn't remember, was probably for the best. I wasn't completely honest with you about that."

"What does that mean?"

She bites her lip as she thinks. "My memories started comin' back to me. Bits and pieces. Glimpses of what I think my brain had already been keepin' from me before our car accident."

"Memories of what?"

She looks down at her hands. "My pain, mostly. My fall into the grief that threatened to consume me whole." Her eyes meet mine and I see that pain there. "I became someone I was not because I just wanted to—" Her mouth snaps shut, but I need to know.

"You wanted to what?" She hesitates again, but I put my hand on the table. I've resisted long enough. It's such a natural thing for me to do for her. She looks at my hand for a moment, but places hers in mine. From that little bit of give in my favor, I tell her the truth. "Jeann, you know I would never judge you." I rub over her knuckles with my thumb before deciding to bring them to my lips. She's still standing over me, but when my lips touch her skin, she drops into my lap.

Her face is buried in my chest and my arms circle her right away. I hold her tight to me, hoping that whatever it is that she thinks she must keep from me, is irrelevant.

I love this woman. She belongs with me. There is no doubt in my mind.

I will do whatever I have to in order for her to come home and be with me so we can be together.

Kissing her forehead like I've been wanting to do, I let her catch her breath in the comfort of my embrace.

"What is it, sugar? Tell me so I can help."

She buries her face into my neck. The ghost of her breath along my collarbone grounding me in her presence over so long without it. "You can't fix it. It's over now. I want to leave the past where it was. What I want is to be Jeann and that's all."

I nudge her chin to look up at me. "Who else would you be?"

She looks away to the door again. "Can we just go?"

I nudge her chin again, pleading with her to look at me. "We don't know everything about the moon and yet, every imperfection from the long life it's lived is still a marvel." I hold her chin so that she has to look at me. "Whatever it is that happened in the past is just that. It's the past."

Her eyes squeeze tight. "I want to tell you. One day I will, but it can't be today or now."

"Okay." I answer and mean it.

I want to be the one who she tells everything to because she is the person that I would like to do the same with.

I want to be her safe space.

But there is something I still have on my mind.

My hand finds her stomach. With a firm hold on her middle, I can already tell there is a difference there, even though it's so slight I could be making it up.

I know I'm not.

She freezes for a moment, and it's not unexpected. I ask anyway. "Are you gonna make me a daddy, butterfly?"

Silence. All silence that expands throughout the room we're in as I wait for her to answer me.

I'm patient. So patient because I know something that she clearly wasn't ready to tell me just yet.

Finally, she stands, but doesn't get too far from me to keep a hand on her middle. With glassy eyes and a guilty smile, she says, "Hey, I'm havin' your baby."

I already knew. I did. But her telling me is an entirely different experience. There is no stopping the stretch in my cheeks from my own smile.

Standing as well, I walk her back to the table. When her legs bump against the edge I lift her easily onto it. She watches my face with hesitation like she doesn't know how I'll feel about the news.

I haven't said anything and... why haven't I said anything.

The only thing I can think to say is, "I love you, Jeann Barker," before I take her mouth with mine.

Chapter 42

Jeann

His kiss.

His touch.

His light.

I didn't know how much I needed all of it. All of him.

But Mack's here and I am still in disbelief that he's here. That he found me.

I know that I'm still keeping so much from him, but telling him about the little one I'm growing inside feels... It feels better than I could have imagined.

I wanted more pomp or maybe I wasn't expecting to have to tell him at all. Somehow, I didn't really have to. He already knew.

All that I've uncovered today floats away in his presence again. He makes everything better.

I love you, Jeann Barker.

I look into his stormy blue eyes that are still soft as he looks me over. What had he been through to find me? He's seen me among the Duponts, probably suspects something about my truth and yet, "You love me?"

"How could I not?" I just... stare. I keep looking at him, expecting this to be some dream. Expecting the other shoe to drop. "Do I need to make a list?"

"A list would be helpful."

He smirks, "Maybe later. For now, I just want to take you home. Can I do that?"

There is twenty thousand dollars looming overhead that Blue expects from me, but I'll worry about that in time. I'm free to go.

Free from the darkness that I was holding onto before.

"I guess I could..." I tease and he nips at my neck, hands still holding my waist. I don't know if he realizes that he's doing it, but his thumbs are rubbing little circles over my belly.

He smirks. "You did say that you were going to keep me if you took me... So, naturally, you could see why I feel a little bit duped. Where can I ask for a refund?" I smack at his chest, but he catches my hand easily.

"You're a fool, Mack."

I'm swallowed up in a hug that feels like I've already gone home. Somehow, he still smells like leather and fresh cut grass and him. "Not just any fool. Your fool."

"Mine," I agree.

Our moment is quickly interrupted by the door swinging open and Blue stepping in. Just like when he walked into my hospital room all those months ago, the energy changes as soon as he steps inside. Now, I know exactly why. I step out of Mack's hold and in front of him, instinctively shielding him with my body.

Blue doesn't mince words or allow either of us to say anything. "Remember what I told you. It will be easy to find you again."

"I know the score." I cross my arms over my chest. There is no forgetting that he expects something from me that I can't give right now. My life is on a countdown of his choosing because I know too much, or could remember too much and put his entire operation in danger. I don't want anything to do with the operation, let alone rehash what I was a part of.

Geno and Vert step into the room behind him. If Redd is Blue's second, then Vert and Geno share the third command. They are higher ranked than I am, but not by much.

"Sorry 'bout your face," Geno says in a way that doesn't seem genuine at all.

"What's he talking about?" I question, looking between the two larger men.

Vert speaks up, seemingly pleased to tattle on Geno. "Fucking G decided to interrogate with force before we had the full story. Smacked mans around a lil' bit."

I turn to look at Mack's face again. It was a little flushed, but there was no lasting damage. Beside a cut at his lip, that I assumed he had before he got here.

Mack allows me to look his face over, turning it one way and then the other. "It's not the first time I've been hit. I'm fine."

"Mack–"

"I'm. Fine." His eyes shift to the three imposing men behind me and I recognize that he doesn't want me to make him look weak in front of them. But I'm still pissed that they hurt him for absolutely no reason.

I open my mouth to go off on all of them, but know it's unwise. Exercising as much restraint as I can, I say, "You three should be glad I've already made a deal to walk out of here. Fuck you, Geno."

Geno licks his lips and looks me up and down. "Tried that, didn't work before and I don't think it'll work now."

Mack stiffens behind me and I can practically hear his jaw cracking under his restraint in responding as well. *Smart man is smart.* Everyone in this room is packing heat and trained to act quickly in a hostile situation. He's outmanned, outgunned and no one would ever find him if any of the three men in this crime family so desired.

I place a hand on Mack's arm and tell Blue, "I'm ready to leave."

He nods. "Good," Blue says with finality before texting someone on his phone and a set of guards come in to escort us out of the building. Mack grabs my bag from me and we're both silent following Blue's men out.

When the humid Southern air greets us, Mack sweeps me into his arms again and presses his lips to mine. His tongue slips inside my mouth and I let him in. This kiss is my realization that I made it out. I dodged the future that I suspected was coming for me because of my affiliation with the Dupont family.

"Take me home," I tell him and he opens the passenger door for me to get inside. Before I sit, I see the ultrasound image on the seat. Grabbing it, I fall into the seat. He crosses the front of the car quickly and slides in behind the steering wheel. "Where did you get this?"

He looks a little abashed when he tells me, "The day I came home to find you were gone, I found it under the seat when I was putting the car back into the garage. I gotta admit, it hurt finding out like this and not from your lips. Why didn't you tell me before you left?"

He gets onto the long dirt road that leads to the main highway in my hometown. I stare out of the window for a while, trying to decide what to say. The last thing I want is to hurt him even more than my decisions likely already have.

I can see that he hasn't been sleeping and I know I'm probably the reason for that. When I left, I knew it would impact him negatively. Making some sort of resolution with the past-me was far more important that he could realize.

Before I left, I was only the broken woman he saw in the hospital bed. Months later, I know that I was a wolf in sheep's clothing, moments from bringing ruin to his doorstep.

Who knows how long Blue was willing to wait before he decided enough was enough? If I had not come to him, what measures would he have taken to ensure that everything is the way he thought it should be? Even driving away from the warehouse now, I'm still not done there. If I can't come up with the money he's asked for then, I'm still putting Mack's life in danger.

"Jeann?"

I blink out of my menacing thoughts and clear my throat. "I wanted to tell you, but I had too much I wasn't telling you in the way."

He thinks that over for a minute. He taps out an unknown rhythm on the wheel before he says, "I respect that there are things that you can't tell me. And if you think that I'm better off not knowing, that's fine too. These *cryptic, saying nothing, but using words to do it* answers are just as bad as a 'sure'."

I flinch because he's right. I'm not telling him anything even as words come out. "In all honesty Mack, you should not be near me. You know as much as you need to in order to come to that conclusion."

For a second there is complete quiet in the car. Then in a tone too quiet to match the intense emotion apparent from his grip on the steering wheel, he asks, "Do you want me to come to that conclusion? Tell you you're a bad person and that you don't deserve me? *I'm not.* You've said it enough—in every way you could think of—and pissed me off in the process. I should be the one who decides who I do and do not want to be around. Either you accept that I love you, wholly, regardless of everything else, or you don't."

My voice is a whisper, somehow smaller than his, "And I'm telling you that it's too much to ask of you."

"Well, here I am. Still asking it of you. Accept that I'm here, that I'm not going anywhere and I want to be with you. You leaving with the baby and not knowing whether I would see my child again, was... I don't want to ever deal with that again. If you're not ready or you don't want to keep the pregnancy is another situation entirely—"

"It never occurred to me—I'm keepin' our baby, Mack."

He chances a look over at me, but then puts his eyes back on the long road ahead of us. "With me?" His cheeks are tinged pink and I feel even worse for putting him through all this.

"What? Yes! There is no one I would want to have a baby with besides you. How could you doubt that?"

He tilts his head to the side, "I mean... Leaving and not telling me speaks for itself."

My head falls into my hands. "I'm sorry. God, I'm sorry. I wasn't—I didn't think that would..." I turn in the seat so that I can look at him when I say, "Mack, I love you. I want to have this baby with you and start a family. None of that matters when it comes to your safety though. My affiliation and consequently my rankin' with Blue puts a mark on my head and anyone in the way of that could be collateral. Before I came here and got his word, we were—" I don't want to admit that we were in danger anymore than I already have. I swallow the end of that sentence and continue, "I had to go. But, I should have handled it differently."

"Or just picked up the phone when I called." He grumbles.

I hang my head. "I know I said that one day I'll tell you everythin', and I mean that. But I still don't have all my memories. You should know that I should be behind bars many, many times over. I have not been good or reputable for years in the name of retaliation. Petty revenge that destroyed me. Losin' my Nana was the result of some Faye, and more than her life was lost. I linked up with Blue to get back at the people who were responsible... It only got worse from there. I lost myself and wanted out.

"Then we crashed and you came into my life. You showed me that I could be someone else, though I didn't know I was lost long before you came to hold my hand in that hospital room... and never left."

We're finally within viewing distance of the highway. "And I'm not going anywhere still. I meant it when I said I want to be yours. I meant it when I said I loved you. But I need you to promise me one thing."

He parks the car, looking at me with earnestness shining in his gaze on me. "Promise me that you won't leave me like this again. I need to know that I can count on you as much as I hope you can count on me. I'm in this and nothing you say could make me go. You can tell me what's on your mind and what you need. I'll listen. I'm not just some dumb cowboy. I can understand if I'm not the person you want anymore. I can. But the way you left, it took me to a dark place I never wanted to visit again."

Tears fill my eyes. I know I hurt him and I hate myself for doing it. "I promise. You are the person I want. You and only you."

He wipes a tear from my cheek. "Then we're in this. Whatever may come."

"Okay," I nod my head, but the tears keep coming.

It seems like all I've done in Louisiana is cry in cars.

"Tell me what scares you, Jeann. I swear I'll do whatever I have to. Whatever it will take to keep you and our baby with me. Nothing is more important to me than our family."

Our baby. Our family.

"I've lost so many people." I swipe at my nose with the back of my arm. So many emotions coming to me all at once. "When I saw you standin' there with your beat up face, on crutches, smilin' like you just saw your favorite person..." The smile that breaks across his face even now, hurts something deep in my heart. "I can't lose that too. I can't. I refuse to be the reason that you've lost your light again."

"Can't you see that you are the reason for my light? Or whatever the fuck you want to call it. I couldn't explain it then, but I know it now. You and I were meant to find each other. We were meant to be here, right now, together. To get a second chance at life."

"You really think that we were destined?"

"I know it." He reaches for my seat belt to unbuckle it. "Come here. I'm sick of not touching you." I crawl across the seat and into his lap again, settling into his hold. One hand around my shoulders and the other on my belly. Something tells me that we'll be in this position a lot in the future. "I'm gonna hold you like this for a good while and then I'm gonna take you back to my hotel so you can show exactly how much you like what we're doing here."

I chuckle and smirk up at his ridiculously smug face. "Two words, Mack."

"I'm yours, sugar," he says with no hesitation.

Chapter 43

Jeann

THE MOMENT WE STEP into the hotel lobby, the weight in my chest eases just a little. The place isn't much, just another roadside stop with a too-bright sign and outdated decor, but it's the first space Mack and I have walked into together in what feels like months though it's only been a week.

He's beside me, solid and steady, even after everything.

The ride here had been quiet. Heavy with all the things we hadn't said yet, all the emotions waiting just beneath the surface. I'd spent most of it stealing glances at him, trying to memorize the sharp angles of his face again, the cut of his jaw, the softness of those lips I'd missed.

I haven't picked up a pencil since I left his house, but in this moment, I want to draw. I want to capture every version of him and this one, the contemplative and wan version, is new.

Now that we're inside, he studies me, the silence stretching until he finally gestures toward the elevators. "Come to my room."

I arch a brow. "Awfully presumptuous."

"Yeah, but also practical. Yours is probably closer to the vending machine, and I know for a fact my bed is bigger."

I cross my arms, fighting back a smirk. "You really know how to sweet-talk a girl. There is no vending machine on my floor though."

"Oh, that settles it then." He steps closer, voice lowering. "Come on, sugar. I think we've spent enough time apart."

I don't argue. *Can't.*

I feel like I owe this man everything I can give after what I've put him through.

Instead, I follow him, the tension between us crackling as we take the elevator in silence. When we reach his door, he swipes the key card, pushing it open, and steps back to let me in first.

The room smells like him—leather and something warm I can't quite place. The familiarity grips me hard and instantly I miss home, his home—my home. I set my bag on the chair while he closes the door behind us.

"So," I start, turning to face him, "you wanna go first or should I?"

Now that we're in the silence of his room neither of us can ignore what is in front of us.

Mack exhales, rubbing a hand down his face before he sits on the edge of the bed. "I'll go. No way to say it besides the blunt way." He looks up at me, his eyes raw. "I drank, Jeann. More than I should have. More than I want to admit."

I move to sit next to him, waiting for him to continue. For him, I always want to carry the weight of his truth. I know I'm strong enough to handle it and hold him down.

He looks at his hands when he tells me, "I wanted to forget. I wanted to stop feeling like the world beat me up again, like that brief bit of happiness I had with you was a mistake. But the truth is..." He shakes his head. "I've gotta own it. I'm an alcoholic and an addict. I fixate and you were easy to get hooked on. When you left, I relapsed—hard. And I don't say that with shame, but with honesty. I can't keep trying to cure my pain this way."

I press my lips together, my chest tightening. "Baby—"

He takes my hand, threading our fingers together like he needs to anchor himself to something real. Or maybe just to convince himself that I'm real. "I don't want to be the man who drowns in a bottle. I don't want to be the man who loses who he is whenever life gets tough." Mack looks at me then, straight and unwavering. "And there's no shame in that. I have to acknowledge it if I'm going to be better. If I'm going to be a good man for you—for our baby."

My heart aches at the sheer vulnerability in his voice.

"I hate that I left you to face that alone," I whisper. "I came to Louisiana thinkin' I'd find somethin', some missin' piece of myself, but all I found was regret. I learned that nothin' here was worth rememberin'. Nothin' except you has made me feel worth knowing."

I lie on the bed and he joins me. My shirt rises a little and he helps it up over the rest of my middle, looking over my stomach with appreciation. Mack scoots closer, reaching out like he can't help himself, his fingers brushing my cheek. "I don't blame you, butterfly. Not for a second. You had your reasons and I get that. But you're right," His lips twitch, that same Mack smirk that I've always been fond of, only now it's laced with something softer. "There was never a world where I wouldn't find you worth knowing."

I can't keep the sorrow from my voice. It's a heavy, sticky thing that I haven't been able to escape since I got off the plane. "There is nothin' here for me. I thought maybe my past would tell me who I was supposed to be, but all I learned was that I didn't wanna be without you." My voice wavers, but I push through. "I'm sorry for leavin', Mack. I abandoned you just like everyone else has, and I hate myself for it."

He shakes his head. "Don't."

Then his mouth is on mine, slow and deep, like he's trying to make up for every second we lost. I clutch his shirt, pulling him closer, and he groans into the kiss, hands settling at my waist, sliding up my back, anchoring me to him.

His forehead presses against mine, breath heavy, his hands trembling just slightly where they frame my face.

"I love you, Jeann," he murmurs.

I tighten my grip on him, my answer falling between us, desperate and sure. "I love you."

The rest of the night, we prove it to each other.

Clothes are ripped off as quickly as we can manage between the two of us trying to feel each newly exposed area of skin. His skin is flushed and I'm impatient as I search for something, anything to take the edge off.

He smiles up at me as I climb over his arm, pressing his fingers right where I need him.

"You're so good at taking everything. No matter what it is," he praises.

I moan when his index and middle finger slide over my clit. It's so sensitive that I begin rocking my hips, holding his face so I can look at him through the intense sensation.

He's encouraging and awed all while I make a mess of his hand. "Ride my hand, just like that sugar." Squeezing my nipples, the pressure just isn't enough. I want more of him. More of everything.

"Fuck, you've got me so hard." He picks me up like I weigh nothing to straddle his lap.

"Grind your pussy on my leg," he tells me and I obey, grinding as fast as I can, getting close, but not close enough.

He strokes his cock, groaning and whimpering, hard and pulsing with need. The beaded tip is begging for my pussy.

Mine.

Why would I settle for a thigh when I could have him deep inside me already?

I take his length into my hand and rub it through my arousal. We're both hot and sticky with me, but I don't care about being neat and proper.

I care about being connected to him in every way possible.

Taking my time, with each inch as he slides in, my gaze never leaves his. "I want to see your pretty eyes when you stretch me," I demand. Nothing makes me wetter than the blend of his heavy breathing as he tries to hold that whimper in from when I squeeze my inner muscles around him. The blue of his heated stare is nearly lost to the size of his pupils. "Give me all of it, Mack."

"Fuuuck, I missed you," he says into my ear once he's slid deep inside me.

I feel every inch of him filling me, fitting me perfectly. I'm so full and… happy. Joy washes over me like I've never experienced before.

We've fucked around plenty of times before, but this is different. I almost destroyed this connection between us. I almost destroyed him. But we survived. *We made it.* And now we have each other again. I'm not letting our reunion go to waste.

My smile stretches my cheeks, as I work my hips in a circle, my clit rubbing deliciously over his short hair at the base of him. "Show me how much, daddy."

He pulls back and thrusts just once. His eyes sparkle as he looks into mine. Just like when I first saw them, inviting pools I want to dip into and you'll have to drag me out. "Say it again, sugar."

"Daddy?"

He thrusts up into me again. Hands holding my sides. His thumbs rubbing reverent circles on the small bump that's forming our baby.

"Goddamn," he grunts, his hips punching at a rhythm that takes me to my orgasm faster than I'm ready for.

I want to last. For this moment to last.

But my orgasm rips through me violently, all the adrenaline and intensity of the day fizzling away to leave the truth of us, raw and exposed like a live wire. We just make sense together

Positive and negative finally meeting to give light.

In a haze of euphoria, my fingers grip his hair as he places me on my back to find his. I'm coming again when he finally fills me and falls on top of me.

His weight feels good. Just before he slips out of me, I lock my legs around his back.

He tries to pull away, but I tell him, "No, I just want you here."

Mack's chuckle is soft. "I'm not going anywhere but the bathroom to clean us up."

Reluctantly, I let him go before he returns with a towel to clean me. He peels back the blankets and holds them open for me to get under.

We lie under the sheets with his arms around me and his leg locking me into place.

"Mine."

I fall asleep dreaming of scenic mountains and a horse that looks like Barbie's waiting for me to join them again.

I dream of home.

CHAPTER 44

Jeann

THE KNOCK AT THE door is sharp and deliberate, echoing through the house with a kind of impatience that immediately rubs me the wrong way. I glance from my spot at the dining table through the large window beside the door, but the porch is still cast in soft morning shadows, hiding whoever is standing there. I'm too far away to really see who is there.

Mack is in the back room sorting through old baby clothes that he found in storage the other day, leaving me to handle the visitor. With a sigh and a bit of effort since I'm twenty-eight weeks along now and baby boy is lying horizontally across me, I wipe my charcoal-smudged hands on my maternity jeans and make my way to the door. Maybe Chandie or someone from the Ranch is here. All I know is that I'm not expecting anyone.

I am *not* expecting the woman standing on the other side.

She's tall and polished, her blouse perfectly crisp, slacks ironed into sharp lines, and her light hair pinned into one of those intricate twists that looks effortless, but definitely takes half an hour and a lot of expensive hairspray to accomplish. Her makeup is light but purposeful, the kind that says, *I want to look natural, but I also want you to know I put in effort and am inherently superior.*

I don't like it.

She looks me over in one long, slow pass, eyes cool and assessing, and I can already tell she's the kind of woman who walks into a room and expects it to adjust around her. Instinctively a hand goes to my belly and her eyes follow the movement before they double in size.

"You must be Jeann," she says finally, with the kind of smile that's more condescension than greeting.

I raise a brow. "And you are?"

Her eyes flicker, like she can't believe I don't already know. "Rebecca Stewart," she says, her tone making it clear she assumes her name carries weight.

Ah. *Mack's mother.*

Well, this just got interesting... in the worst way.

I cross my arms, leaning against the doorframe. "Nice to meet you, *Rebecca.* What can I do for you?"

Her smile tightens. "Is Mack home?" She's trying to look around my body into the house, but we're close enough in height that she doesn't get a better view.

I had Mack install privacy film on the front windows a couple of weeks back. We can see out of them, but you can't see in. There had been too many close calls of people being able to see exactly what happened on this couch. When my pregnancy hormones are raging and I need him, I don't care that we aren't in bed. I certainly didn't care before and I really don't care now.

When I want him, I need him.

A fact that he is not upset about in the slightest.

Here is yet another reason to pat myself on the back for the idea. His mother has shown up completely unannounced.

I don't move. "What's this about?"

Rebecca exhales, clearly unimpressed with my lack of immediate compliance. *Get used to it, lady.* "I wanted to check on *my son*," she says, voice dripping with martyrdom. "It's been too long."

Before I can respond, footsteps sound behind me, and then Mack is at my side, solid and warm. His presence is grounding, but his body is tense, like he's already bracing for whatever's coming.

Not a good sign.

"Mom," he says, his voice unreadable. "What are you doing here?"

Rebecca's expression shifts, her features softening in a way that feels entirely performative. "Mack, sweetheart," she says, with an air of exaggerated patience. "Can't a mother check on her child?"

Mack's jaw tightens, ticking once and then twice as he takes a deep breath for patience. "You didn't check on me when I was in the hospital. Didn't check on me when I moved back. So, I'll ask again… What are you doing here?"

Rebecca sighs, giving a delicate shake of her head. "I heard some things around town." Her gaze flicks back to me, her lips pursing. "About *her.*"

I stiffen, my fingers curling at my sides, but I don't break eye contact. I've dealt with women like Rebecca my whole life. Ones who wield their words like scalpels, cutting deep while pretending it's all just a polite conversation. She was already on my shit list and now her name is bolded. She's here because of town gossip.

Mother of the year, everybody.

"And?" Mack's voice is clipped.

Rebecca shrugs, the picture of concerned disapproval. "People are just… curious. You've always been reckless, Mack, but moving *some woman* into your home without so much as an introduction to your mother?" She sighs again, shaking her head like she's truly burdened by the weight of my existence. "It's not a good look. For *either* of you."

I let out a low, amused breath. "Wow. That's a lot of words just to say you don't like not being in control of your son's life anymore."

Rebecca's head jerks slightly, as if I'd slapped her with my tone alone. Luck is on her side that I haven't with my hand. She recovers quickly, but not before I see the flicker of irritation in her sharp blue eyes. So like Mack's color, but the wrong shape. He must have gotten them from his dad. I don't know which is better, or worse.

"This isn't about control," she says coolly. "This is about common sense. *Decorum*. I don't expect you to understand—"

"Oh, *Rebecca*," I say, matching her tone with a mocking sweetness, but adding even more drawl into my words. "You really don't have to waste your energy explainin'. I *do* understand. You care a lot about appearances, don't you?"

Her lips press together so tightly they turn white. Her eyes flick toward Mack, as if expecting him to rein me in, but he doesn't move. He just stands there, arms crossed, watching the interaction unfold like he's waiting to see if she's going to dig her grave any deeper.

When she realizes she's not getting backup, she exhales sharply and turns her attention toward the interior of the house. Her gaze sweeps over the space, her eyes lingering on the entry wall where my framed charcoal sketches hang.

I don't miss the way her expression pinches.

"I see you've redecorated," she says stiffly.

I smile. "I *have*. Mack actually loves my work, so it only made sense to put up somethin' meaningful instead of... floral prints and fake family portraits you had before. I'd show you the others, but you haven't been invited in so..."

Rebecca blinks, like she can't quite believe my audacity. But then she speaks again. "So, when are you due?"

The question lands like a stone in the doorway. Neither of us have moved to let her into the house. I don't want her energy in here and I certainly don't want her to say anything more to Mack that might guilt him into allowing her back into his life.

He deserves better.

Mack tenses beside me. My pulse jumps, but I don't give her the satisfaction of reacting. Instead, I tip my head. "Oh, you know, sometime after the next round of town gossip hits your ears."

Rebecca purses her lips. "It's a reasonable question."

"No," Mack says, stepping forward and in front of me, his voice hard now. "It's not." His eyes lock onto hers. "Why do you care, Mom?"

Rebecca straightens. "I just think, if you're bringing a child into this world, you should consider who you're surrounding them with."

Mack's jaw clenches. "You mean like how I was surrounded by a mother who was more interested in social circles or getting back at her husband than her own son?"

Rebecca's cheeks flush, but she doesn't deny it.

Mack shakes his head, exhaling sharply. He's too good of a person and this woman does not deserve the words he is about to say to her.

I know him too well by now.

"I need to know, right now. Are you asking because you actually care, or because you don't like being the last to know things?"

Rebecca lifts her chin. "A child needs family." *Not an answer.*

Mack crosses his arms. "Yeah. A present family. Which you weren't for me."

The silence stretches. Rebecca looks between us, her mouth pressing into a thin line, but she says nothing.

Then, with an air of forced grace, she nods. "Well," she says, smoothing down her blouse. "I can see I'm not needed here."

Mack doesn't stop her as she turns to leave.

Neither do I.

The door clicks shut behind her, leaving a heavy silence in her wake.

I exhale, shaking my head. "Wow. That was fun."

Mack scrubs a hand down his face, muttering a curse under his breath. "Sorry about that."

"Don't be," I say. "That was entertainin'. Also, I think I just made your mom hate me. Which is fair because I'm now sure that I hate her."

He lets out a humorless laugh. "She doesn't hate you. She just doesn't like not being the center of my life."

I tilt my head, watching the tension in his shoulders. "This wasn't just about me, was it?"

Mack hesitates, then exhales. "No," he admits. "My parents' divorce was ugly. I've told you that, but my dad left all the businesses to me to spite her. Every last one. My mom wanted half and he made sure that would not happen. The money, the assets, all of it. I guess he still had other income that wasn't being accounted for legally, so at some point before the proceedings happened and he left, he signed over."

"So, you really don't need to work at Mason Ranch." I state with that realization becoming clear to me.

"No, I don't, but the fact that I do is upsetting for both of them. Like a slap in the face to her and him. Flashing their money around is probably the only thing that brought them together in the first place. But he hates her and I'm sure the reasons why go on forever. I could care less. I do what I want with what he left me. Carriage rides, donating to Mason Sanctuary and several children's foundations..."

All the things that are important to him–horse, kids and now, me.

I frown with my processing. "And your mom?"

"She got a lump sum, but knowing her, it's probably gone." His jaw tightens. "If she's showing up now, it's not because she cares. It's because she needs something. She was staying with her Mom in Arizona because she couldn't bear the reality of all that went down with Reese and Alex. Instead of being a good person and making amends, she went back to what she knew before she met my Dad."

I reach for his hand, squeezing it gently. "Mack," I say, waiting until his eyes meet mine. "It's not your responsibility to take care of people who don't care about you."

His fingers tighten around mine. "It's hard not to feel like I owe her something."

"You don't," I say, firm but gentle. "And you won't do to our son what she did to you."

Something softens in his expression, like he's been waiting to hear those words out loud.

"No," he says, voice steady. "I won't."

I smile and place his hands on my stomach where our son is now moving around animatedly. "We're gonna do better."

His lips tilt into something small but overwhelmingly affectionate. "Yeah. We are."

MACK

I SHIFT IN MY chair, dragging a hand down my jaw as the screen blinks to life. The signal's a little fuzzy, but then the screen shows Dr. Maria Lopez, calm as ever, her voice soft as she greets me like we've been doing this more consistently than we have been. It's been months since I've reached out to her for a session.

"Good morning, Mack. How've you been feeling since our last check-in?"

I let out a breath, not quite a sigh. "Better. Not perfect. But... better."

She nods, encouraging. "Want to talk about what's made it feel better? Or... what's made it hard?"

I glance toward the window. Jeann is somewhere in the house, humming to the music playing while she sketches. That sound alone is a lifeline.

"I slipped up," I admit. "A couple months back. Not a full spiral, but it was a binge. I had a bad breakup." It's as best as I can describe what happened between Jeann and I in a short period of time. "The emotions—it got loud. I told myself I could handle one drink, and it turned into three. And then it was a couple days of heavy drinking."

Maria doesn't flinch or write anything down. She just waits, patient. Present.

"I hated myself the second I stopped and tried to win her back," I continue. "But I told Jeann, my girlfriend. I told her before I tried to hide it. I don't want to hide anything anymore. She deserves to see all of me if I want the same from her. That matters, doesn't it?"

"It matters a lot, Mack," she says gently. "Relapse—or slips—are a part of recovery. What matters most is how we respond to them. And you reached out. You were honest. That's huge."

I nod slowly. "Then yesterday, my mother showed up unannounced."

Maria raises a brow. "Rebecca?"

"Yeah," I mutter. "I haven't seen her in months, and suddenly she's at our front door pretending it's about checking on me. But I know what it was. She's nosy and proud and only came because she caught wind of town gossip. I could feel it all pressing in—like I was sixteen again, like nothing I ever did would be good enough for her or for him. Like the only way out was a bottle."

"And what did you do instead?"

I look up at her. "I called Reese. Just... let it out. Then I held Jeann's hand and took a damn walk around the pasture. That helped."

Maria smiles. "You chose connection over isolation. That's a powerful shift, Mack. And it's not just about staying sober. It's about retraining your instincts."

"Sometimes it still feels like I'm dragging a boulder uphill," I admit. "Like any day I could fall back and become them. Rebecca. Or worse, like Alex. I'm trying to be better. For Jeann. For my baby boy. For myself."

"You are being better," she says firmly. "You're practicing vulnerability, setting boundaries, and reaching out. And that matters. You don't have to be perfect—you just have to keep choosing growth."

I nod. "Jeann said something like that last night. She said... it's not about being healed, it's about staying in the fight. She sees the good in me even when I can't." She sees too much good in me. But I'll never discount how much I need her opinion of me to stay the same as I fight for my sobriety again. "She's the gift that the snow gave me."

"That's a gift," Maria says, smiling. "But you deserve support from more than just her. Jeann is your partner, not your entire lifeline. Keep your circle open. Reese, Cory, the friends who've been there through the grit and grief. They can carry pieces of this with you. You're not alone anymore, Mack."

That hits me in the chest, hard and true.

I nod again, slower this time. "Yea. I think I'm finally starting to believe that."

"Have you opened that door to anyone else in your life?" She's led me exactly where she wants to go in this conversation.

Rubbing my chest, I say, "I... uh, have been more vocal about my feelings to the guys."

"When you say the guys, who are we referring to?" Maria asks with openness in her tone and expression.

"Quincy. Ellis... Tyson." The last one still kills me a little.

"Would you like to elaborate? We don't have to, but this is a big progression for you. I'd like to hear more about it."

"There isn't much to share. I told them how I felt ostracized because they picked Melody's side instead of seeing both sides. How what happened to us, hurt us both when we were already broken. There were conversations had, but ultimately, I think that awkwardness... The unsureness of my standing with the whole group is less shaky. I think Jeann has helped show how I've moved on and am no longer the loose cannon, grumpy piece of shit that everyone knew when I was drinking heavily."

"So communicating has improved, not only your relationship with your yourself and Jeann, but with your sister's friends who are also your friends. That distinction is still present?"

"Quincy and Ty were my boys. I knew they woud follow whatever their women wanted most. Aren't we all being led by the woman in our lives? I'm pretty sure. But no, they aren't just Reese's friends. I'd like to believe they are becoming mine again, too."

"Are you happy about that?" My therapist asks, unable to keep the hope off of her face.

"I am. I think everyone is happier about trying to mend that disconnect. I like it for Jeann, too. I love that it's given her the community she deserves. That I, in someway, am able to make her life better and more full."

There is a moment where she thinks about my words before responding, "Even without your friends, you are enough. She isn't with you because of any other reason than her love for you. You must acknowledge that, as well."

"I am." Maria doesn't react but I amend, anyway, "I'm working on it."

She nods and we talk more about the upcoming birth of my son. We wrap up, and after the screen fades to black, I just sit there a minute. The house is quiet except for the music down the hall and Jeann's voice singing something off-key.

I could've ended up just like them—my parents–alone, angry, bitter. But I didn't. I don't.

I get to break the pattern.

And damn if I'm not grateful every day that I still can.

CHAPTER 45

Mack

I NEVER THOUGHT I'D be standing in a nursery, holding a damn mobile with little hand-carved horses dangling from it, trying to figure out how the hell to attach it to the crib.

But here I am.

After everything I went through with Callan, I never thought I'd get another chance to be a father.

Life shows you different paths if you let it.

Jeann's sitting in the rocking chair by the window, one hand resting on her round belly, watching me with that amused little smirk she gets when she knows I'm struggling, but won't ask for help.

"You sure you don't need the instructions?" she asks, arching a brow.

I shoot her a look. "I don't need a damn pamphlet to put together a baby's mobile."

She hums, resting her head against the back of the chair. "That's what you said about the crib, and yet..." She gestures toward the wooden frame, where I nearly lost my mind putting it together last night. I don't know who's nesting, *me or her*. I've read a few books and still, I can't stop feeling like I'm not prepared.

I grumble under my breath, finally securing the mobile in place, then step back, hands on my hips. "See? Perfect."

Jeann snickers, but when I look over at her, I see the way she's staring at the crib. Not just looking but *feeling* it.

"You okay, butterfly?" I ask, crossing the room to her.

She nods slowly, rubbing her belly. "Thirty-five weeks," she murmurs. "Five more to go."

I kneel beside her chair, pressing my hand to the swell of her stomach. Her body has changed so much in the months leading up to now and I can't believe that she could be even more beautiful. Keeping my hands off of her is not an option. "You ready for him?"

She nods and her eyes flick to mine. "Are you ready?"

I don't hesitate. "Yeah," I say, voice rougher than I mean for it to be. Clearing my throat, "Yeah, I am."

She exhales, nodding again. "I think I am too. My sister was this far along when we rushed over to the hospital. I should be panickin', but I don't feel it. Not like I expected to."

I know she's still scared. She has every reason to be after Lauren. But we've taken every precaution to make sure she will have a successful delivery. Hell, I'd be lying if I said I still wasn't nervous.

It hits me all over again how damn much I love this woman, how much I love this baby we made together.

I glance around the room, taking it all in. The crib, the shelf lined with books I'd never have thought to buy, the soft blue and cream blankets folded neatly over the rocking chair. And then my eyes land on the wall across from the crib.

There's a drawing Jeann made and hung herself at some point without me knowing.

It's a breathtaking piece.

Black and white with just the faintest hint of blue for depth. A foal standing in the middle of a vast field, its mother close by, the sky endless above them. It's simple but striking, the kind of thing that sticks with you long after you look away. She always has had a way of creating emotion with her work.

I swallow hard. "You made that for him?"

She nods, fingers curling over the arm of the chair. "I wanted somethin' personal. Somethin' that means somethin'."

I stand and walk over to it, running my fingers lightly over the frame. "It's beautiful, sugar."

"Do you think he'll like it?" she asks quietly.

I turn back to her, watching the way she's absentmindedly rubbing her belly, her lips pressed together in something too close to worry.

I cross the room, kneel in front of her again, and take her face in my hands. "He's gonna love it," I say, my thumbs brushing over her cheekbones. "And if he's anything like his mama, he's gonna love making his own, too."

Her eyes soften. "You think so?"

I nod. "I do." Then I glance back at the piece, shaking my head. "Damn. He's not even here yet, and you're already showing him what love looks like."

She lets out a breath, blinking a few times like she's trying not to get emotional, then she lets out a little laugh. "*Great.* Pregnancy hormones weren't enough. Now, you're gonna make me cry, too?"

I grin. "Maybe."

She shakes her head, but she's smiling.

I lean in and press a kiss to her belly, right where our son is resting, where he's listening. "You got a hell of a mama, little man," I whisper to him. "She's already got the world waiting for you."

Jeann runs her fingers through my hair, her touch light and steady. "And he's got a Dad who's gonna teach him everything that matters."

I look up at her, feeling something in my chest pull tight. "Damn right, I am."

She smiles, and for a long moment, we just sit there. Her in the rocking chair. Me kneeling before her. Our hands on the life we're about to meet.

And for the first time, it feels like we're really ready.

"It's real now," she murmurs.

"It was always real, butterfly," I say, pressing a kiss to her temple.

She leans into me, exhaling a slow breath. "I never pictured this," she admits. "Not the nursery. Not the normalcy. Not you."

I smirk. "What, you thought you'd end up with some city guy?"

She scoffs. "I thought I'd end up alone."

Something in my chest tightens at that, but I don't let it settle. I just press another kiss to her scar and hold her a little tighter. "Well, you're stuck with me now."

She turns in my arms, tilting her head up to look at me, eyes filled with something softer than she usually lets show. "Good," she says simply.

We spend the rest of the morning organizing the nursery, unpacking boxes of tiny clothes and placing decorations around. Every time I catch her looking at something for too long, I can tell it still surprises her that she gets to have this.

A safe home.

A baby she wants.

A future she chose.

And hell if I don't feel the same way.

By the time we're done, we're both covered in dust and sweat, but Jeann stands in the doorway, hands on her hips, surveying the room like she just conquered a battlefield.

"Alright," she says, nodding in satisfaction. "We've done enough for to-day." Then she glances at me, eyes flickering with something unreadable. "But there's one more thing I want to do before he gets here."

<hr>

THE TOW YARD LOOKS even rougher than I remember.

The SUV still sits in the back lot, wrecked beyond repair. Seeing it again sends something cold through my chest. I remember that day too well.

The crash.

The blood.

The pain.

All of it.

Jeann, on the other hand, just looks at the vehicle like it's an annoying loose end she's finally getting to tie up.

She walks up to it, fingers tracing the battered edge of the door, then pulls out the key and pops the glove compartment. A few papers flutter out, but she ignores them. Then she checks the floor, reaching deeper until she pulls out a dented metal box.

My brows furrow. "What's that?"

Jeann exhales sharply, turning it over in her hands. "Somethin' I've been thinking about for too long."

She tries the latch, but of course, it's locked. She stares at the numbers for a long moment, then presses them in.

0-3-0-1.

Lauren's birthday.

The click is quiet, but she lets out a shaky breath like she wasn't sure it would work.

She lifts the lid. The sight of the pistol shouldn't shock me at this point, but there is sits. Next to it, neatly stacked and secured, are papers, bank information, and notes scribbled in Jeann's careful handwriting. My eyes catch numbers—large numbers.

Accounts.

Transactions.

And then I see it.

A folded piece of paper labeled "Money Bags" with an address.

She lets out a breath, then leans over... with laughter. It's quiet and almost disbelieving. "I did it," she murmurs. "I actually did it."

I look at her, waiting. She glances up, and there's just relief.

"I hid everything," she says. "All the money Blue ever funneled through to me, everythin' I earned, everythin' I kept—it's all there. Untouched. And now I can use it." She laughs again, this time louder, like the weight of those years are lifting from her shoulders. "I don't owe him anymore."

I take the box from her hands, looking at the contents. "And you trust this is still where you left it?"

She nods. "I was careful. I never touched it. Never wrote the location anywhere except in my head. And now?" She breathes deep, straightening. "Now, I'm getting it back."

Slowly, Jeann had shared what she remembered. She continued to dream her memories, but it seemed that most of them were the ones linked to the times she had gotten a tattoo. They were the stories of the life she had lost. Many of them were shocking, even to her. But we honesty and judgement-free conversations were our specialty at this point. I'm grateful that she was willing to be so open with me.

When she told me that Blue wanted twenty thousand to walk away, I told her I'd liquidate whatever I had to so she could get the money to him. Jeann, being Jeann, declined and wanted to do it herself. She knew he wouldn't ask for it if she didn't actually have it to give.

I smirk. "Damn right, you are."

She turns to me, eyes bright and alive in a way I don't think I've ever seen. "Mack," she says, voice steady, "I can buy back my freedom."

I pull her close, pressing my forehead against hers. "You were always free, butterfly," I murmur. "Now, you just got the proof."

She smiles, and makes my own stretch wide across my face.

And standing there, in the wreckage of the past, we make a promise. To each other, to our son, to the life we're building.

No more ghosts.

No more debts.

Just this family we made together.

Epilogue: Mack

I'm used to waiting.

Waiting for fences to be fixed, cattle to mosey along through the gate, for colts to learn the feel of a saddle, for storms to roll in and roll back out again.

But this?

Sitting in this hospital waiting room while the woman I love is preparing for surgery?

This is the kind of waiting that damn near kills a man.

The waiting room is packed. I didn't expect this many people, but when I look around, I see every part of our life sitting in these hard plastic chairs, drinking vending machine coffee, pacing the floors.

Over the months since Jeann's return, I knew there was much to mend and much to let be water under the bridge. When it came down to it, I knew that there was as much love available to us as we needed from each other. When we were good, it was easy to have perspective on what the people outside of me, Jeann and the baby were. Our friends and family grew stronger and healed. I was able to make amends by way of honesty about the hurt I felt and she was there, holding my hand, as I voiced the pain I had once smiled through.

It was tough, but everyone has been better for it. Jeann deserved community as much as I deserved resolution. So now, we have an abundance of love in our lives, when before neither of us had much.

Reese is here, standing near the window, arms crossed, looking like she's about two seconds from demanding a nurse give her an update. My sister has been my rock more times than I can count, and right now, I can tell she's barely holding it together for me.

Cory's sitting beside me, leaning forward with his elbows on his knees. The kids are tucked around him. Kelsie's braiding Kyra's hair, and CJ's pretending not to be nervous by scrolling on his phone. Gabe is already walking toward his mom at the window, attuned to her anxious mood. Bren… not sure where he is, but if his mom and dad aren't worried, neither am I.

Tony and Drea are in the corner, their daughter, Mireya, asleep against Tony's chest. Drea catches my eye and gives me a reassuring nod, the kind that says, "She's strong. She's got this."

Even Ellis and Cammie are here. Ellis, looking like he'd rather be wrangling cattle than sitting under these fluorescent lights, but he showed up anyway. Cammie, soothing his high energy, her arm linked through his as they talk quietly to Taylor and Josh who sit across from them.

And then there's Tyson and Melody, Zeke, and Rob. A group I never thought would be in my corner, but here they are. Tyson claps a hand on my shoulder as he passes, his way of saying, "You're not alone." Though I know he won't say it aloud. My ex-wife just nods to me from where she sits with the other two bandmates.

Chloe and Quincy are bustling in with bags upon bags in their hands. "I'm running late, but rich auntie vibes dictate that I come with gifts. Did I miss it?"

Quincy takes the bags from her hands, "There's no baby in here so I'm gonna say no."

"He's right," I say, "I'm just waiting for them to call me back so I can scrub up."

Everyone settles a little more at my announcement. It's overwhelming, having this much love in one room, and yet, it's the only thing keeping me sane.

I run a hand over my face, exhaling slowly. "Should've started drinking coffee for this."

Cory chuckles beside me. "First-time dad nerves?"

I shake my head. "Nah, I just want her to be okay. We both have had so much loss around—"

Reese makes a quiet sound, then crosses the room and drops into the chair beside me, looping her arm through mine. "She's okay," she says firmly. "And so are you."

I nod, but it doesn't feel real until a nurse finally steps into the room, scanning for me.

"Mack Stewart?"

I shoot to my feet. "Yea?"

⟨•••⟩

Jeann didn't make the decision lightly.

We'd gone back and forth for the past few weeks, weighing the risks, listening to the doctors, talking through every possibility. She wanted control—needed it, after everything she'd been through—and this? Choosing a scheduled C-section instead of waiting for the unpredictable nature of labor? It gave her that.

I saw the relief in her eyes when she finalized the decision. She wasn't afraid anymore. She was confident.

That meant everything to me.

So when the day finally arrived, I'm by her side, dressed in surgical scrubs that are too stiff, a cap covering my hair, and a mask dangling around my neck.

She's nervous, even if she won't admit it outright. I see it in the way her fingers twitch against the hospital sheets, how she keeps adjusting the IV line taped to her hand.

I take her hand, running my thumb over her knuckles. "Hey."

She looks up at me, her copper eyes meeting mine. "Hey."

"You good?"

She exhales slowly. "I am. Just...ready."

Soon enough, they wheel her back to the operating room. I walk alongside the bed, never letting go of her hand.

Once we're in, everything moves fast. Blue drapes go up, dividing the room. Machines beep in steady rhythm. The surgeon explains what's happening as they go, and I stay right by Jeann's head, whispering to her, grounding her.

"You're doing great," I murmur, pressing a kiss to her forehead. "Just a little longer."

She nods, gripping my fingers tighter. "I can feel pressure," she says, her voice a little tight.

"That's normal," the doctor reassures her. "Baby's almost here."

I don't look over the drape. I can't. I'm not the squeamish type, but I'd rather keep my focus on her and not the scalpel I saw the doctor pick up.

Then, after a moment that stretches forever, I hear it.

A *cry*.

Sharp, new, and the most incredible sound I've ever heard.

Jeann gasps, her whole body going still before she lets out a shaking breath.

"Oh my God," she whispers.

"He's here," I say, voice thick.

My son.

Everything in me goes tight, the kind of feeling that breaks a man open and puts him back together all at once.

The nurses clean him up and neither Jeann or I take our eyes off of him all the while. At some point a nurse hands her a stick of gum.

"Just a little trick for after. I've done many of these procedures, trust me. It helps." She flits off to help the other nurse and finally—FINALLY—she returns with our little boy wrapped up in a blanket with a little knit cap over his thick head of curly hair.

I stare at the new life in my love's arms and the nurse continues saying something, but I'm not listening. Thankfully, Jeann is.

"We're good," she tells the nurse before she leaves. Then she looks down at the baby, nudging him slightly toward me. "Wanna hold him?"

I nod, unable to speak past the lump in my throat, and she carefully hands him to me.

The moment I have him in my arms, something inside me shifts. This tiny, squirming boy is mine. *Ours.* His little fingers curl instinctively against my shirt, and my chest aches with the weight of it all.

"Damn," I breathe. "He's perfect."

Jeann watches me, exhaustion in her eyes, but love flickers there, too. "He is."

I run a careful finger over his little cheek, then glance back at her. "Ready for everyone to meet him?"

She exhales a quiet laugh. "They're probably about to break down the door, so yea, might as well."

When I walk into the waiting room, baby in my arms, the entire room stills.

Reese's hand flies to her mouth. Cammie's eyes shine. Cory grins, nudging his girls forward. Drea practically beams. At some point Chandie, Danny, Janet and Sammie joined the waiting party and are already making their way to the boy in my arms. Tony nods, quiet approval in his gaze. Tyson, Melody, Zeke, and Rob all lean in, waiting.

"Everyone," I say, my voice thick, "come meet our son." They all follow us into the room where Jeann has been covered and moved to another bed for the next few days of our hospital stay. It feels a little nostalgic to be planning on being here by her side again.

"Surely, you've named that baby now," Chandie hedges. We kept the name we chose a secret, just for us until this very moment.

The room holds its breath as I sit in the chair beside my girl.

I look down at him, then at Jeann, who's resting against the pillows, smiling at the scene before her.

I clear my throat. "This is Levi Daniel Stewart."

Reese lets out a choked sound, wiping her eyes. "Mack."

I give her a small smile. "Yea," and look at the man who leans on his cane beside his wife.

The grumpy man comes over to see all Levi's sweet baby glory. "I'm honored," he admits, and gives my son a little squeeze on the arm.

Cory claps a hand on my shoulder, "Hell of a name."

Tony nods. "Strong one."

Ellis pipes up. "Gonna be a cowboy like his old man?" His usual teasing grin gone, a reverent smile in its place.

I glance down at my son, my chest full to bursting. "I guess we'll see."

Kelsie steps closer, peering at him with wide eyes. "Can I hold him?"

Jeann gestures from the bed. "Come sit with me, sweetheart."

Kelsie rushes forward, trailed slowly by Kyra, and one by one, everyone gathers around, taking turns meeting Levi, marveling over him.

Reese touches his tiny hand and lets out a breath. "You did good, big brother."

I exhale slowly, looking around the room at all the people who showed up for us. The people who will show up for Levi, too.

Family isn't always blood. It's the people who love you through it all. And standing here, watching my world expand in ways I never imagined, I know one thing for sure.

This boy?

He's already surrounded by more love than I ever dreamed possible.

THE END

Want more of Mack and Jeann? Check out their bonus epilogue here.
www.zeakayleighgalan.com/b/nZzmO

<hr>

The Shades of Vengeance series, beginning with Blue Dupont's angsty romance is coming soon:

Into the Blue

August 2025

Join the newsletter so you don't miss any updates about new releases.
www.zeakayleighgalan.com/news

Thank You for Reading!

Thank you for joining me on this journey through Roped on the Ridge. Your time and support mean the world to me, and I hope you've fallen in love with the characters and their story as much as I have!

Share Your Thoughts

If you enjoyed this book, leaving a review is one of the best ways to support authors like me. Reviews help other readers discover stories they'll love, and your voice matters! **Leave your review on Amazon or your favorite review site!**

Keep the Love Going

Roped on the Ridge is part of the Alpenglow Ridge series. Dive deeper into the world of Alpenglow Ridge with these other books in the series:
   Saddled with Finesse: Can their unexpected kiss ignite a love strong enough to overcome the shadows of her past and give him the fresh start he's been searching for?
Tropes: Returning to hometown, Single Dad, City Boy/Country Girl, He Falls First, Close Proximity

   Verse to Acclimate: Years after heartbreak tore them apart, a broken small-town girl and country music's rising star must face the scars of their past to find out if love is worth a second chance.

Tropes: Second Chance, Best Friend's Brother, First Love, He Falls First, Mutual Pining

Whisk til Peaked: Trapped by a snowstorm in a luxury resort with only one bed, a single mom and her loyal best friend must confront unspoken desires and buried secrets that could shatter everything they hold dear—or finally bring them together.
Tropes: Best Friends to Lovers, Single Mom, Snowed in/Forced Proximity, He Falls First
You can find all my books on my website: www.zeakayleighgalan.com

Stay Connected

Want to be the first to hear about new releases, exclusive content, and special offers?
Sign up for my newsletter at www.zeakayleighgalan.com/news

With love and gratitude,
Zea Kayleigh Galan

Acknowledgements

Writing Mack and Jeann's story is one that I had been looking forward to since I started writing this series. This couple touched me in a way that I could not wait to put on the page. I loved their chemistry and at times it was hard to stop typing and take care of myself because I wanted to stay in their scenes just a little while longer. This couple is different from the others in the series for so many reasons. They stand apart but still fit my overarching theme of healing through love and understanding. I'm a firm believer that having love and support in your life can transform you in positive ways. I think that this couple shows that the most clearly in the series.

I want to address though of you who sent me messages and emails about Mack: thank you for trusting me to give him an HEA. I know that there was a soft spot for Reese's neighbor and friend, so I hope that you found joy in his resolution. Jeann certainly is.

The biggest thank you to my husband and best friend who has been beyond supportive and encouraging. I love you, Bryan. You are my rock and without you, I would be lost.

I've got to thank my cheerleader, N. She is always a fan of celebrating, just like mama. Thank you for your sweet words and always asking what my book couples are doing... and wanting to listen to the book playlists on repeat as I'm drafting.

Thank you to by BETA team for being patient with me, answering my countless questions, providing me with support and feedback that has been incredibly helpful and invaluable. Thank you Brooklyn, Faith H, Jessica N, Karime and my other BETAs! So many hugs and squeezes for you!

Thank you to my ARC readers! You all are rockstars and I am ever grateful for your time and effort in hyping up this release! You all carry me through the stress of releasing a new story with your enthusiasm!

Thank YOU to the readers and my community! Whether you're returning or are a new reader, I'm so happy that you read this story and went on this journey with me, Mack and Jeann. Really hope you enjoyed this one! My wish is that you will stick around for more stories and join me on socials so we can talk about more books. See you for the next one!

Keep up to date with me and all my new releases by signing up for my newsletter:www.zeakayleighgalan.com/news

Also by Zea Kayleigh Galan

Alpenglow Ridge

Saddled with Finesse
Verse to Acclimate
Whisk til Peaked
Hope by the Horizon
Roped on the Ridge

Shades of Vengeance

Into the Blue

About the Author

Zea is a passionate storyteller who brings small-town romance to life with heartfelt emotion and unforgettable characters. A lifelong lover of love stories, she weaves her background in anthropology into crafting tales where swoon-worthy heroes fall hard for their strong, relatable heroines.

Living in the picturesque mountains of Colorado with her husband, daughter, and a spoiled, posh cat, Zea draws inspiration from her surroundings to create warm, vibrant settings readers want to escape to. When she's not writing, she's indulging in her other loves: cooking, hiking, designing clothes, or curling up with a romance novel and a plate of sweets.

Zea is dedicated to connecting with her readers and invites you to join her on this journey of love, laughter, and happily ever afters.

Want to be the first to hear about new releases, exclusive content, and special offers?

Sign up for my newsletter at

www.zeakayleighgalan.com/news

www.instagram.com/zeakayleigh

www.facebook.com/zeakayleigh

Signed Book Shop